THE
BEIJING
CONSPIRACY

Adrian d'Hagé was born in Sydney and educated at North Sydney Boys High School and the Royal Military College Duntroon (Applied Science). He graduated into the Intelligence Corps in 1967, and was later transferred into Infantry, serving as a platoon commander in Vietnam where he was awarded the Military Cross. His service in the Australian Army included command of the 6th Battalion and Director of Joint Operations for Defence. In 1990 he was promoted to Brigadier as Head of Defence Public Relations.

In 1994 Adrian was made a Member of the Order of Australia for services to communications. In his last appointment as Head of Defence Planning for security of the Sydney Olympics, including chemical, biological and nuclear threats, he worked closely with the NSW Police.

In October 2000 Adrian left the Army to pursue a writing career, moving to Italy to complete *The Omega Scroll* (Penguin, 2005). Now into its fifth printing, *The Omega Scroll* has been voted one of the top 50 books of 2006 (Booklovers Guide) and has been published in over ten countries. Adrian holds an Honours degree in Theology, entering as a committed Christian and graduating 'of no fixed religion'. He is presently a Research Scholar at the Centre for Arab and Islamic Studies (Middle East and Central Asia) at ANU and his doctorate is entitled 'The Influence of Religion on US Foreign Policy in the Middle East'. He is also completing a further degree in Wine Science at Charles Sturt University, and he has recently returned from Austria after successfully sitting the Austrian Government exams as a ski instructor, 'Schilehrer Antwärter'.

Praise for *The Omega Scroll*:

'A provocative book in which every sort of dogma is questioned
and every preconceived idea turned on its head'
Sunday Mail

'A classy action thriller'
Sunday Times

ADRIAN d'HAGÉ

THE BEIJING CONSPIRACY

VIKING
an imprint of
PENGUIN BOOKS

PENGUIN BOOKS

Published by the Penguin Group
Penguin Group (Australia)
250 Camberwell Road, Camberwell, Victoria 3124, Australia
(a division of Pearson Australia Group Pty Ltd)
Penguin Group (USA) Inc.
375 Hudson Street, New York, New York 10014, USA
Penguin Group (Canada)
90 Eglinton Avenue East, Suite 700, Toronto, Canada ON M4P 2Y3
(a division of Pearson Penguin Canada Inc.)
Penguin Books Ltd
80 Strand, London WC2R 0RL England
Penguin Ireland
25 St Stephen's Green, Dublin 2, Ireland
(a division of Penguin Books Ltd)
Penguin Books India Pvt Ltd
11 Community Centre, Panchsheel Park, New Delhi – 110 017, India
Penguin Group (NZ)
67 Apollo Drive, Rosedale, North Shore 0632, New Zealand
(a division of Pearson New Zealand Ltd)
Penguin Books (South Africa) (Pty) Ltd
24 Sturdee Avenue, Rosebank, Johannesburg 2196, South Africa

Penguin Books Ltd, Registered Offices: 80 Strand, London, WC2R 0RL, England

First published by Penguin Group (Australia), 2007

1 3 5 7 9 10 8 6 4 2

Text copyright © Adrian d'Hage 2007

Cover and text design by David Altheim © Penguin Group (Australia)
Cover photograph by George F Mobley/Getty Images
Typeset in Granjon by Post Pre-press Group, Brisbane, Queensland
Printed and bound in Australia by McPherson's Printing Group, Maryborough, Victoria

National Library of Australia
Cataloguing-in-Publication data:

D'Hagé, Adrian.
The Beijing conspiracy.

ISBN 978 0 670 02958 7.

1. Terrorists – Fiction. 2. Olympics – Fiction. I. Title.

A823.4

penguin.com.au

For Robyn

CONTENTS

BOOK ONE Towards the Final Solution   1

BOOK TWO The First Warning Attack   291

BOOK THREE The Second and Third Warning Attacks   391

BOOK FOUR The Final Solution   447

BOOK ONE

TOWARDS THE FINAL SOLUTION

CHAPTER 1

THE WHITE HOUSE, WASHINGTON DC

'We will strike you when you least expect it, beneath Eternity where the windmill has been stolen. This is the first of three warnings. If you do not heed these warnings and if Allah, the Most Kind, the Most Merciful wills it, we will be forced to implement the final solution.'

The mood in the White House war cabinet was tense. The briefing had been hastily convened in the cramped Situation Room beneath the Oval Office in the West Wing. The video being viewed was grainy, but the features of sixty-year-old Dr Khalid Kadeer were clear enough. Like the Hydra of Greek mythology, al-Qaeda had grown another monstrous head, and the terrorist mastermind was calm and chillingly confident. Unlike his thinner and more familiar colleague, Osama bin Laden, the Muslim Uighur from the Xinjiang Autonomous Region in western China was powerfully built. He was tall and his demeanor was menacing. His dark, oval face was etched with the lines of a lifelong Islamic struggle against the West and the Han Chinese, and his narrow, hooded eyes were black and coldly calculating. An elegantly embroidered *doppa*, the traditional headgear of his Uighur people, covered his fine, grey hair.

Kadeer spoke quietly, inviting President Denver Harrison and the members of his war cabinet, the most powerful group of men and women in the world, to dismiss the warning attack as nothing more than rambling Islamic bravado. Agent Curtis O'Connor wasn't so sure. Kadeer was a brilliant microbiologist who had trained at Harvard University. O'Connor knew Kadeer was very focused.

Curtis O'Connor, an expert on bioterrorism and one of the CIA's most knowledgeable agents on Islam, Central Asia and al-Qaeda, was seated in one of the advisor's chairs that were placed along the dark panelled wall of the White House Situation Room. He was forty-three, fit, with a solid physique and tall, standing at 178 centimetres. His thick, dark hair was roughly brushed into place. His face was tanned and his blue eyes were mischievous, although looks could be misleading. Originally from Ireland, Curtis O'Connor was very much his own man, and he had one of the sharpest minds in the CIA. Some time ago he'd concluded that the President and his advisors were in a state of denial over the war in Iraq. Somehow, he thought, he would have to influence a change to the dangerous and arrogant course the Administration had charted for his adopted country and for the wider western world. O'Connor had little time for presidents and prime ministers who started wars on false premises, or for sycophantic advisors and generals who did their bidding, and he had even less time for religion and the fundamentalists who misused it, whatever their creed.

'The West is increasingly using this so-called war on terror to persecute Muslims all over the world,' Kadeer continued. 'Innocent women and children are being slaughtered in Iraq, in Lebanon, and in the Palestinian territories occupied by Israel. Other government authorities, like those in Beijing, have followed the lead of the United States, Britain and Australia, using the war on terror to eliminate Muslim Uighurs they perceive as a threat. You don't see this in the West, but China executes more people every year than the rest of the world combined. Torture and imprisonment is at the whim of the communists in Beijing, as is the blocking of the internet. Freedom of speech is non-existent, yet you will flock to the Beijing Olympics and show support for a murderous regime. It was the same in 1936,' Kadeer said, a touch of sadness in his voice. 'The Berlin Olympics were opened by Hitler and the Third Reich used sporting teams and the Nazi salute to glorify their regime. You seem to have forgotten that the Olympic charter is concerned with the harmonious development of man and the promoting of a peaceful society and the preservation of human dignity.' With stunning irony, Kadeer warned, 'If you do not change course, where Hitler failed, Islam will succeed.'

Curtis O'Connor wondered if the first attack might be biological and if the athletes and the Games might be the target. 'Beneath Eternity where the windmill has been stolen' didn't sound like a bacteria or a virus, but O'Connor knew that among the terrorists on the United States' most-wanted list, the Muslim scientist and philosopher had few peers, and no one was in a better position to exploit the dark, microscopic world of bioterrorism. Despite the disdain on the faces of President Harrison and the rest of his cabinet, O'Connor had a feeling that somewhere within the coded first warning was a real and present danger that the West would ignore at her peril.

As the video drew towards to its conclusion, President Harrison fidgeted with his expensive gold pen. He'd not long returned from his ranch on the banks of the Bitterroot River in Montana, and it was clear that he would rather be back there. Instead he was being forced to sit through a video of threats from some two-bit Muslim terrorist. Harrison's square face was tanned and his jaw was set stubbornly. The constant criticisms levelled at his Administration for favouring the rich, instead of looking after the poor and an increasingly cash-strapped Middle America, hadn't bothered him in the least – but the disaster that was Iraq and the war on terror was taking its toll. His once dark hair was now noticeably grey. President Harrison glared at the figure on the screen.

Kadeer's demeanor softened, and he appeared almost reasonable as he directed his remarks towards the ordinary citizens of the West and China. 'The people of the West and the people of China are in mortal danger. I wish it wasn't so, but your leaders are arrogant and stubborn, and they refuse to negotiate with many of the key states in the Muslim world, such as Syria and Iran. In Iraq, the invasion by the West has resulted in the deaths of over 400,000 innocent Iraqi citizens. Your leaders dismiss these figures, but they come from your own prestigious Johns Hopkins University. Beijing maintains very tight controls over the media and the internet and many in the West are unaware of what is happening, but hundreds of my people in Xinjiang province have been murdered by ruthless Han Chinese government soldiers,' Kadeer continued, his dark eyes now flashing with anger as he remembered the slaughter of his own family. 'The

Beijing government has been persecuting the Muslim Uighur people in the Xinjiang Autonomous Region for decades, and the West's war on terror has provided those in authority with the excuse they need to legitimise murder and imprisonment without trial. Beijing is only doing what the West sanctions at Guantanamo Bay.'

The President's thin mouth turned down as he struggled to comprehend Kadeer's message. He seemed to be taking the threat to a sinister new level.

'The Prophet, peace be upon him, predicted that the end times would be very near when you, the Mushrikeen, and the Jews amongst you "swarmed against Islam from every hill". You are swarming against us today from every hill in all the four corners of the earth. If your leaders persist with the destruction of the Muslim people; if you continue to humiliate the Prophet, peace be upon him, your civilisations will be destroyed in the final solution, as it is predicted in the noble Qu'ran.' The Muslim microbiologist closed his holy book.

'September 11 was the forerunner of much worse to come. Very soon you will be given your first warning and we will attack you beneath Eternity. This will be followed by a second and a third warning, and if you do not heed these warnings from Allah, the Most Kind, the Most Merciful, you will perish when the single strand meets its double.'

CHAPTER 2

THE CENTERS FOR DISEASE CONTROL, ATLANTA, GEORGIA

naked beneath her sterile surgical gown, Dr Kate Braithwaite was protected by a blue biosafety spacesuit. When anyone left a Biosafety Level 4 laboratory, nothing was allowed past the decontamination showers. Although it was already after 9 p.m., Kate was not ready to leave yet, and she moved towards the door at the far end of the deadly hot-zone laboratory, shuffling in the galoshes that protected the soles of her spacesuit from any wear from the floors.

Only thirty-four, and Australian-born, Dr Kate Braithwaite was one of the most respected biochemists and virologists in the United States and she was one of the few scientists in the world who could claim to be an expert on *Variola major,* otherwise known as smallpox. Her long, blonde curly hair was held in place with a hairnet to keep it from falling across her eyes behind the heavy plastic face mask. Her lightly freckled face was tanned and, even behind a visor, Kate Braithwaite was clearly a very attractive young woman, although on this night her normally sparkling green eyes smouldered with anger. Kate was usually based in Maryland at USAMRIID, the United States Army Medical Research Institute for Infectious Diseases, but a week ago she'd received a top-secret directive ordering her to divide her time between Maryland and the CDC, the Centers for Disease Control in Atlanta. Dr Braithwaite had been instructed to prepare some of the most dangerous experiments ever conducted in the history of biological warfare.

CDC's main Biosafety Level 4 laboratory in the western sector of the complex was one of the deadliest laboratories in the world. The floors and walls were tiled and kept immaculately clean. There were dozens of red, coiled air hoses hanging from the ceiling. The air in the lab was at negative pressure and was constantly replaced. Telltale banks of chimneys on the roof expelled micro-filtered air that was also super-heated to make doubly sure any pathogens like Ebola and Marburg, for which there was no known cure, were well and truly destroyed before they reached the outside world. Alone in the lab, Kate had put in an exhausting fourteen hours hunched over Petri dishes that contained India-1, one of the most lethal strains of smallpox known to man, but she wanted to check on her beloved chimpanzees before she left for home.

To go ahead with these experiments was utterly irresponsible, she thought angrily, as she eased open the heavy steel door to the animal room. The world had already seen enough horror without risking another outbreak of smallpox. Kate knew there were only two repositories of smallpox left on the planet. One was in the Russian laboratories in Koltsovo in Siberia and no one was really sure that the Russians could account for all of their lethal stocks. The other repository was here at CDC, which was surrounded by concrete barriers to prevent anyone driving a truck bomb into the building. The smallpox was kept under the tightest laboratory security found anywhere in the world.

Kate's thoughts turned briefly to Professor Imran Sayed, her immediate boss from her home base in Maryland. She had supported both her Professor and the old Colonel Commanding USAMRIID, the three of them arguing passionately for the destruction of the world's two remaining stockpiles of the deadly virus, but each time they had been firmly rebuffed by those in power. They had argued just as passionately that experiments on the great apes should not proceed, but last week a new Colonel Commanding had been posted in – Colonel Walter C. Wassenberg III; and it was he who had issued the orders for the experiments. She would no doubt get to meet him when she returned to Maryland, but she had already heard enough from her colleagues back at 'the RID', as USAMRIID was known to the inmates, and the news was not good. Wassenberg was a stickler for military discipline and a staunch supporter of White House policy, and Kate had a terrible feeling that neither she nor Professor Sayed would be successful in getting the dreadful experiments stopped.

Kate closed the heavy steel door behind her and reached for one of the red air hoses, plugging it into her regulator. The cool air pressurised her suit with a loud hiss and she shuffled over to the first of the cages that held the small family of chimpanzees brought in from Gabon for the research.

None of the chimps had settled into their new homes; half-eaten persimmons, bananas and paw paws were scattered among the green leaves on the floors of the cages. Kate had named the alpha male

Maverick and as she looked into his soulful brown eyes, her anger softened. He was sitting at the far end of his cage thoughtfully stroking his chin. His big, black nose was squashed onto his wrinkly old face, and his powerful arms and the rest of his body were covered in black hair, although there were grey touches on the top of his head. As Kate continued to hold eye contact, he got up and ambled over to the bars of the cage, pressing his face between them, looking at her quizzically. Although he was well built, the alpha male wasn't the biggest in the group. In many ways, families of chimpanzees mirrored their human communities. In Maverick's case, he was the most politically astute and he had ascended to the position of alpha male because he possessed the best social skills and was the most capable of maintaining order within the group. He had the respect of all the others, which gave him first feeding rights, as well as mating rights.

Kate felt a strange connection to the big primate. It was not the first time she had wondered about DNA and the inter-connectedness of life. She knew that, unlike gorillas, chimpanzees' DNA differed from human DNA by only 1.6 per cent, but that didn't mean she agreed with the Administration's view that chimpanzees provided the best chance of success in the deadly experiment. The gentle primate seemed troubled, Kate thought. She could see the sadness in his eyes. It was almost as if he had some inkling about what was going to happen to him and his family, and Kate shared his concern. As skilled as she was in handling *Variola major,* the experiments she had been ordered to conduct had never been tried before and she had no way of knowing how they might turn out or how dangerous they might become.

CHAPTER 3

GEORGIA SPORT SHOOTING ASSOCIATION, ATLANTA

President Denver Harrison's emergency war cabinet had been scheduled less than two hours after Dr Kadeer's video had been aired by al-Jazeera. As yet unaware of either the video or the war cabinet meeting, Vice President Charles 'Chuck' Bolton had been addressing a meeting of the National Rifle Association in one of the big conference rooms at the Georgia International Convention Center. Vice President Bolton was driven by just two forces: power and money. He was the principal attack dog for the GOP or 'Grand Old Party' as the Republicans had been known since *The Boston Post* had dubbed them that in the late nineteenth century. The Vice President was feared by GOP Republicans and Democrats alike for his 'take no prisoners' approach to politics. Chuck Bolton was slightly built and of medium height; his oval face was pale and his fine grey hair was thinning. His blue eyes were hard and metallic, and his pencil moustache was greying above needle-thin lips. Vice President

Bolton's demeanor held not a scintilla of warmth. The Vice President was one of the most powerful men in Washington, and although the top job had so far eluded him he was widely acknowledged as being the real power behind the Presidency. No one was in any doubt as to what the Vice President stood for, be it his abhorrence of homosexuals, his unflinching support for bans on abortion and stem cell research, or his conviction that America was destined to reshape the world; and for Bolton, that world was defined by a projection of American power. As he concluded his address an aide approached him and whispered in his ear.

'al-Qaeda have released another video and there's an emergency meeting of the war cabinet scheduled for the White House Situation Room. We're arranging for you to view it down at Atlanta's FBI Headquarters with secure video conference facilities. It'll be a bit more comfortable than the back of the communications van.' Like the President, the Vice President's convoy included a communications van bristling with state-of-the-art equipment that could connect both men anywhere in the world.

'Air Force Two?' the Vice President queried. Flown by the Presidential Airlift Group assigned to 89th Airlift Wing at Andrews Air Force Base in Maryland, Virginia, the Boeing 757 used by the President and designated Air Force Two was sitting on the tarmac barely 10 minutes away at Hartsfield-Jackson Atlanta International Airport.

'No time. They're meeting within the hour. You'll need to wrap this one up, Mr Vice President.'

The Vice President nodded and turned back to his audience, every member of which had been handpicked and screened for the occasion. With the possible exception of the President's chief political advisor and election strategist, Dan Esposito, no one in the Administration was more aware than Vice President Bolton that in a few short weeks the people of the United States would go to the polls. The mid-term elections would decide who controlled the Congress in both the House and the Senate. In American elections, where voting was not compulsory and low turnouts could spell electoral disaster, the support of groups like the National Rifle Association and the massive churches on the evangelical right was crucial. As he prepared to wind up his address Vice President Bolton made a mental note to get a message to Dr Richard Halliwell. His private meeting with the CEO of Halliwell Pharmaceuticals would have to be put back until after the video conference. It would mean a very late night, but Bolton thrived on late nights and the meeting was crucial to both of them.

'We're still safe!' the Vice President joked to the audience. 'Terrorists think twice these days before attacking the United States of America!' He was not yet aware of the content of the latest video release by Dr Khalid Kadeer, but Bolton's remarks would come back to haunt him. 'We need to ensure that we *keep* America safe,' Bolton continued. 'The Second Amendment and the right of every law-abiding American to carry a gun is not negotiable!' The pro-gun audience erupted with foot-stamping applause. 'We need to keep America safe from terrorists like bin Laden and Kadeer. The only thing these Islamic terrorist thugs understand is the point of a gun. Debating societies like the United Nations and the Democratic Party only embolden these terrorists to commit more atrocities against the American people, and I'm not about to stand by and let that happen!'

As with every speech, Vice President Bolton was subtly positioning himself for another run at the White House.

The audience leapt to their feet cheering and whistling, and they were still applauding as the Vice President headed into the convention center's cavernous foyer. His Cadillac DeVille with an attendant convoy of black Chevrolet Suburbans and heavily armed secret service agents was waiting in the driveway.

As the Situation Room beneath the Oval Office came into focus on the screen, the Vice President made a mental note of who was present. The President was yet to arrive, but the Secretary of State, Secretary of Defense, Secretary of Homeland Security, National Security Advisor, Director of National Intelligence and the Chairman of the Joint Chiefs were all at the table, as was the White House Chief of Staff. The advisors' seats crowded against the panelled wall were occupied by his own Chief of Staff and the Deputy National Security Advisor, as well as the Director of the Central Intelligence Agency. This video must be causing more concern than usual, Bolton thought. Ever since the new super Office of the Director of National Intelligence had been established, the CIA had lost its longstanding direct access to the President, causing more than a deal of angst amongst the die-hards at Langley, but today the Director of Central Intelligence had been summoned as well. The Vice President's eyes hardened when he noticed that the DCI had brought along one of his principal advisors, Curtis O'Connor. Officer O'Connor and the Vice President had clashed more than once when O'Connor had had the temerity to disagree with him. Bolton had recognised early that O'Connor was dangerously articulate and he'd added O'Connor's

name to his long list of people to be watched carefully. The little shit
seated against the opposite wall, Dan Esposito, was also on the list.
Bolton was annoyed that the President's powerful electoral advisor
had also gained access to the war cabinet. Homosexual faggot, he
fumed. Chuck Bolton had reluctantly decided to tolerate Esposito's
sexual proclivities, but only for as long as he remained useful. Bolton
knew that should anything happen to this president, he was only a
heartbeat away from the White House. Every time Chuck Bolton had
raised the prospect of running for the top job, Esposito had evaded
the issue. If the Republican Party did as badly in the mid-term elections as the polls were predicting, Bolton had already decided that
the first head to roll would be Dan Esposito's.

As he waited for the President to arrive, Bolton's thoughts turned
to his meeting with Richard Halliwell. Halliwell Pharmaceuticals
was now the biggest of the world's 'Big Pharma', the none-too-
flattering epithet used to describe the largest of the drug companies,
and although it had been officially denied, the Vice President still
held a substantial interest in the company. In the last two years,
Halliwell Pharmaceuticals had become larger still. Washington's top-
secret decision to quietly fund a new $500 million Biosafety Level 4
laboratory in the far corner of Halliwell's sprawling 100 acre Atlanta
complex had been pushed through by Vice President Bolton as part
of the war on terror. The decision was so sensitive that several of the
President's closest advisors were still unaware of it.

Dr Kadeer brought his warning to a quiet but menacing conclusion.
The video faded to an ominous black and an equally ominous silence
settled over the Situation Room.

Curtis O'Connor reflected that the President seemed to be running out of options. Most Americans had long ceased to believe the White House spin on the war in Iraq and the Harrison Presidency was looking increasingly weak, even impotent. Once the chilling message from al-Qaeda had been broadcast by the big western media outlets, the public had become increasingly alarmed. Messages like this from the enemy would need a response. O'Connor glanced towards Dan Esposito. Curtis O'Connor knew that Esposito would ensure that the response was immediate. On the first day he'd met the short, fat, balding advisor the dislike had been mutual. Arseholes and Esposito had a lot in common, O'Connor mused.

'What the hell does all that mean, and where the hell is Xinjiang,' the President demanded, breaking the silence and directing his question to Curtis O'Connor. President Harrison was clearly feeling the pressure.

'We're not sure what this means yet, Mr President,' Curtis replied calmly. 'We've done a preliminary imagery and voice analysis and there's no doubt that the video recording is genuine, although the location is open to question. al-Qaeda are meticulous in ensuring a nondescript background for recordings like this, and those rocks behind Dr Kadeer could be just about anywhere in Central Asia, of which Xinjiang – a large province in Western China – is a part.' He could have added that at 1,600,000 square kilometres, Xinjiang was more than three times the size of France and it had common borders with Pakistan, India, Afghanistan, Mongolia and three of the 'Stans' – the Central Asian states that had been part of the old USSR – Tajikistan, Kazakhstan and Kyrgyzstan. He could also have added that the deserts, lakes and the Tianshan or 'heavenly mountains' of Xinjiang were stunningly captivating and that the Muslim Uighurs who had lived in the area for centuries had a deep spiritual attachment to their lands. He might have mentioned that the province was rich in oil and minerals, but he didn't. The average man in the street might not know or care where Xinjiang or the 'Stans' were, but Curtis O'Connor was talking to the most powerful man in the world and Curtis figured that he should have known. Perhaps an atlas for Christmas, he mused wryly. But right now there were more pressing things to get across.

'So where will this first warning attack occur?' President Harrison seemed rattled, as if events were spiralling out of his control. 'Does it have anything to do with the threat from anthrax and smallpox?' he asked, looking around the table for answers.

'The content of the message is something of an enigma, Mr President,' O'Connor continued. 'This is the first time al-Qaeda have employed this sort of vague coding and we're uncertain if Kadeer's been able to develop any biological weapons. Our initial impression is that the first warning attack will be carried out either here in the United States or against either of our two major allies – Britain or Australia.'

'And the Chinese?'

'The Han Chinese Government see the Uighur Muslims in western Xinjiang on the border with Kyrgyzstan and Kazakhstan as 'different' and a threat to the unity of the country, and they're determined to crush them. For decades the Chinese police and armed forces have been carrying out brutal attacks against Muslims in Xinjiang, which is so remote from the rest of the world the attacks are not widely reported, Mr President. Kadeer's final attack will not only be directed against the United States, Britain and Australia, but at the Chinese as well.' Curtis O'Connor had no way of knowing just how large and devastating that attack might be.

'And this business about eternity?' the President asked edgily.

'Depending on the translation, Mr President, the Qu'ran mentions eternity in only eighteen of its suras or chapters, mostly in relation to gardens of eternity, although some scholars translate the Arabic as gardens of Eden. Interestingly enough, in six of those suras, the Qu'ran speaks of rivers flowing beneath these gardens or beneath eternity. We're now looking at possible attacks on major rivers, perhaps with the aim of poisoning our water supplies. The Qu'ran also makes it clear that where the rivers flow under eternity, the righteous dwell there as a reward from Allah, rather than as a punishment, so at first glance, the theory on the rivers doesn't seem to add up.' Without realising it, O'Connor was getting tantalisingly close.

'You seem to be forgetting the stolen windmill and that the country most associated with windmills is the Netherlands,' the Secretary of Defense interjected. 'An attack on the dykes would devastate vast low lying areas and cause untold damage.'

'We haven't ruled that out, Secretary,' Curtis O'Connor replied evenly, 'but the Netherlands were not one of the three original members of the coalition.' O'Connor disliked the pompous Secretary of Defense almost as much as Esposito, and he would have liked to add that the Dutch had not reported any of their windmills as 'missing', but he held his tongue.

'And the mushrikeen and what was it – strands?' the Secretary of Defense asked, his irritation palpable.

'When the single strand meets its double has got us puzzled as well,' O'Connor responded candidly. 'That would appear to be associated with Kadeer's final solution and we're still working on that, although the use of mushrikeen is clear enough. Mushrikeen is Arabic for those who worship more than one God. The Islamists in particular reject any notion that Allah can be worshipped in conjunction with any other God. For example Hindus and Buddhists who partner their idols with God, or Christians who also worship Christ and the Holy Spirit.' O'Connor knew that he was trespassing on dangerous ground with President Harrison, but he didn't back off. In O'Connor's mind, a quick readiness to wage brutal and debilitating wars on behalf of various versions of a God was dangerous nonsense. Unless something was done to get religion out of the foreign policy equation, the resultant clash could lead the world to an unmitigated catastrophe.

As night fell over Atlanta, Richard Halliwell was waiting for the Vice President in his office on the thirty-seventh floor of the Halliwell Tower situated on the outskirts of the central business district. For Richard Halliwell the new laboratories represented another significant step in his own quest for power. The sinister tentacles of the huge international conglomerate reached into the very top echelons of power in the United States and into intelligence agencies and governments in a hundred other countries around the globe. None was more important than China.

CHAPTER 4

THE HINDU KUSH, PAKISTAN–AFGHANISTAN BORDER

The dusty city of Peshawar, the capital of the wild and remote North-West Frontier Province of Pakistan, was bathed in the eerie light of a half moon. Nearly 18 kilometres to the west of Peshawar, the ancient Khyber Pass began its narrow, steep and stony journey up towards the border with Afghanistan. In 1893, when Pakistan had been part of India, the British Foreign Secretary of the colonial government, Sir Mortimer Durand, had drawn an arbitrary line on a rudimentary map. The establishment of the Durand Line as the border between Afghanistan and India had been typically colonial and typically designed to serve British interests. With little consultation, arrogant hands had once again ignored centuries of culture and tribal lands. The new border sliced through the middle of the Pashtun tribes, dividing them between two different countries. The vehemently disputed area now provided sanctuary for a resurgent Taliban who were attacking the coalition and NATO forces

...stan on a daily basis. The lawless North-West Frontier ...nce also provided sanctuary for an even more sinister group, al-Qaeda.

In the foothills of the Hindu Kush, a few kilometres to the north of the Khyber Pass, the forward scout of the patrol protecting one of al-Qaeda's most senior generals had seen a movement in front of him. He held up his hand, signalling those behind him to stop. Instinctively, twenty of the fiercest fighters in the world fanned out silently over the snow-covered rocks, taking up positions on either side of the path, their Kalashnikovs loaded and ready, their dark eyes calmly scanning the rocky hills. Each wore two bandoleers of 7.62mm rounds over their shoulders and the dull brass casings glinted menacingly in the moonlight. The donkeys carrying the other supplies, together with their handlers, propped obediently on the path. The small group had come from Xinjiang, and they'd been moving through the soaring mountains of the Hindu Kush for nearly two months, travelling at night and retreating to rest in the caves during the day. The infidels with their noisy helicopters were clumsy and easily avoided, but Khalid Kadeer's fighters were taking no chances. The Taliban who provided the guides through each of the areas they controlled were jumpy. Taliban fighters needed to be approached with caution.

Kadeer sat calmly on an icy rock at the side of track. In the distance, a thousand metres below them, he could see the lights of Peshawar, shrouded among the smoke from the house fires. He looked back behind him. The moonlight was reflected on the snow and granite of the higher peaks, and despite the enormity of what he was planning, Khalid Kadeer felt strangely at peace. He reflected on the different moods of the mountains. Sometimes thick clouds would roll in, swirling around the peaks and foothills, signalling an angry change. The blizzards would howl for days, with temperatures plunging to minus 40 degrees centigrade. The stinging sago snow would tear at the flesh of anyone who was foolish enough to try and move, then just as quickly the anger would dissipate. Tonight, Khalid mused, the towering mountains were majestically peaceful. They reminded him of another mountain and his thoughts turned to the Prophet Muhammad and the Archangel Gabriel. God's message, Kadeer knew, had been delivered to the Jews through Moses and the prophets, and the Christians had received theirs through Christ, but for centuries it seemed that God had ignored the Arab nations. Rabbis and priests had been quick to ridicule his Arab country-men, preaching to anyone who'd listen that the Arabs were not part of God's divine plan, but in the year 610, Gabriel appeared before Muhammad on the top of Mount Hira in Arabia and the balance had been restored. God's revelations had finally been delivered in the Arab language. If only the West would accept those revelations as being the equal of the messages of Moses and Christ, Khalid thought bitterly, it might be a different world. Instead, evangelists in the United States and elsewhere in the West had described Islam as an evil religion and the die was cast. If humankind would not accept the various religions' core messages and embrace the beauty of diversity and difference, those very same religions would become the source of humankind's destruction.

Khalid breathed in deeply, absorbing the power of the mountains. Just as the Prophet Muhammad had felt when he retreated to Mount Hira in what was now Saudi Arabia, it was here in the mountains of the Hindu Kush that Khalid felt closest to Allah, all praise be upon Him. It was here that he had received the messages to deliver the world three warnings, and it was here that Allah, the Most Kind, the Most Merciful, had directed him to prepare the final solution in case the West stubbornly refused to alter its present course. Khalid remained hopeful that China, the United States and her British and Australian partners would negotiate, but hope was slowly fading for the Muslim world. Kahlid recalled Sura 71 of the noble Qu'ran when Allah had given a similar mission to Noah and sent him to warn the people to change course. The message for Muslims from the Qu'ran had been the same message as the Christians had received in the Bible. 'Warn your people before some painful torment comes to them!' but Noah too had been in despair. 'My Lord,' he had said, 'the people have defied me . . . they have hatched a great plot . . . do not leave any disbelievers with homes on earth . . . do not increase wrongdoers in anything except destruction.' Kadeer could understand Allah's disappointment with the conduct of his children, and if Allah willed it, as he had with Noah, the final solution would be implemented.

Dr Kadeer turned back towards Peshawar. As the moon faded and the dawn broke, the indigo of the night cloaking the surrounding hills was slowly tinged with hues of soft purple and pink. The ancient city was stirring. Kadeer's thoughts turned fleetingly to the meeting he'd scheduled for later in the week with his chief lieutenant, Amon al-Falid. It was rare for Kadeer to meet with his top operational planner from the United States, but Peshawar was no ordinary city and the mission Allah had directed him to prepare was no ordinary mission. Kadeer leaned back against the rocks and closed his eyes to take a short nap. It was a habit of a lifetime that enabled him to stay alert through the long days and nights. As he dozed, he drifted back to his childhood spent in the little village near Kashgar in the far west of the vast autonomous region of Xinjiang, not far from China's border with Kyrgyzstan. A time when Khalid was eight and he'd been playing with his cousin after school.

It was October 1955. Mao Tse-tung had been in power for just six years but it had been long enough for the ruthless dictator to establish control over the far-flung western Xinjiang region with the establishment of the *Xinjiang shengchan jianshe bingtuan*, the Xinjiang Production and Construction Corps. The small, peaceful villages to the west of the city of Kashgar were under the control of a young, ruthless and ambitious Peoples' Liberation Army officer, Captain Ho Feng. Ho Feng had been ordered to keep the Muslims under control and he was determined to make his mark.

Like Kadeer's simple mudbrick house, his cousin Abdul Rasal's house was built in a square, with a dirt courtyard in the middle. An old pump stood in one corner of the courtyard, from which the family gathered water. The roof of the house was decorated with colourful Uighur motifs, and on the other side of the courtyard weathered wooden pillars supported a high veranda. In the room beyond it, Abdul's family slept on a carpeted platform, but for now, the family's cotton-filled mattresses made from Uighur silk were rolled up against the mud wall.

'Abdul! Khalid! Where is the wood, you two?'

'Coming, Mama!' Abdul grinned as he took another shot at Khalid's marble in the dirt pitch they'd made, but his marble missed.

'I win!' Khalid yelled, pocketing his cousin's marble and getting up to cut the wood for his aunt. Hayrinisahan was stoking the fire in the kitchen in readiness for the evening meal. Khalid always looked forward to staying with Hayrinisahan. She was like a second mother, although more fun. As he put the pile of kindling he'd cut next to the wood-fired stove his aunt smiled at him, but her smile faded as first one truck, and then another, followed by several more roared past the house. Khalid and Abdul rushed to the door and peered through the beads at the convoy of Han Chinese soldiers tearing down towards the village square. A staff car was travelling in the middle of the convoy and Khalid caught sight of the most hated man in Xinjiang, the ruthless Chinese Captain Ho Feng. His skin was oily and his fine, black hair was parted in the middle and fell either side of an oval face. Ho Feng's dark eyes were inscrutable. He was responsible for the murders of hundreds of Uighurs and even the mention of his name struck fear into the peaceful Muslims.

'Khalid! Abdul! Come back inside, both of you!' Hayrinisahan scolded, covering her mouth and nose as a thick cloud of dust swept into the house, settling on the elegant Uighur carpets covering the walls.

A short while later, Hayrinisahan's face paled as the sounds of systematic gunfire rent the air. Friday prayers at the little village mosque would have finished and although she'd expected her husband, Ali, to be home by now, he often dropped in to see Khalid's parents and was sometimes a little late. She hadn't worried unduly.

The day before, one of Ho's soldiers patrolling in the village square had been knocked down and killed by a runaway horse.

'Make an example of them!' Captain Ho ordered. 'That house over there!'

Twenty Chinese soldiers stormed into Khalid's house, rounding up Khalid's mother, father, uncle, brother and his little sister. With his mother crying and his sister screaming in fright, they were roughly paraded in front of the captain.

'String them up!' he commanded, 'and leave them there for three days, so these people learn how to keep their animals under control.' Captain Ho caught sight of the village Imam in the door of the little mosque. 'And set fire to their mosque,' he added with a sinister smile. 'Perhaps Allah will help them put it out.'

Khalid woke with a start. The images of his mother and father, uncle, brother and baby sister, their heads twisting grotesquely as they swung from wooden poles beside the burned down mosque were seared indelibly on his soul.

Khalid's forward scout scanned the foothills below. He'd seen a movement behind a large rock that stood sentinel-like on a bend ahead. The scout moved forward cautiously, keeping off the narrow, rocky track, alert in case the infidel had chosen to put in an ambush. He caught the movement again, a shadowy figure with a weapon, and he stopped, holding his position on the dominating high ground.

CHAPTER 5

THE SITUATION ROOM, THE WHITE HOUSE, WASHINGTON DC

As Agent O'Connor had predicted, his explanation of the mush-rikeen and the Muslims' belief in only one God infuriated President Harrison, especially when he compared it with the Christian worship of the Trinity: God, his son Jesus Christ and the Holy Spirit.

'This is a Christian country with Christian values, and we need to smoke these little Muslim terrorists out of their hideouts and round 'em up,' the President responded angrily, in no mood for a theological discussion on the Qu'ran.

As a plan, it was a little short on detail. O'Connor said nothing.

'I couldn't agree more, Mr President.' The video link to the Vice President in Atlanta, despite going through a complex series of unbreakable encryptions, was clear and the image of the Vice President seemed to dominate the entire room. 'I've just finished addressing the National Rifle Association, and you have their full support. This is just bluff.'

'In the meantime, Mr President, we'll need to make a public response,' Dan Esposito stipulated.

Curtis O'Connor reflected that it had not taken President Harrison's powerful and cunning little advisor long to reduce a discussion on a terrorist threat that might affect millions of lives to one of politics and votes.

'We will need to reassure the public that Kadeer is bluffing and stick to the agreed line that we are winning this war on terror and that it is a war that is crucially important for all freedom-loving people around the world.' Dan Esposito's voice had a touch of steel, daring anyone, including the President, to disagree with him.

'I don't think Kadeer is bluffing, Mr President,' Curtis O'Connor said quietly, glancing towards the camera so that the Vice President would also be left in no doubt as to what O'Connor thought of his views.

'And what facts do you have to base that on, Officer O'Connor?' Esposito spat the words across the room.

Curtis O'Connor suppressed a wry smile. The use of his CIA rank was a none-too-subtle reminder from Esposito that opinions that did not support the White House line were not welcome. The Administration and the Party's private polling was probably a lot worse than what was being published, Curtis thought to himself.

'I've been involved with Islam and Islamic terrorists for nearly twenty years, Dan,' Curtis replied, ignoring Esposito's bullying rank tactics. 'Dr Kadeer is not only a brilliant microbiologist, he is a deep thinker and philosopher and his threats should not be dismissed lightly. He trained as an undergraduate in Beijing and he did his doctorate at Harvard. He knows this country well and knows how to strike fear into the population. His hatred of both the West and the Han Chinese is deep-seated, but his struggle is not confined to the West and the Chinese. Kadeer is first and foremost a Sunni, and although he is very tolerant of other religions, he is committed to a return of the Caliphate.'

'Meaning?' President Harrison's exasperation was reaching breaking point, but he wasn't the only one in his Administration who was struggling to comprehend Islam. Most of his senior advisors and his own cabinet had completely misjudged what might be driving *Jihad*, the call to action amongst the Islamic fundamentalists or Islamists as they had become known. Some of the cabinet, including the President, had not realised there was a difference between a Sunni and a Shiite.

Curtis again answered calmly. 'Islam is translated literally as "surrender". A true Muslim surrenders his or her entire being to Allah, and strives to meet Allah's demand that human beings treat each other with justice, equity and compassion.'

'You've got to be fucking joking,' Esposito muttered.

O'Connor ignored him. 'For Kadeer, the future of Islam depends on its ability to return to its past. For thirteen centuries, until 1923, Islam was always responsible to a supreme authority. The last such authority able to trace his lineage back through Baghdad and Damascus to the Prophet Muhammad was the Ottoman Sultan Mehmet VI in Istanbul. In 1922—'

'Mr President,' Dan Esposito interrupted, irritated that they were straying from the main game of winning the next election but the President held up his hand for silence.

'In 1922,' Curtis continued, 'Ataturk overthrew the last Sultan and replaced the Caliphate with a secular government and moved the Turkish capital to Ankara. Kadeer is a Sunni, and he wants to re-unite Muslims under a single Caliphate which not only pits him against the West but also against Shiite countries like Iran and large parts of Iraq and Lebanon.'

The President and more than one member of his cabinet were still looking puzzled.

'The Sunni–Shiite divide dates back to the death of Muhammad in 632,' Curtis explained. His mind was racing as to how he might distill the long-running feud into a few simple sentences. 'The Sunni are those who accept that the Caliph can be elected for his qualities of being the most competent and knowledgeable to lead Muslims by the Sunna – or the laws of the Prophet – and when the Prophet died they prevailed with the election of the first Caliph, Abu Bakr, as Muhammad's *khalifah* or representative. The Shia, on the other hand, have always believed that the Caliph should have a lineage back to Muhammad's family, and the Prophet's cousin Ali, who was not elected as the fourth Caliph until 656, only to be murdered in 661. Kadeer knows it's a huge ask to achieve unity but despite the arguments over succession, in terms of what they believe, Sunnis and Shiites have much in common and he's still prepared to try. In that sense Kadeer and bin Laden are united. Both are Sunni and for them the end of the Caliphate was a catastrophe which the West has only exacerbated by attacking Iraq and supporting Israel against Lebanon and Palestine.'

It was too much for the Vice President, and once again he domi-nated the room from the video screen. 'Mr President, is any of this relevant? A Muslim is what a Muslim does and that's attack our freedom and our democracy!'

'What's your point, Mr O'Connor?' the President asked, looking even more confused.

'Not long after September 11, on 7 October 2001, bin Laden made a video broadcast over al-Jazeera, not unlike the one we have seen today. In it he declared that "What America is tasting is only a copy of what we have tasted . . . Our Islamic nation has been tasting the same for more than eighty years of humiliation and disgrace, its sons killed and their blood spilled, its sanctities desecrated." Like bin Laden, Kadeer is deeply offended by the presence of our troops in the revered and holy lands of Saudi Arabia, and his speech today only underlines his outrage over what has happened in Iraq and Lebanon.' O'Connor could feel the hostility of those around the table but he didn't hold back. This was a rare opportunity to urge the President of the United States to change course. Curtis O'Connor had an uncommon ability to look at any given situation through the eyes of his enemy, and he was convinced that if he let this cabinet believe Esposito's spin that Kadeer was bluffing, it would be another deadly mistake.

'Whatever you may think of Kadeer's religious beliefs,' O'Connor said, 'he holds to them strongly, including the belief that the end times have been predicted in the Qu'ran.' O'Connor was tempted to observe that Dr Kadeer was not the only one who believed that the twenty-first century and the looming clash of civilizations heralded the end times. Biblical prophecies about a rapidly approaching Armageddon and 'the rapture' were also being aired by some of the President's own equally fanatical religious advisors. Advisors like the

Reverend Jerry Buffett who had unprecedented access to the Oval Office. Curtis noticed that the President was becoming increasingly agitated, and he decided to bring his forceful briefing to a close.

'Kadeer has made a number of lesser threats in the past, and,' O'Connor concluded solemnly, looking at Esposito and towards the camera at the Vice President, 'he has always carried them out. The only difference this time is his final solution. When he issued the threat of a single strand meeting its double, he used the words "if Allah wills it". He has not used that terminology before and it may mean he has yet to complete his plans for the final attack.'

O'Connor was not to know that he had got that part of the puzzle right. Although Kadeer had not yet secured everything he needed to put his final solution in place, he was ready to implement his series of warnings. He had not only issued a demand for coalition forces to be withdrawn from Muslim lands, he had brazenly pinpointed the exact location of the first warning attack. Neither Curtis O'Connor nor anyone else in the CIA had yet been able to decipher the deceptively simple code that gave this location. There was also a clue to the final deadly assault and if the nature of it wasn't yet clear, it would be in time; a conspiracy that would have its zenith in Beijing, driven by the threat from Islam and by the rise of China. With chilling calm, Dr Khalid Kadeer had revealed he was close to acquiring the means to annihilate a large part of the human race.

CHAPTER 6

ATLANTA, GEORGIA

Kate Braithwaite tossed restlessly in her sleep in the small, one-bedroom apartment the government had provided for her in Atlanta. She'd drifted back to her boarding school days at St Catherine's in Sydney and, as usual, her challenging mind had got her into trouble, this time with Sister Agnes, the history teacher. The lesson had been on wars and violence in the twentieth century. In 1987, Kate was in her third-last year at high school.

'In summary,' the stout and severe-looking Sister Agnes said, 'Idi Amin was responsible for the murder of nearly a half a million of his countrymen; Pol Pot murdered three million people – a third of Cambodia's population; Joseph Stalin was responsible for the deaths of twenty million, a million of whom were executed; Mao Tse-tung, somewhere between fifteen and twenty million; and Hitler, sixty million as a result of the Second World War, including six million Jews murdered in his Nazi gas chambers. In the twentieth century, somewhere between 170 and 200 million people have already been murdered or killed as a result of war and violence, and with Islamic fundamentalism on the rise, that number is likely to increase. On that rather depressing note, does anyone have any questions? Yes, Katherine.'

'Sister, the one common denominator in all this carnage is that the perpetrators were all men, and in more recent wars, such as those in Northern Ireland and the Middle East, where religion is a major factor, once again those inciting the violence and bloodletting are men. It doesn't seem to matter whether it's Islam or Christianity. In our own church the leadership is always male. Don't you think we females deserve a go, surely we couldn't do any worse than the men?'

A titter rolled around the room.

'I'm not sure what you mean by deserving a go, Katherine, but I will thank you not to cast any aspersions against the leadership of our Holy Church,' Sister Agnes sniffed haughtily. 'Now, for homework . . .'

Kate was invariably at the top or second-top of her class in every subject except one. Every annual report had marked her down for religion.

Kate tossed onto her side as her dream changed tack.

'What's this "Religion – a disappointing attitude"?' her staunchly Catholic father demanded after he had summoned Kate into his study on 'Bulahdelah', the family's 30,000 acre sheep property on the New England Tablelands west of Armidale.

Kate shrugged, unable to tell her puritanical father that she'd lost the faith he'd instilled in her since as long ago as she could remember.

'Well?' her father demanded. Dalton McKenzie was a big man in every sense of the word. His square, weatherbeaten face was flushed, as it always was when he was angry. He'd been elected Mayor of the Armidale Dumaresq Council on no fewer than three occasions and was known throughout the district for his no-nonsense conservative National Party views. Once again, his disappointment with Kate surfaced. When Kate's diminutive mother Muriel had produced a son and heir for her husband, the baby had been stillborn. Kate's father had made no effort to hide his disappointment when the doctors told Muriel McKenzie she would not be able to have any more children.

'I don't see why we always have to agree with what the nuns teach us,' Kate replied finally. 'Why are the leaders of religions all men?'

'There's only one true religion, Katherine, and that's the Catholic faith,' her father replied angrily. 'The leaders are men because the Bible says so, something you would obviously do well to read more often, young lady.' Dalton McKenzie reached for the old family bible with its cracked and worn leather cover that held pride of place on his desk. Opening it at Saint Paul's First Letter to Timothy, he began to read from Chapter Two. 'Let a woman learn in silence with full submission. I permit no woman to teach or to have authority over a man; she is to keep silent. For Adam was formed first, then Eve; and Adam was not deceived, but the woman was deceived and became a transgressor. Yet she will be saved through childbearing . . .'

'One day you will meet someone and be able to establish a home for him and provide him with a family. Until then, I suggest you guard that unruly tongue of yours. Now go to your room!'

Kate stormed out of her father's study, angry that she was fighting back tears and determined he wouldn't see them. She had long ago come to terms with having a father who hardly gave her the time of day, although if she was honest with herself, deep down she still craved his approval. Kate slammed the door to her room and, as she often did when she felt alone in the world, she sat down at her desk, took the cover off her most prized possession and switched on the Nikon microscope that had been a Christmas present. Her father had been puzzled by her request but in the end he'd agreed. Cookbooks would have been far more appropriate, but if his daughter wanted to muck about with bugs, maybe it would make her happy. Kate's tomboyish qualities only made him feel more acutely the disappointing loss of a son.

Kate tossed again in her sleep as her dreams shifted to Tiananmen Square. Standing at the Tian'an Gate, which separated the square from the Forbidden City, Kate gazed south across the vast flat snow-covered expanse of the largest paved square in the world. It had been designed to hold a million people, yet today the square was eerily deserted. In the distance people were fleeing the city in their tens of thousands. A 38-metre high obelisk, the Monument to the Peoples' Heroes, stood in the centre of the deserted square. Beyond it, on the southern edge, Kate could see Mao Zedong's Mausoleum – a large, low building supported by pillars where the great tyrant's embalmed body lay in state in a rose-coloured glass enclosure. To the west, the Great Hall of the People dominated while the eastern side of the square was flanked by the National Museum of China, the roof adorned with dozens of huge red national flags with the big yellow star and four smaller stars in one corner. The large paving stones seemed to be moving, and the reason for the people taking flight soon became clear. The snow on the great square was covered in millions of wriggling, deadly Ebola viruses. The long thin strands were curled at the end and Kate could see that the capsids – the protein covering that protected the virus' nucleic acid – were finely textured, another characteristic of the filovirus with no known cure.

The images of Tiananmen Square faded to the Forbidden City and the huge pagodas of the old Imperial Palace. Knobbly, grenade-like smallpox viruses were bouncing down the steps of the Taihe Dian, the Hall of Supreme Harmony, and into the vast snow-covered courtyard. Thousands more people were fleeing in front of the smallpox and Ebola, their bodies covered in raised, bleeding pustules, blood streaming from every bodily orifice.

Kate sat up in bed, shocked by her dream and wondering what it meant. She looked at her watch to find that she'd been asleep for less than two hours. Had she known about a meeting that was about to take place between the Vice President of the United States and Richard Halliwell she would have realised that the cosmos was warning her of what was to come.

CHAPTER 7

HALLIWELL TOWER, ATLANTA

The report was entitled 'The Chinese Threat: an Asian Tsunami'. Richard Halliwell pushed the analysis he'd commissioned on the Chinese to one side of his huge walnut desk and leaned back in his leather chair, the back of which was embossed with the Halliwell logo – a big gold 'H'. Like the yellow 'M' of McDonald's, it was a trademark that was recognisable anywhere in the world.

The CEO of Halliwell Pharmaceuticals towered over most men and he had a personality to match. His nose was sharp, accentuating his arrogance, and his grey eyes were steely. Richard Halliwell was in his fifty-fifth year, and his reddish hair was greying but a fortnightly visit to his office by Romano, his personal hair stylist, kept that hidden from the outside world. For a long time now Halliwell had also been putting on weight and there was a flabbiness around his paunch. The weight-loss pills hadn't worked, and despite the irritating urgings of his personal physician, he had not visited the well-equipped gym in the basement of the Halliwell Tower since he'd opened it five years earlier. Two years ago he'd had a facelift from one of the most expensive plastic surgeons in Los Angeles. The flab and wrinkles had been stretched out and, apart from a slight tightening around the eyes and the extremities of his square face, Halliwell was confident the rest of the world was none the wiser about that either, although there was one other physical attribute that he'd never been satisfied with and he'd always struggled to keep those insecurities at bay.

Halliwell swiveled in his chair to face the floor-to-ceiling windows of his vast office complex which took up the entire thirty-seventh floor of the Halliwell Tower. Halliwell's office afforded sweeping views of Stone Mountain National Park and the world's largest low relief sculpture on one side of the mountain cliff – the 30-metre high granite carvings of the Confederate leaders Robert E. Lee, Jefferson Davis and Stonewall Jackson on horseback. He gazed unseeingly towards the evening lights of Atlanta's central business district. Obsessed with the threat from the Chinese and driven by a deep belief in the superiority of the United States of America, he again contemplated the implications of the report. The population of Atlanta was a mere 470,000 and in the whole of the United States there were only nine cities with a population of more than a million. According to the report on his desk China's population was rapidly approaching the one and a half billion mark. The population of Beijing and its surrounds was nearly fourteen million, a staggering 27.3 per cent increase over the last decade, and aside from Beijing, China boasted more than 150 other mega-cities. Halliwell had sent a copy of the analysis to the Vice President.

The report had been compiled by some of the most astute business, economic and security researchers in the United States and their

findings only confirmed Halliwell's fears. The analysts were all predicting that in two decades, perhaps less, the yuan would take over
from the dollar as the world's principal currency. More importantly,
the Chinese were beginning to make huge inroads into world trade
markets, and the biggest single threat to the international dominance
of Halliwell Pharmaceuticals now came from the Orientals. Richard
Halliwell's demeanor was cold and calculating. If something wasn't
done to stop these slant-eyed little bastards in another twenty years,
perhaps less, they would take over from the United States as the most
powerful nation on earth. Oil prices had already gone through the
roof because of China's insatiable appetite and Washington was doing
absolutely fuck all about it, he reflected angrily. The media might see
terrorism as the biggest threat to the American way of life, but Dr
Richard Halliwell had absolutely no doubt that the Chinese juggernaut
was a much bigger threat than any backward towel-headed terrorist. Halliwell had already resolved that the Chinese must be stopped
permanently. Nothing less was at stake than America's pre-eminent
place of leadership in the world. For Richard Halliwell a world led by
the Chinese was unthinkable.

As the black, bullet-proof Cadillac DeVille made its way along Route
20, shadowed by just one black Suburban secret service van, Vice
President Bolton's thoughts turned away from the al-Qaeda video
threats to the long-term menace posed by the Chinese. He switched
on the reading light in the back seat and extracted the Halliwell
analysis from his leather briefcase. Sinking back into the soft leather

upholstery, he began to re-read the executive summary. This analysis, he reflected, matched the top-secret reports he'd received from the State Department, Treasury and the Department of Defense, but the White House was totally consumed by the war in Iraq and mid-term elections. The warnings on the Chinese were very clear, but like the CIA and FBI warnings on al-Qaeda before September 11, they were being ignored.

Richard Halliwell glanced at his diamond-studded Rolex as one of the dozens of lights on his Commander telephone console flashed. Simone, his well-endowed secretary, would normally have answered it but he'd made sure she'd taken the night off.

'I'm on my way,' Halliwell grunted. The palm trees flanking the mile-long drive that led to the white security gates at Halliwell were softly lit by hundreds of floodlights and the palm fronds were waving in a light breeze. The guardhouse had been alerted to the tripping of the security sensors near the big Halliwell logo that adorned the sandstone entrance just off the highway and the night vision cameras were tracking the Vice President's progression up the drive.

Richard Halliwell pressed the button for the lift that had been installed for his personal use and the doors opened immediately. At the moment Vice President Bolton had his uses, he reflected, as the lift plunged smoothly down towards the marble entrance foyer below, but Halliwell knew that Vice President Bolton's burning desire for the White House would eventually confront his own and that might require action. As the lift doors opened, Halliwell stepped out and reflected on the Kennedy assassination in Dallas. No one could be protected absolutely.

'I don't like this,' the team leader of the Vice President's personal protection detail muttered, as his partner parked their van close to Halliwell Pharmaceutical's imposing main entrance. Special Agent Brown watched closely as the Vice President shook hands with Richard Halliwell and then he scanned the areas of darkness on either side of the headquarters building with his night-vision goggles. Normally, on a visit like this, they would have maintained close personal protection and accompanied the Vice President to the outer office of the person he was visiting. Tonight the Vice President had insisted that would not be necessary. The visit was a personal one and Vice President Bolton was determined that it be kept low key. Not even the President knew he was here. Above all the visit was to be kept from the media. From time to time there had been heated speculation in the media as to whether or not the Vice President's association with Halliwell Pharmaceuticals included substantial shareholdings, forcing Chuck Bolton to send a personal explanation to Capitol Hill.

His shareholdings in American companies were indeed substantial. His soothing announcements always followed a similar tack; he believed in supporting American enterprise, but he'd assured both the House and the Senate that all of his shares had been placed in an 'arms length' trust. That part of his remuneration from Halliwell could easily be checked but there were more substantial benefits. Bolton was confident that even the most dedicated journalist would find those special bank accounts hard to trace.

CHAPTER 8

THE HINDU KUSH AND PESHAWAR

Khalid Kadeer's forward scout caught the movement down the track again. He quietly clicked his safety catch to the 'off' position and rested his gloved hand lightly on the trigger of his Kalashnikov and waited, scanning the ground below. If he revealed himself to the infidel the forward scout knew from bitter experience that the servants of the Great Satan would retreat but in their place the B57 bombers would appear overhead, their vapour trails reflected in the moonlight. A whistling sound would herald a rain of death, tons of high explosive shattering the peace and beauty of the Hindu Kush. At first light the helicopter gunships would appear like a swarm of angry wasps combing the hillsides for any sign of life. Suddenly three pinpricks of light appeared in quick succession. It was the simple pre-arranged signal from a Taliban sentry. Kadeer's scout reached for his pencil torch to reply.

Khalid Kadeer stood up and stretched as his protective party moved silently back onto the snow-covered track to resume the move down the mountain. The Khyber Pass was faintly visible in the distance as they prepared to be escorted through the last of the Taliban-controlled areas.

A small scout party pressed on towards Peshawar tasked with ensuring that neither the infidel nor the Pakistani authorities were waiting for them and that the al-Qaeda safe house was indeed safe. Not that there was likely to be a problem, Kadeer thought. The Taliban and al-Qaeda had long ago made the North-West Frontier Province their own and the American infidel was so bogged down in Iraq that Afghanistan was slowly being reclaimed. Occasionally the Pakistani government would make a token gesture and deploy the military into the border area so that the Pakistani President could claim they were doing their utmost to support the war on terror, but Khalid Kadeer and the rest of al-Qaeda and the Taliban always had ample warning. Just the same, Kadeer had vowed that the Pakistani government would pay the ultimate price for their treachery.

With the soft pink of the pre-dawn sky appearing, the shrill exhausts of the first of the *tuk tuks,* the three-wheeled, two-stroke rickshaws of Peshawar, began to echo through ancient bazaars that were stirring to life. The first of the *tongas*, horse carts with big rubber tyres and impossible loads, were making their way onto the streets, as were Peshawar's garishly coloured buses, belching clouds of thick, black exhaust. Emerging from beneath dirty cardboard shelters, dozens of beggars, many of them deformed, prepared to face another day of abject poverty. Suddenly the pall of smoke and gathering exhausts that enveloped the old city was shattered by the call to prayer by first one muezzin and then the echo of others, their messages to the faithful blaring discordantly into the surrounding hills.

Allahu Akbar! Allahu Akbar!
Allah is Greatest, Allah is Greatest

Allah ash hadu allaa ilaaha ill Allah
I bear witness that there is nothing worthy of worship but Allah.

As salaatu khairun minan maum.
Prayer is better than sleep.

Dr Khalid Kadeer moved a little away from his bodyguards who were reaching for their prayer mats. He laid his own prayer mat on a patch of rocky ground and pressed his forehead on the mat, then rose to the sitting position.

At the end of *Salat al Fajr*, the dawn prayer, one of the first of the five prayers of the day, Kadeer looked first over his right shoulder, towards the angel recording his good deeds. *As Salaamu 'alaikum wa rahmatulaah.* Peace and blessings of God be upon you.

Then he looked over his left shoulder towards the angel recording his wrongful deeds, of which he strived to ensure there were none. The three warning missions against the infidel and the final mission were not considered wrongful. They were after all ordained by Allah. *As Salaamu 'alaikum wa rahmatulaah.* Peace and blessings of God be upon you.

His prayers completed, Kadeer rolled up his prayer mat and settled down to wait for his scouting party to return. He smiled his thanks as one of his protective party appeared with a battered tin mug of steaming green tea, and he turned his mind to the discussions he would have with al-Falid. Hopefully the preparations for all of the warning attacks were well advanced. He already knew from the coded messages he and al-Falid had exchanged in anonymous internet chat rooms that the ocean-going tugs had maintained schedule and several of their precious cargos had been delivered safely. He allowed himself a grim smile. *Beneath Eternity where the windmill has been stolen.* It would be driving the infidel mad.

CHAPTER 9

HALLIWELL TOWER, ATLANTA

'Good to see you again, Chuck,' Richard Halliwell said without any depth of meaning, as he showed Bolton to one of the leather couches at one end of his vast office. 'Meeting go well?' he asked as he pressed a button on a remote and crossed the thick-piled carpet to where a well-stocked liquor cabinet was slowly rotating from behind the far wall.

'Very well,' Vice President Bolton replied in his southern drawl. 'At least the fucking National Rifle Association is on side, which is more than I can say for some of the treacherous bastards who inhabit the beltway around Washington,' he added, still furious at O'Connor disagreeing with him over the Khalid Kadeer threats.

Halliwell nodded as he handed the Vice President a crystal tumbler of Elijah Craig bourbon and ice. 'Our problem, Chuck, is that we're too honest and open in this country. If we're not careful Americans are going to pay a very heavy price. It's not the terrorists I'm worried about. It's the fucking Chinese. Did you read my report?'

The Vice President nodded as he savoured the eighteen-year-old bourbon. They were two of the most influential men in the United States, both driven by a lust for power and an unshakeable belief that the United States of America set the standard for the rest of the world. As the Presidential primaries to decide the next Republican candidate for the White House drew closer, their intense rivalry would surface, but for the moment, the Chinese threat to US dominance had them singing from the same deadly sheet of music.

'I agree with you. The Muslims are a backward and fragmented lot with a false religion.' Vice President Chuck Bolton wasn't the least bit religious but where the war on terror was concerned he played to the ordinary Americans' strong sense of the Almighty in their country's destiny and it suited him to denigrate Islam at every turn. 'But the Chinese are not constrained by religion, and that makes them more dangerous still.'

'You won't get any disagreement from me on that score,' Halliwell said, taking a hefty swig from his glass.

'Your report corresponds with other reports that have passed over my desk, and as of last week,' the Vice President continued, 'our gross domestic product stood at just over $10 trillion a year. That still puts us where we should be with the biggest share of the world's total of $36 trillion, but the damn Chinese are catching up and catching up fast. $1.5 trillion might put them in seventh place but unless we find a way to reign these little slopes in, they're going to overtake us within the next fifteen years, maybe ten.'

'It's worse than that, Chuck. That figure of $1.5 trillion is grossly misleading,' Halliwell said, his eyes steely. 'You can't take it in

isolation. Provincial governments in China routinely file very low productivity figures so they can continue to be classified as poverty zones
and remain eligible for large Central Government funding injections.
The internal regional productivity figures I've seen are much higher.
On the poverty correction factor alone, the Chinese GDP is closer to
$2 trillion. Our economy is growing at somewhere between 2 and 4
per cent, and the Fed thinks that's healthy? For fuck's sake, Chuck,
China is growing at three times that!' Dr Halliwell's passionate dislike
of the Chinese was on full display.

'Last year,' Halliwell went on, 'we bought $150 billion more in
goods from China than they bought from us. While the deficit here
is going through the roof, our dollars are pouring into the Chinese
treasury faster than they can count them. Believe me, Chuck, the
Chinese GDP is closer to $7 trillion a year.'

Both men were incensed that dumb-arsed Americans and millions
of other people around the globe were scrambling over one another to
buy Chinese imports. They knew that in reality the Chinese economy
was already the second largest in the world and it was threatening to
swamp the lead position of the United States. 'Tsunami' was a very
accurate metaphor.

The Vice President nodded. 'The Chinese are going to use the
Beijing Olympics as their passport to credibility, Richard. They're
putting so much into it that for the first time in history the International Olympic Committee has had to tell a host nation to slow down
on construction. The IOC's actually worried that they'll have a white
elephant sitting around for a year before the Games. Without the
drama in the lead-up the media will lose interest.'

The Vice President drained his glass and Halliwell reached over to refill it. 'If the Beijing Olympics is an outstanding success,' Bolton said, 'we can forget about attacking them over human rights and Tiananmen Square, so I was thinking that we ought to try and find another way to slow these little bastards down.' In a macabre parallel with Khalid Kadeer's plans, the Beijing conspiracy of Richard Halliwell and Vice President Bolton was taking on a sinister shape.

'Have you got something specific in mind?' Richard Halliwell already had something very specific in mind but he was missing a vital element.

The Vice President lowered his voice. 'Has the office been swept?'

Halliwell nodded. 'Just last week.'

Halliwell's Chief Financial Officer, still in his office two floors below, adjusted his headphones. The sweeping of the CEO's office was a security routine that Alan Ferraro made sure he was well aware of.

'I was thinking that if Beijing was to be subjected to a nasty health scare a couple of months before the Games that it might take some of the gloss off the event.'

'It would take more than a health scare, Chuck,' Halliwell replied. 'It would take something like Ebola or smallpox, although there are problems with Ebola.' Dr Richard Halliwell, one of the most ruthless and nationalistic men ever to wield corporate power in America, had already given the scenario a great deal of thought and he watched for any sign of squeamishness in his equally ruthless Vice President. Bolton didn't flinch.

'Unlike smallpox, which can be transmitted by a sneeze or a cough, Ebola can only be transmitted through direct contact with an infected person or their body fluids,' Halliwell explained. Although most of his time was taken up with maintaining Halliwell Pharmaceutical's domination of the global pharmaceutical market, Richard Halliwell was a very experienced biochemist, and one of only a few scientists among the hundreds Halliwell Pharmaceuticals employed around the world qualified to work in a Level 4 hot-zone laboratory. He had every intention of keeping his hand in. 'If we just used smallpox on its own the Chinese would put the weights on us for a smallpox vaccine. While that might be profitable,' Halliwell added with a sneer, 'eventually vaccines and strict worldwide quarantine might bring it back under control. On the other hand, there's no vaccine for Ebola. If Ebola was crossed with smallpox the Chinese would have to contend with a super virus that was easily transmitted. We could claim that the vaccine for that was still being worked on – even if it was ready for our own people.'

CHAPTER 10

CIA HEADQUARTERS, LANGLEY, VIRGINIA

Curtis O'Connor leaned back in his chair, clasping his hands behind his head. The sun had long since departed from the placid surface of the Potomac and the lights of the New Headquarters of the CIA probed the night around the lawns and the fishpond in the courtyard. The latest threat from Dr Khalid Kadeer was not making any sense and Curtis had an uneasy feeling that Kadeer was deadly serious. The Secretary of Defense was making even less sense, he thought, and his whacky views on windmills and an attack on the Netherlands were in keeping with the low opinion O'Connor reserved for most politicians.

O'Connor swung on his chair, turning to stare out into the night, switching his attention from possible targets towards the types of attacks al-Qaeda might mount. His mind went back to a fiery cabinet meeting in the White House Situation Room a few months earlier when he'd briefed the war cabinet on two reports. The first on the possibility of another biological attack against the United States using anthrax and a new strain of smallpox and the second from one of the CIA's agents in Moscow on the possible defection of a scientist from Russia.

Both reports had come from a single source and O'Connor had urged caution. Single source reports, especially those whose reliability was unknown, needed to be confirmed by at least one other source. It was one of the intelligence community's cardinal rules and he had wanted to check it before informing the White House, but the new DCI had overruled him. Dan Esposito was insisting on being kept informed of each new threat as it occurred. The hawks – the Vice President, the Secretary of Defense and Esposito – had led the others, demanding a 'fight fire with fire' retaliation and once again, Curtis had found himself backing the Secretary of State, a lone voice of reason in a cabinet convinced that America's overwhelming military strength would prevail. O'Connor remembered it well. The anthrax meeting had been heated almost from the start.

As that war cabinet meeting got underway, Curtis O'Connor hadn't had to consult his notes. He could recall both the anthrax and smallpox threats that had allegedly come from al-Qaeda and the cables from Moscow, word for word.

'We have two reports, Mr President. The first one, purporting to be from al-Qaeda, warns that the United States will be attacked with new strains of smallpox and possibly anthrax sometime in the next twelve months. Several cities will be targeted, but the threat does not indicate which ones or whether they will be attacked with anthrax or smallpox or both.'

'Purporting to be from al-Qaeda? What do you mean by that?' Dan Esposito demanded.

'I will come to that in a moment, Dan,' O'Connor replied, not phased by Esposito's challenge. 'The second report is connected with the first and indicates that a Georgian scientist who is working for the Russians on the weaponisation of smallpox wants to defect. Both reports should be treated with caution, especially the defection.'

'Why?' Dan Esposito asked. 'You seem to forget, Agent O'Connor, that 9/11 could have been prevented if we'd taken a little more notice of what you people in the CIA and the FBI were sitting on.'

'I agree, Mr President!' the Vice President interjected passionately, tapping the table with his pen for emphasis. 'If we've got information on possible anthrax and smallpox attacks we can't afford to ignore it.'

The President turned towards O'Connor, his left eyebrow raised.

'I'm not suggesting we ignore it, Mr President, just that you should be aware that we are dealing with raw intelligence here, and it can be dangerous to treat it as fact. For starters, al-Qaeda normally broadcast their threats through al-Jazeera or one of the other Arab channels but this intelligence has come from a Muslim activist in Georgia. al-Qaeda are known to be active in the Pankisi Gorge area, about 48 kilometres from the Georgian capital of Tbilisi, close to the border with Muslim Chechnya. As a matter of principle, Mr President, single source reports always need to be checked for accuracy. We need to know whether this really is from al-Qaeda or from a Georgian group that might have its own agenda, especially where stirring up trouble with the Russians is concerned.' O'Connor knew the hawks would see the need to double check reports as weak and bureaucratic but years of experience had taught him the wisdom of the process.

'What do we know about the scientist who wants to defect?' President Harrison asked.

'A Dr Eduard Dolinsky. The last time he was seen in public was in Vienna at the 2003 International Conference on pox viruses. The Georgian Muslims are claiming that he's been sent to Russia's Koltsovo laboratories in Siberia to work on a top-secret program weaponising anthrax and smallpox.'

'It wouldn't be the first time the Russians have had a crack at weaponising smallpox,' the Secretary of Defense broke in, glaring at O'Connor. 'I seem to remember when that Stolichnaya-swigging Yeltsin was at the helm the Kremlin was busy telling us that they had all their stocks of smallpox locked away in a freezer in Moscow.' He turned towards the President. 'They got caught out at a World Health Organization meeting in Geneva in 1999, Mr President, when one of their scientists let slip that the smallpox viruses had been moved to the Siberian desert for testing.'

'That's true, Secretary,' O'Connor responded, 'but this is the first time this source has contacted us and we don't know whether or not he's reliable. As yet we've not been able to corroborate his information.'

President Harrison looked confused. 'This Eduard Dolinsky, he's a Muslim?'

'He is, Mr President, but he's also one of the world's leading authorities on the genetic engineering of viruses,' Curtis replied bluntly, barely controlling his frustration that even here, the word 'Muslim' was automatically associated with terrorism and another planet. With the media continually painting every Muslim as a terrorist, what hope was there for the wider and much less informed public, he thought grimly.

'The employment of Muslim scientists in this area is not without precedent, Mr President.' The Secretary of State's voice was calm and reasonable. 'One of the most respected virologists in this country, and indeed internationally, Professor Imran Sayed, is also a Muslim. He was born in Pakistan, and he's employed by the US Army at USAMRIID.' Curtis O'Connor was grateful for the Secretary of State's wise counsel, although he immediately regretted the comparison as he watched the Secretary of Defense make a note.

'If this threat gets out, Mr President, and if the past record of some agencies is anything to go by, it will,' Dan Esposito said, glancing at O'Connor, 'we will need to be in a position for you as President and Commander-in-Chief to front the cameras and tell the American people that in the event of an anthrax or smallpox attack you will have the situation under control. The anthrax attacks on Senator Daschle's office and the others just days after 9/11 unnerved the entire population.' Esposito's jowls were wobbling like a turkey's wattle as his gaze shifted from the President to the other members of the war cabinet. 'If the terrorists can get hold of bioweapons they will and if this new threat materialises we will need to be a damn sight better prepared than we were for the first anthrax scare,' he said, looking back at O'Connor. Dan Esposito never missed an opportunity to direct the blame away from the White House towards those he disliked; everyone in the room knew that Esposito disliked the calm, confident O'Connor. That said, O'Connor saw things from both sides and he knew that Esposito was right about one thing; releasing a deadly biological weapon into the atmosphere could ultimately wipe out hundreds of millions of people. There was no doubt that the original anthrax attacks directed at Senator Daschle and others had signalled a new phase in the war on terror.

'You will need to be in a position to tell the American public that we have enough vaccine stocks to vaccinate every man, woman and child who has not already been inoculated, Mr President,' Esposito concluded, his face flushed and agitated. 'That will send a powerful message that we have things under control.'

'It might not be as simple as that, Mr President,' Curtis O'Connor argued, ignoring Esposito's glare of disapproval. 'Once smallpox was eradicated we stopped vaccinating people. That was over twenty-five years ago. Vaccinations for smallpox only last twenty years, so most people are now out of date. Furthermore, the India-1 strain, which the Russians are known to possess, is the most virulent of all the smallpox viruses we've encountered to date. We only hold enough vaccine to vaccinate about one-tenth of the population, keeping in mind that our armed forces and emergency responders have first priority. But even then our current vaccines would most likely be ineffective against strains like India-1.'

President Denver Harrison was looking decidedly uncomfortable and he abruptly brought the meeting to an end. As Dan Esposito walked past O'Connor on his way out of the room, he stopped and leaned towards him.

'I'm beginning to wonder whose fucking side you're on, Agent O'Connor,' Esposito hissed.

Curtis O'Connor swung wearily back to his desk. A stolen windmill, he mused. It wasn't making much sense, but it would in time.

The first of Khalid Kadeer's devastating warning strikes was planned for the target city's most vulnerable point; cruelly designed to paralyse one of the most beautiful cities in the world.

CHAPTER 11

HALLIWELL TOWER, ATLANTA

'Has anyone ever tried to cross Ebola with smallpox?' Vice President Bolton asked.

'The Russians have but I'm not sure they ever cracked it,' Halliwell replied. 'You remember that guy who defected, Dr Kanatjan Alibekov.'

'Changed his name to Alibek.'

'He's the one. Used to be the number two in the Russian biological weapons program, Biopreparat. After he spilled his guts on just what the Russkies had been up to there was a lot of speculation in the media. There's no doubt they weaponised anthrax and smallpox. Alibek confirmed that but they also had a go at genetically engineering different strains. With a DNA virus like smallpox that's no mean feat. It took years to perfect but the Russians were eventually able to combine the DNA of smallpox with Venezuelan equine encephalitis or VEE – a brain virus that causes a blinding headache that's so bad it puts you in a coma; the problem is it doesn't usually kill you. There was speculation that one of their key scientists, a guy by the name of Dolinsky, might have been able to combine smallpox with Ebola, which is an RNA virus. Unlike the double stranded smallpox, Ebola's RNA consists of a single strand of ribonucleic acid and I've not seen anything to confirm he was able to put them together – not on the open record anyway,' Halliwell added, hoping that the Vice President might disclose more information from classified sources. Halliwell had long been fascinated with the prospect of a super virus and he'd followed the open speculation as closely as anyone at Langley or USAMRIID.

'Dr Eduard Dolinsky?' the Vice President asked.

'That's him. Pity he's on the wrong side. He's one of the best virologists medical science has ever produced.'

'Interesting you should raise him. Dolinsky's name came up a few months back when cabinet was discussing the Daschle anthrax attacks,' the Vice President said. 'We've got some intelligence that he might want to defect, although an agent called O'Connor and the CIA are putting their usual negative spin on it.'

'Any idea why he'd want to defect?' Halliwell asked, his interest well and truly aroused.

'Not sure, although I gather that he's working somewhere in Siberia so that might have something to do with it. Would he be useful to you? If he is, O'Connor and his friends can be tasked with getting him out,' Bolton said with a sneer, not for the first time letting his vindictiveness override the need for security.

'Someone like Dolinsky would be very useful. If we could overcome the technical problems, Chuck, a super virus like Ebolapox would not only spell the end of the Beijing Olympics, it would put those little bastards back years, perhaps decades.'

'A super virus is no respecter of international borders, Richard,' the Vice President said. 'I don't give a shit how many millions of Chinese we wipe out – the more the better – but we'd want to make damn sure we had a vaccine to protect Americans, especially our athletes, before we released it.'

'You've hit the nail on the head, Chuck,' Halliwell agreed, reaching again for the bourbon bottle. 'Dolinsky is one of the few people, perhaps the only one, who could develop both the virus and its vaccine quickly. I can look after the distribution in Beijing,' Halliwell said, knowing that money would fix that problem, 'but I'd need your help to get the virus in through the black bag.' Halliwell's voice was strangely energised. The pieces were starting to fall into place and Halliwell could sense his destiny as the saviour of a grateful nation. Dolinsky was the missing link he'd been looking for. Provided the American nation had a vaccine for protection, a super virus would not only cause tens of millions of deaths, devastating the Chinese and their rampant economy, but the entire world would be clamoring for a vaccine that only Halliwell would be able to deliver.

'That won't be a problem,' Bolton replied.

'Dolinsky would be able to lead the development program but he would need two of our top scientists to help him,' Halliwell said.

'Just two?'

'The fewer people that know about this, the better, Chuck. Genetic engineering has come a long way and provided they're at the top of their field, two will be enough. You think you can sell it in Washington?'

The Vice President's smile was cold and humourless. 'I sold the idea of a new $500 million Biosafety Level 4 complex for you and I'll be working on the contract for the production of smallpox vaccines as well, which comes in at another half a billion. The last time I looked your contracts in Iraq this year topped $300 million,' he added meaningfully.

'You will find there will be $10 million of that in your Bahamas account by the end of the week,' Halliwell replied, just as meaningfully.

'How vulnerable is the Beijing Olympics to this sort of attack?' the Vice President asked.

'I'll find out next week,' Halliwell replied. 'I'm going to Beijing to meet with the Executive Vice President of the Beijing Organising Committee, General Ho Feng.'

'You know him?'

Halliwell nodded. 'Ruthless little bastard but he's open to, shall we say, "persuasion", and he's been pretty useful in helping us get contracts with the government. He's had a rapid rise through the Peoples' Liberation Army. When he was a young captain, they put him in charge of part of the Xinjiang Military District, with specific instructions to suppress the Muslims up on the border. Did it very effectively I gather. Used to string up whole families in village squares to give them the message.'

Alan Ferraro took off his headphones and moments later moved to the window of his darkened office on the thirty-fifth floor. From the shadows he watched as the Vice President's vehicles left, followed shortly after by Halliwell in his red McLaren Sports. The infidel, he reflected contemptuously, might have swallowed the bait.

CHAPTER 12

BEIJING ORGANISING COMMITTEE FOR THE OLYMPIC GAMES COMMITTEE TOWER, BEIJING

The driver of the Mercedes hire car held the door open for Richard Halliwell outside the impressive new headquarters of BOCOG, the Beijing Organising Committee for the Olympic Games on Beisihuan Zhong Lu. The Chinese had attached a 20-metre high logo to the front of the building and Halliwell smiled wryly as he looked at it. If the Chinese thought that the red logo of a runner embodied peace, they were in for a very nasty surprise. The BOCOG headquarters, which would double as the command centre for the Games, was not far from the impressive National Stadium, a doughnut-shaped building with a maze of steel girders that interlocked like twigs, earning the stadium the nickname of 'The Birds Nest'.

'Welcome, welcome, Dr Halliwell, we are very pleased to see you.' Ho Feng's personal assistant spoke perfect English, and she nodded slightly and shook Halliwell's hand before ushering him past the long reception counter and into the lift.

'Welcome to Beijing and to BOCOG, Richard, it's very good to see you again.' General Ho Feng was a slightly built man with an oval face and dark brown eyes. His fine, black hair was oiled and parted in the middle. When he smiled, his thin lips parted fractionally to reveal yellowing teeth. Halliwell knew that the General's feigned politeness was a mask that hid one of the most calculating personalities in the Chinese Communist Party.

'Thank you, Feng, thank you. I know you are a very busy man and it is very good of you to give me so much of your time.' General Ho was not the only one practised in the art of feigned politeness. Halliwell understood the Chinese culture of *guanxi* better than most. Loosely translated, it meant 'it's who you know'. Good *guanxi* in China was a very powerful asset.

The marketing pitch was the first in the series of briefings General Ho had arranged. Halliwell listened politely.

'Beijing will be the green Olympics and the high-tech Olympics,' the young and attractive marketing executive concluded. 'We want to show the world that these games are environmentally friendly.' Not for nothing had the cluster of venues nearby been named the 'Olympic Green' and the goal of high technology had been specifically designed to demonstrate China's new-found prowess. It was a goal that was not lost on Richard Halliwell.

'And finally, this is the peoples' Olympics, Dr Halliwell. The people in China have very positive attitudes.'

Richard Halliwell smiled and focused his laser-like brain on his own plans for the Beijing Olympics as the briefing on security got into full swing.

'Are you worried about terrorists disrupting the Games?' Halliwell asked blandly.

'We have the best security of any games,' General Ho replied. 'How do you say it in your country, Richard . . . Beijing will be locked down tighter than Fort Knox,' the general laughed. 'Especially the Athletes Village and the venues so you need not worry, Richard, your athletes will be perfectly safe here.'

The official doing the security brief unsuccessfully tried to hide his surprise at his general's frank disclosure. He knew well that the police, the Peoples' Liberation Army and counter-terrorism units would total more than 20,000 and thousands of hidden cameras were being installed to monitor every move in the ancient and modern city. For months the official line had been that Beijing would not be turned into a fortress. On the wall behind the briefer, the slogan for the Beijing Olympics 同一个世界，同一个梦想 – 'One World, One Dream' was displayed prominently. The slogan embodied a vision of 1.3 billion people reaching out and sharing in the global community, hand in hand with the rest of the world, creating a bright and peaceful future.

'Thank you so much for such an informative briefing,' Halliwell said, nodding slightly to the briefing staff, 'and for your gift.' Halliwell held up the gold plaque that BOCOG reserved for powerful dignitaries and Heads of State. 'And this is for you in appreciation, General Ho,' Halliwell said as he handed over a gold plaque with the Halliwell logo. The envelope containing 10,000 Halliwell shares remained in his briefcase. He would present that when the General and he were alone.

As Ho Feng led the way to a private luncheon that would

feature the General's favourite dish of bear bile soup, Halliwell was, as always, deep in thought. As he expected, the venues would be closely guarded but the city's hotels were far more vulnerable. Tomorrow he would work on the distribution system for the virus. Despite the Chinese government's efforts to portray the new China as a beacon for the twenty-first century, corruption was endemic and money always talked. The hired Triad thugs would not have the faintest idea what they were pumping into the air conditioning systems until it was too late.

'You must come and visit Atlanta, Feng. I would like to return some of your hospitality,' Halliwell said. Good *guanxi* was something to be nurtured.

CHAPTER 13

DETROIT INTERNATIONAL AIRPORT, WAYNE COUNTY

Kadeer's chief operations planner in the United States, Amon al-Falid, walked past the fountain in the McNamara terminal of Wayne County's new Detroit International Airport and continued on through the changing lights of the tunnel that connected with concourse A. The handler of a sniffer dog gave him a long look as they passed, even though the German shepherd took no notice. Perhaps the dog had not yet been trained to check out people of 'Middle Eastern appearance', al-Falid thought bitterly.

He had chosen Detroit as a departure point to add another layer of deception, but before he had even reached the customs barrier, two US Customs and Border Protection officers suddenly appeared at his side, the big blue 'Department of Homeland Security' flashes prominent on their sleeves. al-Falid turned to face them. The older of the two must have been nearly 18 stone, he reflected, the officer's stomach hanging over his heavy, black pistol belt, scalloping the buttons on his dark blue uniform. The other officer was a young woman al-Falid judged to be about twenty-five, and from the bars on her shoulders, she was the senior of the two.

al-Falid fought to keep his anger in check at the sight of the infidel flaunting her sexuality. Her blonde hair hung over her shoulders and her lips were covered with a purple gloss. An outline of the customs officer's breasts and nipples strained against the flimsy blue material of her uniform. al-Falid took a deep breath. The Imams in Australia had been right, he thought, yet they had been roundly criticised for sermons about scantily clad women.

'Mr al-Falid?' the young woman asked briskly.

'Yes.'

'You will come with us – now,' she demanded.

Amon al-Falid forced himself to remain calm. Even though he was inwardly incensed that he was being ordered about by a woman, he had trained himself for situations such as this. Now that the US Customs and Border Control had swept up the old Customs, Immigration, Plant and Animal Health into one powerful organisation, al-Falid had found himself being subjected to more and more interrogations and strip searches, even on domestic travel. He knew that computer crosschecks now linked more than twenty different federal agencies, including the FBI and the CIA databases, but he reassured himself that in the tens of thousands of movements that occurred each day, his Egyptian passport had yet to be linked to his United States passport. Nor had the infidel given any indication they had any inkling of his membership of al Qaeda.

'You were born in Egypt?' the young woman asked, looking first at al-Falid, and then at the photo in his passport. The photo showed a man with a swarthy complexion, the lower part of his face covered with a short black beard and a neatly trimmed moustache. He had a hooked nose, black hair and full lips. Behind the large black-rimmed spectacles, his eyes were dark and alert.

'As you can see, Cairo 1954,' al-Falid replied evenly. al-Falid had long ago decided that the best way to deal with one of the infidel's interrogations was to answer all of their inane questions firmly but politely.

The customs officer placed al-Falid's passport under a microscope to check it for any sign of forgery. The microscope and the nearby computer looked strangely out of place in the starkly furnished and windowless interrogation room with its grey, bare walls. The interrogator's obese colleague was leaning against the opposite wall. A third officer, thin and wearing thick glasses suddenly entered the room and extracted al-Falid's laptop from its black leather case. He plugged it into the wall socket, switched it on and pushed it towards al-Falid.

'Activate it,' he demanded. al-Falid shrugged and began to type in his codeword. His face was inscrutable. al-Falid had the ability to break into all but the most sophisticated of computer databases and wiping the internet searches that might incriminate him from his laptop had been child's play. He'd kept all his research results on the weak points of the various target cities on his computer in his office behind firewalls. al-Falid had constructed them to be as safe as any bank and much safer than any notes on paper. He watched as the customs officer scrutinised a mind-numbing array of sites on the architecture of the Silk Road.

'What is your reason for travelling to Pakistan,' the female officer asked.

'I'm on a sabbatical from Michigan State University. I have an interest in Asian history, especially the early architecture of Pakistan,' al-Falid said as he faced his interrogator. Keep calm, and keep your answers short and accurate, he told himself. Short, but not too short. Give out the absolute minimum of information without appearing to hold anything back.

'Why did you leave Egypt,' she asked suddenly. al-Falid recognised the question for what it was. It was a question out of left field that was designed to throw him off balance and elicit any sign of nerves. He was ready for it.

'I came here to study for my doctorate at Harvard University,' he replied calmly. 'When I completed it the university sponsored me for a green card and I was lucky enough to be accepted,' he said. 'Lucky enough to be accepted' was al-Falid's first lie of the interview but it was a well-practised one. Momentarily his thoughts flashed back to a time when he'd been taunted by American students at the university. A time when Khalid Kadeer had befriended him as he'd walked past one of the student bars. A group of Harvard footballers, joined by their scantily dressed cheerleaders, had taken over the tables on one of the balconies and called out to him.

'Hey towel head!! Why don't you let your hair out of your towel and come and have a drink!' The footballers were celebrating their win and their loud laughter encouraged the verbal barbs of their quarterback, one of the more arrogant of their number.

'I'm talking to you, dickhead!' the Harvard quarterback yelled after him, as al-Falid kept walking.

'Why don't you go back to your stinking camels and your sand-pits, you arrogant asshole!' another one yelled.

'No wonder you prefer vestal virgins! You wouldn't know what to fucking do with it!' yelled another. The cheerleaders broke into a fit of the giggles.

'Ignore them. Like many Westerners, they're threatened by difference. They have shallow minds and think that theirs is the only society worth living in.' al-Falid turned to find a tall man beside him. The man was slightly older than al-Falid and was dressed in western clothes but wore an elegant handwoven cap, the culture of which he didn't recognise. 'I'm Khalid Kadeer. I'm doing a doctorate in microbiology. There is a quiet coffee shop around the corner that sells green tea.'

Had it not been for the friendship and support of the brilliant Uighur microbiologist, al-Falid was certain he would have returned home to Cairo without completing his MBA. Kadeer had convinced him that one day the infidels and the Chinese would pay for their ignorance and for their contempt of Islam. The need for 'sleeper cells' to deliver warnings had been one example of Kadeer's vision for the future, and al-Falid had given thanks to Allah, the Most Kind and the Most Merciful, that such a need had finally come to reality. Although as he put the master freedom fighter's complex plans in place, al-Falid also found himself at odds with his mentor. Even after the humiliation at the hands of the West and the Han Chinese, Khalid Kadeer still seemed ready to forgive. If only the West and the Han Chinese would give Islam the respect it deserved. For al-Falid, forgiveness didn't come into it. al-Falid was convinced that there was only one true path, the path of Islam, and the great Prophet Muhammad, peace be upon him, had laid out that path very clearly. The United States, Britain, Australia and all other western countries would be taken over by Islam and operate under strict Sharia law. Eventually the one true religion would take over the world with a wondrous encompassment of pan-Islam, the way Allah, the Most Kind, the Most Merciful had always intended.

'What places are you going to visit in Pakistan, exactly?' The customs officer's exasperation at al-Falid's calm responses was beginning to show. She pushed her hair over her shoulder with a contemptuous flick.

'I will be spending some time studying sixteenth and seventeenth century architecture in Islamabad,' al-Falid replied, fighting to hide his disgust at a woman doing the job of a man, 'After that, provided the authorities will give me a permit, I hope to spend some time in the North-West Frontier Province as I have a great interest in the area and I'm writing a book on architecture and the Silk Road.' al-Falid reminded himself that there was no need to mention the specifics of Peshawar, although he still needed to be prudent. al-Falid knew that the results of the interrogation would be fed into the CIA's computers and if they followed him in Pakistan, he wanted his trip to look as close to the way he had described it as possible. Except for his planned visit to Darra Adam Khel, the mountain village where you could buy anything from an AK-47 to a stinger missile. It would be very necessary, al-Falid reminded himself, to make sure he wasn't being tailed when he visited Darra Adam Khel.

CHAPTER 14

CIA HEADQUARTERS, LANGLEY, VIRGINIA

Curtis O'Connor read through the summary of airport interrogations, signed off on the file and threw it into his out tray. In the last 24 hours, Customs and Border Protection had plucked no fewer than 141 people out of queues waiting to board aircraft and passenger liners. The interrogations had not been entirely random with most being American citizens of Muslim background or of Middle Eastern appearance. The results were no different from any other day. Three people had been detained for visa irregularities, and a petty thief wanted by police in Las Vegas for assaulting a prostitute had been arrested but nothing of substance had caught O'Connor's attention. Based on their destinations he marked five citizens for routine surveillance – two in Syria, one in Jordan, one in Indonesia and an academic who was writing a book on the architecture of the Silk Road and who was trying to get into the North-West Frontier near Pakistan's border with Afghanistan. The war on terror was taking its toll, increasing the demand for surveillance. Out in the field CIA agents were struggling to cope.

In a basement of the US embassy in the Diplomatic Enclave in Islamabad, Washington's relentless demands for information on Osama bin Laden's whereabouts had been flooding in on a daily basis. The White House was also fending off mounting complaints in the US media that the Taliban were avoiding capture in Afghanistan by slipping across the border into Pakistan's North-West Frontier Province. The Administration had assigned too few troops to Afghanistan, repeating the mistake ten times over in Iraq, but the White House had dismissed the criticisms and, despite the lack of resources, Esposito was pushing for something concrete the President could use to rebut his critics. In Islamabad the pressure was beginning to tell. Rob Regan, a big man with close-cropped grey hair was the CIA's Chief of Station and he had been pulling some appalling hours. He read the latest 'Top-Secret' cable from Washington with disbelief.

'Fuck me!' he muttered.

'No thanks,' Tony Carmello, his younger, dark-haired and ever cheerful deputy said. 'Washington?' he asked.

'Got it in one. We're up to our armpits in alligators here and now they want us to mount a surveillance operation on some obscure academic who's writing a book on Islamic architecture and the Silk Road. Another riveting bestseller. I don't think those dickheads back in Washington would know if a Foggy Bottom bus was up their ass,' Regan grumbled.

'Well, not until the people got off,' his deputy said with a grin, 'and in the Secretary of Defense's office you'd have to ring the bell.' Neither of the CIA men could understand why the politicians and generals in the Pentagon had gone into two wars in the region without enough troops or equipment to do the job, and now the whole of the Middle East was in danger of going up in flames.

'Who've we got spare?'

'Only the new guy.'

'Crawford? I don't think he's started to shave yet. He's only been here five minutes.'

Regan's deputy shrugged. 'Bit wet behind the ears but he's all we've got left. He has to learn sometime.'

O'Connor leaned back in his chair, thinking about what would be happening out in the field. In many ways he envied agents. Field-work had always been his forte and he longed to be back there.

The CIA's most experienced counter-terrorism officer had no way of knowing, but he would get the opportunity much sooner than he expected, and in a part of the world that was as inhospitable and dangerous as it got.

CHAPTER 15

UNITED STATES ARMY MEDICAL RESEARCH INSTITUTE FOR INFECTIOUS DISEASES, FORT DETRICK, MARYLAND

Dr Kate Braithwaite flung her backpack into a corner of her small, ramshackle office in USAMRIID, and flopped down behind a desk that was almost totally covered with files and papers. The wall behind her had floor-to-ceiling bookcases that were crammed with books and file boxes that detailed some of the most deadly pathogens known to man. Weary from the early morning flight, Kate ran her hand through her unruly curls and leaned back in her battered leather swivel chair with a sigh. Her jeans were spotlessly clean but faded, as was her favourite cream-coloured sweatshirt with 'Sydney University' written across the front.

The US Army Medical Research Institute for Infectious Diseases, or USAMRIID, had been set up by President Nixon in 1969 to protect America's armed forces from biological attack. The Fort Detrick campus was nestled in the distant shadow of Catoctin Mountain and the Appalachians on the outskirts of Frederick, Maryland. With the whole country on edge since September 11, USAMRIID's role had widened and Fort Detrick was under heavy guard. Even so, Kate was pleased to be back albeit only for a short while. The encounter with Maverick and the other chimpanzees had depressed her more than she realised and she'd asked her boss, Professor Imran Sayed, to make one last attempt to have the experiments stopped. With a sigh she began clearing a space on her desk.

'Goodness! Not tidying up are we?' Imran Sayed's smile was warm and genuine. Imran was dressed in an expensive suit, his shirt a soft, understated pink. His olive skin was slightly pockmarked, his short dark hair brushed roughly into place. Imran had a long, aquiline nose, and his tortoiseshell glasses gave him a serious demeanor; his dark eyes were keen and alert. Kate knew that he also possessed a wicked sense of humour, particularly when they were alone. At sixty-three, he radiated the quiet confidence of a professor at the height of his powers. Kate had first met him when she was one of his post-doctoral students at the Yale School of Medicine and she had immediately warmed to him. Despite impressive international recognition for his stunning achievements in the world of virology, Professor Sayed still managed not to take life too seriously.

'Don't you start,' Kate responded with another sigh.

'How are your charges at the CDC?' Imran asked more seriously. He had mentored this young scientist right from the start, carefully nurturing her career. After years of working with her he was immediately sensitive to her mood.

'Still restless. I can't put my finger on it, Imran, but Maverick in particular seems to sense something's about to happen.'

'The alpha male?'

Kate nodded. 'Because he's restless, it's keeping the whole group off balance. It's crazy, Imran. We're going to subject these wonderful creatures to insane doses of the virus, yet in all the centuries that smallpox has ravaged the planet there's never been a single case of that virus infecting the animal kingdom. It doesn't make sense.'

Imran nodded. 'I agree, but making sense is not this Administration's long suit right now. Next time you go down to CDC I'll come with you to see for myself, although I'm not holding out much hope of stopping this. You will have heard about the new Colonel?' Imran asked, raising his eyebrows. 'He's just sent around a memo demanding key scientists sign an endorsement for the retention of our stocks of smallpox. No doubt they want that as ammunition for the Secretary to wave at a bunch of journalists next time he gets quizzed.'

'I got mine while I was in Atlanta but I'm not going to sign it. I sent it back with a strong argument for those stocks to be destroyed.'

'Good for you. I haven't signed mine either and I'm going to have one last try this morning to get them to see sense. The new Colonel has a daily meeting now,' Imran said, rolling his eyes.

'I'd heard that,' Kate said with a grin, feeling some of her anger dissipate. She would always be grateful that no matter how tough things appeared, Imran invariably managed to make her laugh.

'For Heads of Departments and senior scientists who have charge of particular programs, so shelve whatever you had planned this morning and we'll have another go at them.'

'You want *me* there? I'm hardly a senior scientist, Imran.'

'You know more about *Variola major* than anyone else in this complex, and you can back me up. Besides, it will be good for your education,' he said with a smile.

'Do these meetings really include intelligence briefings on the enemy?'

'Lurking under everyone's bed apparently and we have to stay alert. Even the lab technicians may not be what they seem.'

'Sounds like the Colonel was brought up in the Stasi.'

'Ex-marine. Although I've got my doubts about how "ex". He's had his office sandbagged. It looks like something out of Desert Storm.'

'You've got to be kidding!' Kate said, shaking her head.

'Colonel Cluster is a man's man.' Professor Sayed's nickname for their new boss was destined to stick. 'And single too. A drop-dead gorgeous blonde like you should be a shoe-in.'

Kate made a face. 'If he's even remotely like his reputation there's a reason people like him are single, Imran.'

'Ah, but you haven't met his J3.'

'Have you all gone barking mad while I've been away. What the bloody hell's a J3?'

'The Colonel's new right-hand man, Captain Donald Crawshaw. He's pretty hot. If things don't work out with the Colonel, perhaps you two should get together.'

Kate could hear her irrepressible Professor still chuckling as he walked back to his office. She hadn't had a serious relationship since she'd left her husband, Malcolm, after he had found God or God had found him, she wasn't sure which. Shortly after his 'Road to Damascus' conversion, Malcolm had been elected President of the Young Liberals in her home state of New South Wales. Kate shuddered at the memory of a brief marriage turned into a nightmare by a dangerous mix of religion and politics. To get away she had moved from Sydney and thrown herself into her post-doctoral studies at Yale. Despite a couple of flings 'Mr Right' had been elusive. Not that she really wanted another marriage, just a decent partner. 'J what's-his-number' didn't seem like he was about to break the drought, although if he was as hot as her professor made out, she mused, her love life might be about to pick up.

CHAPTER 17

CIA HEADQUARTERS, LANGLEY, VIRGINIA

Curtis O'Connor reached for the report on 'The Netherlands: Dyke Vulnerability' and began to read through it again, looking for anything he might have missed. Could the Dutch be one of the targets? O'Connor knew that the deployment of over a thousand Dutch troops to Iraq's southern Muthanna province after Saddam Hussein had been toppled had infuriated some sections of the Arab world. He was also privy to the details of the resultant terrorist threats to Amsterdam's Schiphol Airport and the Dutch parliament, as well as the reports on the murder of the Dutch filmmaker, Theo van Gogh, whose criticism of Muslims had enraged the Islamists. Despite his contempt for the Secretary of Defense, O'Connor was a true professional who never let personal animosity cloud his judgement; he had already accepted that a failure of the Netherlands dyke systems would lead to nearly half the country being flooded. He reflected that the last time that happened had been in 1953, when a catastrophic North Sea storm surge had breached the dykes in over 500 places.

O'Connor leaned forward in his chair and took another look at the Maeslantkering, the engineering marvel that had been opened by Queen Beatrix in 1997. In the event of another storm surge like the one in 1953, two massive gates the size of the Eiffel Tower and weighing four times as much would be swung towards one another. The Nieuwe Waterweg – the new waterway canal connecting the port of Rotterdam with the North Sea – would be sealed off until the danger had passed. O'Connor rested his chin in the palm of his hand and thought again about the Secretary's preoccupation with the Dutch and their windmills. It had obviously been some time since the Secretary had visited the low countries, he thought wryly. With the invention of diesel and electricity, the windmills that had kept the vast reclaimed polders dry since the thirteenth century had been replaced by sophisticated pumps. Curtis frowned. 'Beneath Eternity where the windmill has been stolen.' Was the Defense Secretary right for the wrong reasons, he wondered. Was it perhaps the role of the windmills that had been stolen? He shook his head in frustration. Between Osama bin Laden and his mad mullahs on one side, and the neocons on his side who saw every Muslim country as a potential threat, planet Earth had become a lot less safe.

The satellite imagery from the National Reconnaissance Office KeyHole and Lacrosse satellites, some of which were the size of a bus and orbited as high as 36,000 kilometres above Earth, was over four years old. Had one of these satellites been footprinted over Rotterdam just eighteen months earlier, O'Connor could have been provided with the images of three massive ocean-going tugs that he would come to realise were of extraordinary importance. With disaster upon disaster unfolding in the Middle East all of the KeyHole and Lacrosse satellites had much higher priorities over Iraq, the border between Afghanistan and Pakistan, the Hindu Kush and Iran, not to mention North Korea.

The *Winston Churchill*, the *Montgomery*, and the *Wavell* had each undergone extensive engine refits at one of the huge shipyards in the second busiest port in the world. Like three large ugly ducklings they left Rotterdam line astern, passing the old Verolme Botlek shipyard. This vast complex was a hive of activity as the welders and shipwrights worked on a huge oil rig in the widest graving dock in Europe. The tugs were heading towards the Maeslantkering. From there they would keep company through the English Channel before turning east through the Strait of Gibraltar, across the Mediterranean, through the Suez Canal and the Red Sea and across the northern Indian Ocean to the teeming Pakistani port of Karachi. The *Montgomery* and the *Wavell* had been tasked with collecting and delivering missiles for the first and second warnings. The *Winston Churchill* had a mission of a different nature that would come into play if the third and final warning was necessary. She was tasked with visiting third world countries where regulations governing the disposal of old radiotherapy machines were less than stringent. al-Falid had not only been relentless in his sourcing of the obsolete machinery, he had also been aware of the tiniest of details, giving instructions that the tugboats were to be renamed with British names when they had been purchased. He calculated that the names might cause precious indecisiveness when the tugs appeared in the binoculars of any western port authorities who might be wondering what they were up to. A fourth ocean-going tug re-named the *George Washington* was undergoing a refit in Rotterdam. al-Falid had a different purpose in mind for her and then it would be the American authorities he would want to lull into a false sense of security.

Curtis O'Connor racked his brain trying to crack the secret meaning of the code. Across the Potomac in the Oval Office, the hawks in the Administration were about to try and convince President Harrison to elevate the war on terror to a frightening new level.

CHAPTER 17

THE OVAL OFFICE, THE WHITE HOUSE, WASHINGTON DC

President Harrison leaned back into one of two long, cream-coloured couches that faced each other in the Oval Office. A large blue and gold Presidential seal was woven into the caramel carpet between them. Dan Esposito sat at one end of the President's couch, and the Vice President and the Secretary of Defense sat opposite. Three trusted advisors who all thought along the same lines; it was an arrangement that this President had long been comfortable with. A sort of inner 'kitchen cabinet' whose time was not wasted in dealing with opposing views that came from people like the Secretary of State.

'So what are we going to do about the production of smallpox vaccines?' President Harrison asked.

'I'm looking into that, Mr President,' the Vice President responded smoothly. 'I'll have some recommendations to you later in the week, but the development will need to be done by a pharmaceutical we can trust that has a proven track record. One with the right facilities because they'll need access to the smallpox we're holding in CDC and they'll need to produce this on time and on budget.' The Vice President knew well that the only pharmaceutical with Biosafety Level 4 facilities outside of CDC and USAMRIID was Halliwell.

The President nodded approvingly. The contract would be worth nearly half a billion dollars and would require the production of 300 million doses of vaccine for the American people. The prospect of it being done 'on time and on budget' was the sort of uncomplicated news the President liked to hear.

'Which brings us to the related issue of today's agenda, Mr President,' the Vice President continued. It was not an agenda that would ever be recorded on paper.

'Quite frankly we were caught with our pants down on 9/11 and we took a lot of hits over the anthrax attacks afterwards. If we're attacked with anthrax again and, heaven forbid, with smallpox as well, and if it ever gets out that we had prior warning, your presidency will be history. As far as Kadeer goes, I'm with Dan, I think the bastard's bluffing, but Eternity and stolen windmills have got the media's attention. The public is worried and we need to get into a position to reassure them.'

The Secretary of Defense nodded. 'This town leaks like a sieve, Mr President,' he said. 'If the report warning of another anthrax and smallpox attack surfaces, the media and those bastards up on the Hill will have our balls in a vice.'

'I agree.' Vice President Bolton seized his chance to push the argument on the development of biological weapons to restore the United States to a position where they were leading the world in the deadly research that could only be carried out in hot-zone laboratories. 'We need to fight fire with fire, Mr President, and to do that we need to reintroduce our own bioweapons research program so that we've got some idea of what these little Muslim bastards might be up to. And it's not only the threat from the Islamists we should be worried about, Mr President. The Chinese have massively increased their spending on Defense, and just like the Russians in the 1970s, I wouldn't put it past them to develop biological weapons.'

'We're a signatory to the Biological Weapons Convention, Mr President,' Dan Esposito interjected. 'That prohibits us from developing the kind of weapons we're talking about here.' It wasn't the ethics that was bothering Esposito; he was more concerned that the President obey one of the first maxims of a successful modern day politician, 'thou shall not get caught'. The other two had missed the point.

'For fuck's sake, Dan!' Vice President Bolton's anger was never far from the surface and it always erupted when anybody dared to disagree with him. 'The report on Dolinsky is more than credible. You and I both know the fucking Russians started a huge bioweapons program before the ink was even dry on that convention. When that fellow Alibek defected from Russia in 1992 we discovered that at the same time the Russians were telling us and the rest of the world they wouldn't develop any biological weapons, they were actually building Biopreparat!'

'Chuck's right, Mr President,' the Defense Secretary said. 'Not only did they move their stocks of smallpox to Koltsovo without telling us but after they signed the 1972 convention, they employed tens of thousands of bioweapons experts in fifty different laboratories.'

'And just in case you might think it odd that the Russians are employing a Georgian like Dolinsky, Dan,' the Vice President continued, building on the unsolicited support from the Defense Secretary and pre-empting Esposito, 'I'll remind you that Alibek is Asian. He was born in Kazakhstan for fuck's sake! This is war, and if the Russians ignored the convention, do you think a bunch of backward bloody Muslims are going to take any notice of any paper agreement? If they can get their hands on biological weapons, they will, and they'll use them against the American people. Our own research stopped when that little shit Nixon canned it in 1969. Right now we haven't got a clue what these bastards might be up to because we're the only turkeys playing the game!'

'You're missing the point, Mr Vice President,' Dan Esposito responded coolly, speaking from a position of power that infuriated Bolton. Esposito turned towards the President. 'I'm not saying that we shouldn't be in a position to strike first, Mr President, far from it. The point I'm making is that we need to make damn sure this doesn't leak. The two organisations that have Biosafety Level 4 laboratories most capable of this sort of research are the CDC and USAMRIID. USAMRIID employs over 700 people, including 200 Doctorate level scientists, and the CDC employs even more.' Dan Esposito absorbed facts and figures like a steel trap, something that hadn't been lost on the Vice President.

For Vice President Bolton knowledge was power. The Vice President had briefed the Secretary of Defense but as yet, he hadn't allowed Esposito into the compartment dealing with the top-secret construction at Halliwell. To the construction workers it was just another laboratory complex and only a handful of engineers with a need to ensure the hot-zone laboratory met strict tolerances were in the compartment – and even they had only been given a bare outline of the laboratory's ultimate purpose.

Esposito glared at the Vice President, determined to protect his man and the Republican Party's interests. 'Not only that,' Esposito said, 'but the Colonel Commanding USAMRIID is on the public record as wanting the stockpiles of smallpox destroyed for hell's sake, so if you think we can keep this quiet in USAMRIID, Mr Vice President, you've got more faith in them than I have.'

'The Colonel Commanding USAMRIID has been replaced with an officer who shares the Administration's views and, more importantly, who will do as he's told,' the Secretary of Defense responded bluntly. A silence descended on the Oval Office.

President Harrison was normally absolutely sure of his mission in the world but his trusted electoral advisor had put him in two minds. His Administration had taken a lot of hits and Denver Harrison knew that the American people would probably be against this. To authorise the development of biological weapons, even if they could later claim it was in self-defense, was a huge step into uncharted territory. Perhaps O'Connor was right. It might be prudent to go with the development of the vaccines and wait for confirmation of the threat. After all, he reasoned, no one in the media or on the Hill was likely to criticise him for not wanting to develop biological weapons. For a moment he let his mind wander, distracted by a higher mission. The one thing President Harrison was sure of was that at a time like this God would guide him. All the great Presidents had been god-fearing men, he reflected, and none more so than his hero Abraham Lincoln. As the Reverend Jerry Buffett, the charismatic televangelist from Atlanta, had often said, in this war on terror God was on the side of those who believed in freedom and democracy. The Reverent Buffet had reminded the President that it was no coincidence that America's motto was 'In God We Trust'. Discussions with Jerry Buffett always gave Denver Harrison a sense of purpose and resolve. Perhaps the debate that was swirling around him might be clearer once he'd had a quiet chat with the evangelist.

The Vice President was equally thoughtful, although not in any religious sense. Despite the seeming uncertainty of the President, Bolton felt a sense of satisfaction over the direction in which the conversation was heading. Although it was by no means a done deal, at least the President's advisor had taken the bait on CDC and USAMRIID. If the proposal to get back into research on biological weapons got up, CDC was a logical choice for the assignment, but earlier in the day he'd casually floated the idea of the dangers of media leaks from USAMRIID and CDC with Esposito. Bolton smirked inwardly. He would shortly play another card and bring Esposito up to date on the Halliwell construction, but for the moment the little advisor hadn't disappointed him. Esposito was only too well aware that lately several highly sensitive top-secret documents, including the FBI's surveillance on ordinary American citizens, had become public and the damage to the Republicans' chances of retaining both houses in the mid-term elections had been considerable. Any development of biological weapons at either CDC or USAMRIID in defiance of the international Biological Weapons Convention would be a very high-risk strategy.

CHAPTER 18

UNITED STATES ARMY MEDICAL RESEARCH INSTITUTE FOR INFECTIOUS DISEASES, FORT DETRICK, MARYLAND

Although the Surgeon General had personally assured him of the importance of his new post as Commanding Colonel of USAMRIID, Colonel Walter C. Wassenberg III, US Army Medical Corps, was in a foul mood. The promotions list for Brigadier General had been published the day before, and once again his name hadn't been on it. He was short and fit, his uniform was immaculate, but time was running out. Underneath the black hair dye, his 'jarhead' Marine crew cut was now very grey. Colonel Wassenberg had once thought he would make four stars as Commandant of the Marines but an accident in Somalia had brought his career as a marine to an ignominious end. He'd never got over it and, although he'd accepted the Army's offer to put him through a degree in medical administration, a deep and grudging bitterness was never far from the surface. Promotion in the Army Medical Corps had a ceiling of three stars – Lieutenant General – but Wassenberg knew that you had to be a goddamn poodle-faking doctor to get that job. Walter Wassenberg had not even made his first star.

Colonel Wassenberg turned the next page in the folder containing the biographies of USAMRIID staff, finding himself confronted with a photograph and profile of a Dr Kate Braithwaite. 'The day they have women playing in the Super Bowl will be the day I accept front bums have something meaningful to offer the Army,' he muttered to himself. Ignoring her string of degrees and doctorates he focused on the photograph, and as he did his eyes narrowed and his thin lips pressed even more firmly together. The scientist's untidy hair irritated him and he made a mental note to have her fix it. In Walter Wassenberg's world haircuts and discipline went hand in hand, and in the short time he'd been at USAMRIID he'd been appalled at the lax attitude to both. He was infuriated by what he'd decided was a 'fifth column' in the ranks of the long-haired scientists. His early morning parades for the academics had not lasted more than a week before there'd been a damaging revolt. Word had filtered back to the Pentagon and he'd been told by some flunky in the Surgeon General's office to modify his style.

Walter Wassenberg continued to browse through the pages until he got to Professor Sayed's profile and his pulse quickened. Here was a man of Middle Eastern appearance who had unrestricted access on a top-secret US base. Incensed at the entry 'Muslim' beside the heading of religion, Colonel Wassenberg never made it past the first page. Had he bothered to turn that page and read more than the executive summary of Sayed's details, he would have discovered that Imran Sayed had been born in Karachi to a Pakistani father, and an American mother. He would have also discovered that Imran's wealthy shipping merchant father had been killed in an accident on Karachi's docks when Imran had been just four years old. The detailed biography recorded that after the accident, his mother had brought the very young Imran back to the United States and raised him in New York. He had graduated summa cum laude at the Yale School of Medicine and after a distinguished international career in some of the world's most desperate health trouble spots which included outbreaks of smallpox, dengue fever, typhoid and malaria, Imran Sayed had returned to Yale as a visiting Professor of Epidemiology. Professor Sayed was now on contract to USAMRIID and to the World Health Organization, and the Secretary General of the United Nations valued Imran as a friend and a trusted advisor. Wassenberg buzzed for his J3.

'Sir!' Tall and gangly to the point of being awkward, Marine Captain Donald Crawshaw appeared inside the Colonel's door in an instant and snapped to attention. Crawshaw wasn't the sharpest spine on the porcupine but he'd worked out quickly enough that the very short ex-Marine Corps Colonel was a man of explosive action who detested being kept waiting. Captain Crawshaw aimed to please. His performance report from his last unit hadn't been too complimentary and he had also missed out on the last round of promotions, but he figured that all was not lost. A strong recommendation from an ex-Marine like Colonel Wassenberg might help him to replace his two bar insignia for Captain with the coveted oak leaf of a Major.

'We have a security problem on this base, Crawshaw. A security problem!'

'Sir!' The colour drained from Crawshaw's face as he wondered whether or not he was responsible.

'Come around here, son. You see this man – he's a goddamn Muslim! This is a Christian country. A Christian country that is at war with these motherfucker Muslims and now I find that we've got a goddamn Muslim scientist in the middle of a top-secret base. I want a security review done on every one of these motherfucker scientists without delay. Without delay d'ya hear!' Colonel Wassenberg slammed the folder shut and shoved it towards his J3.

'Yes SIR! USAMRIID SIR!' Captain Crawshaw rammed the folder under his left arm, snapped to attention again and saluted before marching back to his small desk just outside the Colonel's door.

Walter Wassenberg breathed in deeply. His predecessor had not only been pushing for the destruction of the country's stocks of smallpox, for chrissake, he'd allowed a Muslim on his staff. Another poodle-faking-motherfucker doctor who'd never seen a shot fired in anger, he thought resentfully. The Muslim would have to go and the stocks of smallpox would be destroyed over his dead body. For the third time in as many minutes he checked his watch. On his first day he'd timed the walk from his office to the conference room down the hall at precisely 59 seconds and his watch now showed 0858 hours, just over a minute before he would leave the office.

Colonel Wassenberg got up from behind his desk and stood in front of the full-length mirror he'd had installed behind the door of his office and adjusted a shirt fold above his belt. He also made an adjustment to the position of the large nameplate that took pride of place in the front centre of his desk, specially made in polished silky oak, with WALTER C. WASSENBERG III embossed in large gold letters, and COLONEL COMMANDING underneath. On the wall behind his desk he'd had two flags installed in a polished wood cabinet. The Stars and Stripes always had pride of place, but in a breach of protocol for a medical unit Colonel Wassenberg had insisted on installing the Marine Corps flag, as well as the Marine Corps seal on the wall above – a huge bald eagle atop the Western Hemisphere with a foul anchor behind it. In its beak the eagle carried a scroll with the Marine Corps motto – *Semper Fidelis* 'Always Faithful'. Satisfied, Colonel Wassenberg ran his hands over his Marine Corps combat gear that he kept hanging on two wooden pegs inside the door, just in case he got the call. He made a final check of his watch and as the sweep hand passed the hour he strode purposefully through his J3's office and down the corridor towards the conference room.

CHAPTER 19

THE OVAL OFFICE, THE WHITE HOUSE, WASHINGTON DC

President Harrison broke the silence. 'So if you think CDC and USAMRIID might leak, where does that leave us?' he asked.

'There is another option, Mr President,' Vice President Bolton said smoothly. 'You will recall that we agreed that from time to time, Halliwell might have to work on Level 4 pathogens and the classified contract for Halliwell Pharmaceuticals included the construction of a full Biosafety Level 4 laboratory.'

Esposito's jowls trembled alarmingly as he jerked his head up from his folder of notes. A surge of white-hot anger pulsed through his veins. He seethed, wondering why he hadn't been told. It wasn't the first time the arrogant and ambitious Vice President had kept him in the dark on classified projects. As Esposito brought his fury back under control he made a mental note to remind the President that his electoral advisor needed to be aware of absolutely every-thing that crossed the President's desk – everything. There had been a great deal of resistance from the Vice President, but one of the reasons Esposito had insisted on being present at meetings of the war cabinet was to ensure that the Republican Party's re-election strategy wasn't threatened by foreign policy decisions. Bolton's day would come. The Vice President's chances of gaining the Oval Office lay somewhere below zilch and fuck all.

President Harrison nodded. The Vice President had informed him that the Halliwell laboratory was now protected by security guards, motion alarms, triple fencing and CCT cameras that were monitored 24 hours a day from Halliwell's main operations centre.

'That area is completely secure but we need to keep things small,' Vice President Bolton said, a quiet insistence in his voice. 'The scientists will have to be leaders in their field and we'll have to disguise the funding, but I'm sure Richard Halliwell can be trusted to keep access to an absolute minimum. If there is a leak, any scientist on the project will know we won't be looking very far.'

Dan Esposito's piggy little eyes narrowed even further. He already had a separate long-range plan for Richard Halliwell. As the Vice President outlined the proposals for bioweapons research, another idea quickly took shape in his agile mind.

'The funding will have to be black, Mr President,' Esposito said calmly, looking at the Vice President, giving the impression he already knew about the Halliwell construction.

'CIA?' the President asked.

Esposito nodded. 'It has to be deniable. It can be funded out of O'Connor's budget and that way you're at arms' length.' Dan Esposito felt a surge of satisfaction at his stroke of genius. This way all the risk would be carried by O'Connor and if anything went wrong he could hang him out to dry.

'And what do we do about this Dolinsky guy?' the President asked.

The Vice President had already ensured the Secretary of Defense was on side and he let him make the running.

'I've had my people check him out independently,' the Secretary of Defense replied authoritatively. Not satisfied that the other agencies that had served the United States for decades were giving him the answers he wanted to hear, the Secretary of Defense had set up his own top-secret cell that provided more palatable intelligence. It would prove to be another disastrous mistake.

'He's a brilliant molecular biologist and virologist, Mr President,' the Secretary of Defense continued, 'and quite frankly I'd rather he were on our side than al-Qaeda's. If he wants to defect we should ensure he comes over to us, and the CIA should be told to make that happen.'

'I agree, Mr President,' Vice President Bolton said, sensing that even if the President might still be against the development of bio-weapons, he would be reluctant to allow al-Qaeda and the Islamists to get their hands on someone like Dolinsky; not to mention that Dolinsky also held the key to his plans for the Beijing Olympics and the dominance of the United States as the world's only super-power. 'If you approve the re-introduction of research into biological weapons and I don't think we can afford not to in light of the latest intelligence reports,' Bolton pressed, sensing that the President was not yet convinced, 'Halliwell is going to need the best.'

Vice President Bolton was determined to back the intelligence that best suited his aims of maintaining US supremacy – and his own personal power. Little did Bolton realise what he was unleashing on the world.

CHAPTER 20

UNITED STATES ARMY MEDICAL RESEARCH INSTITUTE FOR INFECTIOUS DISEASES, FORT DETRICK, MARYLAND

'Shit!' Kate Braithwaite looked up at her wall clock, grabbed her notebook, locked the door to her office and hurried off to her first meeting with the new Colonel, annoyed that to have any chance of being on time she would have to run.

Two minutes later Kate slowed to a deliberate stroll as she turned the corner of the drab green corridor that led to the conference room, only to find that the door was guarded by a tall, thin Marine Corps Captain with pimply skin, nervously tapping a ridiculously polished boot on the cement floor.

'Quickly,' he hissed as Kate approached. 'The Colonel's coming.'

Bully for the Colonel, Kate thought, as she smiled sweetly, rolling her eyes and guessing this was the new J 'what's-his-number'. Imran caught her eye and winked as she took her place with the advisory group of scientists sitting along one wall. 'I'll get you for that,' she mouthed at him, her eyes twinkling as she made a show of silently sucking in a breath through pursed lips.

Kate exchanged glances with a couple of her closest colleagues. Clearly there was an undercurrent of conspiracy running, and she wondered what 'Colonel Cluster' might have in store for them. If the stakes hadn't been so high it would have been comical. Another Captain was sitting bolt upright against the opposite wall. Kate surmised he was the duty briefer and she shuddered at the prospect of a mind-numbing exposé on some obscure mad mullah in outer Baluchistan. The young Captain from the Pentagon was probably too shit-scared of the Colonel to offer anything other than the military line that the United States was winning the war in Iraq, she mused. After Imran had left her office earlier in the day, a colleague had confided in her that not only had Imran's nickname for the new Colonel caught on, but while she'd been away at the CDC her fellow scientists had enhanced it. She'd been assured that Colonel 'Clusterfuck' was infinitely more appropriate and the scientists were running a book on who would get the vote at the end of the year for the most incompetent; the military moron who'd taken over command or the pimply-faced jerk of a captain he'd brought with him as his sidekick. At the moment Captain Crawshaw was marginally in front, not least for his bizarre habit of saluting the Colonel from as far as 100 metres away while at the same time yelling 'USAMRIID Sir!' Kate reflected that 'Panic Palace', as the scientists called the headquarters, had been taken over by dumb and dumber. Dumber was now hovering nervously inside the conference room doorway.

'Atten..hun! The Colonel Commanding!' Captain Crawshaw saluted as Colonel Wassenberg strode into the room. 'All present and accounted for Sir! USAMRIID Sir!'

Kate and the other civilian scientists half rose in their chairs as the military members snapped to attention.

'At ease!'

Jesus Christ, I'm in the middle of a military circus, Kate thought, suppressing a grin. The circus ringmaster immediately reminded her of some sort of latter day Napoleon, except this one was even shorter. She didn't dare look at Imran for fear of getting a fit of the giggles.

Colonel Wassenberg snapped open his folder that was embossed with a blue and gold Marine Corps seal. Without speaking he scrutinised those on the left and right of the table, then he did a slow visual inspection of the advisory group sitting along the walls.

'I'm still not satisfied with the standard of dress on this base,' he said finally, looking directly at Kate. Innocently she blinked her green eyes at him, which infuriated him as she knew it would. Here they were in USAMRIID on the cutting edge of research into some of the most dangerous pathogens on the planet and all this dickhead could find to worry about was what people wore.

'I want an instant improvement,' the Colonel demanded, looking around the room again before glancing down at his notes. The first item on the agenda was his newly instituted requirement for a daily report from Heads of Departments.

'Epidemiology!' Wassenberg snapped, glaring at Professor Sayed.

'No change from yesterday, Colonel,' Imran replied quietly and pointedly, but the message went straight over Walter Wassenberg's closely cropped head.

'What do you mean "no change"?' the Colonel demanded, his face colouring.

'Dr Braithwaite returned this morning from the CDC and I'm

sure she will be able to brief you on her work, but other than that our programs are all proceeding on schedule.'

Colonel Wassenberg turned towards the advisors, singling out Kate with his stare. In the silence that followed, Kate again blinked at the Colonel with a calculated touch of insolence. As soon as he'd walked into the room she'd concluded that he was the type of man who would be very uncomfortable around women. It was an advantage she was determined to press.

'And what have you got to add, Ms Braithwaite?' the Colonel demanded.

'It's Doctor, actually,' Kate replied icily, any sense of mischievous amusement extinguished. She was not sure what the Army could have been thinking when they appointed him, but at a place like USAMRIID a military automaton could be a disaster.

'As I'm sure you're aware, Colonel, research into areas like *Variola major* does not normally herald daily results. I've responded to your memo on smallpox and I've sent it back unsigned with a recommendation that we strongly support the World Health Organization's efforts to have the world's smallpox stocks destroyed. I've also requested that the series of experiments on the Great Apes not go ahead.' Colonel Wassenberg looked as though he was about to give birth.

'I've not signed mine either, Colonel,' Professor Sayed said, taking the heat away from Kate. 'And I know there are many other scientists in this room who think along similar lines. The World Health Organization has voted on no fewer than three occasions to have the last remaining stocks of this virus in Atlanta and Siberia destroyed; first in 1994, then in 1996, and again in 1999. Each time the United States has been instrumental in delaying that destruction. If smallpox ever falls into the hands of terrorists, Colonel, with thousands of aircraft criss-crossing the globe every day, the resulting epidemic could kill hundreds of millions of people. It would make 9/11 and bird flu look like child's play. Smallpox is one of the most deadly diseases on the planet, one that took D. A. Henderson and others a lifetime to eradicate,' Professor Sayed added pointedly. He was wasting his breath.

'I'll remind you all that the United States of America is at war. At war!' Colonel Wassenberg slammed his fist on the table. 'Those stocks of smallpox are vital to the protection of this country and they'll be destroyed over my dead body!' Wassenberg glared again at Professor Sayed before turning his attention back to Kate. 'The experiments on the monkeys are essential for the development of vaccines and not only will those experiments proceed but I want fast results!' Wassenberg's face was flushed with anger as he unknowingly exposed his total lack of knowledge of the painstaking nature of research involving deadly viruses. He fixed Kate with a stony stare. 'I'll see you in my office, Braithwaite, tomorrow at 1700 hours.'

At the end of the morning briefing Colonel Wassenberg marched back to his office and sat behind his desk. His anger was still at boiling point. Impertinent woman. Far too sure of herself and her clothing was appalling. Her relationship with that Muslim professor had not escaped him either; too cosy by half. A far more disciplined approach was needed for the entire base and where others had so obviously failed, he, Colonel Walter Wassenberg III, would succeed. In the light of the feedback from the Surgeon General's flunky he would have to tread warily, but at the first opportunity he would find a way to get rid of both of them.

CHAPTER 21

THE OVAL OFFICE, THE WHITE HOUSE, WASHINGTON DC

'There's something else you might like to think about, Mr President,' Dan Esposito said, after the Vice President and the Secretary of Defense had left. 'Your second term still has a while to run, and you will have left this country and the world an enduring legacy, but we need to give some consideration as to who you're going to support to succeed you in this office. If the Democrats run someone like Hillary Clinton or Barack Obama, we're going to need a candidate who is tough and uncompromising on the war on terror, someone who represents the values of the American people.'

'Do you have anyone in mind?'

Dan Esposito nodded. He'd already quietly canvassed the idea on the Hill and when he'd put forward Richard Halliwell's name the response from the Republican heavyweights, already nervous over the war in Iraq, had been overwhelmingly positive. Esposito's research had revealed that Richard Halliwell had started his career working in CDC's Level 4 labs as a biochemist. The President's advisor had noted that it hadn't been long before Halliwell had been attracted by the bigger bucks on offer in private enterprise. Paralleling the staggering rise of Enron, in a little over three decades, Halliwell had taken a medium-sized biotech and turned it into the world's biggest pharmaceutical. Halliwell had a reputation on Wall Street for being a ruthless, successful and mega-wealthy businessman and 'ruthless' was something Esposito understood and could work with. The Halliwell conglomerate was more than a match for GlaxoSmithKline and the rest of Big Pharma combined, and Halliwell shares had just reached a new high of $141 on the New York Stock Exchange.

There was something else that attracted the politically astute Esposito, who was forever looking for an advantage over the Democrats. Esposito had discovered that Halliwell was a prominent Southern Baptist and a member of one of the largest churches in the country; the Buffett Evangelical Center for Christ could seat 15,000 worshippers. America was overwhelmingly a Christian country and Esposito's latest research indicated that over 50 per cent of the population were Protestant, 25 per cent Catholic, and another 11 per cent described themselves as Christian without specifying a denomination. Esposito had separate plans for the Catholics, but he knew that with evangelical preachers like Jerry Buffett on side a big part of his next election campaign could be fought from the pulpit. In a country where voting wasn't compulsory, voter apathy was an ever-present danger but if the evangelical right were convinced a candidate was one of them, several thousand preachers could be brought into play. The growing power of the Christian Right could be harnessed to get over 30 million evangelicals, who were in church on a Sunday, down to the polling booth the following Tuesday.

'Richard Halliwell,' Esposito replied, endorsing his candidate without hesitation. 'I know he would have a lot of support on the Hill, and he would also have the support of Jerry Buffett and a lot of the Reverend Buffett's colleagues,' he added, appealing to the President's relationship with his spiritual advisor. 'It will be important for your place in history, Mr President, for the country to continue to support the Republican ideals that you've set in place.'

'What about Bolton?' the President asked, more than well aware of his deputy's ambitions.

'He's a good Vice President,' Esposito replied carefully, 'but he's made a lot of enemies over the years, and frankly, Mr President, he's carrying too much baggage for an election campaign. The Democrats would re-raise his share portfolio and we'd spend the whole campaign defending him.' Esposito did not go so far as to air his intelligence from his contacts in Inland Revenue. Should that ever surface the President needed to be in a position to employ the time-honoured defence of 'I wasn't told'.

The President looked thoughtful. Esposito was right. Although he wasn't eligible to run again it would be important that his legacy continued.

'Halliwell's smarter than the Vice President and he's clean,' Esposito said, sensing he had won the President's support. 'For now we'll need to keep this under wraps. Halliwell's a pretty good golfer, so I suggest you and I have a quiet round with him and that way any suggestion that we met for other than social reasons will be deniable.'

President Harrison grinned. 'He's good,' he said, 'but not that good. I whipped his ass the last time we played.' There was nothing the President liked better than a game of golf. It not only got him away from the war on terror and any one of a dozen other crises that seemed to constantly swirl around the White House, but it was a much more likeable form of combat. On the golf course you could see your enemy and assess his every move.

Dan Esposito allowed himself a smile. He hated golf with a passion but it wasn't a complete waste of time. Whenever Esposito wanted to get the President's complete attention on something, he could often achieve far more over eighteen holes than he could in the Oval Office. It was a small price to pay. Richard Halliwell was a man after his own heart, he mused. Yes, ruthless and uncompromising, but the war on terror and a strategy to deal with the raging Chinese required nothing less.

For once Esposito's research lacked its usual depth and thoroughness. He'd been blinded by Halliwell's business acumen and membership of the big Southern Baptist Church. If Dan Esposito had carried out his research into Richard Halliwell with the same meticulous attention to detail that he gave the poll data that flooded into his office each week, he might have discovered that Richard Halliwell's reputation on Wall Street, like his membership of the Buffett Evangelical Center for Christ, was not all it seemed.

CHAPTER 22

DELTA AIRLINES FLIGHT 1874, WASHINGTON

The Captain of the direct service from Atlanta, Georgia to Reagan Airport beside the Potomac River in Washington DC, listened as the direction from the Control Tower crackled in his headset.

'Delta Flight 1874 you are cleared to descend to 10,000 feet. On leaving level 190, switch to primary approach on 119 decimal 85.'

'Descending to 10,000 feet. Thank you and have a good day.' It was a fine, clear morning and the dome of the Capitol building was faintly visible in the distance. A great day for flying, the Captain thought, as he prepared to ease back the twin throttles on the Boeing 737-800 and his co-pilot reached for the radio console to change frequencies.

In the cabin behind them the purser took the intercom. 'As we've now begun our descent into Washington, would you please ensure that your seatbelt is fastened, your tray table secured and your seat is in the upright position.' The most powerful Christian televangelist in America, the Reverend Jerry Buffet, seated in row 1A, reluctantly obeyed the purser's directions and pushed the armrest button that controlled his comfortable leather seat. The powerful turbofan engines quietened and the nose of the 737 dipped towards the ground.

Jerry Buffett smiled politely as he accepted the warm face towel from the young flight attendant. Of just average height, the Southern Baptist televangelist was in his early sixties but he looked ten years younger; his tanned, square-jawed face was one of the most recognisable in America. He wiped his hands and face and then turned to look at the countryside below. He had seen the broadcast by Dr Khalid Kadeer and when the President had asked him for his advice he had caught the first available plane that had a first-class seat. Jerry Buffett had no doubt that the threats from Kadeer were real, but as he would explain to the President, the real threats facing America had very little to do with Kadeer's explanations from a false religion and the Qu'ran. The warnings were in the Bible and the Lord continued to bring these to America's attention. When Ariel Sharon, supported by the President, withdrew Israeli troops from the Gaza Strip, the land that had been promised to Israel, the Lord had felled Sharon with a mighty stroke for daring to divide the Promised Land. The Bible warnings were crystal clear but God's chosen people in Israel and the United States continued to ignore them.

As the 737 banked away from a distant Chesapeake Bay, Jerry Buffett reflected on the two greatest threats he saw facing the United States, both predicted in the Bible. The coming threat from China was made clear in Revelations 9:15–16. 'So the four angels were released, who had been held ready for the hour . . . to kill a third of humankind. The number of troops was 200 million.' There was only one country in the world capable of raising such an army and Jerry Buffett knew that the CIA fact book on China indicated that the number of men of military service age in China had passed the 200 million mark in 2001.

The other threat, the one from Islam, had already appeared on September 11, and the rise of Osama bin Laden had also been predicted in the Bible over 2000 years ago, when Daniel said that a great Islamic leader would appear. A 'Mahdi' who would galvanise Islam against the West. 'And there shall be a time of trouble as there never was before,' Daniel had said.

The Reverend Jerry Buffett had warned his massive congregation more than once about the threat from the evil religion of Islam and his mind turned to Matthew's description of Christ's time on the Mount of Olives and Christ's prophecy to his disciples of the world's coming destruction. 'What will be the sign of your coming again, and the end of the age?' the disciples had asked, and Jesus had answered, 'You will hear of wars and nation will rise against nation.' Since the end of the Second World War, the number of wars around the globe had increased dramatically, Jerry Buffett mused. Christ had also said there would be famines, storms and earthquakes just before His coming. Those too had increased dramatically. The tsunami in the Indian Ocean had killed tens of thousands, as had the devastating earthquake in Kashmir. And now, like the Jews of ancient Jerusalem, the people of the United States had been warned again. The Apostle Paul had forecast as much in his second letter to Timothy. 'But know this,' he had said, 'that in the last days, perilous times will come: for men will be lovers of themselves, lovers of money. Lovers of pleasure rather than lovers of God.' Buffet reflected that more than most cities in the United States, New Orleans epitomised man's increasing lust for drugs, sex and alcohol, and other pleasures of the flesh. God had sent Hurricane Katrina as another warning against loose living.

As the 737 settled on its final approach into Washington's Ronald Reagan Airport, Reverend Buffett knew that God was using him to deliver a message to the President. God was calling on the President to act now and act fast to save the chosen people of America. The end times were frighteningly close.

CHAPTER 23

UNITED STATES ARMY MEDICAL RESEARCH INSTITUTE FOR INFECTIOUS DISEASES, FORT DETRICK, MARYLAND

Captain Donald Crawshaw waited until he saw Colonel Wassenberg drive into the car park at 0555 hours. Crawshaw could set his watch by it and he had quickly learned to be in the office before the Colonel arrived, even if it did mean getting up at 0330 hours. The Colonel had pulled some strings in the Pentagon and somehow managed to have USAMRIID's normal staff car replaced with a camouflaged four-wheel drive Marine Corps Humvee, complete with machine gun mounts and a massive fuel consumption of less than 4 miles per gallon. 'In this war on terror, you have to be ready, Crawshaw. You never know when these little Muslim bastards will appear next!' the Colonel had reminded him.

'Yessir! USAMRIID Sir!' Captain Crawshaw had replied. It wasn't always easy but Crawshaw had learned to think before speaking and, if he did venture a comment, he tried to make sure it was one that the Colonel would agree with. He ducked through the Colonel's sandbagged doorway to check that he'd turned the coffee percola-tor on – 'I take my coffee heavy-duty, boy, black and strong' – and that the morning papers were neatly folded and laid out in a fan on the right-hand side of the Colonel's desk; *The New York Times* on the left, overlaying *The Washington Post*, overlaying *USA Today*. Satisfied, he checked his running uniform in the Colonel's mirror. His white T-shirt was starched as were the creases on his camouflage trousers and his boots gleamed in the half-light of the early morning. Timing his exit Captain Crawshaw jogged out of the main entrance doors as the Colonel switched off the huge V8 diesel.

'Morning Sir! USAMRIID Sir!' Crawshaw shouted as he saluted on the run.

'No pain, no gain, Crawshaw!' Colonel Wassenberg yelled, feeling back in control for once, towering over the world in his Humvee.

'Yessir! USAMRIID Sir!'

Colonel Wassenberg strode in through the main entrance and down the corridor that led to his office. He checked that his combat gear was ready on the hooks just inside the sandbagged door and placed his black briefcase with its heavy brass locks on the rack he'd had made for it. He poured coffee into his mug embossed with the Marine Corps seal and then eased himself into his large leather chair behind his sandbagged desk; Colonel Wassenberg always took great care not to disturb the creases in his uniform. He picked up the *New York Times*; the news from Iraq dominated the front page. October had been the worst month for the US forces since the invasion over three years before, with the bodies of over a hundred young men and women shipped back to the States in body bags, bringing the total close to the 3000 mark. Nearly 300 Coalition soldiers had been maimed and wounded, bringing that total to well over 20,000. Another 1200 Iraqi civilians had been killed at an average of forty a day as the country sank deeper into civil war and the Shia and Sunni death squads took control of Baghdad and the provinces. If only he could get back into a real combat command, he thought wistfully, he would turn this war around. Kick ass and bring in the B-52s and flatten the goddamn place. By the time he'd finished with them there wouldn't be a Muslim terrorist or a stinking camel train within a hundred miles of the borders.

Colonel Wassenberg had always wanted to follow in the footsteps of his hero, General Patton, and Wassenberg imagined the headlines as he pictured himself as General Walter C. Wassenberg III, a four star general in command of the entire operation. 'General Wassenberg Declares Victory in Iraq – Mission Accomplished' would be splashed over the front pages of newspapers around the world. He could see the headlines that would follow, almost on a daily basis. 'General Wassenberg Establishes Military Government In Iraq – Democracy For Iraqis On Track', 'Wassenberg Brings Oil Supplies Back On Line – SUV Sales Surge', 'Wassenberg Declares Muslim Threat Over'. He closed his eyes and saw himself in Baghdad, shaking hands with the Reverend Jerry Buffett as American democracy and the true faith of Christianity took hold in the once pagan, but now liberated country of Iraq. In a reversal of the invasion of Constantinople by the Ottoman Sultan Mehmet the Conqueror on 29 May 1453, when he converted one of the greatest Christian cathedrals in the world, Hagia Sophia, to a grand Mosque, Wassenberg would have Iraq's mosques converted into Christian churches. He opened his eyes and, as he often did when he was alone, he raised his chin slightly and looked towards the ceiling, seeing himself at the White House with the cameras of the world's press flashing incessantly. 'A Grateful Nation Awards Wassenberg the Congressional Medal of Honor'; it was something he had prayed for often.

Colonel Wassenberg finished devouring the news and turned to the opinion page. A prominent headline caught his attention. The sub-editor had headlined the article 'The Fear of Difference' but the opinion piece was signed by Professor Imran Sayed. Wassenberg's face reddened and he gripped the edge of his desk as he read the article.

As the war on terror continues around the globe, a dangerous divide is opening between Islam and the West. We in the West are consumed by a fear of difference. It is a fear that is fuelled by the media's incessant references to men and women of Middle Eastern appearance and an insistence on describing terrorists as Muslim. Fear in the community is fuelled by prominent Christian leaders in this country and other Western countries who misinterpret the Bible as the only revelation from God, and who themselves fear that Christianity is threatened by Islam. In the United States, the Reverend Franklin Graham, the son of Billy Graham, has described Islam as a 'very evil and wicked religion', the Reverend Jerry Vines has described Muhammad as a 'demon-obsessed paedophile' and the Reverend Pat Robertson has described Muslims as 'worse than Nazis', prompting other influential Christian leaders like the Reverend Jerry Buffett to follow suit. This is causing anger and frustration in much of the Islamic world. One can only imagine the reaction here if an

Imam were to interpret Christ's fondness for women as devious or describe the Christian Saviour as 'the Womanising Christ'.

Colonel Wassenberg tightened his grip on the desk. Professor Sayed's even-handed criticism of his own faith of Islam that followed did nothing to restore the blood flow to Wassenberg's white knuckles.

On the other side of the fence, the Islamists continually misinterpret another of God's revelations, the Qu'ran. Like their Christian counterparts many Imams claim that Islam is the only true religion, denouncing those who are not Muslims as infidels, and they ignore the Prophet's command in the verses of the Spider Sura, to treat the 'other people of the book – the Jews and the Christians' well. *Jihad* is dangerously misinterpreted by both sides.

Both sides fear differences in dress. Here in the United States and in Britain and Australia, two of our staunchest allies in this war on terror, Muslim women are criticised for covering their bodies with the veil and the *hijab*, the head scarf; but Christians think nothing of wearing a gold cross around their neck and brook no criticism of nuns wearing habits. The Jews would be appalled if anyone suggested banning the *yarmulke* or the ringlets and broad black hats of their more conservative cousins.

Wassenberg was approaching meltdown. Although the Professor had not disclosed his appointment as a scientist at USAMRIID in the article, there would be many in the Surgeon General's office who would know him. Not only was this Muslim scientist profoundly wrong in his thinking, for which Wassenberg had already decided he would be disciplined severely, but to have this sort of open criticism of the West by a member of his own staff might put that elusive first star even further out of reach. With his blood pressure rising to a dangerous level, he continued to read Imran Sayed's final paragraphs.

Religion is an accident of birth, and if you were born in Pakistan, as I was, you were taught from a very young age to believe in Muhammad's ascension into heaven from the Dome of the Rock in Jerusalem. If you were born in this country and you are a Christian, you are taught to believe in Christ's ascension a short distance away, from his tomb near Calvary over which the Church of the Holy Sepulchre now stands.

Muhammad and Christ, peace be upon them both, had much in common. Both called for justice, equity and compassion. Instead of fearing difference moderates on both sides need to embrace it, and celebrate the diversity of culture we have inherited. Unless the growing influence of Islamic, Christian and Jewish fundamentalists is marginalised, along with their differing but unshakeable beliefs that they alone have the only answer to our salvation, our future as a species is bleak.

'Crawshaw! I want that motherfucker Muslim scientist in my office immediately. Immediately, d'yer hear!'

At the far end of the sprawling compound Captain Crawshaw was sweating profusely in the half-light of the dawn, struggling to put one boot in front of the other, mercifully out of hearing of his incandescent Colonel.

CHAPTER 24

ISLAMABAD, PAKISTAN

As the British Airways 747 taxied after landing al-Falid caught a glimpse of the faded blue 'Islamabad International' sign above the low white building that served as the gateway to Pakistan's capital. The airport was shared with the Pakistan Air Force Chaklala Transport Base, and al-Falid had mixed emotions as he watched two American-made F-16 fighters roar down the main runway. The jets' single afterburners blasted a long orange fire trail behind them, the green and white decals of the Pakistan Air Force on the fuselages and the white crescent and star of Pakistan on the tail fins clearly visible. One day, al-Falid thought resentfully, we will not need your aircraft. One day we will be making our own and pan-Islam will stretch across Europe and Asia, and across the Pacific to the Americas. The world's aircraft, along with everything else, will be made by Muslims for the benefit of Islam. al-Falid silently thanked Allah, the Most Merciful and the Most Gracious, that such a day was fast approaching.

al-Falid spotted the CIA agent immediately. This one was standing way too close to the baggage carousel, nervously scanning the passengers arriving to pick up their bags. It looked like the young man was on his first assignment in the field. He was wearing black wrap-around sunglasses and al-Falid judged him to be in his mid-twenties, about 175 centimetres tall, with a long oval face and very short, blond hair. al-Falid sensed that, behind the sunglasses, their eyes met and the American infidel immediately looked away. 'Never make eye contact' would be in the manual, al-Falid thought wryly. After a few minutes, with the baggage carousel remaining obstinately stationary, al-Falid turned abruptly and walked up to the newsstand at the far end of the terminal. After he had bought a copy of the *Pakistan Observer,* he turned back to find that the American infidel was only 30 metres away looking at the departure screens. Suspicions confirmed, al-Falid moved back towards the baggage carousel. This was not going to be too difficult, al-Falid thought, but then his mood changed abruptly as he checked his BlackBerry to find that he had an email. Most communications were sent via innocuous blogger sites on the internet, and he made a mental note to remind his cell leader in the city targeted for the first warning attack that the Americans, along with their British and Australian counterparts, could now read emails with ease.

Authorities reacted to TCDD and community worries. Half-life a concern. Normal activities suspended and no longer able to use them as cover. Cork in bottle approach will be limited and will need to concentrate on HEAT for surface attack.

Conscious of being watched by the CIA agent, al-Falid kept his expression neutral as he deleted the incriminating message. The authorities' decision to cease normal activities, the activities which would have provided his cell in the target city with the perfect cover for delivery of large amounts of explosives for the first of Kadeer's warning attacks was a blow, but canny operational planners like al-Falid always allowed for the unexpected. The email had suggested his alternative plan be put into operation. Several high explosive anti-tank rockets had been acquired from the infidel's own forces and they would now be used in the major manoeuvre. The fishing boat al-Falid had purchased would have to be reconfigured to deliver its part in the attack on the surface, although time was running out. al-Falid knew the schedule of the supertanker off by heart, and two of the tugs would already be preparing to leave their base for the long voyage to the target. As the baggage carousel rumbled into life, al-Falid pondered the change in plan. The anti-tank missiles would have to be accompanied by a bigger shaped charge, but that had been allowed for and al-Falid was confident that the welding operations could be carried out in broad daylight. That sort of activity was perfectly normal around a boatshed and it might still be possible to position smaller charges on the bottom. If the charges on the bottom were also successful the disruption to the target would be complete. al-Falid's eyes narrowed at the memory of the long hours he had spent poring over the map of the infidel's city. The cork in the bottle might yet be possible, he thought, as he moved to collect his battered suitcase.

Amon al-Falid had chosen a large hotel off Gomal Road, not far from the huge Shah Faisal Mosque at the base of the majestic Magalla Hills. The hills overlooked the thoroughly modern capital of Pakistan which had been moved from Karachi in the late 1950s. High-rise buildings separated by wide, tree-lined avenues gave a false image of a stable, prosperous and peaceful Islamic nation. Many of the large hotels had loading docks staffed by Muslims and al-Falid's hotel had a member of the Faith who had been only too happy to help. The day after his arrival al-Falid had been quite content for the American infidel to follow him to the Islamic University where al-Falid had perused documents on Islamic architecture, but today he planned to visit the arms traders in Darra Adam Khel. His first visit eighteen months ago to the dusty, lawless outpost in the foothills of the Hindu Kush, where you could buy anything from an AK-47 to the most sophisticated weapons the international arms black markets had to offer, had been highly successful, and the resources for the second and third of Kadeer's warning attacks were in position in various parts of the world. Today he would complete the purchases for the first attack. Like the last visit, his visit today was something that had to be kept from the infidel at all costs. al-Falid carefully eased back the window curtain. The young CIA agent was keen. Not yet 7 am, and already he was sitting in a battered Suzuki Potohar parked across the street. Probably thinks it is non-descript and unobtrusive, al-Falid thought contemptuously. Every so often, the infidel would look up from his newspaper and glance anxiously towards the hotel entrance. Well, he was in for a very long day, al-Falid mused, as he headed down to the basement and the loading dock.

Already the temperature had reached 40°C and it was going to be one of those very hot and humid days the sub-continent was renowned for. al-Falid allowed himself a rare smile. The trip out of the hotel in among the big calico laundry bags belonging to the Hyderabad Laundry Company had been quite comfortable, and he had then changed into a loose-fitting *shalwat kameez,* the traditional flowing robes of the Pashtuns. He was now in the passenger seat of the laundry company's four-wheel drive Toyota that was speeding towards the Afghan border. Two of Khalid Kadeer's fighters were in the back of the Toyota with their AK-47 Kalashnikovs, loaded with two full magazines taped together, between their knees. Following close behind was a truck from the same company with six more of Kadeer's bodyguards. The two heavy metal suitcases in the back contained US$10 million in non-sequential $100 bills, and both Kadeer and al-Falid were determined that it would not fall into the wrong hands. The money had come from one of al-Qaeda's global charities, for which the Hyderabad Laundry Company in Islamabad was just a front. al-Falid had become an expert in hiding money trails and not all the banks in Islamabad were what they seemed.

al-Falid felt a surge of satisfaction as the avenues of Islamabad gave way to the Indus River Valley, then two hours later, to the Peshawar valley. To the north he could pick out the hazy foothills of the Hindu Kush, and if Allah, the Most Kind, the Most Merciful was willing, the money in the back of the Toyota would soon be exchanged for sophisticated American-made weapons that would be used for the glory of Islam. Fleetingly he wondered about the young CIA agent and he allowed himself another smile.

Bill Crawford looked over his newspaper and glanced at his watch, nervous that he might have blown his very first assignment. It was mid-afternoon and there was still no sign of the target. Could the man have slipped out through another entrance, he wondered, and then he reassured himself. That wasn't possible. There were only two exits from the hotel, either the main revolving doors or out of the loading dock that fronted on to a dusty side alley, and he had positioned himself so he could see both. The only movement at the loading dock had been a four-wheel drive laundry truck and that had been hours ago. With the temperature still hovering around 40°C and the air thick and oppressive, he started the Suzuki again in a vain attempt to get some relief from an air conditioner that was way past its use-by-date. His thoughts drifted back to the States where he'd left his young wife Natalie and three-month-old daughter Tabatha, and he wondered when he would see them again.

The Toyota came to a halt at the border to North-West Frontier, the Pakistani province that bordered Afghanistan, where the law of the gun was paramount, and where not even the Pakistani military held any control. The dirty sign read 'Attention: Entry Of Foreigners Is Prohibited Beyond This Point'. Despite the Pakistan Office of Home Security permit produced by the driver, the guard appeared agitated, but when al-Falid produced his Egyptian passport the guard relaxed and the gates were opened with a fisted salute.

'Allahu Akbar! God is Great!' Even among the Urdu and Pashto speaking tribes the Muslim war cry in Arabic bridged a multitude of languages.

An hour and a half later, they reached the outskirts of Darra Adam Khel and they were challenged again, this time by Kalashnikov-wielding Pashtun tribesmen. After another brief exchange of words between them and al-Falid's driver, and another cry of '*Allahu Akbar!* God is great!' the Toyota was allowed into the dusty main street of the town. al-Falid's driver headed for the crowded and noisy market at the far end. Had the Pakistani government been serious about hunting down the Taliban who had fled from the US forces in Afghanistan, they would not have had any trouble finding a sizeable number of them on the streets of Darra Adam Khel, all easily recognisable in their robes and turbans. The air was hot and heavy, and the smoke from charcoal-burning braziers on which the store holders were cooking spiced meats hung thickly alongside the hashish and exhausts of the *tuk-tuks*. Eventually they came to a dirty canvas bazaar in the centre of the market. Pictures of Osama bin Laden and Mullah Omar were fixed to either side of the entrance to the tent, and two Pashtun tribesmen stood in front, their ubiquitous Kalashnikovs at the ready. After a word from one of Kadeer's bodyguards al-Falid was quickly ushered inside.

al-Falid nodded with approval as he was shown four long, green metal boxes, one of which was open. Nestling on the grey moulded foam inside was an olive-green tube about 1.5 metres long and 14 centimetres wide. Smaller boxes holding the grip stocks for each missile were stacked separately. The stingers were going to be used in the first of Khalid Kadeer's warning attacks. This batch of missiles would facilitate just one small but essential part of the overall plan, and al-Falid already knew that the infidel's forces had been training for just the sort of assault Kadeer had ordered him to mount against one of the world's most beautiful cities. The infidel's training exercises had been faithfully reported and well publicised in the target city's media. al-Falid smiled grimly at the infidel's foolishness. The media coverage was undoubtedly a political ploy to convince the city's population that everything was under control, but the infidel's political arrogance had provided al-Falid with a very good idea of what his men might face. Although the infidel's soldiers were among the best in the world, they were only lightly armed. He now knew that the more heavily armed tugboats would be absolutely critical in neutralising the city's police and the military.

The arms dealer offered al-Falid a battered armchair and then excused himself to count the cash from the two trunks that had been unloaded from the back of the truck. Out here in the wilds of the border area nothing was taken for granted.

The arms bazaar at Darra Adam Khel had become one of the CIA's and the Pentagon's worst nightmares, but it was a nightmare of their own making. The sale of sophisticated arms had its genesis in the United States' support for Osama bin Laden and the Muja-hadeen, the Islamic holy warriors in Afghanistan, many of whom held to very austere forms of Islam. Afghanistan was one of the poorest countries on the planet, and in the nineteenth century the British and the Russian empires had competed for control of a geography that was dominated by some of the highest and most inhospitable mountain ranges in the world. In December 1979, with the British out of the picture, the Soviets were fearful that Islamic Mujahadeen factions hostile to the USSR would gain power. The Soviets invaded Afghanistan and installed a puppet government in Kabul. The

United States immediately threw its massive firepower behind the freedom fighters, as Ronald Reagan preferred to call Osama bin Laden and the Mujahadeen, arming them with large numbers of some of the most sophisticated small arms available, including the stinger missiles that could down any aircraft that was flying below 10,000 feet. When the Soviets withdrew in 1989, yet another army defeated by the mountainous Hindu Kush, Afghanistan had been once again bombed back into the Stone Age. Over a million of its citizens were killed and millions more fled to Pakistan and neighbouring Iran. The United States withdrew, leaving the opium fields and the rest of the country to disintegrate as the warlords turned on each other in fierce inter-tribal fighting, paving the way for the appearance of the Pakistani-supported Taliban who emerged from their *madrassas*, the austere Islamic schools that operated in the no-go border areas of Pakistan's North-West Frontier Province. More importantly for Khalid Kadeer and al-Falid, in the vacuum left by the United States over 500 of the feared stinger missiles that had been supplied to the Mujahadeen had gone missing, and now, for a price, they were available in Darra Adam Khel.

A young boy brought a tin mug of green tea and while the arms dealers counted the stacks of US$100 bills, al-Falid sank back into the armchair, grateful for a small respite in what would be a very long and complex campaign. His mind went back to the time he had been in the very same tent, eighteen months before, at the time the *Churchill,* the *Montgomery* and the *Wavell* were leaving Rotterdam, each bound for Karachi. Back then, al-Falid's first visit to Darra Adam Khel had gone surprisingly smoothly and fifteen of the stinger missiles had been purchased. The purchase of the tugs had also been a masterstroke. al-Falid's assessment that tugs were only subjected to cursory customs inspections, if at all, had turned out to be correct. The weapons al-Falid had just purchased for the first warning attack beneath Eternity would be now moved to Karachi where they would be collected by the *Montgomery* and the *Wavell*. The third tug, the *Winston Churchill* had been assigned to putting resources in place for a later warning. Slowly but surely the entire plan was coming together.

Khalid Kadeer had chosen the target cities with great care, betting that none of the huge spy satellites belonging to the United States would be focused on any of them. The Great Satan, Allah be praised, had played into his hands.

CHAPTER 25

THE OVAL OFFICE, THE WHITE HOUSE, WASHINGTON DC

The secret service agent outside the entrance to the Oval Office in the West Wing nodded politely to Jerry Buffett, one of the President's most trusted advisors on domestic and foreign policy. The Reverend Buffett was a frequent but unpublicised visitor to a White House where regular prayer sessions and the word of the Lord held sway.

'Jerry, come on in,' President Harrison said, getting up from behind his desk and taking the evangelist warmly by the hand. 'Dan Esposito, you know,' he said, as his advisor also proffered a hand in welcome.

'Thank you, Mr President, thank you.' Despite the relaxed rapport and an absolute trust between them, Jerry Buffett always stuck with protocol. Unless they were alone or in prayer and he was asking God to bless the Presidency, he never addressed the President by his first name. 'These are difficult times, Mr President, but a lot of folk are praying for you and we all think you're doing a first class job,' he added encouragingly.

'Well I appreciate that, Jerry. Sometimes it's not easy but I get a lot of strength from the Lord.'

'Amen to that, Mr President, Amen to that.'

'Take the weight off your feet,' the President said, sitting down on one of the two lounges and gesturing towards the other.

'What do you make of this latest threat from Khalid Kadeer and al-Qaeda, Jerry?' the President asked after the secret service agent had left the room.

Jerry Buffett nodded gravely and leaned forward, lowering his deep southern drawl, which seemed an entirely unnecessary precaution in what was arguably the most secure office in the world.

'We should be doing something about this threat before it overwhelms us, Mr President. It isn't the false prophecies of the Qu'ran that we should be concerned about here but the real prophecies in the Bible. We face one of the most serious times in the history of mankind and that's why God has put you in this office. Yours is a mission from God,' he said, making sure he emphasised his point, 'and there are two separate threats, Mr President. The greatest threat will come from the Chinese and the massive armies of Gog, as Ezekiel makes clear, but that will come later. The more immediate threat will come from the false religion of Islam. The Muslims are demanding that the Palestinians be given their own State, Mr President, but that will only be a small start. They want nothing more than for Israel to be pushed into the sea. But the Bible tells us, Mr President, that before Christ can return, all of the biblical lands must be returned to the Israelites, *all of them*,' the Reverend Buffett said determinedly.

'The Palestinians must be relocated to Jordan and any other country that will take these pagans. In Ezekiel, God says to us "But you, O mountains of Israel, you will put forth your branches and bear your fruit for my people Israel, for they will soon come. I will cause you to be inhabited as you were formerly". God has also warned us that in the last days, Mr President, just before the return of Christ, the Muslims will try and destroy Israel and Jerusalem.'

President Harrison looked thoughtful.

'The Bible is quite clear, Mr President,' Jerry Buffett pressed on. 'Attacks on the United States by Islamic terrorists are predicted in both the Old and the New Testaments. What we're seeing is the beginning of the end times that herald the return of Jesus himself, and I very much fear that Khalid Kadeer will carry out his threats, exactly as it's been laid out for us in the Bible.'

Dan Esposito was sitting at the opposite end of the President's couch and he shifted in his seat uncomfortably. First that little shit O'Connor from the CIA and now this meddlesome preacher, both espousing the view that the threats from Kadeer were genuine. It was not a line that he wanted aired in public but for the moment he said nothing. Esposito knew that, for now, he needed Buffett to galvanise the voters in the southern bible-belt and in the swing states like Ohio. If Buffett's preachers urged them to vote for a godfearing President who took his guidance from the Lord, they would turn out in droves.

The Reverend Buffett reached inside his soft leather briefcase and pulled out his well-thumbed Bible. 'God has told me that the Muslim nations are preparing to strike our nation, Mr President, and our Lord revealed how they would do this when he spoke with

John on the Greek island of Patmos.' Jerry Buffett turned to the Revelation to John. '"And I saw a pale horse and its rider's name was Death." The Greek for pale is *chloros*, which stands for disease. The Bible could not be more clear, Mr President. It's there in Daniel, in Matthew and in Revelations. I have no doubt that these Muslims are planning to launch an attack that spreads disease and that can only be a biological attack.'

'The State Department and our Intelligence agencies don't think they've developed that capability yet,' the President said, glancing over at Esposito.

'Our State Department and our Intelligence agencies all do an excellent job, Mr President, no doubt about it, but unlike you, they don't have a direct line to a higher authority. Like Hitler, Kadeer speaks of a final solution. As God's man in the White House, Mr President, you're privy to the greatest source of intelligence there is. There can be no higher authority than the word of the Lord and the Holy Book. We not only need to prepare this country against a devastating Islamic biological attack, Mr President, we need to deter them from even thinking about launching one. The only thing that prevented the Soviet Union from launching a nuclear attack during the Cuban missile crisis was our own nuclear capability. Khrushchev knew that if he attacked, his own country would be annihilated. We need to develop our own biological weapons, Mr President, and leave the Muslims in no doubt that if they attack us we not only have the means to destroy them, but we will not hesitate to use them.'

'I hear you, Jerry,' President Harrison replied, his mind wavering, 'I hear you, but it would be a very big step to re-introduce that research.'

'These are desperate last days, Mr President, and you need to get yourself into a position to strike first. If you strike in the name of the Lord you can rest assured that God will be on your side.'

The Reverend Buffett was using the same persuasive bible-based rhetoric he used on his centre's big stage back in Atlanta; skills he had spent a lifetime perfecting. After pausing for more thought, the President nodded in agreement, as he reflected that the urgings of the Vice President and the Secretary of Defense may well have been God's way of getting his message through; a message that was now being confirmed by his spiritual advisor.

Before he left, Jerry Buffett joined hands with the other two men and led them in prayer. 'Lord Jesus, we thank you for this godfearing President that you have placed in the White House, that your will might be done here on earth. We ask that you continue to protect this President, that he might overcome the Islamic forces of evil in this world. We ask that you will guide all those who are tasked with the preparations for our defense, that your light might shine forth from this nation to illuminate the world. We ask this in Jesus' name, Amen.'

Earlier in the day, and some 900 kilometres to the south, evil of a more sinister nature had been gathering strength.

CHAPTER 26

ATLANTA, GEORGIA

Dr Richard Halliwell waited impatiently for the man from the City Pound. It was not yet 6.30 a.m. and apart from the occasional jogger, the park in downtown Atlanta was deserted, or at least Halliwell thought it was. This was a meeting that, if the worst happened, had to be deniable and could not be delegated. Halliwell smiled to himself. It appealed to his sense of justice that he might employ someone from the City Pound. They were, after all, no better than mangy dogs.

Halliwell thrust his gloved hands into the pockets of his expensive cashmere overcoat and tapped his Italian leather shoes in frustration. He was not a man who was accustomed to being kept waiting. His planning was, as usual, meticulous. The previous month he had tasked his long-time private investigator to report on several of the city's employees. His private detective had understood the sensitivity of the task perfectly. As he always did, Halliwell had insisted on a verbal briefing and payment was in cash, which meant there was no paper trail. Halliwell had decided on a Mexican illegal immigrant. Married to a fiery wife, with two children, the man was a regular visitor to one of the city's seedier bars where he was often seen in the company of equally dubious women. Why anyone would bother with him was beyond Dr Halliwell's imagination as he watched the fat, dark-haired little Mexican make his way furtively across the park. Some women obviously had no taste, he thought, but in the end, the more disgusting his private life the better. Richard Halliwell liked to have control over people. When the man was 45 metres away, Halliwell slipped a thin balaclava over his face.

'You took your time,' Halliwell challenged.

The Mexican jumped, a startled look on his face.

'In here,' Halliwell commanded, appearing from behind the hedge that encircled a small private area of the park.

'Why all the secrecy?' the Mexican asked.

'Because that's the way I like it,' Halliwell responded curtly. Leaving his fine leather gloves on, he withdrew a plain envelope from his cashmere coat. 'Inside there is a thousand dollars cash. There will be a lot more where that came from, provided you cooperate.'

'And if I don't?' The Mexican was now very wary of the tall, well-dressed man behind the mask, but he sensed he had the upper hand and his coal-like eyes gleamed with greed. Whatever he was about to be asked to do was important enough to be cloaked in extraordinary secrecy. His sense of the upper hand did not last long.

'If you decide not to take the task on, this meeting never took place and you don't get your thousand dollars. If you do take the task on, which is a relatively simple one, you will be very handsomely rewarded. Either way you keep your trap shut. There are some photographs in the envelope as well. Taken in the motel behind Hungry Jacks. They are copies. If you don't remain silent the originals of the photographs will be delivered to your wife.'

The man's dark face went pale. 'Who the hell are you?' he rasped.

'That's none of your concern. Do you want the money?'

'Depends on what you want me to do,' the man replied glancing around, like a large rat cornered at the end of a sewer and looking for a way out.

Richard Halliwell gave the man a quick outline of what was required.

The man paused, as if something was bothering him, as well it might. '$5000 a delivery?' he asked.

'Cash.'

Again he paused before answering. $5000 dollars would buy a lot of women and a lot of hooch, and it would keep that bitch he married in order too, he thought hungrily.

'No skin off my nose,' he said finally. 'When do you want your first delivery?'

'The barman will give you a message to contact your uncle. That will be the signal for you to come here. Your instructions will be in purple ink on a piece of paper at the bottom of that bin.' Halliwell pointed to the refuse bin he had chosen as the dead-letter drop. 'There is an entrance to the laboratory compound that is normally kept locked. You will be given the time for delivery and you are to stick to it exactly.'

Richard Halliwell waited until the man had driven away in his van before he removed the balaclava, then he walked out of the park in the opposite direction.

Unseen by either Halliwell or the Mexican, a shadowy figure on the far side of the hedge waited a full five minutes before he too walked out of the park.

CHAPTER 27

UNITED STATES ARMY MEDICAL RESEARCH INSTITUTE FOR INFECTIOUS DISEASES, FORT DETRICK, MARYLAND

As Professor Imran Sayed entered the new Commanding Colonel's office, the pungent odour of fresh sandbags assailed his nostrils. Not only had the door been arched with the freshly filled sacks, but the front and sides of the desk looked like something out of ancient Giza with the green bags packed up to the top of the desk in a pyramid.

'At ease!' the Colonel snapped.

Professor Sayed had wandered in with one hand in his suit pocket, and he was somewhat taken aback by the Colonel's order for him to relax. 'Expecting an attack anytime soon, Colonel?' he asked with a grin, unable to resist baiting the military commander.

'I'll remind you again, Professor, this country is at war. At war, d'yer hear, and we can never be too prepared. This is a top-secret base and another 9/11 might be just around the corner,' Wassenberg fumed, momentarily distracted from the Professor's opinion piece and the reason he had summoned the recalcitrant academic.

'Perhaps that might be a good reason to sit down and talk with people like President Ahmadinejad and Bashar al Assad,' Imran replied more seriously. 'Instead of treating them and their people like pariahs and threatening to bomb them all out of existence. We might get better results if we sat across the table and got to know one another a little better. You never know, we might even find some common ground we can work from.'

'Iran and Syria are part of the axis of evil, Professor. Haven't you been listening to President Harrison?'

Not if I can help it, Sayed thought.

'Chamberlain tried that with Hitler and look where that got us. We don't negotiate with terrorists, Professor, and one day you and the rest of the academics on this base will learn to leave war fighting to the President and people like me who know something about it.'

Sayed was tempted to observe that neither Iran nor Syria had shown any sign of the territorial ambitions of either Hitler or the United States, nor did the President and his generals seem to know a great deal about the implications of starting a war in places like Iraq. He was beginning to think that the IQ of his Colonel and the sandbags had alarming similarities and he let the comments go through to the catcher.

'Which brings me to your opinion piece in today's *New York Times*. Who authorised that?' Colonel Wassenberg demanded.

'I wasn't aware that an opinion piece, being one man's opinion, required authorisation from anyone, Colonel,' Sayed replied, his own anger starting to rise. 'One of the cornerstones of this democracy, a democracy that we are very keen to impose on the Middle East,' he added pointedly, 'is supposed to be freedom of speech, but it seems to me that for conservative governments like this one, freedom of speech only applies if you happen to agree with their policies.'

Colonel Wassenberg was apoplectic. 'You're employed by the United States government to adhere to the policies laid down by the President, the Pentagon and myself, and that does not include writing to the papers with criticism that is way above your pay grade. In future you will clear all correspondence through me. Through me, d'yer hear? Dismissed.'

Sayed shrugged, turned and walked from Wassenberg's office shaking his head. Not only did the Commanding Colonel have some interesting delusions of grandeur, but Professor Sayed judged that Wassenberg was a prime candidate for a stroke or a heart attack. He rolled his eyes and winked at a bemused Kate who was waiting to go in.

'Crawshaw! Is that Braithwaite woman here yet?'

'Yessir! USAMRIID Sir!' Captain Crawshaw shouted. 'Quickly, the Colonel's waiting,' he urged, waving his hand back and forth as he shooed Kate towards the door.

Kate tilted her head, raised her eyebrows and made cross-eyes at the captain before wandering in to Colonel Cluster's inner sanctum.

'You wanted to see me, Colonel?' Kate asked, blinking innocently at the red-faced Wassenberg who was drumming his fingers on the top of his desk.

'At ease.'

'Thank *you*, Colonel,' Kate said condescendingly, infuriating Wassenberg even further.

'I said this morning that I wasn't happy with the standard of dress on this base, and one of the main offenders is you! Jeans are not an acceptable form of dress and your hair is to be cut short or tied in a bun. Crawshaw is sending you a copy of the dress manual.'

'This may come as a surprise to you, Colonel,' Kate responded angrily, 'but I'm not part of your army, or anyone else's. If I wanted to parade at six o'clock in the morning and tie my hair in a bun I would have gone to West Point, but from the little I've seen of that institution's product,' she said, glaring at the small man sitting behind his bombproof desk, 'I'm quite happy with my decision to be a microbiologist!'

Incensed, Kate turned on her heel and strode through the sand-bags, leaving Colonel Wassenberg speechless but more determined than ever to demolish the fiery young scientist's career. He reached for the letter he'd received in the afternoon post, signed personally by the Secretary of Defense, requesting two high quality scientists skilled in Level 4 laboratory work be temporarily assigned to Halliwell Pharmaceuticals as liaison officers on the smallpox vaccine project and added Braithwaite's name to Sayed's. This would be a backwater that would at least stall her career until he could think of something more permanent.

CHAPTER 28

HALLIWELL TOWER, ATLANTA

Dr Richard Halliwell parked his red Mercedes-Benz SLR 722 McLaren Sports in his private car park underneath the Halliwell Tower. With a top speed of 208 miles an hour and a price tag of over $400,000, the sports roadster was just another symbol of Halliwell's relentless pursuit of power; although for church on Sundays he conveyed a more subtle if no less powerful image with the big black Mercedes S600 sedan he allowed his wife to drive. Simone Carstairs, Halliwell's personal assistant of nearly eight years, preferred the McLaren.

Halliwell inserted the key to his private lift and rode it to his office. The gleaming monolith of chrome and glass symbolised the 'Big Pharma of Big Pharma'. Halliwell Pharmaceuticals had offices and factories in sixty-three countries.

Dr Halliwell took off his coat and hung it in the walnut-panelled cupboard adjacent to his private bathroom. Deep in thought, he wandered over to the windows of his office and, as was his habit, stared out towards the early morning mists that hovered over the lake below Stone Mountain. The day before, Vice President Bolton had telephoned to congratulate him on being awarded the Administration's half-a-billion dollar contract for the production of 300 million doses of smallpox vaccine. Keeping Bolton on the books as a consultant, albeit on a separate set of books, had been a stroke of genius. Fleetingly he reflected on the expertise of his Chief Financial Officer, Alan Ferraro, who was away on leave. He'd never warmed to him, but then again, with the possible exception of his secretary, Halliwell didn't warm to anyone. As long as Ferraro managed to keep the company clear of the Securities and Exchange Commission and the rest of the Wall Street regulators, Halliwell would continue to pay him his exorbitant salary and tolerate Ferraro's need to disappear from time to time to explore the stupidity of his private interests. His thoughts were interrupted by a knock on the inner doors to his spacious suite.

'Come in, Simone,' he said, moving back to his large walnut desk.

'Morning, Richard.' Simone Carstairs was tall and fit. Her striking red hair contrasted arrestingly with her deep tan. She was universally referred to as 'Big Red' around Halliwell Pharmaceuticals, although no one ever used the nickname in earshot of either her or the company's chairman. Simone guarded the moat around Level 37 with an iron fist in a velvet glove. If you wanted to get to the chairman, you had to get past her. She had an oval face and her immaculate teeth were a brilliant white. Simone Carstair's orthodontist was one of the most expensive in Atlanta, although there was nothing artificial about her cleavage, a fact that had never been lost on Richard Halliwell. Simone was wearing a loose-fitting top; she bent over his desk, lingering for a fraction longer than she needed to as she placed a cup of freshly percolated coffee on his desk. 'Sleep well?'

'Like a log – you?' he asked meaningfully. Although he knew better than to quiz her, Halliwell often wondered what Simone got up to out of hours, or when she was on one of her numerous holidays to the Caribbean. So far his private investigator had not turned up any attachments. Where possessions were concerned Richard Halliwell was not one to be crossed.

'I would have slept better if you'd been around,' Simone replied none-too-subtly. It had been a constant source of irritation to her that Richard would not countenance leaving Constance, his depressingly boring and very religious wife, but she'd reluctantly learned to live with it.

Richard Halliwell had married into one of the most well-connected families in American politics, although if Halliwell thought he might benefit, he'd been sadly mistaken. Constance Halliwell was the daughter of Congressman Davis Burton. The Congressman had failed in both of his attempts to win the Republican nomination for the White House, but as one of the most respected and erudite congressmen on the Hill, he'd risen to lead the Republicans in the House. Speaker Davis Burton was now second-in-line to the Presidency after the Vice President, and a very astute judge of people. With years of experience in dealing with lobbyists and other characters of dubious pedigree swimming in the murky waters of politics, Davis Burton had taken an instant dislike to the young Halliwell. He'd been opposed to the marriage from the very beginning, and as time had gone on, that opposition had strengthened to the point he would no longer tolerate Halliwell in his house; but Richard Halliwell continued to believe he could win the congressman over. At the start of their marriage, when Halliwell discovered his wife was a complete waste of time in the bedroom, he'd nevertheless decided Constance was worth keeping. His difficulties with her father were not in the public domain and there were advantages in having a wife to whom middle-America could relate. To the voters, Halliwell was the 'all-American boy' made good, with powerful connections on the Hill and to the White House. Richard Halliwell had no doubt that when the time came, his prominent membership of an increasingly politically savvy Southern Baptist Church would also be a factor. Dan Esposito was not the only one to notice that the new Christian Right in America had become a powerful political force.

'Your wife rang a few minutes ago. She said to tell you that Randy Baker has been offered a congressional page's place. He's going to work with your father-in-law.'

Halliwell nodded in satisfaction. Randy Baker, a young member of the Buffett Center, had recently expressed to Halliwell he had an interest in politics. Richard Halliwell had immediately recruited Constance to put in a word with her father. For the cost of a mobile phone and a few nickels out of petty cash, Halliwell had no doubt he could recruit the impressionable young Randy Baker to report on the comings and goings in the Speaker's office. Information was power. Halliwell made a note to ring the young man and congratulate him.

'She also asked me to remind you that you're having lunch with Jerry Buffett after church next Sunday. He's asked a Marine Corps

Colonel to come down from Maryland and give the sermon as part of his "Wake Up America" program.' Simone raised her eyebrows ever so slightly in a 'that should be fun' expression. 'And the White House rang. They wanted to know if you are free for a game of golf with the President on Thursday this week at The Vineyard Country Club in California. Dan Esposito will be there as well.'

Richard Halliwell nodded, a look of satisfaction on his face. Nestled amongst stately old coastal oaks and towering redwoods not far from the Napa Valley north of San Francisco, The Vineyard was one of the most exclusive golf clubs in the United States and with less than 400 members, it was a club membership that Richard Halliwell had coveted for a long time. A 'males only' club, it had been designed in the early 1930s and played host to one of the world's greatest golf tournaments. The average age of the membership was 76, most of them billionaires and although Richard Halliwell qualified on the latter count there was a problem. You couldn't apply to be a member of The Vineyard, you had to be invited, and despite some quite intensive lobbying, that invitation had been elusive. Perhaps this might be an opportunity to make some useful contacts, he thought. 'Sounds interesting, I think you should tell the pilot to stand by.'

'Already done.' Simone Carstairs was not just a pretty face. She was also ruthlessly efficient.

'Did they say who else might be playing?'

'I asked that, just you three.'

'Interesting,' Richard mused. 'Very interesting.' A quiet game of golf with the President and his most trusted political advisor was more than a little intriguing.

'They apologised that the President can't stay for dinner as he has

a speech to deliver at the American Faith-based Policy Institute.'
Like Vice President Bolton's address to the National Rifle Association, the President's speech to the right wing think tank would be
preaching to the converted, but the Institute was one of the White
House's more important constituencies, plus the audience could be
relied on to applaud in all the right places.

'We'll just have to dine alone,' Halliwell replied, his smile a quick,
unemotional action.

'I've booked us adjoining suites at The Vineyard Resort,' Simone
said.

Richard Halliwell watched his PA walk from his suite. There
was no doubt about it, Simone Carstairs had a great pair of legs and
a great fanny.

CHAPTER 29

CALIFORNIA

The President of the United States was the only leader in the world who used a 747 to get him to a golf match, and the domestic and air travel arrangements for the President had not been lost on either Khalid Kadeer or al-Falid. al-Qaeda had spent many hours looking to exploit any weakness.

The arrival or departure of Air Force One was the stuff of security nightmares. It invariably involved a total air exclusion zone and a closure of taxiways which wreaked havoc with normal domestic and international schedules. If there was an option, airport authorities around the world were always keen for an air force base to be used. Since September 11 the protective screen around Air Force One had been strengthened even further and for the first time in the history of the United States, the US Air Force flew regular combat air patrols over major cities. Although it hadn't been the practice in the past, if the threat level rose even slightly, Air Force One would be given a

fighter escort and the Air Force was confident that the series of security screens around the President's aircraft would be very difficult for
a terrorist to penetrate. The most dangerous time was on take off and
landing when the aircraft was vulnerable to a missile strike, but the
extra deployments of heavily armed secret service agents around an
airfield provided additional protection. Earlier in the day, the 89th
Airlift Wing at Andrews Air Force Base had received an anonymous
threat to destroy Air Force One which would normally be put down
as one of many hoax calls, but this morning's caller had used the US
Air Force's classified codeword 'Angel' for the President's aircraft,
and the Air Force had scrambled two fighters, just in case.

It was a beautifully clear autumn day. In the cockpit of Air Force
One, as President Harrison's chief pilot Air Force Colonel Mike
Munro and his crew went through their routine briefing for landing at Travis Air Force Base in California, the vapour trails of two
F-16s were visible as they kept a vigilant patrol high above the President. The two young US Air Force pilots were watchful, ready to
escort any intruders out of the area, or shoot them out of the sky
if it was necessary; in the brave new world post-September 11, the
rules of engagement were brutal. This morning only one civilian
aircraft had clearance into Travis and that clearance had come from
the White House. A black Learjet 60 with the Halliwell Pharmaceuticals logo on the tailfin was scheduled to land 30 minutes before
the President.

Richard Halliwell's personal flight attendant finished clearing away
the light lunch of crayfish salad and the nose of the Learjet dipped as
Halliwell's pilots eased back the power. Simone Carstairs leaned back
in the red leather of her armchair and raised her champagne glass.

She was wearing a dark blue linen dress with a plunging neckline that exposed the top of her tanned breasts. Halliwell's eyes were focused on her cleavage. Beneath the blue linen he could make out the faint outline of her nipples.

'To tonight,' she mouthed seductively, allowing her tongue to flick over her lips.

'I'll hold you to that,' Richard Halliwell replied, raising his glass in response. 'What are you doing this afternoon?' he asked, curious to know her every move.

Simone smiled. 'Well, since The Vineyard doesn't seem to be too fond of women,' she replied meaningfully, 'while you're out hitting little white balls with the President of this country, I'm sure I can put your black American Express card to good use in San Francisco,' she replied evasively. One day she would get him to ditch that boring little wife of his, she mused, reflecting that when Constance Halliwell wasn't in Church singing hymns, she was devoting the rest of her time singing the praises of that even more boring bible-bashing preacher Jerry Buffett. Simone drained the last of the vintage Krug and again licked her lips. Richard Halliwell, she knew, was calculating and powerful, and she was attracted to that in a man. She was sure that, one day, Halliwell would be on the presidential plane that was following them in, and she intended to be on it with him.

As Halliwell went back to reading one of the reports on China – an analysis of the security arrangements for the Beijing Olympics – she watched him as her thoughts turned again to his marriage. For the life of her she couldn't see what Richard saw in his wife. He'd once confided in her that Constance had resisted anything other than the missionary position, recoiling in horror on their wedding night when he'd attempted oral sex. Simone suppressed a smile. She'd never been able to get her mind around Constance on top, let alone having oral sex, and Constance's reticence in the bedroom was something that Simone Carstairs knew how to turn to her advantage. Simone would continue to ensure that Richard Halliwell got what his wife could never give him, even if that contained an extraordinary irony. He was quite possibly the most selfish and ill-equipped lover she'd ever encountered. In his case she'd reluctantly concluded that size did matter; it was just that for Simone Carstairs, power mattered much more. When he came to his senses, she and President Richard Halliwell would make a very powerful team. JFK and Jacqueline had taken the world by storm, and soon there would be a new Camelot, one that the world would have to take notice of.

Puffs of light blue smoke wisped from the tyres of the Learjet as Halliwell's chief pilot eased the aircraft on to 21 Left, one of two long parallel strips at Travis Air Force Base in Fairfield just outside San Francisco Bay. The sprawling 5000 acre base was home to the 60th Air Mobility Wing and the massive C-5 Galaxy and C-17 Globe-master cargo aircraft and today, like every other day, it was busy. As Secret Service agents scanned the perimeter in preparation for the arrival of the President's plane, three huge KC-10 Extender refuelling jets were banked up behind one another waiting to land.

Halliwell's pilot taxied towards the special arrivals area where a black Bell Jet Ranger helicopter was waiting, rotors already turning. A hundred metres away, close to the orange cross that marked the spot onto which Colonel Mike Munro would nudge Air Force One's nose wheel, two more of the President's pilots were already strapped in and going through their pre-flight checks on Marine One, the

President's olive-green and white helicopter. Her much bigger fixed wing sister was only 20 minutes out of Travis and had commenced her descent toward finals.

CHAPTER 30

CIA HEADQUARTERS, LANGLEY, VIRGINIA

Curtis O'Connor glanced at the clock on his wall. It was just before 6 p.m and he was contemplating an early night when a quiet buzzing on his private line interrupted his thoughts.

'I'm on my way,' O'Connor said, wondering what crisis had arisen that had the CIA's Deputy Director of Operations, Tom McNamara summoning him. Tom McNamara was the second most senior officer in the Agency and was responsible for running all of the CIA's spies and foreign clandestine operations, including the insertion of CIA paramilitary teams into places like Afghanistan and Iraq, and more recently Iran.

'Come in, buddy, have a seat,' McNamara said, motioning Curtis towards one of two comfortable brown leather couches. The leather on each of them was torn and cracked. The furniture had been scheduled for replacement more than once, but each time Tom had told 'those wankers down in the Director of Administration's Office' that he'd garrote the first person who laid a hand on them. His exploits in the field in his younger days were already the subject of folklore at Langley, with more than one foreign agent known to have breathed his last as McNamara had silently wielded a short length of chicken wire. The furniture had stayed put. The seal of the CIA – an eagle atop a shield with a sixteen pointed compass star representing intelligence from all points of the globe converging on Langley – hung proudly on the wood-panelled wall behind a desk covered in crimson files. The DDO's powerful reading light was off and the office was lit by a number of elegant table lamps.

'I've just come from the Director's office,' Tom McNamara said, rolling his eyes up towards the seventh floor and taking the other couch. The DDO had a big, round face, grey hair which he kept very short and piercing blue eyes. Weighing in at 120 kilograms, the ex-Marine had a huge barrel chest, and for such a big man, he moved with surprising grace and agility. 'The new wunderkind's been on the phone to the Vice President,' he added disparagingly. Curtis and Tom had worked together for many years, both in the field and at Langley, and they enjoyed an easy rapport. The deep trust between the two men had been forged in adversity. Each would trust the other with his life but neither man trusted the new Director who'd been sent over by the White House to 'sort the joint out'.

'There are a couple of issues. For whatever reason the Vice President seems to be obsessed with China and the security of the Olympics. I've explained to the Director that we've already established an intelligence task force which will work closely with the US Olympic Committee to protect our athletes and officials, but I'd like you to sit in on their meetings when you can, just to keep an eye on things.'

Curtis grinned. Given his current workload, provided they met between midnight and dawn, that shouldn't be a problem, but he said nothing as his DDO continued.

'More importantly the brains trust down in Pennsylvania Avenue have hatched a brilliant new scheme to carry out research on biological weapons and you and I are about to get the football.'

'Sounds like a hospital pass to me,' Curtis observed, becoming serious.

'Got it in one. The program's black, so it'll be run out of your office. If it fucks up you and I will wear it. It's got that slime ball Esposito's name written all over it.'

'USAMRIID or CDC?'

'Neither. Ever since that memo on phone tapping ordinary citizens hit the media, they're paranoid about leaks. It'll be done in that new lab we built for the Vice President's mate down in Atlanta at Halliwell Pharmaceuticals. What do we know about this guy?'

'One of my old buddies, Rob Bauer down at the FBI in Atlanta, has an interesting file on Halliwell,' Curtis replied. Despite the intense public rivalry between the FBI and the CIA, true professionals like Deputy Director McNamara and Officer O'Connor had contacts that flew under the radar of the raging jealousies at the top. Those contacts sliced through red tape in an instant and were worth their weight in gold to both sides.

'Outwardly Halliwell's a pillar of the Southern Baptist Church, all-American boy made good, turned a piss-farting little biotech into a multinational, darling of the Wall Street set and the brokers worship the ground he walks on.'

'And?' Tom McNamara asked with a grin.

'He'd assassinate his grandmother if he thought there was a buck in it. Right now he's pushing on with that court case in Africa to prevent cheap generic AIDS drugs being distributed, even though the rest of Big Pharma have backed off. He's also trying to dominate the AIDS drug market in China.'

'Wife and kids?'

'The kids are pretty smart; they left home first chance they got,' Curtis replied cynically. 'His wife Constance is as boring as bat shit and she's a pillar of the church what's-his-face runs, that crackpot evangelist mate of the President.'

'Buffett?'

'He's the one. For $10,000 he'll pray for you and throw in a plaque as big as a postage stamp on a porch about the size of the fucking Super Bowl. Halliwell turns up there with his wife every Sunday, and then he spends the rest of the week porking the ass off his secretary. Mind you,' Curtis added with a grin, 'I've seen a photo. She's got a very nice ass and I wouldn't crawl over her to get to you.'

'I'm relieved to hear that, O'Connor,' McNamara said with a wry smile. 'So other than that you're quite fond of Halliwell.'

'He's a prick. More dangerous than a warren full of rattlesnakes on heat,' Curtis replied. 'He'll probably make a good politician one day, although he won't get any help from his father-in-law.'

'Who is?' Tom raised an eyebrow.

'The Speaker of the House, Davis Burton.'

'Halliwell's married to the Speaker's daughter?'

Curtis nodded. 'Burton can't stand him although the Speaker's out of step with his colleagues. Halliwell throws some of the biggest parties in Washington and he's got a lot of support in the Republican Party.'

'Wouldn't be the first time Davis Burton's been out of step,' Tom observed, his admiration for the veteran politician coming to the fore. 'I've briefed him many times. He's a thorough gentleman and very sharp, and he's about the only one who's making any sense on Iraq,' he added.

'Neither the FBI nor Inland Revenue are convinced Halliwell's operating within the law,' Curtis concluded, 'and they're quietly watching him, but given Halliwell's connections they're very wary. He and the Vice President are as thick as thieves.'

'What's your view?'

'I think there's a lot more to Halliwell than the current intelligence indicates. My gut feeling says he needs watching.'

CHAPTER 33

THE VINEYARD COUNTRY CLUB, CALIFORNIA

Richard Halliwell's helicopter preceded the President's onto the landing pad at The Vineyard Country Club in the Napa Valley. No one in the imposing clubhouse took the slightest bit of notice. Helicopters landing at the club were almost as common as the large black limos in the car park. The Vineyard Country Club boasted three 18-hole championship courses set in a forest and vineyards that took up 40 hectares of some of the most expensive land in Napa County. The President's visit had been kept quiet, and the Secret Service had deliberately chosen the third of the three courses, which for the last two days had been closed for a 'visiting dignitary'. Although it was lined with tall redwoods and coastal oaks, the 'new 18' was more easily protected as the surrounding countryside beyond its boundaries was more open. Nothing had been left to chance. Dog squads had combed the rough and the bushes on the course the day before. They had found nothing more sinister than 40 new golf balls their owners had been too lazy to look for. A military helicopter manned by snipers equipped with long range rifles and stabilised mounts was patrolling in the distance. For those charged with the President's security even a game of golf was an expensive logistical nightmare. Not that a visit by the President of the United States could be kept secret for long.

One of the club's billionaire octogenarians, Otis J. Lynberg II, had lodged an official complaint with the Chairman, Palmer Weinberger. Visiting dignitaries should be invited to play elsewhere, he'd snorted. Later, when he'd spotted the President alighting from Marine One, Otis had immediately sought out Palmer again, wholeheartedly endorsing the President's visit but expressing his displeasure that members were given no advance warning. He'd become even more irate when he was told that members were not going to be presented to the President. It was precisely the sort of scenario Dan Esposito wanted to avoid.

'What a pity the cameras aren't around when you want them!' the President said, his voice raised in enthusiasm as he watched his drive off the first tee bounce down the middle of the long par five fairway.

'Nice shot, Mr President,' Richard Halliwell acknowledged grudgingly, as he prepared to tee up behind his host. The first tee was nearly half the size of a bowling green, and the immaculately kept turf was on top of a raised mound, three sides of which were pro- tected by weathered sandstone. Halliwell stepped back from his ball and assessed his drive. For the first 200 metres the fairway dropped away towards a treacherous hazard – a deep creek that could only be crossed by walking over a quaint little stone-arch bridge. From there the fairway climbed a gently undulating slope to a huge green nestled in among stately redwood pines that were more than a hundred years old. He lined up his driver and adjusted his stance. He stared at the white ball imagining it represented GlaxoSmithKline. The silence of the first tee was broken by a sharp whistling sound as Richard Halliwell tried to get his ball past the President's.

'That's big trouble in there, Hal!' President Harrison shouted with the enthusiasm of a small boy in the middle of a marbles match. Halliwell's lips compressed into a hard, thin line as he watched his ball take on a vicious hook and disappear into the thick rough underneath the trees just short of the creek.

'It's not over until the fat lady sings, Mr President,' Halliwell replied, struggling to keep the jocularity in his voice. Much to the President's amusement, Dan Esposito nearly put his ball in the creek but at the last moment it bounced into the trees on the opposite side of the fairway to Halliwell's.

Halliwell combed the thick rough, trying to keep his agitation in check. Finding his ball in here would need a small miracle, he thought, and he was not one to believe in miracles. He took a quick glance back towards the fairway. Dan Esposito was in the rough on the far side and the President was giving him stick from his cart about 20 metres away. The Secret Service agents were all scanning the sides of the fairway ahead. Choosing a small clear area, Halliwell put his hand in the pocket of his golfing slacks, undid the zip that he'd had his tailor sew in the pocket and dropped a brand new ball down his trouser leg. He always played with a number one that was embossed with the gold Halliwell 'H', and as the ball rolled into a depression he gently moved it into a better lie with his foot.

'Want some help, Hal?' the President called.

'Got it thanks, Mr President.' Richard Halliwell walked back to the cart he was sharing with the President and selected a five wood. Moments later he watched with satisfaction as he drilled his ball over the creek and up the slope to within striking distance of the hole.

'Nice recovery, Hal,' the President shouted. Richard Halliwell waved his golf club in acknowledgment.

'Number three, Mr Esposito?' the Secret Service agent asked, looking at the partially buried ball. The Secret Service agents assigned to protect the President detested the arrogant little advisor. Esposito waddled over and grunted. 'Stupid fucking game,' he muttered, but 'Whatever it Takes' was Esposito's motto in politics and in life and if today that was a golf game, then so be it.

While the President and Richard Halliwell played golf, both men yet to discuss their plans to change the course of history, satellite imagery from the top-secret National Reconnaissance Office in Chantilly, Virginia was on its way to Pakistan where a more violent and menacing history was about to be written.

CHAPTER 32

THE NATIONAL RECONNAISSANCE OFFICE, CHANTILLY, VIRGINIA

The National Reconnaissance Office or NRO top-secret satellite ground station connected to NORAD, the North American Aerospace Defense Command inside Cheyenne Mountain, and to many other similar stations besides – had a large plaque on the wall of the command centre. It was inscribed around the edges with 'National Reconnaissance Office: We Own The Night'. The logo looked like something out of science fiction, but since September 11, a lot of science fiction and reality had become indistinguishable. The inner circle of the plaque was black with a pair of sinister-looking owl's eyes peering out from behind a silver mesh that was identical to that on the Lacrosse series of satellites' wire mesh antennae. The logo was a reminder to the operators hunched over their high-resolution screens that dozens of sophisticated US satellites were orbiting between 300 and 40,000 kilometres above the Earth, their cameras turning night into day. Some, like the Defense Support

Program satellites controlled by the US Air Force operated in the infra-red spectrum to detect missile launches. Others were capable of reading the numbers on a letterbox. In the NRO command centre, Iraq was still dominating collection priorities, and the KeyHole and Lacrosse satellites were sending back real-time information as they passed over Baghdad, Fallujah, Mosul, Tikrit and other Iraqi cities every hour.

The Lacrosse satellites, codenamed onyx, vega and indigo, and weighing a massive 15 tonnes, were in a relatively low orbit – 650 kilometres above the earth. Travelling at over 6 kilometres a second, with huge power-generating solar arrays the size of the wings on a 747, the synthetic aperture radars were peering through clouds and weather that might have made targets hard to detect. Right now, a satellite from a sister program – the highly classified advanced KeyHole series KH–11 – was directly over Baghdad on its midday pass over the city. Launched from a massive but expendable Titan IV rocket and costing more than $1.5 billion, KH–11 was also the size of a school bus and its cameras operated in the near infra-red and thermal infra-red spectra, which enabled it to see at night, as well as operating in the visible light spectrum for daylight surveillance. The photostream could detect someone wearing a pistol, but even though the satellite cameras could pierce through clouds and bad weather, there was still no way for them to determine what vehicles might contain explosives.

Iraq was not the only place in the world being examined in minute detail, and another bank of computers further over was linked to the KeyHole series footprinted over the Pakistan–Afghanistan border. A few hours ago the huge satellite had passed over Peshawar and the nearby foothills of the Hindu Kush. The real-time photos of a white van with Hyderabad Laundry Company emblazoned on the side, approaching what looked like a dirt-poor village didn't mean anything to the operator, but like thousands of other images that might be connected with the new war on terror, the file was marked for transmission to Langley, just in case.

Rob Regan ran his hand through his hair and stared at the imagery on the screen in front of him. The satellite photographs were grainy, but he could clearly make out the words 'Hyderabad Laundry Company' on the side of the white four-wheel drive.

'What do you think a fucking laundry truck would have been doing in a place like Darra Adam Khel and why would it now be headed for Peshawar?' he mused out loud.

'Not collecting the sheets would be my first guess,' his lanky deputy, Tony Carmello said, getting up from his own desk and ambling over to his boss's.

'Precisely. This war on terror would be a fucking sight easier if the Pakis got off their black asses and cleaned out this cesspool on their border,' Regan grumbled.

'Fat chance,' his deputy responded. Both men knew that the Pakistani government had been unwilling to exert any serious control over the border with Afghanistan. Despite intense pressure from the United States and the UN, Pakistan had refused to regulate the *madrassas*, the Islamic schools that were financially supported by the puritanical Wahhabis from Saudi Arabia and other equally fanatical Islamists. Hundreds of the Taliban schools were flourishing in the North-West Frontier Province. The invective from furious and often illiterate Imams filled impressionable young minds with a burning hatred towards the West. The world was being flooded with a seemingly inexhaustible supply of suicide bombers, but any Pakistani leader who tried to rein in the *madrassas* and restrict their teaching to the real messages of the Qu'ran risked losing office at the hands of Pakistan's Islamic hardliners and the ISI, Pakistan's Inter-Service Intelligence agency, which was a strong supporter of the Taliban. In Pakistan's relatively short history a coup was an ever-present possibility.

'Have we heard from Crawford?' Regan asked.

'Not since yesterday; I'll check what's happening.'

A minute later, Tony Carmello handed his boss a handset that was connected through an encryption system that no terrorist would be able to break. 'Crawford. He says his target hasn't left the hotel.'

'Back entrance?' the station chief asked his latest recruit bluntly.

'There's a loading dock but I've got that in view as well,' the young CIA agent answered confidently. 'The only movement out of there has been a laundry truck and that was early this morning.'

'Would that have belonged to the Hyderabad Laundry Company?' Regan asked.

'I think it might have,' Crawford replied, less certain now.

'If you're going to be successful in this game, Crawford, you're not only going to have to think, you're going to have to know!' Regan barked down the phone. The long hours were taking their toll. 'How big was the truck? What colour?'

'A Toyota four-wheel drive and it was white,' the young agent replied nervously.

'Get yourself up to Peshawar and find it because right now I've got satellite imagery that tells me a white four-wheel drive Toyota belonging to the Hyderabad Laundry Company is headed towards there and something tells my end of nose that it might be the same four-wheel drive you watched leave this morning. When you do find it, I don't want any fucking heroics. Just keep it under surveillance and see if you can find out what they're up to. And be careful. Peshawar isn't a tourist resort.'

'Whatever they're up to, I think you're right, it's got fuck all to do with delivering clean linen,' Regan said when he'd hung up the phone. Sometimes, all a CIA agent in the field had to go on was a hunch, but hunches based on years of experience sometimes paid off.

CHAPTER 33

CIA HEADQUARTERS, LANGLEY, VIRGINIA

When will the contingency plan for a terrorist attack on the Beijing Olympics be ready?' Tom McNamara asked O'Connor, turning the focus away from what Richard Halliwell might be up to.

'We're still developing the possible scenarios and our responses, but the head of the Olympic Task Force will have a draft for you within the next couple of months,' Curtis replied.

'How's it shaping up?' McNamara asked, keen to get the views of an agent he knew to be a straightshooter.

'The biggest worry is a biological attack. Genetic engineering of viruses is a very real threat and we may not have the right vaccines. I haven't seen anything to confirm my suspicions, but if someone like Kadeer can get hold of a bioweapon and we don't take notice of his warnings to start negotiating, I think he'll use it.'

'At the Olympics?'

'The Beijing Olympics are particularly vulnerable because for two weeks in August over three million people from hundreds of thousands of different places around the world are going to be concentrated in the one spot. Once they leave the area, if they're carrying a deadly virus it would be like exporting a far more deadly bird flu all over the world. Although it's not as simple as the media make it sound, Tom. You and I know that in the 1980s and 1990s Aum Shinrikyo were successful when they put plastic bags full of sarin on the Tokyo subway trains and punctured them with umbrellas, but you might remember they carried out at least nine other attacks and the only one of those that was successful was another sarin attack. The anthrax and botulinum attacks all failed.'

Tom McNamara nodded grimly. 'Shoko Asahara. Another fucking crackpot who thinks the world's about to end. He and that raving lunatic Buffett make a good pair,' he grumbled. 'What gets me is that otherwise sane and intelligent people believe all this shit. If the Japanese police hadn't tumbled to these whackers, they might have killed a lot more than nineteen people and what was it . . . 1000 wounded?'

'Plus another 4000 "worried well"; although I guess we can't blame them for being worried. When you see hundreds of people lying on the ground with blood pouring out of their noses and mouths, it's not a pretty sight. And you're right, if they'd had more time and if their university whiz kids had isolated the virulent strain of anthrax rather than the vaccine strain, it might have been a very different story.'

'Hmm,' the DDO grunted, 'but did you see the final report on the Daschle anthrax?'

Curtis nodded. 'I've got my own theory on that and that *was* a different story. That stuff was weapons grade.'

Curtis O'Connor and Tom McNamara had both been startled

when, just six days after September 11, someone in New Jersey had mailed anthrax to the *New York Post*, to CBS, ABC, NBC and the offices of Senate Majority Leader, Tom Daschle. Two mail workers in the Brentwood mail-sorting facility in Washington had died and epidemiologists from the CDC had frantically tested over 5000 employees from Capitol Hill for exposure to the deadly spores.

'Whoever mailed that stuff, Tom, not only had a very high degree of professional expertise, but he or she had access to some pretty sophisticated laboratories.' The perpetrators had been able to achieve what Aum Shinrikyo and other terrorist organisations had not. They'd been able to refine the anthrax to the point where it was lighter than air so that it would float like an aerosol mist. 'That anthrax was not only very pure and concentrated but whoever did it found a way to coat the spores.'

'Is that hard?' the DDO asked, deferring to his younger colleague's earlier years as a biochemist.

'Very difficult. The Daschle anthrax would have had to come from a state-run facility. Outside of here and some of our allies, there are not too many labs that have that capability,' Curtis added pointedly, suspicious that the attack had originated from somewhere within the United States. 'Anthrax spores are ovoid, like a headache capsule, except they're measured in microns or millionths of a metre,' he explained. 'You can't see them with the naked eye but someone found a way to coat them with even smaller superfine particles of silicon dioxide.'

In a chilling discovery that had been kept under wraps, the scientists at USAMRIID had discovered that the tiny anthrax spores used in the Daschle attack had been coated with microscopic particles of glass that were thousands of times smaller again than the spores themselves. It was the equivalent of being able to place a grain of sand on an apple, but in dimensions that an ordinary compound light microscope would not be able to detect. It would take the extraordinary resolution power of an electron microscope to even see it.

'It was the silicon dioxide that caused the spores to break up and crumble. If you can achieve that, the anthrax not only becomes lighter than air, it can pass through the holes in the paper of an envelope.'

Tom McNamara whistled. Both men knew that while *Bacillus anthracis* occurred naturally in cattle and could lie dormant in the soil for years, once anthrax was inhaled by a human, the spores broke open, germinating into energised bacilli – rod-shaped cells – that multiplied with astonishing rapidity, migrating to the lymph nodes in the chest. The first symptoms would be deceptively similar to flu – headache, fever, cough, chills, sometimes vomiting, and a deadly attack was easy to miss. If treated for flu, the patient would begin to feel better but that would happen even if they weren't treated. Anthrax had a characteristic 'ellipse' and for a while the deadly anthrax bacteria would retreat to re-group. When they returned, blood vessels would burst in the brain, the victim's skin would start to turn black and the chest cavity would fill with fluid. Victims had been known to drop dead mid-sentence.

'I will read the report on Olympic security with interest,' Tom said, reaching behind him for another crimson file. 'In the meantime do you remember that single source report we had on Eduard Dolinsky? The White House wants him on our team.'

'You're kidding, Tom.' Curtis O'Connor shook his head in disbelief, his expression matching that of McNamara's.

'I wish I was. I suspect this is another little gem being pushed by the Vice President. He wants Dolinsky in our tent rather than in the Russkies' or Kadeer's. I don't think the President was convinced at first but he's suddenly come around big time.'

'Esposito?'

'I don't think so. That little turd's still shit-scared of something leaking before the next election. Iraq's been bad enough, but this would be the last straw and the Democrats would have a field day. My spies tell me, and I suspect they're right, that the President changed his mind after he had a message from God via that whacky evangelist.'

'I don't get it, Tom. Apart from the Georgian source I haven't seen a single piece of intelligence that would indicate al-Qaeda have got the means to launch a biological attack. The way the Secretary of Defense and his neocons are carrying on, you'd think it's already a clear and present danger. You and I both know it's a long way short of that.'

'I know, but the President's convinced that apart from China's growing economic clout and the Beijing Olympics, the biggest threat to the United States is a biological attack, and he's worried that if we don't get Dolinsky out, Kadeer and his mad mullahs will.'

'We?'

'You to be precise.' Tom smiled. Koltsovo was very remote and neither man was under any illusions as to just how dangerous such a mission might be, if not impossible, but somehow humour served to relieve the tension. 'You always said you'd rather be back in the field.'

'Yeah but I'm fond of living too,' O'Connor replied, his mind going back to another desert years earlier. The rescue of US hostages in Tehran, ordered by President Jimmy Carter, had been a disaster and it had sealed the fate of his Presidency. He lost to Ronald Reagan in a landslide in 1980. 'Siberia's never been at the top of my list of assignments.'

Tom McNamara was still smiling. 'We're in the process of buying a Russian Mi-8T transport helicopter on the arms market in the hope that the Russians will mistake it for one of theirs, although we'll have to recondition it.'

Curtis pulled a face. He'd flown in Russian helicopters before.

'Once that's done,' Tom continued on, ignoring him, 'a couple of our special forces pilots will be trained up. They're working on getting a route in over at the Department of State, which will probably be a bit tricky,' he said in a masterful understatement. It would involve flying out of Canci Air Base, rented by the United States, in Bishek, the capital of Kyrgyzstan. Kazakhstan would have to be provided with enough incentive to allow Curtis' rescue helicopter to refuel and fly along Kazakhstan's 500 kilometre border with China to where the Kazakhstan, Chinese, Russian and Mongolian borders converged high in the Altai Mountains south of the Siberian steppe. It was some of the most mountainous, isolated and dangerous flying territory in the world.

'I imagine you'll want to go in and make contact with Dolinsky first?'

'I'll have a think about that,' Curtis responded, the vaguest of plans starting to take shape, a plan that had flashing red lights all over it, 'but I'm still not convinced about Dolinsky's defection. Getting him out of fucking Koltsovo won't be a cakewalk and I'd feel a lot more comfortable if we knew whether this intelligence could be relied on.'

The DDO could only nod his head in agreement. Both men had years of experience and were well equipped to tackle the most dangerous of missions, but there was something about Dolinsky's defection that made them both very wary.

'And just to make your day,' Tom said, reaching for another crimson file, 'the Director tells me that Halliwell wants two scientists to assist Dolinsky, once you get him out of Koltsovo.'

This time the file was marked 'Top Secret – NOFORN – Limited Distribution'. The 'No Foreigners – Limited Distribution' caveat was not surprising. The Administration was about to disregard one of the most important international treaties the United States had ever signed – the Biological Weapons and Toxin Convention. The consequences of a biological weapons attack were considered to be so devastating to the wider world that the Biological Weapons and Toxin Convention had been signed and ratified by nearly 150 countries. Like so many other conventions, including the Geneva and United Nations conventions against torture, this one was going to be disregarded because of this war on terror.

'The Halliwell lab is pretty isolated,' McNamara continued, 'but even so, they want the number of scientists working on the genetic engineering of the viruses kept to a minimum.'

'Have the scientists been nominated?'

'The Colonel Commanding USAMRIID, a guy by the name of Wassenberg, was asked to provide two of his top people, although he wasn't told the real reason. He was asked to provide Level 4 qualified scientists to work with the pharmaceutical industry on vaccinating the public against smallpox. You'll need to check his nominations out. They look okay on paper but I remember Wassenberg when he was a lieutenant. Complete fuckwit and a god-botherer to boot.'

'I didn't think you allowed fuckwits in the Marines,' Curtis said. When it came to the Marines, O'Connor never missed an opportunity to jerk his boss's fiercely patriotic string.

'We don't!' For a moment, Tom was serious, then he grinned, realising that Curtis was having a lend of him. 'Wassenberg's grandfather was an admiral and his father was a four-star general, which probably explains how he got into the Marines, although I don't know where they got Wassenberg number three from. I think his mother must've been having it off with the pool man. We put him ashore from a submarine one night on a clandestine insertion, only to have him find there was a bunch of television cameras waiting for him with lights blazing on the beach. That wasn't his fault but then he turned around and gave a fucking press conference. Moron!' Tom McNamara shook his head at the memory of it. 'I was in the ops room on the *Abraham Lincoln* watching it unfold. Got half his platoon wiped out as a result, and he was wounded so we packed him off to the Medical Corps.'

'How did he finish up running a place like USAMRIID?'

'I suspect the Secretary of Defense thinks he's a bright cookie. Takes one to know one,' Tom said. 'Have you heard of a Professor Imran Sayed?'

'If it's the same Imran Sayed I think it is, they've at least got that nomination right. I met him a few years back. Sayed's one of the best virologists in the world, although it's a bit odd that Wassenberg would give up a scientist of that calibre, no matter how sensitive the liaison job. It's even odder that the Professor would accept it.'

'He hasn't yet,' Tom replied. ' Neither has the other scientist. Part of your job will be to remind them both of their duty to their country.'

'Who's the other one?'

'A Dr Kate Braithwaite. Both their details are in there,' Tom said, handing Curtis the file.

'Pretty easy on the eye,' Curtis said with a grin, looking at Kate's photograph on the inside cover.

'Sometimes, O'Connor, I think your brains are in the end of your dick,' McNamara said, a resigned look on his face. 'I need hardly remind you that the system hasn't quite got over your little contretemps with the Russian.'

'She gave me some very useful information,' Curtis protested, still grinning.

'That's not all she gave you,' the DDO replied, looking over the top of his glasses. 'I want you to run these two in the same way you'd run a couple of agents out of Moscow.' O'Connor smirked and Tom immediately regretted the analogy. 'Or Baluchistan, which is where you'll be sent if you fuck this up. Once you're convinced they can do the job, and looking at their background there's probably not much doubt about that, bring them into the compartment and make it happen.'

'It's the funding that's black, Tom,' O'Connor replied, more serious now. 'If I try and run these two in the same way you and I have run agents out of Moscow I'll finish up meeting them separately in Lafayette Park and they'll freak. I think we ought to do this with as much normality as possible. It's not exactly a secret that I talk to a lot of scientists about biological threats. I go to conferences with them for Christ's sake.'

Tom McNamara grunted. 'I'll leave that up to you as long as what goes on at Halliwell is watertight. As far as vaccines are concerned, the Vice President seems particularly keen on ensuring that the athletes and officials in our Beijing Olympic team are protected, so without disclosing what we're on about, you'll need to liaise closely with the US Olympic Committee.'

'Do we have a codeword yet?'

'Operation PLASMID and this one is about as tightly held as it can get. Apart from you and I and wunderkind on the seventh floor, not even the Secretary of State's been told – just the President, Vice President, Secretary of Defense and that little turd Esposito.'

'What about Halliwell?'

'From what you've told me about him, if there's a buck in it he'll come on board.'

Dr Richard Halliwell had been on board the day the top-secret laboratory had been certified as safe, but not in a way that either Tom McNamara or O'Connor could ever have imagined.

Back in his office Curtis scanned the files on the two scientists. Given the White House's wildly unreasonable demands for the program to be up and running yesterday, he would need to get them in tomorrow and he pondered his approach. Both of them had been staunch opponents of the retention of the smallpox stocks, and talking them into being part of the top-secret Operation PLASMID might not be easy although his own sympathies lay with the scientists. Unlike an Administration that had no idea how dangerous this could be, the two scientists would know what they were letting themselves in for.

Curtis O'Connor looked at his watch and prepared to drop and lock after another long day at the farm. The photograph of Kate Braithwaite reminded him of how long it had been since he'd been in the company of a beautiful, intelligent woman. His line of work made it difficult to have a longstanding relationship with anybody and he knew that too much emotional involvement with someone could make him lose focus on the job he had to do. Fleetingly, he wondered what it might be like to live a more normal life; one that was not dictated by work and would allow him to have someone to go home to. He ran his hand through his hair and let out a deep sigh of frustration, his thoughts turning back to the other part of his mission. 'While you're at it, O'Connor, could you rock over to Koltsovo in Siberia, and hole up in the Altai Mountains where it gets down to minus 40 degrees fucking Celsius and give this Dolinsky guy a lift back to the States? Sure. The Russians might get a bit pissed about it, and there's no guarantee it won't all turn into a shit box, but you'll manage, you always do.' O'Connor shook his head and spun the combination on his safe.

'We never seem to learn,' he muttered. Hot extractions were inevitably messy, as Oliver North and Ronald Reagan had found out after the Ayatollah Khomeini had overthrown the Shah of Iran in 1978. The following year, sixty-six hostages had been taken prisoner in the US Embassy in Tehran. O'Connor again reflected on a rescue attempt that had been an unmitigated disaster. One of the Marines' Stallion helicopters had crashed into a C-130 transport in the Iranian desert and, in the panic to get out, top-secret plans which identified all of the CIA's agents in Iran were left behind. Curtis knew that it had taken years to recover from that disaster and here was another one on the cards, but rescuing Dolinsky from the clutches of the Kremlin would have to wait until he sorted out Halliwell and the scientists, he thought. As he headed towards the security desk at the main entrance and out into what was left of the night, he reflected on a world that was going barking bloody mad.

CHAPTER 34

THE VINEYARD COUNTRY CLUB, CALIFORNIA

Richard Halliwell watched in amusement as Dan Esposito duffed his third shot, but his smile soon vanished. Instead of disappearing into the creek, the ball hit the middle of the stone-arch bridge and bounced fiendishly, landing halfway up the middle of the fairway on the other side. Halliwell and the President reached the first green in the regulation three shots and while they were waiting in their cart for Dan Esposito to take his fourth, the President quietly raised his plans for research into biological weapons.

'I think the Reverend Buffett is absolutely right, Mr President,' Richard Halliwell responded. Halliwell had concluded some time ago that the shortest route to the inside circle of this White House was a biblical one. 'These Muslims will not stop until they've achieved their goal of a pan-Islamic society, and we need to do everything we can to ensure that doesn't happen. It would be an honour to take on the task, Mr President.'

'You'd be doing this nation a great service, Hal. A great service.'

Dan Esposito wobbled his flabby arse and then swung his club like a baseball bat. Somehow the club connected with the ball, which sizzled off the fairway, along with a sizeable chunk of The Vineyard's best turf. Had Esposito's ball not immediately developed a vicious slice it would have finished up on the next fairway.

'Oh shit!' Esposito's expletive carried across the course. If any of the members had been within earshot, there would have been an instant complaint of 'ungentlemanly language'.

Halliwell smirked with satisfaction as he watched Esposito's ball veer towards trouble among the tall pines on the right-hand side of the green, but his smirk faded as a resounding *thwack* reverberated across the course. Esposito's ball had slammed into a large redwood, bounced back onto the green and into the hole.

'Yes!' Not one usually given to show any emotion, Dan Esposito gave a full-fisted salute.

'I suppose you're going to claim that one, Dan,' the President yelled.

'It's not how, Mr President, it's how many. Whatever it takes.' The campaign trail was not the only place Esposito adhered to his ruthless dictum.

Richard Halliwell fought to retain his composure as he watched his putt rim the hole and then stay out. Hitting off last on the next tee was not something he was going to enjoy.

'Have you ever thought about running for office, Hal?' President Harrison asked, as he drove their cart off the tee on the par 5 second.

'I've sometimes toyed with the idea, Mr President, but when

you leave office there will be a lot of challengers for the Republican nomination and it's difficult to judge my support base,' Halliwell replied enigmatically, leaving the President plenty of room to frame his reply.

'You see that guy over there,' the President said. Dan Esposito had parked his cart on the edge of the fairway and was once again searching for his ball among the trees. 'He may not be the greatest golfer in the world but when it comes to getting people elected he knows every trick in the book and then some. This country is going to need a strong man to carry on the work we've started. Someone like you who can stand up for American Christian values. Someone who isn't afraid to take the fight to our enemies and make sure they don't succeed.'

As the three men shook hands at the end of their round and walked off the eighteenth green, Palmer Weinberger was waiting for them. 'I hope you had a very good game, Mr President. It's been an honour and a privilege to have you as our guest.'

'Well, the result could have been better, Palmer,' the President said, looking at Halliwell with a twisted grin, 'but there's always next time. Dan Esposito I think you know, and this is Richard Halliwell. '

'A very fine course, Palmer,' Halliwell replied. 'You and your committee are to be congratulated.' His response was as calculated as it was insincere. Halliwell's dossier on Weinberger and his committee had not revealed anything he could use in his quest to gain a membership invitation, but Halliwell was not one to give up easily.

'Here's my card. If ever you're in Atlanta give me a call. I'd be happy to look after you.'

Weinberger smiled thinly and pocketed Halliwell's card without looking at it. 'The members were wondering, Mr President, now that they know you're here,' Palmer said, 'if you might join them for a drink in the clubhouse? I know your schedule is tight but they would really appreciate meeting you.'

'Well . . .' The President was uncertain, and he turned towards Esposito.

'Mr President, I'm sure that would be fine.' Esposito moved closer to the President and spoke more quietly. 'I think if you said a few words about being in California for a meeting with the Faith-based Policy Institute, and what better place than a country club like The Vineyard to take a little time out. A club that epitomises American values and success in the world, and,' Esposito concluded, speaking a little more loudly, 'how much we appreciate the club's discretion at keeping a private visit in-house. Would that keep the members happy?' Esposito looked inquiringly at Weinberger.

Richard Halliwell took in the nuances of the conversation immediately. Up until now his feelings towards the powerful little advisor had been ambivalent, but he decided that as long as he remained useful, Esposito was someone he could work with. Sharp and ruthless. Esposito's emphasis of 'a few words' had not been lost on Halliwell either.

'No questions though,' Esposito stipulated, as if reading Halliwell's mind. 'While you're greeting the members, Mr President, Richard and I will grab a quiet drink on the breezeway.'

'I want to talk to you about the announcement of your campaign which I think we should do sooner rather than later,' Esposito said, as they followed the President and the Club Chairman towards the historic clubhouse. 'I'd also like to talk to you about the threat from Islam and get your views on how you're going to handle the threat from China.'

'I have some ideas,' Halliwell replied, still smarting over Weinberger's perfunctory response to his card and invitation, 'but I think China is by far the most serious,' he added, his thoughts turning momentarily to the defection of Dolinsky. If he could put his program in place, and then gain the White House at the next election, he mused, America's dominance of the world would be unassailable.

The jaws of Kadeer's trap were starting to close.

CHAPTER 35

THE VINEYARD RESORT, CALIFORNIA

'How was your golf?' Simone asked, giving Richard Halliwell a lingering kiss on the cheek.

'Beat the b'Jesus out of both of them,' Halliwell boasted, his words a little slurred after several Ancient Reserve Glenfiddichs. The President had been able to relax among like-minded Republican friends and the visit had lasted for quite a bit longer than Esposito had scheduled. The Lincoln Penthouse on the thirtieth floor of The Vineyard Resort boasted sweeping views, and out beyond San Francisco Bay and the Golden Gate the fiery red rim of the sun was just disappearing below the horizon.

'Is that wise, darling, to beat the b'Jesus out of the President of the United States?' Simone asked, reverting to a term of endearment she only ever used when they were alone.

'It is when he's just asked you to run as the next one,' Halliwell said, squeezing Simone's bottom.

'He's going to back you?' Simone felt a surge of excitement.

'Wants me to throw my hat in the ring for the Republican nom-ination,' Halliwell replied, careful not to mention the President's other request for him to re-commence research into the dark world of biological warfare.

'I had a private drink after the game with his advisor, Dan Esposito, and he thinks I've got all the right cards. Solid business credentials, runs on the board, good family background and not only that,' Halliwell added enthusiastically, 'Esposito has told me quietly that my links to Jerry Buffett and his church won't do me any harm either. Buffett's likely to get behind my nomination and he'll bring thousands of other churches on board with him. And that,' Halliwell said, helping himself to a large bourbon, 'is a very big plus.'

'I think this calls for champagne,' Simone said. A little while later she emerged from the penthouse's stylish kitchen with a bottle of Krug, vintage 1964.

'To Richard Halliwell, the next President of the United States,' Simone said, handing him a slender crystal flute and raising her own in a salute.

'President Halliwell. I think the business world will get behind me, don't you?' he asked.

'Of course, darling. They couldn't wish for a better champion. Who's going to run your campaign?' she asked, already alert to any threats to her own position.

'Esposito. There isn't anyone better,' Halliwell replied, raising his chin arrogantly and staring out over the hills. Around the foreshores lights were glimmering in the distance.

'It would be good to meet this Dan Esposito,' Simone said

provocatively as she leaned against Halliwell. 'What would you like for dinner? I thought we'd eat in tonight.'

'You don't want to eat in the restaurant?'

'You've just had a game of golf with the President of the United States, Richard,' Simone replied, immediately taking control of image and PR. 'The golf club members know about it, so it won't be long before the rest of the world does. As the next President of the United States, you have a reputation to protect,' she said, adjusting the collar of his golf shirt and letting her hand slide over his chest. 'Can you imagine what the Democrats would do with a photograph of you and I having an intimate dinner? That's an ad campaign we don't need, darling, even if I am going to be your private secretary in the White House. Besides, I thought a dinner with just the two of us would be rather nice.'

Richard Halliwell walked unsteadily across the penthouse to where Simone was now reclining on the lounge that faced the big windows overlooking the vineyards far below. Simone's red hair cascaded over her shoulders, the low-cut, black evening gown accentuating her generous cleavage.

'I think we should fuck,' Halliwell said thickly, grabbing at her breast.

Simone groaned inwardly. She never missed an opportunity to exploit Halliwell's weakness for sex but when he was drunk, and he was now very drunk, it was a case of humouring him and getting it over with, although drunk or sober, getting it over with was the usual.

Halliwell put his drink on the coffee table, spilling champagne on the polished glass. He unzipped his fly and fumbled for his small, half-erect penis.

'Suck my cock,' he demanded, pushing his groin towards Simone's face.

'More comfortable in the bedroom,' she answered in a throaty voice.

Halliwell fell over while he was trying to get his trousers off and had to clamber into the bed from the floor. He crawled on top of Simone and, to her surprise, she found that he was hard, despite the alcohol. Even though his erection was tiny she winced as he forced himself into her.

'Fuck me, Mr President, fuck me,' she whispered huskily. 'Oh yes! Yeeesss.' It was a well-practised routine for Simone Carstairs but tonight the faked orgasm was not really needed. Richard Halliwell groaned as he came almost immediately, farted, rolled off her and fell asleep.

CHAPTER 36

PESHAWAR, NORTH-WEST FRONTIER

Bill Crawford slowed his vehicle as he approached the Old City of Peshawar and the Street of the Storytellers. The narrow road was almost impassable. Pashtun tribesmen mingled with the Taliban as donkey carts competed with brightly coloured buses, *tuk-tuks* and bicycles. The air was thick with the aroma of spices, pomegranates, goat cheese and the smell of greasy slices of mutton sizzling on braziers beside the crowded thoroughfare. In the back of the shops and bazaars that were crammed together, hot forges were fired by old tyres and hundreds of gunsmiths were turning scrap metal into rifles of dubious quality. An acrid smoke hung heavily over the city. Every few minutes the sound of gunfire could be heard as the gunsmiths took their life into their hands and tested their newly manufactured wares. Photographs of Osama bin Laden, Mullah Omar and al-Zawahiri hung proudly above stalls that offered tea brewed in Russian samovars. Alongside the gunsmiths other merchants were peddling fruit, ceramics, carpets and prayer mats.

Instinctively Crawford felt for his shoulder holster. Every man in the city was armed with a Kalashnikov and a lot of them had bandoliers of ammunition over their shoulders. The few women around were covered from head to toe in black burqas, their eyes hidden behind fine mesh. Suddenly, in among the chaos, he saw it. The Hyderabad Laundry Company Toyota pulled out of a laneway about 100 metres ahead, scattering a herd of goats that had added to the impossible congestion on the Street of the Storytellers.

A more experienced agent might have held back and wondered if this sudden appearance was mere coincidence or something more sinister, but Crawford was keen to make up for his mistake earlier that day. He forced his car past the goats, ignoring the shouts and remonstrations of the gnarled and bearded goatherd.

The Toyota turned left and Crawford followed it down a narrow dirt road. As they headed towards the more upmarket area of University Town, the gunsmiths' bazaars and roadside stalls gradually gave way to large villas on spacious grounds, hidden behind big whitewashed walls. Bill Crawford slowed as the Toyota stopped 200 metres ahead of him. Unfamiliar with the area, and with the lectures on Pakistani culture a distant memory, Crawford unwittingly pulled over past a set of iron gates. If he'd had more experience he would have chosen a safer place to stop. The gates shielded the driveway and entrance to one of Osama bin Laden's *madrassa* compounds. He might also have locked his doors, but he didn't.

Sitting in the passenger seat of the Toyota, al-Falid dialed a number and allowed it to ring three times. He hung up and moved his head slightly so that the side mirror gave him a clear view of the infidel's red Suzuki. Three minutes later twenty students slipped out of the front gates of the *madrassa* and approached the Suzuki from behind. al-Falid knew the infidel would be totally focused on his Toyota and he watched with satisfaction as the young Islamic students closed in on their quarry. One of the CIA's newest recruits was about to discover how dangerous Peshawar could be.

Bill Crawford concentrated on the Toyota ahead of him. Suddenly his thoughts were interrupted as the door of the Suzuki was wrenched open and he was dragged onto the dirt road. He tried to reach for his shoulder holster but his arms were being forced behind his back and his hands were securely tied, the thin wire tearing into his flesh. His assailants turned him around, slamming his head against the Suzuki's door pillar with bone-crunching force. Searing pain flooded his body.

Bill Crawford tried to keep his focus on the group of young men that surrounded him. There seemed to be a big crowd of them all dressed in loosely fitting robes and black turbans and they were seething with anger, their chants getting louder and louder. '*Allahu Akbar*! *Allahu Akbar*! Allah is Great! Allah is Great!

Young Taliban, Crawford thought, but how . . . where had they come from? He knew there were still remnants hiding in the mountains of the Hindu Kush, yet here they were in broad daylight on a public road in the capital city of the North-West Frontier. The station chief's last words about Peshawar not being a tourist resort suddenly came home. Crawford looked from left to right vainly hoping for assistance. He fought against a rising panic as he saw a man get out of the passenger side of the white Toyota and walk towards him. There was no mistaking who he was – al-Falid, the Cairo-born American whom he'd been assigned to tail from the Islamabad International Airport.

'*Allahu Akbar*! *Allahu Akbar*! Allah is Great! Allah is Great.'

Crawford felt a chill run down his spine as the chants echoed off the whitewashed walls.

'Death to the Infidel! Death to the Infidel!'

As al-Falid reached the group the chanting died down and the young Taliban parted respectfully.

'Why are you following me?' al-Falid asked. Crawford was taken aback at the hatred in the man's dark eyes and he remained silent.

al-Falid nodded to one of the young students wielding an AK-47. Crawford grunted in pain as the butt of the rifle smashed against his chin.

'I asked you a question, infidel. Why are you following me?' al-Falid demanded, the fury of his hatred for America and her allies colouring his voice.

al-Falid again nodded to the gun-wielding student and the young CIA officer choked back a bellow of pain as the rifle butt smashed into his face again, breaking his jaw. Bill Crawford began drifting in and out of consciousness as the group once again started up their chant.

'*Allahu Akbar*! *Allahu Akbar*! God is Great! God is Great!'

al-Falid spat on Crawford's bruised and shattered face, then nodded to one of the young students fingering a *jambiyyah*, a viciously curved dagger. The young Islamist started to chant 'Buzkashi! Buzkashi! Buzkashi!' As the realisation of what the chant meant penetrated through the mists of pain, Bill Crawford could feel his legs beginning to give way. Buzkashi was the traditional game of polo that was played in Afghanistan, and the students wanted a ball.

Bill Crawford's eyes widened in horror as the huge blade whistled through the air towards him, taking his head off in one brutal sweep. Bill's head bounced twice before rolling into a dusty hole in the road, leaving a trail of blood. Jerky streams of bright red blood sprayed out of his aorta as his still frantically beating heart found little resistance.

al-Falid stepped back as the students bundled the headless corpse of the infidel back into the Suzuki and doused the small four-wheel drive in petrol. Just before the match was lit Bill Crawford's mobile rang but al-Falid motioned for the students to ignore it. As the phone rang out, it beeped as Natalie left a message. 'Tabatha wanted to say goodnight, darling. We both love you very much and we miss you.' The Suzuki burst into flames.

al-Falid looked on in satisfaction as he watched the students tossing the infidel's head to one another as they walked back up the drive of the *madrassa*. One of them stepped back and dropped the head, laughing as he tried to avoid the spattering of blood. The discarded head lay facing the clear blue sky, the last moments of pain permanently frozen in the lifeless eyes.

CHAPTER 37

CIA HEADQUARTERS, LANGLEY, VIRGINIA

Back in his office the next day Curtis O'Connor scanned the satellite photographs of the burning Suzuki. There was something about the grainy image of the older man in the loose-fitting *shalwat kameez* that bothered him, but the late nights were taking their toll and even the best could miss a vital clue.

O'Connor read the short report on the loss of another agent with a rising sense of anger. Both he and Tom McNamara had warned the new Director not to send young and inexperienced agents into countries like Pakistan, but their warnings had fallen on deaf ears. It was an arrogance that was costing America dearly, O'Connor thought bitterly. Another widow, another child without a father.

'Fucking politicians,' O'Connor swore softly. Islamabad had their suspicions about who was responsible but the academic had disappeared and there wasn't anything concrete to link him with the gruesome murder. Curtis made a note to issue instructions to

Homeland Security for al-Falid to be detained and questioned on his return to the country. His thoughts were interrupted by a knock on the door.

'Professor Sayed, it's good to see you again,' Curtis said, nodding his thanks to the Professor's escort.

'Please, take a seat.' Curtis O'Connor shook Imran's hand firmly and offered him a chair. 'I suppose you're wondering why you're here?'

Imran Sayed smiled. 'Nothing surprises me anymore, Curtis, but yes, it did cross my mind. I hadn't realised Halliwell's links included the CIA.'

'Up until a few days ago they didn't, or at least not official ones,' O'Connor replied. 'Do you know Richard Halliwell?'

'Only by reputation,' Imran replied enigmatically.

Curtis looked the Professor in the eye, realising that they could spend the next hour fencing or cut to the chase. He already knew that, quite apart from Sayed's unsurpassed international reputation, the Professor held top-secret clearances at the highest level, which meant he'd been positively vetted – an exhaustive process involving referee's reports, scrutiny of bank accounts, credit cards, spending habits. In short, Sayed's public and private life had been put under the microscope. There wasn't much about Imran Sayed that the FBI, the CIA and Curtis O'Connor didn't already know, and O'Connor's respect for the man had only grown as he'd looked through his file. Even though he'd been described as a devout Muslim, Sayed seemed prepared to question anyone whose actions in the name of Islam didn't benefit the *ummah* or community, especially fundamentalists like Osama bin Laden. Sayed was a widower and Curtis noted that he had never remarried nor did he seem to have anyone special in his life, preferring instead to devote himself to the pursuit of medical science. Imran's love of wine was perhaps unusual for a Muslim but then Imran was one whom O'Connor classed as a moderate, and in O'Connor's view, the world needed as many moderates as could be found, not just from Islam. He decided to come straight to the point.

'What I'm going to tell you, Imran, is for your ears only, regardless of whether or not you agree to become part of the program, and I want your agreement that you won't disclose this to anyone,' Curtis emphasised.

'If that's going to save time, Curtis, I appreciate your candour. You have my agreement,' Imran replied with a knowing smile.

Curtis grinned. Here was a man he could work with, Curtis thought, and he gave Professor Sayed the background to PLASMID.

'Halliwell Pharmaceuticals has been chosen because of its isolation, and unlike CDC or USAMRIID, access to the Halliwell Level 4 laboratory can be restricted to those on the program. Once the current experiments with smallpox at CDC have been completed, the staff at CDC will be told those experiments are being closed down. What they will not be told is that the program, together with Dr Richard Meyers, a veterinary surgeon who I think you know, and one or two assistants from the animal room, will shift to Halliwell. Essentially I will provide you and Dr Braithwaite with top-secret briefings on what we think the Russians and the Islamic fundamentalists might have achieved to date, and what they might be capable of in the future, including the genetic engineering of viruses. Your task will be to replicate those experiments, together with whatever other experiments you yourselves might deem necessary to give us a feel for what we're up against and what vaccines can be developed to protect us here in mainland United States and overseas. That also includes the protection of US and other western teams at the Beijing Olympics.'

Imran took a deep breath. 'That's a pretty broad brief, Curtis. I appreciate you have a strong background in this field, but does the Administration have any idea how dangerous this might get? Let me give you one example. If the genome of the India-1 strain of smallpox ever fell into the wrong hands, it would not be beyond a state-sponsored laboratory to completely replicate it using polymerase chain reactions. Today's genetic engineering of viruses makes Huxley's *Brave New World* look like a kids' picnic, and combining something like Ebola with smallpox doesn't even bear thinking about.'

'Which is precisely why we do need to think about it, Imran,' Curtis responded, with more conviction than he felt.

'How much time do I have for this decision?'

'Not a lot. The President is pretty toey so I'll need your answer by the end of the week. I'm talking to your colleague later this afternoon.'

Imran nodded. 'I think I should warn you, Doctor Braithwaite is likely to tell you guys what you can do with the rough end of a pine-apple,' he said with a smile, remembering one of Kate's expressions. 'She's Australian and not afraid to speak her mind. Braithwaite is more than a little upset over the present experiments on the Great Apes at CDC, and not without justification.'

'What's she like as a scientist?'

'Kate Braithwaite is undoubtedly the best young scientist I have encountered in my entire career. I would not be at all surprised if one day we see her in Oslo being awarded a Nobel.'

'That good?'

'That good.'

'Then I will do my best to get her on board. Do you have any influence with her?'

'A little and if I'm going to be a part of this she would be my first and last choice as a colleague, but that would involve me being able to talk to her.'

'From what you've told me it may come to that, and if that will make the difference I'll authorise you to do it.' O'Connor had never been afraid to bend the rules if it meant getting a result. 'After I've spoken to her, I'll let you know.'

CHAPTER 38

PESHAWAR, NORTH-WEST FRONTIER

Amon al-Falid walked unhurriedly down the Street of the Storytellers and through the teeming Kissa Khawani Bazaar. He was in good spirits but he remained alert and watchful; where there was one CIA agent there were likely to be more. Another infidel had been dealt with and the Americans still had no idea who he really was. Like the London bombers, he was one of their own, and he said a silent prayer of thanks for Kadeer's foresight in persuading him to stay the course and endure the campus taunts against Islam, something for which the infidel would now pay and pay dearly. al-Falid was very confident that Kadeer's plans could be executed successfully, and at last, Allah be praised, the one true religion of Islam could be spread the length and breadth of the earth.

He paused at a leather goods stall in the crowded bazaar and casually looked around to make sure he wasn't being followed. The Urdu-speaking al-Falid mingled effortlessly among the teeming

humanity of the Old City. He moved on, glancing at a sign outside what passed for the lobby of a hotel. It read 'Guns cannot be
brought into the hotel. Gunmen must check their arms at reception'.
al-Falid smiled to himself. The wild west of Pakistan was one that
the US would come to fear, and unlike the Dodge Cities of US history, Peshawar and the North-West Frontier Province would never
be tamed. A little further down the Street of the Storytellers, he
passed a barber's shop. The first customer was already seated in the
old wooden chair out the front, his head resting on a tattered leather
headrest that had been tied to a stick poking up from the chair's back,
and the barber was sharpening a fearsome-looking blade on a black
leather strop. Next to the barber's, above a grubby corrugated iron
awning, an alarming 2-metre high painting of gleaming white teeth
and garish pink gums announced that a dentist was open to those
who might be brave enough to enter. al-Falid shook his head good-
naturedly to yet another offer of 'tuk-tuk?', and he stopped briefly
in front of a brazier stall, feigning interest in the kebabs that were
sizzling on the grate. Again he mentally photographed the narrow
thoroughfare with its brightly coloured *tuk-tuks* competing with the
donkeys pulling *tongas* that were overloaded with sacks of spices,
seeds and potatoes. Satisfied, al-Falid turned off into a twisting side
alley, pausing for a final check before he reached the entrance to the
al-Qaeda safe house. The doors were solid teak and the understated
but delicate carving was an exquisite example of the very architecture
he claimed to be studying.

After the pre-arranged knock, the heavy doors opened and one
of Kadeer's bodyguards beckoned him inside with a wave of his
Kalashnikov. al-Falid followed the man down some worn wooden

steps into a cellar that was nearly 12 metres below the ground. It was similar to those of many of the houses in the Old City, designed to keep food and other stores cool during the scorching summers. This one served the same purpose, but it also provided protection against eavesdropping.

As al-Falid entered the cellar, the unmistakable figure of Dr Khalid Kadeer rose from the big cushions scattered on the matting covering the dirt floor. He greeted al-Falid with a traditional hug and kisses to both cheeks.

'Welcome Amon. Your trip was without incident?'

'Not entirely,' al-Falid said.

'They are very arrogant and stupid, these Americans,' Kadeer observed when al-Falid had finished filling in his spiritual leader on the events of the past 48 hours. 'That is one of the reasons they will probably not heed the warnings I am about to send them,' he said, a touch of sadness in his voice.

'I hope they don't,' al-Falid replied angrily. 'Their religious leaders are now describing Islam as an evil religion. One of them referred to the great Prophet Muhammad, peace be upon him, as a "demon obsessed paedophile"!' al-Falid almost choked on the words, determined that his leader should understand what was happening in the land of the great Satan.

'I heard those remarks,' Kadeer said quietly. 'al-Jazeera, Allah be praised, is now providing us all with a great service.'

'Then you have seen the cartoons Khalid!'

Kadeer nodded. 'We should not be so concerned about those, Amon,' he said, cautioning his lieutenant against emotion. 'Islam is bigger than that. As Muslims we should not forget *ahl al-kitab,* the

Jews and the Christians, the People of the Book. The great Prophet, peace be upon him, was always mindful of the earlier revelations of Abraham, and he always instructed us to treat the people of the earlier revelations, the Jews and the Christians, with respect. It is not the People of the Book with whom we quarrel, Amon. Our quarrel is with the corrupt and lying western and Chinese leaders who persecute our people in the Middle East and in Xinjiang. Our quarrel is with the western Imams who denounce the Angel Gabriel's revelations to the Prophet, peace be upon him, and who ridicule Islam and the way we dress, encouraging the Jews and the Christians to rise up against us.' The great Muslim philosopher still hoped for a peaceful solution, but not at the expense of his people and his faith.

'The plans for the attacks are on schedule?' he asked al-Falid.

CHAPTER 39

CIA HEADQUARTERS, LANGLEY, VIRGINIA

Kate Braithwaite fought to keep her anger in check as the government car that had been sent for her sped along Route 123 into McLean, Virginia, but she kept reflecting on the day's events. The jerk of a Colonel in charge of USAMRIID had refused point blank to see her. After she'd got his letter of reassignment as a liaison officer to Halliwell Pharmaceuticals she'd demanded an interview but she hadn't got past 'J what's-his-number'.

'The Colonel is very busy with matters of state, Dr Braithwaite, and he regrets he'll be unable to see you,' Captain Crawshaw had said very seriously, standing in front of Colonel Wassenberg's sandbagged door and barring her entry to the inner bunker.

'Did you have to rehearse that, Crawshaw, or does that sort of official bullshit just come naturally,' she'd replied, before storming off. Sycophantic fuckwit, she thought. She'd felt like decking him and if it hadn't been for Imran's counsel to 'go with the flow' to see what the system was up to, she would have resigned on the spot. Kate had enormous respect for the Professor's judgement; perhaps there was a need to stay and fight the system from within but for the life of her she couldn't see much chance of changing things. Halliwell Pharmaceuticals, she knew, concentrated on one thing, and one thing alone – profits. Kate Braithwaite's sense of foreboding increased as the government car slowed, turning into the main entrance to the Central Intelligence Agency.

'Why are we turning into the CIA?' she asked the driver.

'Sorry Ma'am?'

'This is the Central Intelligence Agency. Why are we stopping here?' Kate demanded.

'I'm sorry Ma'am, my instructions are to bring you here.'

Kate said nothing. No point in taking her frustrations out on the driver, who was only doing his job. Her anger was not diminished by the speed with which she was ushered through security, only to find a rugged and impossibly good-looking man she judged to be in his late thirties to early forties waiting for her just past the main reception desk.

'Dr Braithwaite. Hi, I'm Curtis O'Connor.'

Kate shook his hand, taken aback by the warmth of his smile and intrigued by the touch of Irish brogue in his voice, but considering the events of the last 24 hours she was not about to be beguiled by anyone. She glared at Curtis, saying nothing.

'I can understand that all of this will be somewhat of a surprise, Doctor, but I promise all will be revealed shortly,' Curtis said easily, ushering her across the 5-metre wide granite seal of the CIA that was set into the floor.

'Can I get you a coffee? It's brewed, my own machine,' O'Connor said with a boyish grin, indicating the Faema espresso machine that he'd somehow squeezed into a corner of a bookcase. 'The Agency stuff's undrinkable.'

'Black, thank you,' Kate replied, relaxing a little. Curtis O'Connor was charming and she felt her anger subsiding. The few Agency people she had encountered had been excruciatingly boring and bound by regulations, but this man seemed very different. Kate quickly reminded herself that he was probably part of the same team that the Colonel was on, and she remained on her guard.

'You have an impressive résumé, Doctor.' Curtis O'Connor had decided he would play the feisty Australian by the book. No first names until he had gained her confidence. As he was about to find out, it would be a wise strategy.

'What I'm about to tell you is classified above top secret, so I'm going to need your agreement that regardless of your decision it doesn't go out of this room, and that you don't mention it to anyone without my permission.'

'You're calling the shots here, Mr O'Connor.'

'I'll take that as a yes,' Curtis said, flashing another disarming smile.

It was hard not to warm to this guy, Kate thought, but as Curtis outlined the real reason for her secondment to Halliwell Pharmaceuticals any softening of her opinion of him disappeared. Kate waited until Curtis had finished. Yet again she had to fight to control her anger over the stupidity of this Administration.

'Have you *any* idea of how dangerous this sort of meddling with viruses is?'

Curtis O'Connor looked at her and nodded.

'I don't think you do, Mr O'Connor!' Kate said, her exasperation coming to the fore. 'I doubt that you people in your cloistered little world have ever heard of polymerase chain reactions, but let me tell you what that technique might produce in the wrong hands.'

He held back a grin. Fascinated by the mysteries of DNA, Curtis O'Connor had done his honours thesis in biochemistry on the very subject he was about to get a lecture on, albeit a lecture from one of the world's most promising virologists and a very angry one at that. Curtis O'Connor did have strong sympathy for Kate Braithwaite's views, and her gorgeous looks hadn't escaped his notice either. He wisely decided against letting her know too much about his background. He wanted her on the program. For the moment it was better to let this explanation run. It might even pay dividends later on, he thought mischievously.

Kate reached across his desk and took the blank yellow pad and pen that were lying near Curtis' in-tray. She drew the helix for DNA. 'Deoxyribonucleic acid or DNA, Mr O'Connor, is made up of four nucleotides – adenylate, guanylate, thymidylate and cytidylate.' Kate's pencil flashed down the page as she drew the complex structure of phosphodiester bonds and pentose rings that made up the exquisite helix that Watson and Crick, with the help of some others, had discovered in 1953.

'Otherwise known as A, G, T and C. A always pairs with T, and G always pairs with C. That's important because if even a minute amount of India-1 strain of smallpox ever gets into the wrong hands, a single strand of smallpox DNA will always pair off with its complimentary sequence, and the bioterrorists can use a probe of known DNA to analyse that sequence. Not only that, Mr O'Connor, using a technique known as polymerase chain reactions, or PCR, means that we only need tiny amounts to produce all of the original DNA. In short, we are getting very close to being able to manufacture the complete genome of smallpox or any other deadly virus.'

Curtis O'Connor listened with wry amusement as Doctor Braithwaite filled three pages, making extremely complex chemistry look simple. She explained the PCR laboratory techniques that would enable a bioterrorist to manufacture new DNA using enzymes that would replicate sequences between primers bound to highly specific sites on the original DNA strand, much the same as DNA replicated itself within a normal cell. As she finished outlining the chilling possibilities of the 'brave new world' of biochemistry, her green eyes flashed at him with fury. Doctor Braithwaite would, Curtis thought, make an outstanding Professor if she ever chose to go down that route. Right now he wondered how he might get her on side. He needed her expertise in what would be the most lethal laboratory on the planet.

Kate finished her 'lecture' with a final and simple diagram. 'It's now possible, Mr O'Connor, to replicate deadly viruses like Ebola, Marburg and smallpox by taking a single strand of nucleic acid and joining it to another to make a double.'

Listening to Kate, Curtis O'Connor almost kicked himself. Of course! Where the single strand meets its double. The chilling words of Khalid Kadeer had suddenly become very, very clear. The final attack would be biological, involving the synthetic manufacture of a virus whose DNA the terrorists had access to.

Curtis O'Connor was only half right. Throughout history science had always had a dark side, and Kadeer was close to harnessing a power that would crush the human race.

CHAPTER 40

PESHAWAR, NORTH-WEST FRONTIER

Khalid Kadeer reached for a date in a bowl on the low table, listening intently as al-Falid outlined his plans for the first warning attack.

'My original plan was to detonate a large amount of explosive on the bottom of the harbour, to be delivered at night by rolling 44-gallon drums off the back of a slowly moving fishing trawler. The infidel has changed the rules and trawling at night is no longer possible. I'm still hoping that we can get some explosives into position, and we've been carrying out tests with small aluminium pontoons that have inflatable airbags attached to them. The main attack will have to be carried out on the surface using HEAT – high explosive anti-tank rockets. But don't worry, Khalid,' al-Falid said with a sinister smile. 'I'm having the trawler modified into a floating shaped charge, and it will follow the HEAT rockets to the target, although the timing will be crucial as it can only happen at high tide.' al-Falid pushed one of the mats aside and drew a diagram of the target city on the dirt floor, using two candlesticks to mark the extremities of a world-renowned icon. 'Even though they're minor, the preliminary attacks on the shore will still cause the infidel untold grief. The land attacks are all scheduled to occur just minutes before the major sea-borne attack. If the first ship fails for any reason, a second ship will be following in reserve. The reserve ship's target is here,' al-Falid said, pointing to another well-known landmark.

'The crews for the two ships are in place?' Khalid Kadeer asked.

'It's taken more than four years to bring this to fruition, Khalid, but we have a man on the *Ocean Venturer* and the tanker makes regular trips from the Middle East to the target. If Allah is willing he will succeed. The plan for the reserve ship is also well advanced. We've secured a long lease on the *Jerusalem Bay,* a 7500-ton container ship. It's only small but it will suit our purpose.'

Khalid smiled. The name of the second ship held a powerful irony. 'And the fertiliser?' he asked.

'We have a contract with the UN to deliver fertiliser to Liberia. The infidels weren't interested in such a small contract, so it has worked out perfectly.' It had indeed been a masterstroke. 'We're also in the process of having the *Jerusalem Bay* registered in the target port. As a regular visitor to the port the harbour authorities will get used to it coming and going and they will relax the need for entry with a pilot.'

Nearly 9000 kilometres away, the *Jerusalem Bay* was to the north of the port of Monrovia, maintaining a steady 12 knots in the pre-dawn darkness. The cargo had been provided by UN funding for the struggling war-torn nation of Liberia. In amongst the badly needed water pumps and generators were twenty containers of fertiliser from the target country. Not all of the contents of the containers would be delivered to the farmers who desperately needed it. Five very special containers would be filled with fertiliser explosive in a heavily guarded warehouse on the outskirts of a Muslim ghetto in Paynesville, 16 kilometres down the coast road from the capital, Monrovia.

'The regional seed and fertiliser company that we purchased in the target country two years ago is producing everything we need, and we've also started up a small trucking company in the city itself. It's not making much money though,' al-Falid smiled ruefully, 'because the infidels are corrupt and the big contracts are always worked out in advance.'

'That's not a bad thing for us, Amon. If we're not competing too hard, then no one will be taking much notice. Do we have enough stingers for the first attack?'

'I purchased them in Darra Adam Khel and,' he said, looking at his watch, 'they should have been transferred to one of the Pakistan Intelligence Agency's own trucks. The ISI will deliver them to Karachi. The stingers for the other warning attacks have already been delivered by tugboat. You were right, Khalid. The infidel's security concentrates on container ships. Tugboats don't attract much attention; and if the first attack is to succeed the tugboats and the stingers will be vital,' al-Falid acknowledged, pointing to a critical weak point in the Islamists' plan. 'The infidel's soldiers are among the best in the world, Khalid, and they've been training for an event such as this.'

'The infidel's soldiers are formidable, Amon, but they're only lightly armed. You're confident of getting the stingers out of Pakistan?' he asked.

al-Falid nodded. 'If Allah, the Most Kind, the Most Merciful is willing, both the tugboats and the stingers will make it to their destination. We have many friends in the Pakistani Intelligence, Khalid, and all of them are dedicated to Islam resuming its rightful place in the world. I'm hoping that the wharves of Karachi will not be a problem.'

It was one of the CIA's and the US Administration's great frustrations. The ISI, the powerful Pakistani Inter Service Intelligence agency had its own hard-line Islamic agenda and it was not about to change for even the Pakistani President, let alone a country like the United States which provided India with so much support against the Muslims in Kashmir.

'The tugs are ready?' Khalid asked, pouring some green tea from the ornate Russian samovar standing on a brass tray.

al-Falid nodded. 'My son, Malik is in charge of them,' Amon said proudly, then his face darkened at the thought of his son. Malik had lost his wife and two young daughters at the hands of the notorious Egyptian secret police that were part of the US Administration's 'Extraordinary Rendition Program'; a program that used secret prisons in third countries around the world to get around the Geneva convention on torture. Amon's daughter-in-law was caught up in a demonstration near the Sa'd Zaghlul shrine in Cairo. The opposition party Kifaya, or 'enough' in Arabic, had been protesting against twenty-five years of the dictatorship in Egypt when the riot police had waded into the crowd. The two little girls had been trampled and when Malik's wife had tried to shield them, she had been beaten to death by plainclothes security men. It had not escaped either al-Falid or his son Malik's notice that the Egyptian regime received more than US$2 billion a year from the United States, the second highest funding support in the world after Israel. Now al-Falid and his son Malik would get their revenge.

In the port of Monrovia, three battered-looking ocean-going tugboats, the *Winston Churchill,* the *Montgomery* and the *Wavell*, were preparing to put to sea. The *Winston Churchill* was completing a final delivery of radioactive teletherapy heads in case a subsequent warning attack became necessary. The *Montgomery* and the *Wavell*'s first destination was Karachi, where they would pick up the consignment of stinger missiles. From there, after some stinger missile training en-route, they would head towards one of the world's finest harbours and set in devastating motion the plans for the first warning attack.

CHAPTER 41

PORT OF MONROVIA, LIBERIA

The 1800-ton ocean-going tug, the *Montgomery*, and her sister tugs, the *Wavell* and the *Winston Churchill* rode uneasily on the restless harbour swell that alternately pushed and pulled at the United Towage Company berths in the capital of Liberia. The thick mooring ropes strained and creaked against the rusted bollards on the broken concrete of the dimly lit, dilapidated main wharf in the Freeport of Monrovia. Low asbestos warehouses, holes in the roofs, garish green paint peeling from their sides, stretched the length of the 600-metre pier. Halfway down the pier the wreck of a small 5000-ton container ship lay on its side. It had been there for over three years and rusted containers were still half submerged on the decks and in the holds, the result of a disastrous miscalculation on ballast. Like the piles of rotting rubbish in the main streets of the city, the Port of Monrovia was a symbol of more than a decade of civil war. For al-Qaeda, the location was perfect.

Below the decks of the *Montgomery*, Hani Bassnan, a wiry, wizened engineer of indeterminate age, was going through the start up procedures for the two huge, reconditioned Daihatsu diesel engines. The turquoise paint gleamed under the soft lights of the engine room. The massive diesels each put out 5000 horsepower to two enormous propellers that were encased in large nozzles beneath the hull. Rudders were now unnecessary. Protruding deep into the ocean, the propellers could swivel through 360 degrees in an instant. The engine room was spotless and packed with air and hydraulic hoses and a myriad of other pipes connected to heavy gearboxes, hydraulic pumps and steering. Towards the aft of the engine room, a small soundproof control room served as Hani's office; a mass of warning and control lights quietly winking on the console. Further aft, a hydraulically controlled watertight steel door was open. Once they were underway the hydraulic door would be sealed. If the aft compartment housing the propeller units and the engine room were to flood the *Montgomery* would go straight to the bottom.

Hani checked the big sumps on the diesels. The oil was constantly circulated through a purifier and it looked clean. He opened the sea valves that provided the seawater cooling, then he checked the big steering pumps. Next he started one of two huge caterpillar generators, checked that the banks of compressed air cylinders were full, and disconnected the shore power. Satisfied, he moved back to his control room and pushed the 'Start' button for the starboard main engine. A burst of compressed air exploded into the number one cylinder and then into successive cylinders as each massive piston passed through top dead centre. The fuel–air mixture followed and the main engine burst into life, the big flywheel settling down to just under 100 revs per minute. Hani grinned to himself as he went through an identical procedure for the port engine, doubling the noise in the confines below decks. Hani had been around tugs for nearly fifty years and nothing gave him greater satisfaction, other than doing the will of Allah, than to be below decks among the diesel and the oil, the raw power pulsating beneath his feet.

On the bridge, nearly 18 metres above him, Captain Malik al-Falid was preparing to put to sea. In this cell, he knew how critical the tugs were to the success of the mission. He scanned the weather forecasts with an increasing sense of foreboding and glanced at the black gradations inside the brass casing of the barometer above his head – 980 hPa and falling. Beyond the breakwater lay two oceans, both of them renowned for angry mood swings.

Malik al-Falid had just turned 28 and was young for a tug captain. His dark face was pockmarked and his hair was black and curly. His alert brown eyes reflected a deep sadness that could never be eased, at least not in his lifetime. Malik glanced at the framed photograph that had a permanent place to the left of the depth sounder on the polished marine ply console. It was a photograph of his wife and two daughters aged four and five. It wouldn't be long now and if Allah willed it he would be able to avenge their death at the hands of the hated secret police and their American allies. In just a few weeks he would join his wife and daughters in paradise.

As Malik al-Falid waited for the massive diesels below him to come up to operating temperature, he pulled open the chart drawer beneath the table on the starboard side of the wheelhouse and took out the chart for the approaches to the target city. It was highly unlikely that anyone in Monrovia would ever ask why he might have that particular chart, but just in case, the drawers held the charts of forty other major cities that an ocean-going tug might need at short notice. Malik had already committed this one to memory but somehow it gave him a sense of satisfaction to have the details of the infidel's city out on the chart table, and he scanned it once again. The traffic in and out of the port was tightly regulated and the *Jerusalem Bay* would be restricted to an arrival through area Alpha to the north. Departures came out of the port through area Bravo. A new separation zone was marked on the chart between Alpha and Bravo, brought in because of a rivalry between incoming and outgoing vessels seeking to use the same set of navigation leads, and the port authorities had imposed a strict requirement for arriving ships to keep to the north of the leads at all times. Both he and the masters of the *Wavell* and the *Jerusalem Bay* would obey the regulations to the letter, and so would the Captain of the *Ocean Venturer*. He would have no choice. A pilot would board the big tanker at a point 4 miles due east from the lighthouse on the very edge of area Alpha. Malik traced the route they would take. The tanker would be allowed in first and once it reached the sea buoy inside the entrance, the pilot would turn the lumbering giant from area Alpha towards the Western channel, a channel that was 210 metres wide with a minimum depth of 13.7 metres at low water. The *Jerusalem Bay* would be next on the schedule. The authorities would log that the *Montgomery* and the *Wavell* were midway through an ocean voyage and that they were scheduled to visit for refueling. With a bit of luck, their arrival at the same time as the tanker and the *Jerusalem Bay* would be put down to coincidence. If Allah willed it, Malik mused, when the port authorities discovered that the *Montgomery* and the *Wavell* were no ordinary tugs, it would be too late.

Malik put the chart away leaving the chart table bare. There was
no chart for the soundings of Monrovia Freeport. In a country like
Liberia one had to depend on local knowledge. Taking hold of one
of two radio microphones dangling from the roof of the wheelhouse,
Malik acknowledged his engineer's signal that control of the big
diesels had been transferred to the bridge and he radioed the deck-
hands to cast off.

Malik grasped the two gleaming throttle levers in his left hand
and the steering joystick in his right and expertly moved the big
tug sideways away from the pier. Rather like the control stick in a
modern jet fighter, the joystick spun the big enclosed propellers in
any direction and the dial on the console enabled him to read the
precise direction of thrust. Malik eased the big throttles forward and
10,000 horsepower of diesel throbbed into life. The massive steel bow
on the *Montgomery* was protected by huge tractor tyres. It dipped
and then rose on the swell of the inner harbour, parting the waters.
The *Wavell* followed in her wake as they powered towards the gap
between the two rocky breakwaters where, beyond the entrance, a
stormy Atlantic was waiting. In the half light of the approaching
dawn, Malik could make out a bank of dark clouds rolling down
the coast of Africa from the north and he checked his watch: 4.30
a.m. The *Jerusalem Bay* would have left the waters of Sierra Leone
about midnight but he calculated that she would still be a good 40
nautical miles to the north-west. This would be the last delivery of
fertiliser they would need. Malik had no idea that thousands of kilometres away two other cells were already inside the targeted country,
preparing for attacks that would be launched at the same time. He
steadied himself as the *Montgomery* reached the breakwater and the

bow rose alarmingly against the first of the Atlantic swells before it smashed back down in a cloud of spray. The foam crashed against the reinforced glass that encased the wheelhouse and the big wipers worked furiously to clear the excess water as the two tugs headed into the gathering storm.

CHAPTER 42

UNITED STATES ARMY MEDICAL RESEARCH INSTITUTE FOR INFECTIOUS DISEASES, FORT DETRICK, MARYLAND

Professor Sayed took a seat beside Kate's desk.

'This is my resignation, Imran,' Kate said, holding up a piece of paper, furious at what the Administration was up to and the deception of people like Wassenberg. Ever since his meeting with Curtis O'Connor, Imran had concluded that the Administration had no real idea of the catastrophic implications of their decision to restart the biowarfare program. He had decided that it would be far safer for the whole program, and ultimately perhaps even humanity, if he stuck around to influence things.

'So you told him no?' he asked.

'In a way that there wasn't any part of "no" he wouldn't understand,' Kate replied angrily. 'I even drew him a diagram, Imran, and explained how science can replicate even the smallest strand of DNA. Didn't make a scrap of bloody difference.'

'You drew him a diagram of DNA?'

'Pentoses, phosphates, pyrimidine bases, the bloody lot!'

Imran grinned, his eyes twinkling.

'I don't see what's funny!' Kate remonstrated, letting out a loud sigh.

'I think the diagrams on DNA and polymerase chain reactions might have been a touch superfluous,' Imran replied, still smiling.

'Why?'

'Because although Curtis O'Connor might be a CIA agent he did his honours chemistry thesis on polymerase chain reactions and he's a Doctor of Science. He did his Doctorate on the probable effects of lethal viruses and biological weapons. He's one of the few people in the CIA qualified to work in a hot lab.'

Kate put her head in her hands. She could feel her cheeks burning as she pictured Curtis O'Connor looking on at her furious explanations of hydrogen bonding, hydroxyl ions, monophosphates and a raft of other structures. 'Oh fuck,' she said softly. She looked up at Imran through her fingers. 'You're kidding!'

'He was awarded his postgraduate Doctorate by the School of Biochemistry and Immunology at Trinity in Dublin.'

Kate shook her head in acute embarrassment. 'Double fuck,' she whispered, mortified.

'Come on,' Imran said. 'It's been a very long day. I'll shout you dinner at that little restaurant in Foggy Bottom. I could do with a drink too.'

Imran held the wine glass against the white linen tablecloth and inspected the colour. He savoured the bouquet and tasted the wine before nodding to the waiter.

'One of yours,' he said, clinking his glass with Kate's.

'Pardon?'

'Australian. A shiraz from Pepper Tree in the Hunter. Wine-maker seems to know what he's doing,' he said, tasting the dark cherry and blackcurrant flavours.

Kate smiled wanly. 'Sorry, I'm a little distracted and still embar-rassed. I can't believe O'Connor let me rabbit on like that,' she said, taking a healthy sip from her own glass. 'It's lovely.'

'Don't be embarrassed. He isn't.'

'How do you know?'

'Because he called me. He really wants you on this team.'

'Team?'

'He's asked me to come onboard as well and he's authorised me to talk to you. I've given this a lot of thought over the last few hours, Kate. You and I both know that this Administration hasn't got a clue what they might be unleashing, which is all the more reason for trying to control it. O'Connor's got a barn full of things on his plate already and he's not going to be able to oversee what goes on in that lab every day.'

'Maybe,' Kate agreed reluctantly. 'But if he's so up on all of this how come I've never heard of him,' she said.

Professor Sayed waited until the main course of Chesapeake Bay scallops and crabs in a creamy wine sauce with a hint of parsley was served and the waiter had retreated. Imran had chosen a discreet booth that was to one side of the main restaurant, but even so, he lowered his voice. 'CIA agents don't go around advertising them-selves or who they work for.'

'I guess not,' Kate agreed, 'and if they come up with reports and facts that don't support this Administration's policy the White House will blow their cover anyway,' she added ruefully. Her cynicism towards politicians who so easily turned on their own was deepening. 'Do you know O'Connor well?' she asked, intrigued by the charming and intelligent man who worked in the shadows.

'Only by reputation, and if that's anything to go by, he's one of the best. He's not only highly intelligent but he's also one of the few non-Muslims in this Administration who understand that it is not Islam that threatens the West, but the fundamentalists who mis-interpret it.'

'Do you think this Kadeer really wants everyone to be under Islamic rule?' Kate asked, keen to explore her mentor's knowledge of a subject she knew little about.

Imran shook his head. 'Some of his more fanatical lieutenants are convinced that's the only path. If they have their way, ultimately western countries like the United States and Australia will be taken over by pan-Islam and subjected to Sharia law. To counter that we need ordinary Muslims onside. O'Connor knows that in addition to preparing defences against biological attacks, which is where you and I come in, the key to getting those moderate Muslims onside is to take a more even-handed approach.

'To Muslim countries generally?'

Imran nodded. 'Starting with Palestine. Those who support the fanatical view come from desperately poor backgrounds like the Israeli Occupied Territories. The West should have given much more support to the Palestinians,' Imran explained, 'because to escape from the misery imposed by the Israelis and the West, young Palestinian men and women are now attracted to *madrassas* like those on the Pakistan–Afghanistan border.

'I know very little about Islam,' Kate admitted, 'but I've some-times wondered if the Qu'ran encourages suicide bombings.'

'Quite the opposite, and if you're interested, I'll give you one of my Qu'rans. Verse 46 from Chapter 29 in the Qu'ran is called "The Spider". It should be compulsory reading for anyone who wants to understand Islam, although I don't want to turn dinner into a lecture on it,' he said with a smile.

'You're not,' Kate assured him, intensely interested.

Imran quoted the verse. '"Do not argue with the People of the Book unless it is in the politest manner, except for those of them who do wrong. Say: We believe in what has been sent down to us and what has been sent down to you. Our God and your God is the Same One, and we are committed to observe peace before Him." In essence, what Muhammad is making very clear is that Muslims must respect other religions unless the people that profess those faiths attack Islam. Unfortunately the huge numbers of innocent Muslims who've been killed since we invaded Iraq is enough to convince even the moder-ates that Islam is under attack from the West, and particularly from the United States, Britain and Australia.'

'I think Islam is under attack, Imran. President Harrison's on the record as saying he's on a mission from his Christian God and the Australian Prime Minister is backing him all the way.'

'God's entitled to be a little confused,' Imran replied with a grin. 'Were you ever religious?'

'My father was and so was my ex. The President would get along very well with both of them,' Kate said, shuddering at the memory of it all. 'I agreed with your opinion piece. For me, religion is an acci-dent of birth. If I'd been born in Baghdad, I'd probably be a Sunni or a Shiite or if I'd been born in Jerusalem I might be a Jew. Yet people like Jerry Buffett storm the airwaves claiming that if you're not a Christian, when the Christian "rapture" comes around, you're stuffed. What sort of a God would create six billion people, only to condemn most of them in the afterlife?'

'You think there is an afterlife?'

'I think there's a force around us, and forgive me, Imran, but for me it's not what the various religions call Yahweh or God or Allah . . .'

Imran waved his hand with a deprecating smile to indicate that far from being offended, he was enjoying the depth of their friendship and conversation.

'I don't think you can immerse yourself in what you and I do, Imran, without giving some thought to the exquisitely intricate design of cells that can't be seen by the naked eye. I don't think the design of the universe is just some gigantic accident, which is what makes this threat from Kadeer so scary. If he ever harnessed the microscopic world I think it has the potential to destroy the human race.'

Imran nodded. 'It is hard to get that across to those in power. It underlines the need for negotiation more than ever. Did Curtis mention the Beijing Olympics?'

'No, did he raise it with you?'

'Only in passing. If I were going to mount a biological attack, the Games would be my first choice as a target because of the huge number of different nationalities the airlines are going to fly in and out.'

'Thousands of those will be from Muslim nations, Imran.'

'So were the workers in the Twin Towers,' Imran replied, 'but Curtis O'Connor may have a point. However much you and I disagree with trying to get something like smallpox to jump species, unless we try and find out what is possible, it might be too late.'

For the next hour the two of them quietly talked about the deadly proposal. Save for a Georgian biochemist working in Koltsovo, no two scientists had more experience or more ability.

'If it were anyone else, Imran, I doubt that I would have anything to do with this,' Kate said finally. 'I want you to know that, but I guess you're right. They're going to go ahead with this anyway and it's better to be inside the tent. If this ever got into the hands of the terrorists . . .' Kate let her words trail off before she took another sip of wine.

'O'Connor wants to brief us tomorrow on what he thinks al-Qaeda might be able to achieve. Thank you,' Imran added, taking her hand.

Their eyes met and their hands lingered together.

'Another time, another life,' Imran whispered, conscious of their difference in age. Kate nodded, turning away to hide the tears in her eyes.

CHAPTER 43

CIA HEADQUARTERS, LANGLEY, VIRGINIA

Curtis O'Connor opened Kate Braithwaite's security file. It contained the results of the exhaustive checks that were required for her clearance to work at USAMRIID, and he read them with more than a passing interest. Dr Braithwaite's scientific credentials were impeccable and her research was at the cutting and dangerous edge of microbiology. Looking at her photograph again, Curtis recalled how he had long ago drawn a boundary around himself. For a CIA agent affairs of the heart were a dangerous distraction

The young scientist had been positively vetted and Curtis skipped over the thin reports on her financial affairs, unusually conscious that he was intruding into her private life. The reports on the FBI interviews of her referees however, including one from Professor Sayed, were something that he did need to know about, and they were all overwhelmingly positive, except one. Kate Braithwaite, Curtis discovered, had once been married to an up-and-coming Australian politician from the Liberal Party. It was an episode in her life that Kate had been completely honest about. The long reach of the US security system had gone into the US Embassy in Canberra and from there to the US Consulate in Martin Place in Sydney. Malcolm Braithwaite, the former President of the Young Liberals and now member of the NSW Legislative Council, had painted a scathing picture of his ex-wife, but the FBI's man in Sydney had reached some skillful conclusions about the divorce. During the interview Malcolm Braithwaite had asked the FBI agent if he was a Christian, quoting the letter of the Apostle Paul to the Ephesians at him: 'Just as Christ was the head of the church, a husband was the head of the wife.' Braithwaite had let slip this was something that Kate had not been too keen on. Can't imagine why, Curtis thought, smiling to himself as he closed the file and headed down to the entrance foyer to greet Kate and Professor Sayed.

'I want to thank you both for your decision to come onboard,' Curtis began. 'I could not have hoped for two more qualified people to join me. For the duration of Operation PLASMID you will be sworn in as officers of the CIA. I also want you to know that I understand your concerns over this and for what it's worth, I've opposed this from the very start,' Curtis said, after Imran and Kate had settled into a small briefing room down the corridor from his office.

'I owe you an apology,' Kate responded. 'I've discovered that my explanations on what can be done with polymerase chain reactions might have been a touch superfluous,' she confessed, smiling sheepishly, then glancing at Imran.

'I enjoyed the refresher,' Curtis replied, his eyes twinkling. Kate found herself attracted to the irreverent Irishman. He was smart, seemed to have the same sensibilities, and was impossibly good looking; but she quickly reminded herself that this was not the time to be dropping her emotional guard and losing focus on the work ahead.

'More importantly you helped me find something I missed.' Curtis picked up a remote control and re-ran Dr Khalid Kadeer's video threat of the first warning and the final attack.

'It seems to me that "when the single strand meets its double" might be an indication he's trying to engineer RNA and DNA viruses,' Curtis said, switching on a PowerPoint presentation. 'Operation PLASMID will involve a series of experiments that will be conducted in the Biosafety Level 4 laboratory suites at Halliwell Pharmaceuticals. The existence of these laboratories is classified top secret,' he added, flashing up a screen display of the sprawling complex. 'The Level 4 laboratories are here,' he said, indicating the north-west corner of the Halliwell acreage. What went unnoticed by the three scientists was the number of super-heated exhaust vents — too many for the single laboratory to which Imran and Kate would be assigned.

'While the program and its funding is being run out of my office, the actual experiments in the labs will be coordinated by the CEO of Halliwell,' Curtis explained. The next image of Dr Richard Halliwell dominated the room. Kate was struck by his piercing yet emotionless eyes. Halliwell reminded her of Anthony Hopkins' portrayal of Hannibal Lecter. Little did she know how close to reality her thoughts might be.

'I'll have more to say about Halliwell in a moment, and we'll organise a meeting with him,' Curtis added. He had already decided to bring the scientists into the loop of information he had on the

Pharmaceutical CEO. In O'Connor's world, Halliwell was a man they all needed to be very wary of. 'For the moment, be aware that outwardly he may seem charming but he's ruthless, political, and very well connected to the Vice President and the White House. Athough he's cleared into the compartment I would be cautious about revealing too much of what is shared in this type of briefing,' Curtis warned. He flicked to the next image of a huge intercontinental missile being readied for launch on a pad, vapour coming from various ducts in the nose cone and around the engine cowlings.

'Our mission is to try to discover what the terrorists might be able to achieve in the area of bioterrorism, and to that end, I'm starting with a worst case scenario and assuming that they may have had access to the Russian systems after the collapse of the Soviet Union in 1991. This is a Russian intercontinental missile being readied for launch on the Kamcatka Poluostrov, a 1200-kilometre peninsula that jutts into the icy wastes of the Bering Sea and the Sea of Okhotsk, well to the north of Vladivostok.'

Imran Sayed leaned forward in his chair, staring at the image of the Russian intercontinental missile. 'They look like cooling fins,' he said, staring at the rocket's nose cone.

'They are,' Curtis replied, scrolling through successive imagery that had been obtained from the tracking satellites of the National Reconnaissance Office. The huge R-36M2 Voevoda intercontinental missile with a range of 16,000 kilometres was clearly visible on the launch pad.

'Not only is the nose cone equipped with cooling fins but you can see here that it's also connected to a large refrigeration system on the launch pad. These next images are of the launch itself and you can see as the launch progresses, the fins on the Voevoda nose cone start to glow red hot.'

'Not your average nuclear warhead,' Imran observed.

'Exactly. Russian and US nuclear warheads are all engineered to withstand the extreme heat generated by a missile travelling through the earth's atmosphere and that heat would kill any known virus, unless the nose cone contained an onboard refrigeration system that was fitted with fins that could dissipate the heat.'

'All the hallmarks of a test for a biological launch,' Imran offered, 'but you're not suggesting al-Qaeda are working on missile technology.'

'They no doubt would if they could,' Curtis observed wryly, 'but unfortunately they may not need to. This imagery is only twelve months old and, if it ties in with some other intelligence, the Russians may be testing new forms of biological weapons. We have some recent information to indicate that a Georgian scientist, Dr Eduard Dolinsky, has been working with the Russians on the weaponising of smallpox, and he may also have been working on Ebola.'

Imran let out a low whistle. 'I know him,' Imran said. 'He's one of the most talented virologists in the world.'

'If Dolinsky has been working on the single strand of the RNA Ebola virus, as well as the double strands of the DNA smallpox virus, he may have been trying to engineer one into the other,' Kate said, voicing her thoughts on the single strand/ double strand connundrum.

Curtis nodded. 'A super virus like Ebolapox would be easily transmitted, especially if it were released at an event like the Olympics. More importantly, there is no cure. By comparison, bird flu would be tame. Our task will be to try and emulate that engineering and produce a vaccine.'

A silence fell over the room as Imran and Kate exchanged glances, horrified at the enormity of what they were being asked to do.

'Just to add to this madness,' Curtis continued, 'everything on this program is obviously highly sensitive, but most sensitive of all is some unconfirmed intelligence that Dolinsky may wish to defect. If that comes off, he will join us on the program. He, like some of his illustrious predecessors, will no doubt bring us up to date on what the Russians have been up to, what al-Qaeda has acquired and what they might be able to achieve.'

'You're worried al-Qaeda might have access to the Russian research?' Kate asked.

'It's possible,' Curtis replied. 'Thousands of Russian scientists were thrown out of work after the collapse of the Soviet Union and more than a few of them crossed the line into the dark zone just to survive.'

'Are you going to try and get him out?' Kate challenged with a smile, mischievously putting Curtis on the spot. Kate's and Curtis' eyes met for a moment and in an instant she knew she was right.

'That's another compartment,' Curtis replied with an enigmatic grin. 'If we can do it, it will bring another dimension of expertise to our team. In the meantime, your first task will be to move the small-pox repositories from the Centers for Disease Control to the Halliwell labs. I don't need to tell you how dangerous that might be.'

CHAPTER 44

THE CENTERS FOR DISEASE CONTROL, ATLANTA, GEORGIA

Professor Imran Sayed checked for traffic, and then he and Kate Braithwaite headed out of the hotel car park in Atlanta towards Clifton Highway and the Centers for Disease Control Headquarters.

'God, it's good to be away from the RID,' Kate said, leaning her head against the headrest.

Imran nodded. 'Yep. Even though I don't agree with what we're about to do, I think if I'd stayed around Colonel Wassenberg for much longer I'd have finished up decking him.'

'You'd have to get in line. Where do they find people like that Imran? USAMRIID SAH!' she growled, whacking herself on her forehead, mimicking the pimply-faced Captain Crawshaw to a tee.

Imran grinned. 'You do that very well, Doctor Braithwaite,' he said. 'Are you sure you weren't in the Army in a previous life?'

'Sometimes I wonder about you, Imran,' Kate replied with a

grin. 'For a talented scientist you come up with some very wacky theories!'

Imran grinned. 'I had a call from Curtis last night, wishing us all the best. He said Halliwell wants us to come to lunch in the board-room next week, and don't plan on doing anything in the hot lab afterward – Halliwell's apparently got a very good cellar.'

'Paid for by pharmaceuticals that cost ten times what they're worth,' Kate replied cynically, thinking back to the image of Halli-well. Something about the man had 'warning' written all over it.

The pair fell into a relaxed silence, each wondering how they might best avoid a looming catastrophe over smallpox and Ebola.

'I wonder how Maverick is,' Kate said, as they drove up towards the Centers for Disease Control, the salmon and glass-walled Head-quarters towering over an elegant Japanese garden at the entrance. 'There are times when I look into those big sad eyes that I hope we fail on this one. Smallpox has never been able to infect the animal kingdom and I don't think we should be giving it a helping hand, even if it might mean we get a vaccine out of it.'

Professor Sayed nodded as he produced his pass for the security guard. 'Although,' he said, as they drove towards the car park next to the new maximum containment laboratories where the chimpanzees were kept, 'given what's happened in the last 24 hours, God knows what Kadeer will be up to next. If we *can* get *Variola major* to jump species at least you and I might be able to develop an antiviral drug. If we do, it won't be the first time our predecessors have helped us out.'

'Maybe, but getting this virus to jump species is a very big "if", let alone engineering a super virus with something like Ebola,' Kate replied, reflecting on the utter futility of it all and humankind's bent for self-destruction.

Building 18, the new $160 million laboratory complex at the Roybal Campus at the Centers for Disease Control in Atlanta, had been partially built into the side of a hill that adjoined the old six-storey maximum containment lab. It was close to the underground command centre that would be used during any outbreak of infectious disease or bioterrorist attack on the United States.

Imran and Kate passed through the external security check and headed for the Level 4 laboratories where only a handful of people out of the Centers for Disease Control's 9000 employees were trained and certified to work. Kate gave the guard at the desk a smile as they stopped at the final security point. In turn, they inserted their biometric smart cards and they each looked into the camera which photographed their irises. The iris was like a fingerprint but even more secure. The chances of two individuals having the same patterns were 1 in 10^{78}. That many zeros meant the patterns were about as close to unique as you could get. The light changed from red to green as the computer files matched Kate's irises and Kate followed Imran through the security cubicle into the outer offices and equipment storage areas of one of the most secure laboratories in the world.

The new Level 4 complex at CDC had been constructed meticulously. To minimise cracking, the concrete had been wet-cured for a very long time and then a special coating of sealant had been applied so that the floors, walls and ceilings were absolutely airtight. Like the new construction at Halliwell, the entire complex of filters, plumbing, decontamination and breathing systems and their backup redundancies had been exhaustively tested for six months before the laboratories were certified as safe. The designing engineers had even located any of the systems that might need maintenance outside the hot zone. There was no room for error. Once a laboratory went hot with Ebola, smallpox, Lassa Fever, Marburg, Botulinum toxin or any of the other twenty or so deadly viruses and bacteria for which there was no known cure, maintenance engineers would not get near the place.

In her Level 3 cubicle, Kate stripped and put on a green surgical gown. She taped her latex gloves to the sleeves, put on some thin, green socks and plugged in some ear protection that would soften the harsh 'rushing sound' of the air that would continually cycle through her suit. She sat down on the bench and eased herself into her bright blue spacesuit. Then she stood up, closed the thick, clear plastic face shield which lock-sealed into place, plugged the air regulator into her suit and slung it over her shoulder. Kate shuffled out of her dressing cubicle towards the steel airlock door that was emblazoned with the four bright red concentric circles of the international biohazard symbol. Closing the door behind her, she moved through the decontamination shower room, then into another inner steel airlock where she found Imran waiting for her.

'Your boots Ma'am!' Imran handed her a pair of galoshes, smiling broadly behind the plastic of his faded blue suit. His voice was faint, even though she knew he was shouting in what was standard voice procedure for a hot lab. Kate smiled her thanks, put the rubber boots on and followed him through another air lock into the lethal laboratory.

A door at the far end of the lab opened and the animal keeper,

Dr Richard Myers appeared. Even behind his face shield, Kate could see the grim look on his face.

'I don't like this one little bit, Imran,' he yelled when he'd shuffled up to them.

'Neither do I, Richard.' The two were very old friends. 'Are the chimpanzees ready for the trip to Halliwell?'

Richard Myers nodded. 'And they're not happy either!' he answered sadly.

Kate and Imran prepared to unlock the vault where the stocks of smallpox were stored. A specially designed steel safe had been pre-positioned outside the vault. It would be the first time the smallpox stocks had ever been moved from the Centers for Disease Control. Imran had arranged for a heavy police escort and a truck that was very similar to the armoured trucks that banks used to transfer cash. Having an accident with smallpox didn't bear thinking about.

CHAPTER 45

PESHAWAR, NORTH-WEST FRONTIER

Amon al-Falid spread a map of Beijing on the low table in the safe house cellar. 'Most of the activity during the Games will be centred on the area known as the Olympic Green,' he said, directing Kadeer to the cluster of venues to the north of Tiananmen Square and the Forbidden City. 'Over half the Olympic competition will take place here and it also contains the Athletes' Village, the Main Press Centre and the International Broadcasting Centre.'

'You're focusing just on this area?' Kadeer asked, a little puzzled.

'The Americans, British and the Australians are very keen on their sport,' al-Falid replied contemptuously, 'especially the Australians. The Chinese will obviously have the biggest contingent, but the three countries who first invaded Iraq will also send three of the largest teams and it would be good if we can wipe those out.'

'Don't lose sight of the bigger picture, Amon,' Kadeer replied, cautioning his lieutenant not to let his emotion cloud his judgement. 'Of all the venues, the Olympic Green is likely to be the most heavily guarded and the most difficult to attack. You will need to get some of our own people on staff to get past the security barriers.'

al-Falid nodded, his eyes shining with hatred. 'There will be a large cleaning and maintenance staff, Khalid; my planner in Qingdao is keeping a close eye on that. We're also looking at the airport and the big hotels.'

'The airconditioning systems in the hotels and the airport are the city's weakest point, Amon,' Khalid replied, unknowingly echoing the plans of Richard Halliwell. 'Just as the gram negative bacteria *Legionella*, which causes Legionnaires' disease, is most often spread through airconditioning water towers in buildings, so we can use the same principle for the virus, although we should also look closely at the subway system.'

'For a big city, the subway system is not nearly as well developed as London, but I have been giving it some thought,' al-Falid agreed. 'Line 1 runs from west to east from 苹果园 to 四惠东 – Pingguoyuan to Sidhuidong. That line is important because it's the only subway running through the centre of Beijing and it has stops near Tiananmen Square and the Bajiao Amusement Park; although an additional Line 5 is presently under construction and it will run north–south under the city from 太平庄北 to 宋家庄 – Taipingzhvangbei to Songjiazhuang.' al-Falid produced a map of the Beijing subway system and put it beside the map of the city. 'Line 2, which is known as the Loop Line, will also be important because it runs under the city's second ring road and has four interchange stations for Line 1 and Line 13 running to the north.'

'And the airport line?'

'That is under construction as well, Khalid, and it will connect terminals 2 and 3 to Line 1, although only 4 kilometres is underground. It will open on 30 June 2008. The other line we are looking at is the Olympic branch line which is scheduled to open on the same day. That runs from 熊猫环岛 to 森林公园 – Xiongmaohuandao to Senlingongyuan – and will connect to the new Olympic Park.'

'You've done well, my friend. The bear farm is ready?' With thousands of cameras being installed, Beijing was far too dangerous a place to set up a base. When a bear farm in the western Shandong Province had come up for sale, Kadeer had arranged to buy it. A bear farm would be the last place the authorities would suspect as a planning base for an attack on the Olympics. It had two other advantages. Away from the main roads, nestled among the foot-hills of Laoshan mountain and surrounded by old pines, the farm was hidden from view. And Kadeer had used the bear farm to secure *guanxi* with the most powerful man in the Chinese Olympic movement.

'I will visit the bear farm before the Olympics, Khalid, just to make sure but I'm told that General Ho Feng is very grateful, as you predicted he would be.'

Kadeer was once again drawn back to the brutal murder of his family at the hands of the inhuman then-Captain Ho Feng. Putting the painful memories aside, Kadeer knew well that General Ho believed that bear bile products were a way of prolonging life. Kadeer had arranged for the bear farm manager to send some of the finest products to the general, ensuring that the Qingdao bear farm would enjoy protection at the highest levels of the Chinese government.

More importantly, this gave Kadeer a sense of closure to know that the final solution would be launched from the very place his old enemy protected. Should the final solution become necessary, a special delivery of bear bile soup would be made to his nemesis and it would be a very unusual soup.

'All this will depend on whether or not Dolinsky can successfully engineer the viruses, al-Falid. Have we heard from him?' Kadeer asked. 'His role is key to our plan.'

'We stay in touch through our intermediaries, Khalid. Postings to Koltsovo in Siberia are not highly sought after, and we have several of our people there.'

'How much has he been told?'

'Just that Islam is getting ready to strike against those who are attacking us.'

'What was his reaction?'

'Dolinsky is frustrated and angry about the treatment of Muslim people in Georgia, but he's an educated man and he follows world events closely, even from Koltsovo. He has access to the internet and he's furious about the treatment of Muslims in other countries as well, especially in Chechnya and Iraq. That said, as a scientist Dolinsky might be squeamish about the extent of what we have planned so he hasn't been told the whole story; only that we need him to help us attack those who are attacking Islam and he seems more than willing to do what he can. By the time he discovers the extent of our response it will be too late.

Khalid Kadeer nodded. 'Nevertheless see that we treat him well.'

'If we can get him out and get him into a Level 4 facility, he will be an ideal recruit, although the FSB, the Russian secret police, are watching his every move. They sit outside his apartment at night.'

Dr Dolinsky was part of the Kist people, a minority Muslim group in Georgia, seen as a threat by both the Georgian and Russian governments.

'Because he's a Georgian the Russians have taken him off their top-secret research on smallpox and sidelined him on a project that is looking at genetically engineering a far less deadly strain of cowpox. If he's successful the virus might kill, but smallpox and Ebola are in a class of their own and Dolinsky sees the Russian move as a serious demotion, which it is.'

Kadeer nodded. 'Yes, Georgia and Shevardnadze are not the flavour of the month in Putin's Kremlin right now. How far did he get with his genetic engineering?'

'He was close but the final steps are difficult and the Russians have not yet solved the problem. Dolinsky is a very angry prisoner, and not only is he ready to defect, he is ready to live and work among the infidels and engineer a super virus to be used against them.

'The Americans have bought the intelligence on Dolinsky's defection?' Kadeer asked, intrigued as to how they might be planning to get him out.

al-Falid smiled slowly. 'The American Vice President and the CEO of Halliwell have. The CIA have been told to get Dolinsky out and for operations like this they will probably use a man named Curtis O'Connor.'

Khalid nodded. 'I've heard of him. One of the true professionals and not to be underestimated, but we will need to keep track of this, Amon. If O'Connor tries to get him across the Altai Mountains he may need some help. Dolinsky is absolutely critical to the final solution and those mountains can be very dangerous, even for us. The Russians are not going to be too amused if they discover someone like O'Connor is in their midst.'

CHAPTER 46

MOSCOW

Curtis O'Connor cleared Terminal 2 of Moscow's Sheremetyevo International Airport without incident and headed across to Terminal 1 for his connecting Aeroflot flight to Novosibirsk, the capital of Siberia. Every so often he paused to scan his surroundings. If the FSB was here, then they must have improved on their KGB predecessors, Curtis thought. Tourist class on Aeroflot wasn't going to be a lot of fun, he mused, as he joined a long queue at the check-in desk, but backpackers didn't travel business, although the boys in the passport office at Langley had done some excellent work and Brendan O'Shaughnessy had quite a nice ring to it.

Новосибирск belied its location. Split by the great Siberian River Ob, Novosibirsk was home to nearly a million and a half people and the third largest city in Russia after Moscow and St Petersburg.

The dead letter drop was in a park not far from the trans-Siberian railway station, the massive monument to Russia's imperial architecture that still played host to the famous train. Curtis sat on a bench quietly scanning the surrounding parkland. Satisfied no one was watching he retrieved from under a bush the nondescript-looking bag containing gammahydroxybutyrate, a pistol and an M4 Carbine with a collapsible stock. Curtis walked out of the park and hailed a passing taxi.

'*Rechnoy Voksal*'

'*Novosibirsk ochyen kraseevily gorad.*'

'*Da*,' Curtis replied, agreeing with the taxi driver's assertion that the Siberian capital was indeed very beautiful, but not wishing to get into a conversation. Taxi drivers in Russia were not always all they seemed.

Novosibirsk Mountain Trekking was in a small side street near the Rechnoy Voksal metro, and Vladimir Lebed, a slightly built, likeable Russian in his early forties, welcomed Curtis effusively. It was not every day Vladimir received a request to take just one client on a two-week backpacking expedition to his beloved Altai Mountains.

Curtis handed over 26,000 rubles, half the cost of the tour, and climbed into the passenger seat of the four-wheel drive Toyota. His Russian guide hadn't thought it odd that someone who was backpacking in the Altais might have business in a place like Koltsovo, nor did he quibble about the overnight stay in the one-star hotel Curtis had selected. The Dobrily Dyen, the Good Day Hotel, was in keeping with his new identity, Brendan O'Shaughnessy, and it was only about 500 metres from the apartment block Eduard Dolinsky called home.

Allocating one star to the Dobrily Dyen Hotel might have been optimistic, O'Connor mused. Several Russian workers were playing *Durak* and drinking cheap vodka at a table in the corner and no one took much notice of either Curtis or Vladimir Lebed. As Curtis ordered two Kupecheskoe 1875s, Siberia's popular beer, Vladimir sought out the men's room. Curtis seized his chance, dropping the contents of a small sachet of the gammahydroxybutyrate, more commonly known as GHB, into Vladimir's drink. Curtis knew that by the time Vladimir returned from the bathroom, the white powder would be completely dissolved. GHB was colourless and odourless, which was why it had become popular as a date-rape drug in nightclubs. Uncontrolled doses had been known to cause death, but Curtis wished Vladimir no harm and the sachet he'd taken from the bag he'd picked up at the dead-letter drop had been carefully measured to make sure the likeable Russian was only knocked out for twelve or fifteen hours. Enough time for Curtis to get moving towards the designated helicopter landing zone he'd selected high in the Altai Mountains near the border with Kazakhstan. Curtis felt the exhilaration of being back in the field and away from the politics of Washington. Getting Dolinsky out from under the noses of the old enemy was an almost impossible ask, but he'd been in tough situations before and he was sure he hadn't lost any of his skills. His mind turned to how the Secretary of State might be going with negotiations for the use of Kazakhstan air space for the flight from the big US Ganci air base in Kyrgyzstan, along the border with the Xinjiang Autonomous Region of China. No doubt there would be some incentive, he mused, as Vladimir Lebed returned from the bathroom.

'Приятного аппетита! Good appetite,' Curtis said, as the waiter brought the first course of shchi cabbage soup and set it down on the plastic tablecloth.

Vladimir responded with a broad smile.

Ten minutes later Curtis helped him to his room. When Vladimir woke up, he would find the 26,000 rubles Curtis owed him and quite a bit extra as compensation. 'Who said there's no honour among thieves,' Curtis said softly, as he finished binding Lebed's ankles, arms and mouth.

Leaving the 'Do Not Disturb' sign on Vladimir's door, Curtis looked up the road towards Dolinsky's apartment block. The two gorillas from the FSB were still parked outside. An hour earlier, Dolinsky had assured Curtis that he would be able to get out through a back entrance. al-Qaeda were not the only ones to take advantage of internet chat rooms, Curtis thought, as he felt a surge of adrenalin pulse through his veins.

CHAPTER 47

HALLIWELL LABORATORIES, ATLANTA

Kate followed Imran through the airlock into what would be her home for however long it took to prove or disprove the theory that smallpox could be made to jump species. If they were successful, the gentle chimpanzees would be used as a test bed for developing a vaccine for India-1, and then Ebolapox.

Although the meeting with Richard Halliwell was still a couple of days away, they had already received comprehensive briefings on the layout of the Halliwell laboratories and had been through the security indoctrination; a security that was similar to that at the Centers for Disease Control. The transfer of the viruses and the chimpanzees had gone without incident, although Kate knew that neither the vet nor the chimps were happy. It was almost as if the chimps sensed something was about to happen.

'I take it we're going ahead with this?' Dr Richard Myers was shouting to be heard above the air that was rushing into his spacesuit.

Imran and Kate nodded.

The anger on Richard's face was visible through his heavy plastic face shield. Kate could only sympathise with the Centers for Disease Control's longest serving veterinary surgeon as he made his way back towards the animal room.

Imran and Kate shuffled over to one of two vaults that now housed one half of the world's repository of smallpox. The other half was still in Koltsovo in the wastes of the Siberian desert. The big stainless steel vault that was clearly visible was a decoy. If anyone did manage to break in without setting off the sophisticated *Variola* alarms, they would find a freezer that contained nothing more than smallpox vaccines. A smaller vault behind held the critical freezer.

Imran inserted the special key that partly deactivated the alarm system to the smaller vault, then he stepped back to allow Kate to insert hers. The keys were kept apart and the vaults always had to be opened by Imran and Kate together. Imran dialed in one combination and again stepped back to allow Kate to work on the second tumbler. Kate turned the stainless steel wheel and swung the big door open. At the back of the vault, chained to the floor, was another innocuous-looking stainless steel container on wheels, about the size of a dirty dishes trolley that might be found in any canteen. Kate shivered involuntarily as she fumbled for another key that would unlock one of the huge padlocks.

Imran and Kate pushed the trolley over to the area that was assigned for preparation of the strain of smallpox they would be using on the chimps. The big heavy cylinder set in the middle of the trolley had been fuelled with liquid nitrogen which kept the temperature down to minus 300 degrees. Icy fumes wafted from the container as Kate very gently eased the cover off. Employing a pair of long forceps with the precision of a heart surgeon, Kate located the small plastic box that held the cryovials of the deadly strain of smallpox. It had first been called India-1 by the Russians after a strain that had been discovered in India in 1959 when a Russian tourist had returned to Moscow, infecting nearly 50 people before Russian doctors and scientists had been able to successfully quarantine the outbreak. India-1 was not only the most virulent strain of smallpox, it was more resistant and retained its infectiousness longer than any other, making it an excellent choice for any rogue State that wanted to weaponise it. Kate and Imran prepared the vials of the deadly pathogen for transmission to the monkeys. It was going to be a long, painstaking and very dangerous process.

Maverick, the alpha male, was vocalising loudly towards the other cages as Kate and Imran shuffled into the monkey room, Kate carefully pushing a stainless steel transfer trolley that contained the prepared batches of India-1. Dr Richard Myers and his assistant, Karl Stanford, a postgraduate student, had been unsuccessful in their attempts to calm the small community of Gabon chimpanzees and the floor around the cages was strewn with the biscuits and fruit the chimps had thrown at their captors. Kate connected her suit to an air hose close to Maverick's cage, and as she plugged the red hose into her regulator, Maverick's eyes met hers and something passed between them. The gentle giant calmed and he slowly sashayed over to the front of the cage and grabbed the bars, keeping his gaze on Kate.

Kate fought to keep her emotions in check as she reached for a needle of anaesthetic. She waited while Richard and Karl pulled a stainless steel squeeze screen forward on its rollers, gently bringing the screen up behind Maverick and pinning him against the front bars of the cage. Kate could still feel Maverick's eyes on her as she very carefully moved to his left side. A hot-zone laboratory was not the place to suffer a needle stick, she reminded herself. As gently as she could, she slipped the needle into Maverick's thigh and depressed the syringe.

No one spoke, and the rest of the monkeys became quiet. One by one, Dr Richards and his assistant rolled the squeeze panels forward and Kate anaesthetised all ten of the chimpanzees that made up the community. By the time she'd finished, Maverick was lying on his side, twitching uncomfortably under the anaesthetic and Kate shook her head as she shuffled back to the transfer trolley. She carefully counted all of the anaesthetic needles and placed them in the specially marked biohazard sharps bin, which would be subjected to extremely high temperatures before it was removed from the lab. Working slowly and deliberately, Kate began to prepare a vial of the India-1 smallpox for aerosolisation.

Richard and Karl carried Maverick over to the aerosol chamber where Kate was waiting. Once they had Maverick on the stainless steel table, Kate closed the Perspex cover over him and switched on the aerosol spray. Maverick was lying with his head towards the nozzle, his eyelids twitching as millions of particles of India-1 drifted into his nostrils. After three minutes, Kate switched off the empty aerosoliser and stepped back to allow Imran access to Maverick. The scientists' movements had all been rehearsed. Even though Maverick had been subjected to far greater doses of smallpox than any human would ever be exposed to, it had never taken an animal as a host. For this experiment to have any chance of success, Kate and Imran

had agreed they would also administer the deadly pathogen intra-
venously. The intravenous needle contained millions of the *Variola*
virions, and in the same way that the military only ever allowed one
person to work on a ticking bomb, only one scientist would administer to the chimpanzee.

Kate watched as Imran searched for another good vein on the
chimp's thigh. Maverick moved and gave out a high-pitched groan.
Imran froze and waited for the big primate to settle. He slowly
pushed the intravenous needle into the vein and then connected a
vial of the smallpox virus to the tube and injected Maverick with
India-1. When the vial was empty, Imran disconnected it and turned
slowly towards the other three scientists. In a pre-arranged signal,
they all nodded, indicating they understood what he was about
to do. Imran very carefully turned back and slowly withdrew the
needle from Maverick's thigh. The end was dripping with blood
that contained India-1. Even though all of them had been inoculated
against smallpox several times, the vaccine would be no use against
this strain. A needle stick would mean certain death.

CHAPTER 48

DOBRILY DYEN HOTEL, KOLTSOVO

It was getting on towards 9 p.m. and the temperature had plunged to below zero when Curtis heard the urgent knock on his door. Cocking the Browning 9mm Hi-Power pistol he'd retrieved along with the M4 earlier in the day, Curtis carefully eased the curtain away from the window. From photographs he'd studied, Curtis would have recognised the slim Georgian scientist anywhere. The man with the pencil-thin black moustache, oval face and black hair streaked with grey was clearly nervous.

'Inside,' Curtis commanded softly as he opened the door and checked up and down the ground floor porch. Further up the road the car belonging to the two FSB gorillas was still in position.

'Brendan O'Shaughnessy,' Curtis said, introducing himself. Provided they got out of Siberia in one piece, Dolinsky would come to know his real identity soon enough. For now, it was best that the introduction matched Curtis' passport, just in case.

'Eduard Dolinsky.' Dolinsky's voice was surprisingly soft and his handshake tentative although his English, Curtis knew, was excellent.

'The vehicle's in the car park around the back. Follow me,' Curtis said, grabbing his own backpack and the brown bag he'd retrieved in Novosibirsk.

Three cars followed them out of Koltsovo, but after several kilometres all three had turned off, and Curtis began to breathe a little easier. Any attempts to engage Dolinsky in conversation had been met with monosyllabic answers, which suited Curtis just fine. He was still very wary of the scientist's motives; it would take more than an operation like this before there was any trust.

The four-wheel drive's powerful lights probed a long way down the road, lighting the dusting of snow on either side. Thank God Washington hadn't asked him to attempt this in the middle of winter, Curtis thought as he pulled his parka tighter around himself. Occasionally the Toyota's lights would pick up a fox and once he thought he saw a Siberian weasel. Around midnight, Curtis slowed for the Siberian town of Novo altajsk, just to the east of the regional capital Barnaul on the Ob. Barnaul marked the point where the mighty Ob River, which together with the Irtysh River had its source high in the Altais to the south, began its epic journey north across the Siberian steppes and on towards the Arctic Ocean.

By the time the sun rose, Curtis had passed through Bijsk and Gorno altajsk. The traffic had been light and they'd passed the occasional truck and dilapidated utility. Heavy mists covered the alpine fields, drifting among the spruce and pine trees that clung to the ridges above as the road wound up into the towering snow-covered

Altais; a vast mountain chain stretching across Russia in the north, Kazakhstan in the west, and China and Mongolia to the east and south. Curtis changed down a gear as they passed through a Buddhist Altaian village and the twisting road continued its steep climb into the Mount Belukha region. The 4506-metre high glacial massif was Siberia's highest point and Curtis knew that the helicopters would struggle in the thin, alpine air. The spruce and pine trees had given way to aspen and birch, which later changed to the larch and dwarf conifers that could survive in the freezing altitudes. Three hours later Curtis slowed and pulled to the side of the road, which was now barely more than a track.

'What are you doing?' Dolinsky asked in his thick Georgian accent.

'Piss stop and refuel,' Curtis replied, going around to the back of the four-wheel drive and reaching for one of several jerry cans Vladimir had thoughtfully provided. He froze as he caught a movement on the track up ahead. Signalling Dolinsky to stay down and keeping the vehicle between him and whoever was up ahead, Curtis reached in and grabbed the M4 from the bag in the back seat. Using the light covering of snow to mask his footfall and the thick larch and conifers as cover, Curtis moved silently up the ridgeline.

CHAPTER 49

ATLANTA, GEORGIA

Kate Braithwaite rolled over in the small double bed of her Atlanta apartment, but the phone on the bedside table kept ringing incessantly. She was weary from a sixteen-hour day in the lab, and the night before she'd complained to Imran of a headache and had gone to bed as soon as they'd got back from Halliwell. Kate groped for the handset.

'Kate Braithwaite,' she answered sleepily, mildly annoyed at being rung before she was awake.

'Kate, it's Imran. One of the chimps is down.' Professor Sayed was calm but Kate caught the concern in his voice.

Kate sat bolt upright. 'Which one?'

There was a slight pause. 'I'm sorry, Kate, but it's Maverick.'

'Maverick! God no!'

'I'll meet you in the foyer in half an hour.' Imran had an apartment one floor above Kate's.

'Make that fifteen minutes!' She threw the phone back into its cradle and stumbled toward the bathroom, angry and confused.

Kate found herself struggling into her blue biosuit and she slowed down. Keep calm, she whispered, reminding herself of the extreme dangers that awaited her and Imran on the other side of the airlock. If Maverick was down there wasn't anything she could do about it, although she felt another surge of frustration at what they were being asked to do.

When she emerged from her cubicle, air regulator over her shoulder, Imran was waiting for her outside the airlock door. He handed Kate her boots and she nodded her thanks. Neither of them felt like voicing the concern that both were feeling. Kate snapped the face plate on her suit shut and followed Imran into the decontamination shower airlock, closing the heavy stainless steel door on the level 3 side. When he was satisfied it was sealed, Imran opened the corresponding door opposite and Kate followed him into the hot side, through the main lab to the animal room at the far end where Richard and Karl were waiting for them, their faces pale behind their heavy face shields.

Again Kate forced herself to remain calm as she reached for one of the red oxygen hoses hanging from the ceiling near Maverick's cage. Oblivious to the rush of air into her suit, Kate focused on him. He was lying on his side on the floor of the cage. Kate knew from the grimace of pain on his wise old face that her soulmate from the animal kingdom had suffered a horrible death. His brown, blood-flecked eyes stared back at her lifelessly. Kate could almost see the 'why' in their depths. Turning to Richard, she motioned for the cage door to be unlocked but Imran held up his hand. He shuffled over and retrieved a long pole from its storage position and Kate nodded in understanding. Even though Maverick was dead Imran had to be doubly sure. A tear in a biosuit from the death throes of a smallpox-ridden chimp would be fatal.

Imran and Richard lifted Maverick's body out of the cage and onto a stainless steel trolley, then wheeled him across to the necropsy room. *Rigor mortis* had begun to set in and one of Maverick's legs remained bent as they lifted him on to the stainless steel dissection table. Both Imran and Kate knew that, of all the procedures in a hot lab, an animal autopsy was one of the most dangerous. One slip with a scalpel or cutting tool could be fatal and Kate turned towards Richard and Karl to make sure they were well clear of the table.

Kate slipped a rubber block under Maverick's back so that his chest was pushed up and forwards, then she forced his arms down and out of the way. Imran took a scalpel from the workbench on his side of the necropsy room and made a careful Y-shaped incision from either side of Maverick's neck. Moving slowly, he reached for the stainless steel rib cutters and began to cut through Maverick's ribs.

Kate steadied herself, unprepared for what was lying underneath Maverick's breastplate. Imran looked up and gave Kate a meaningful shake of his head. The *Variola major* had attacked all of the chimpanzee's organs with a viciousness that neither Imran nor Kate expected. Maverick's intestines were haemorrhaging. His heart, kidneys and lungs were speckled and reduced to a red mush and there wasn't a single organ the virus hadn't penetrated. *Variola major*, Kate reflected, was far more deadly than most people realised. No wonder the legendary Dr D. A. Henderson, along with hundreds of others who'd worked for decades to eradicate the virus from the planet, had wanted the stocks destroyed.

Imran worked methodically, cutting out Maverick's haemor-rhaged liver and placing the mushy red tissue into a plastic necropsy container. He stepped back, holding his scalpel clear, and nodded to Kate who reached across for the container so she could label it. The two had worked together for such a long time that each was acutely aware of what the other was doing, but as she turned to place the contaminated plastic container on the bench behind her she collided with Karl, who'd come into the room for a closer look. To her hor-ror, she felt a sharp prick through her glove. Karl was still holding the scalpel he'd been inspecting and it had punctured Kate's glove in an instant. The plastic container splattered Kate's biosuit with blood as it dropped to the floor. Maverick's liver slid over the white tiles, leaving a red stain of hot India-1 virus in its wake.

Karl reeled back, his face white. Despite feeling sick, Kate's training kicked in. Holding her gloved hand steady with the cut downwards to minimise any seepage, she reached up with her other hand and unhooked the coiled red air hose from her regulator. She glanced at Imran who was doing the same and she eased her way past Karl who was now standing back against the stainless steel work-bench, the scalpel still in his gloved hand.

'Please God, oh please God don't let any get to me.' It was an entreaty to a God Kate had not spoken to in a long time. As she turned on the decontamination shower and the blood streaked from her suit, she looked across toward Imran who was turning on the shower opposite. His face was ashen.

CHAPTER 50

ALTAI MOUNTAINS, SOUTHERN SIBERIA

Curtis caught the movement again and he rested his M4 carbine against the trunk of a larch and scanned the forest ahead through the crosshairs of the specially fitted telescopic sights. As a large yak came into view, Curtis expelled the air from his lungs and eased his finger from the trigger. He paused long enough to appreciate the magnificent mountain animal, then returned to the vehicle to check his position on a small GPS receiver the size of a mobile phone.

'50° 41", 85° 32". Less than 100 kilometres to go,' Curtis said, folding up one of the CIA's Russian 1:100,000 maps of the area. The maps were surprisingly reliable, but the GPS system was accurate to within a metre, and two hours later, as they reached the edge of the small clearing at the top of the ridge that the special forces pilots had chosen as the designated landing zone, Curtis nodded with satisfaction. At the bottom of the valley below them he could see a lake, exactly where he'd calculated it would be, one of thousands nestled in among the majestic mountain chain. With his position verified, Curtis backed the four-wheel drive into the forest and pulled out his satellite radio.

'Mountain Goat, this is Antelope, over.'

The special forces pilot responded immediately. 'Antelope, this is Mountain Goat, we have you strength five, over.'

'Antelope is in position, over.'

'Mountain Goat, we're about fifteen minutes out but we've had some radar traffic to your north, over.'

Curtis scanned the horizon and then he saw it. A black dot coming up the valley, moving fast.

'Antelope, wait out.'

As Curtis focused his binoculars, the 'black dot' materialised into a Russian military helicopter – an Mi-8T or 'Hip'. The Mi-8T approaching up the valley toward Curtis' position was the same variant as the CIA was bringing in to extract him and Dolinsky. The rocket and anti-tank grenade launcher pods on the side were only too clear now. Although he couldn't see how many men were onboard, Curtis knew the Hip was capable of carrying twenty-four fully equipped Russian soldiers.

'Russian soldiers, Eduard, and my guess is they're not too pleased at being called out on a Sunday, but this will even up the odds a bit,' Curtis said, handing Dolinsky the 9mm Browning and three spare magazines.

Eduard Dolinsky shook his head. 'I don't use guns,' he said.

'You do now, sunshine,' Curtis replied, shoving the weapon into the scientist's hand. 'I'm sorry if the casualty rate is going to be a bit below the millions you aim for in your profession, but do your best to make each one count,' Curtis added, reaching for the radio.

'Mountain Goat, this is Antelope, we've got company down here.' Curtis had counted sixteen soldiers scrambling out of the big Hip that had landed in a clearing near the lake, about 300 metres below Curtis' position. 'Hip Mi-8T, grid 853504 beside the lake. So far there's only sixteen of them, over.'

'This is Mountain Goat, I'll deal with the Hip first, then we'll see about you and Einstein, out.'

Curtis smiled grimly. Einstein was their codeword for the Russian scientist. By the look of consternation on his face, Dolinsky was not going to lower the odds against the soldiers moving up the hill toward them by much.

Thirty seconds later the CIA Hip roared over the top of Curtis' position. The Russian pilots had made the mistake of staying on the ground and their big transport helicopter exploded in a ball of flame and flying pieces of rotor as two high-powered rockets found their mark.

Amazing what you could buy in the second-hand arms bazaars these days, Curtis thought, but any feeling that he might still get out in one piece was cut short as a withering burst of fire cut through the trees. One of the Russian soldiers had spotted the Toyota.

Curtis got away three quick bursts to make the Russians think twice about storming his position, but as he watched the Russian soldiers spreading out below him, another machine gun started firing from a ridge to his right.

'Shit!' Curtis' first thought was that the Russians had somehow managed to get a gun group into position above him, but then he realised they would have needed a second helicopter to do it so quickly. Another burst of fire from the machine gun echoed around the high mountain peaks and to his surprise, Curtis discovered that whoever was above him was firing at the Russians. A short while later he could see the Russian soldiers withdrawing back down the mountain, carrying several casualties. Through his binoculars Curtis picked out three men, high on the ridge above him, black scarves around their faces and bandoliers of ammunition over their shoulders.

As the CIA's big Hip flared on to the landing zone, Curtis and Dolinsky broke cover, Curtis glancing back towards the ridgeline as he doubled over to get underneath the chopper blades. The pilot hauled on the collective, and as they cleared the snow-covered pines Curtis could see three men moving back along the track towards the border with Xinjiang. He felt a chill run down his spine, wondering if the operation had been compromised and again pondering the possibility that Dolinsky might be a double agent.

As word filtered back along the border that Dolinsky had been safely extracted, many more similar groups started to return to where they came from. Kadeer had no way of knowing which part of the border Curtis would use, but he knew that with over sixty small groups watching there had been a reasonable chance they would be ready to assist him.

'I'm sorry to be the bearer of bad news, Curtis,' Tom McNamara said, speaking to Curtis by satellite phone from Washington to the big US air base in Kyrgyzstan.

'Kate's in the intensive care isolation ward at CDC. A Gulf Five will arrive shortly to bring Einstein and yourself back to Washington and I'll have a plane on standby for you to fly to Atlanta if you want.'

'Thanks, Tom, I'd appreciate that.' To lose a scientist at the start of this operation would raise some very awkward questions, but as Curtis struggled with the devastating news, he realised that the awkward questions were only part of it. He suddenly felt very alone, realising that maybe, just maybe, there was something really special about Kate that he didn't want to lose just yet.

CHAPTER 51

HALLIWELL PHARMACEUTICALS, ATLANTA

The lights on the thirty-seventh floor of Halliwell Pharmaceuticals pierced the pre-dawn darkness surrounding Stone Mountain and Dekalb County. Dr Richard Halliwell had spent the night in the private wing of his opulent office suite. Simone was used to his odd hours and she was asleep in the main bedroom. Her perfume and the faint smell of sex still hung in the air.

Halliwell had risen at 3 a.m. and his waking thoughts had turned to his first critical experiment in his plan to counter the rising threat of China. In a little under an hour he was expecting the first delivery from the pound man. The security command centre had been warned to expect a pre-dawn arrival of urgently required chemicals for experiments that were 'in the national interest'.

He smiled a cold, humourless smile. The dossiers on his guards always made interesting reading, and Halliwell was intimately acquainted with the contents of each of them. The personnel in the

Halliwell security command centre were well paid and bonuses were tailored to meet individual needs. Some of those needs were way outside the norm and Halliwell, a master at latent blackmail, was very happy to facilitate them. As a result, even mundane and routine events like delivery schedules at Halliwell were never discussed outside the compound and Richard Halliwell was very confident that his security was much tighter than Washington where the beltway leaked like a sieve. His small but ruthlessly efficient team of security guards boasted more than a few ex-special forces and FBI officers among their number, all of whom for one reason or another had fallen foul of their previous employer. In a final hiring interview applicants would be confronted with how much the company knew about them. An unwritten requirement for being offered a job in Halliwell Security was a personal history or lifestyle that no applicant would ever want made public.

Halliwell sat down at his desk, deep in thought, but a siren wailing in the distance prompted him to look at his watch. 3.45 a.m. He unlocked a desk drawer and retrieved a dun-coloured envelope. Meticulous in attending to any detail, he double-checked the total of US$10,000 inside the envelope in used, unsequential $100 bills. This morning there would be two deliveries. The low-life pound man had done well, he thought, as he shrugged on his black leather jacket. Halliwell put the envelope in an inside pocket, walked across to his personal lift and pressed the button. It was programmed to remain stationary at his office when it wasn't being used; the doors opened immediately. He inserted a key and pressed another recently installed button. Simone knew that it took the lift to a tunnel and the Level 4 laboratories, but Halliwell had told her that it was an area he didn't want her exposed to, nor did he want the entrance discussed with anyone. Like many other secrets that she was very good at keeping, this one was safe. In Simone Carstair's world, knowledge was power.

The lift descended swiftly and silently. Halliwell had personally designed the Level 4 complex and the small laboratory to which he was now headed was almost completely isolated from the main hot zone. A steel door, hidden behind a large cabinet, connected Halliwell's lab to the main complex, but the door was permanently locked, and Richard Halliwell was the only one who knew of its existence. Even the rear loading dock had been carefully designed to blend in, shrouded with thick vegetation and sealed off by a razor-wire fence that looked as if it was part of the main perimeter fence.

Halliwell stepped out of the lift into a small basement. He deactivated the door alarm and punched in the combination to the lock that secured the steel entrance door to the tunnel. He flicked on the tunnel lights, locked the door behind him and strode toward the far end. The tunnel was nearly a kilometre long, and Halliwell's footsteps echoed eerily on the polished concrete floor. Ten minutes later he punched another combination to unlock the access to the specially built receiving bay. A rush of cold air flooded in as he opened the loading dock. In the distance he could see the headlights of the city pound van as the driver picked his way over the dirt track that skirted the perimeter fence. Richard Halliwell picked up the red phone that connected directly to the security command centre.

'Certainly, Mr Halliwell,' was all the officer on duty said, and the heavy steel back gates moved silently and slowly.

CHAPTER 52

ISOLATION WARD, THE CENTERS FOR DISEASE CONTROL, ATLANTA

Imran woke from his doze in the total isolation ward where they'd transferred Kate after the accident. The small hospital had been constructed in a separate building on the campus of the Centers for Disease Control. Accidents in Level 4 labs were very rare but they were almost always fatal, and this ward had the same level of protection as the laboratories. Imran, like the doctors and nurses, was in his spacesuit, his regulator connected to a coiled red air hose dangling from the ceiling of the ward. He looked across at Kate and mouthed a silent prayer to Allah. She was tossing and turning in her sleep, beads of perspiration covering her pale forehead.

The door opened and the duty sister shuffled in followed by Curtis O'Connor. Both were fully suited and Imran smiled to himself as he watched them both reach for an air hose. Curtis was holding a bunch of white roses with bare stems. He had personally removed every leaf and thorn. It would have taken some smooth talking to get the sister to agree to him bringing them in here, Imran thought. Like any of the waste from this ward, the flowers would eventually be incinerated at ultra high temperatures.

Kate groaned as the sister mopped her brow with a damp cloth, which she then disposed of in a bright yellow waste bin marked with the biohazard symbol. The monitor above the bed showed a heart rate of 120. Imran knew that despite Kate's punishing schedule, she somehow managed to find time to work out in the gym or, when she could manage it, she went for jog at lunchtime. This was one very fit scientist and a resting heart rate of 120 was a bad sign. Her other vital signs were no more encouraging. Her temperature was now 103^0 F, and her blood pressure was 160 over 100. Imran glanced at Curtis O'Connor who was also staring at the monitor, watching Kate's heart rate blips as they raced across the oscilloscope. Both men knew that Kate was still mercifully free of any of the deadly telltale haemorrhagic blood spots underneath the skin, and both men knew that a fever normally occurred after the appearance of either a rash or the blood spots. But if Kate *had* contracted the disease, they would lose her.

CHAPTER 53

HALLIWELL PHARMACEUTICALS, ATLANTA

Dr Richard Halliwell wrinkled his nose in disgust as he curtained off the gurney that had a stinking, drunken vagrant strapped to the stainless steel surface. Still furious at the idiocy of the shifty little Mexican from the city pound, he returned to the second gurney. The young red-haired girl was about sixteen and the pale creamy skin on her arms was a mass of puncture wounds. She had been a very beautiful young woman but she'd succumbed to a heroin overdose. The pound man claimed she'd been breathing when he'd picked her up out of the alley, and he might have been right since the body was still warm, but Halliwell wasn't about to pay anyone for dead bodies and the protesting Mexican had been reminded of the photos and told that if he didn't deliver live flotsam next time, he'd have incineration costs docked from his $5000.

Halliwell ran his hand over the girl's small breasts. He could feel his erection growing, amplified by a mixed surge of power and anger as his mind went back to his days at high school and his first sexual experience.

The gymnasium locker room smelt dank and musty, and the seventeen-year-old cheerleader, Cheryl Konopski, was high on speed. Halliwell was almost as high on bourbon and there was a sense of lustful urgency in Cheryl as she led him into a small storage room. It was a place with which Cheryl Konopski was more than a little familiar and she stepped out of her panties, hitched up her short dress and lay down on a pile of mats.

'Come on,' she urged, undoing her blouse and releasing her breasts from her bra. 'I need to get off!'

Richard Halliwell had only just started to shave, and he felt gangly and awkward as he fumbled with his belt. Somehow he'd imagined he would be in control but it wasn't turning out that way.

Cheryl Konopski stared at Halliwell's penis, her disappointment all too visible to him. 'Can't you get that little wiener of yours any harder than that?' she goaded when he'd finally managed to get out of his trousers. As he lay down beside her she reached for him and three seconds later he came in her hands, his small erection disappearing. The euphoria Cheryl had gained from the speed was also subsiding, replaced by a growing depression that was accompanied by a sudden onslaught of wild anger.

'Jesus Christ! Did anyone ever tell you that you're worse than fucking useless!'

Halliwell could still hear the voice of Cheryl Konopski screaming at him as she stormed out of the locker room. He walked over to the stereo system he'd had installed and turned on Beethoven's Fifth Symphony.

'Da da da da . . . Da da da da' Halliwell hummed along with the famous opening stanza and as he turned up the volume, the music by the New York Philharmonic reverberated off the concrete walls of the Level 3 preparation area. The symphony always gave Halliwell a sense of his own power; it was one of his favourites. He ran his hands inside the top of the young woman's stained and flimsy dress, his anger at Cheryl Konopski's rejection slowly fading as the powerful music took over. This one, at least, wouldn't be able to talk back. Her breasts were still warm but her body was stiffening as *rigor mortis* set in. Halliwell lifted the girl's body off the gurney and placed it on the concrete floor. He calmly removed her panties and pushed her pale white legs apart.

Dr Halliwell pulled on his protective boots, stood up, snapped the seal on his face plate shut and reached for an air regulator. Satisfied, he returned to retrieve the vagrant on the other gurney. The stench was indelibly imprinted in Halliwell's nostrils. As Halliwell stood over him, the man stirred. He blinked, his eyes bleary and bloodshot, then he coughed and gurgled and his eyes widened in horror. He began to struggle violently but realised he was held at his ankles, waist, wrists and neck by heavy nylon straps. His frantic cries were muffled by a heavy surgical bandage taped over his mouth.

Richard Halliwell shook his head in disgust. The man's hair and beard were heavily matted with dirt and lice, and his face was pock-marked and scarred. His bulbous nose had the purplish-blue tinge of a heavy spirits drinker. You disgusting excuse for a human being, Halliwell thought. Giving your filthy, revolting body to science will be the only decent thing you've achieved in your entire miserable existence, he mused, as he wheeled the gurney through the specially designed air lock that connected the Level 3 preparation room with the lethal hot laboratory beyond. Halliwell pushed the gurney into an area of the hot lab that resembled the ward of a hospital. As he passed a freezer, he allowed himself a thin smile. Halliwell knew that bear bile soup was the favourite dish of General Ho Feng. General Ho was yet to accept his invitation to visit, but he'd arranged for the illegal frozen bear bile to be stored, just in case. Some might have thought the security storage arrangements were excessive, but Richard Halliwell never left anything to chance.

There were two tiled bays, each equipped with intravenous drip stands, heart rate and blood pressure monitors and a range of other medical equipment that Halliwell would need for his experiments. The gurneys were equipped with disposal systems for human waste that would wash it into a state of the art drainage system.

His subject was struggling feebly and beginning to sweat. Halliwell disconnected his air hose, shuffled away to the far end of the hot lab where the viruses were stored and reached for another hose dangling from the roof. Even without the Vice President's imprimatur, he had obtained some of the most toxic viruses and bacteria known to man. In Halliwell's world money always talked, and his virus stocks included Ebola and Marburg and his bacteria stock list boasted anthrax, botulinum toxin, and *Yersinia pestis* or plague. Soon, with the transfer of the experiments on the chimpanzees and the addition of *Variola major*, he would have the complete suite.

Halliwell punched the dual combination into the vault, turned the stainless steel wheel and swung open the heavy door. He shuffled towards the trolley marked 'Ebola', wheeled it over to a work bench and extracted a set of plastic well plates from the depths of the stainless steel storage vessel. The Ebola virus was clearly identifiable, a pale red liquid so clear it sparkled under the laboratory lights. He shuffled over to the incubator which held the culture medium he'd inoculated with the virus the previous week. Culturing stocks of the Ebola virus was child's play for someone of Halliwell's skills and resources and he was confident that millions of microscopic strings of the virus would have budded out of the culture cells and into the surrounding soup.

His first task was to test the effects of his virus and compile a database of how it would affect humans in its current form. The subsequent experiments would show whether or not the genetically engineered forms could be made more virulent, and whether or not the RNA that Ebola employed for its genetic code could be engineered into the DNA that was characteristic of smallpox. Halliwell knew the engineering would require sophisticated research at a level above what he was capable of, but with Dolinsky, anything might be possible. The official research that would be done on the Great Apes in the main laboratory would provide no guarantee those results could be replicated in humans, something Halliwell needed to know if he was to put his Chinese plan into action; and Halliwell would ensure that any super virus was tested on the human refuse collected from the streets of Atlanta. He placed a capped needle and a vial of the virus on a steel delivery trolley and shuffled back to the bay where he'd left the subject for his experiment.

Dr Halliwell carefully and unhurriedly filled a syringe with the sparkling red liquid and leaned toward the vagrant. Holding the man's arm in a vice-like grip, Halliwell injected millions of particles of a virus for which there was no known cure.

CHAPTER 54

ISLAMABAD, PAKISTAN

Back in his hotel room in Islamabad, al-Falid checked that the Egyptian passport he would use to depart Islamabad for the city he had chosen for the first warning attack was with his tickets. He packed his American passport into his hold luggage and looked at his watch. By now, if Allah was willing, the tug boats would have reached the Indonesian port of Surabaya. There was still another fifteen minutes before he was scheduled to connect to an internet chat room, so he began to flick through the cable channels on the television. His eyes hardened as a program showing the hated American evangelist came on the screen.

For over a month now, the Reverend Jerry Buffett had been delivering his 'Wake Up America – A Call to Arms' series of sermons on his weekly television show, and the Buffett Evangelical Center for Christ was bursting at the seams. More than 15,000 people had packed into the huge auditorium and hundreds more were standing against the tiered walls, while even more were seated in the aisles. The front two rows were reserved for major benefactors and Richard Halliwell and his wife had the best seats. Constance Halliwell was seated beside her husband, directly in front of the huge stage. She was short and prim-looking, with immaculately groomed auburn hair and she was dressed in a pink Valentino twin-set with beige Ferragamo shoes and matching leather handbag, and around her neck was a string of large, almost flawless pink pearls. As the great evangelist addressed the crowd, Constance Halliwell, like the rest of the adoring congregation, hung on Jerry Buffett's every word, mesmerised by his charisma and the total wisdom of what he had to say. Constance thought that if anyone should run for President, it was definitely this man.

'The Messiah can only return when the Palestinians are evicted and all of the Promised Land is back in the hands of God's chosen people, the Israelis!' the Reverend Buffett thundered, coming to the end of his address. 'This road map to peace is a disaster and needs to be torn up.'

Constance Halliwell turned and whispered in her husband's ear. 'That's so true, Richard. That is so true.'

'We've already been given the map, and it's right here in this book,' Buffett said, his deep voice resonating around the auditorium as he opened his bible on the lectern at the mark for chapter 17 of Genesis.

The Lord said to Abraham, 'I will establish my covenant between me and you, and your offspring after you. And I will give to you, and to your offspring after you, the land where you are now an alien, all the land of Canaan, for a perpetual holding; and I will be their God.'

'What God has promised to his chosen people my brothers and sisters, is the land of Canaan – *all* the land of Canaan, the land we now call Israel and the Palestinian Occupied Territories, and we defy God's commands at our peril.' Jerry Buffett was talking softly now, urgently and persuasively, and Constance Halliwell and thousands of others sat motionless, transfixed as he delivered a warning that was designed to go well beyond the auditorium in Atlanta. Jerry Buffett had no doubts as to what he was doing; he knew his remarks would be picked up and broadcast to the Arab world by television and radio. As well as delivering the word of the Lord to the faithful, Jerry Buffett was delivering a very blunt warning to the Arabs and the other unbelievers he so detested.

Amon al-Falid was burning with anger. His hatred for the Great Satan sank to even darker depths as he listened to the infidel's Imam attack the holy path of Islam, a path that defined al-Falid's very being and the meaning for his existence.

The Reverend Jerry Buffett paced back and forth across the huge stage as he brought the service to its dramatic finale. 'My brothers and sisters be ready! Zechariah warns us in Chapter 14: "For I will gather all the nations against Jerusalem to battle . . . then the Lord will go forth and fight against those nations." Be ready! Only those who believe will be taken up to heaven in the rapture. Those who ignore the one true God of the universe will be left behind. When that terrible day comes, and it's coming soon, trains will crash and planes will fall out of the sky as Christian pilots and drivers and their Christian passengers are raptured up to join the Lord. Wives who believe will suddenly be taken straight from their kitchens, leaving unbelieving husbands begging for mercy in a fiery inferno.'

Constance Halliwell reached across and took her husband's hand.

'The Lord will appear in a blaze of triumphal light, with all the prophets, and Zechariah will be standing there, right behind him. There will be a great trembling across the four corners of the Earth, and our Lord will give the unbelievers one last terrible stare. Then he will shake his head in sadness and vast creaking chasms will open and hundreds of millions of unbelievers will fall, screaming, into the fiery bowels of the earth.'

al-Falid was almost incandescent with rage, and he spat towards the television in the corner of his hotel room. 'Khalid Kadeer was wrong,' he seethed. The infidel with his blasphemous criticism of the great prophet, peace be upon him, must never be accommodated. If Allah, the Most Kind, the Most Merciful was willing, the infidel would surely be annihilated. He flicked the off button on the remote and turned to his laptop, typing in the address for an internet chat room.

The site al-Falid was using to communicate with the tugs was a popular dating site that had private chat rooms, just one of the many al-Qaeda used on a regular basis. Internet chat rooms were the safest way to communicate, although for the tugs, a chat room could only be used when they were in dock. al-Falid logged in and followed the prompts, relieved to see that 'Bald Eagle' was already in the 'bedroom', which meant his son Malik had reached Surabaya. As soon as al-Falid entered the room as 'Red Hot Chili Pepper', someone with the avatar 'Fat, Wet and Hot' tried to engage in conversation.

Fat, Wet and Hot: 'What's your pepper like Chili?'

al-Falid kept his anger in check. Western decadence knew no bounds and 'Fat, Wet and Hot' was undoubtedly an infidel. Amon al-Falid knew that no self-respecting Muslim would even visit a chat room, let alone engage in conversation.

Fat, Wet and Hot: 'Hey! Are you in the bedroom Red Hot Chili Pepper? Speak to me!'

al-Falid maintained his silence and simply remained online, invisible, anonymous and dangerous. Despite the billions of dollars the CIA and other intelligence agencies spent researching and acquiring the latest technology, the anonymity of a chat room was something that even the most sophisticated monitoring systems had so far been unable to penetrate.

al-Falid typed in his invitation.

Red Hot Chili Pepper: 'Can I interest you in a private chat, Bald Eagle?' It had amused al-Falid to assign the American symbol of power for his son to use as a nickname.

Bald Eagle: 'Sounds better than what Fat, Wet and Hot's got to offer!'

al-Falid smiled grimly. He had trained all of his operatives, including his son, to use the infidel's language. Some al-Qaeda cells failed because they didn't blend in. If blending in meant drinking in an infidel's bar that was permitted. If it meant using foul and suggestive language in a chat room in pursuit of the greater cause, Allah, the Most Kind, the Most Merciful, would forgive that too. The next exchange from 'Fat, Wet and Hot' prompted a mild rebuke from the chat room's automated controller.

Fat Wet and Hot: 'Blow your chili pepper out your arse, faggot!'

Itzy: 'Be polite Fat, Wet and Hot.'

Fat, Wet and Hot: 'Blow it out yours too!'

Itzy: Fat, Wet and Hot is being disconnected now.

Red Hot Chili Pepper: 'You have arrived?' al-Falid asked when they were in their private chat room.

Bald Eagle: 'Yesterday, and we are planning to leave within the hour. The weather looks good, and after we complete other activities, we should arrive on schedule.'

al-Falid looked at the screen and nodded to himself in understanding. Malik had learned the lessons well. Always assume the infidel was watching, even in an anonymous chat room. Keep any transmission short and to the point, but vague. Within Malik's banal conversation, a wealth of information had passed between them. Malik's message told al-Falid that the refueling at Surabaya had gone without a hitch, and that the 'other activities', the stinger missile training, was on track and the *Montgomery* and the *Wavell* would arrive on the same schedule as the *Jerusalem Bay*.

Red Hot Chili Pepper: 'Mummy is looking forward to being reunited with her chickens.'

al-Falid had already been in a chat room with 'Mummy', the *Jerusalem Bay*, several days earlier, before the mother ship had left

Monrovia with her deadly cargo stacked on her decks, en route to the target city 21,000 kilometres to the east.

Bald Eagle: 'May the force be with you.'

It was code for 'Allah be praised'.

CHAPTER 55

ISOLATION WARD, THE CENTERS FOR DISEASE CONTROL, ATLANTA

The small light glowed green as the state of the art security camera matched Professor Sayed's iris with the records in the computer bank and Imran passed through into the outer area of the Level 4 ward. He looked at his watch. The Secretary of the United Nations had asked for a personal briefing on the threat of bioterrorism and he was due in New York later that night, but he needed to check in on Kate before he left. Professor Ian Jaegar, CDC's consulting physician on the treatment of Level 4 viruses, had personally overseen and applied every viral test known to modern medicine to Kate's blood. Apart from slightly low white and red blood cell counts, the latter of which the Professor had attributed to a minor iron deficiency, there were no indications that the virus had gained entry through the cut, but Kate still had a fever.

Imran walked into the small isolation ward office to find it very crowded. Professor Jaegar, the duty sister and Curtis O'Connor had also arrived. Ian Jaegar greeted Imran with a smile. He had known both Imran and Curtis for years.

'We've moved her out of Level 4 and back into a normal ward, Imran. I've still got her in isolation but it's been over two weeks now, and I'm confident she didn't contract the virus.'

'The fever?' Imran asked.

Professor Jaegar smiled. 'I don't know what sort of a program she's involved in,' he replied, looking at Curtis, 'but I suspect she's been working far too hard.'

Curtis grinned, but said nothing. Even though Professor Jaegar also had positively vetted clearances above top secret there was no need for him to know, and the PLASMID Compartment would remain tightly sealed to anyone who didn't have a reason to be directly involved. On instructions from Esposito that also included the Secretary of State.

'You think the fever was just a coincidence?' Imran asked.

Professor Jaegar nodded. 'A lowered immune system, coupled with the considerable stress involved in the loss of what I understand was one of her favourite chimpanzees may have left her vulnerable. I'm confident that her symptoms were nothing more than the onset of a fever-based flu, something I suspect she may have had before she was exposed in the necropsy room.

Imran nodded, a sense of relief flooding over him. He recalled that Kate had complained of not feeling well the night before, but in the middle of the incident in the hot laboratory that detail had been forgotten.

'May we see her?' Curtis asked.

'Of course. Sister will take you down.'

'Has Dolinsky settled in, Imran?'

'As well as I can judge, although he doesn't say much,' Imran replied as they followed Sister toward the isolation ward. 'Keeps to himself outside the lab, but we're all due to have lunch with Halliwell when Kate gets out of here so perhaps I'll get to know him a little better.'

'Any idea how far Dolinsky's got with his research?'

'In the first few days I got the impression that he's probably a lot closer to being able to combine the viruses and develop a vaccine than we might have thought. I've helped him insert the primers and the results are frighteningly impressive.'

'A while back I received a couple of invites to next month's international bioterrorism conference in Sydney, Imran. The Chinese are sending a delegation so it will be interesting to see if they canvas a biological attack as a possibility at the Olympics. I was going to invite you to join me, but I see you're down to give the opening address. Have you been to Sydney before?' Curtis asked as they reached Kate's isolation ward.

'No, and unfortunately I won't be able to make the whole program. I've got some urgent things to tidy up at the World Health Organization in Geneva so I can get a clear run at the Halliwell research. If you've got a spare invite why don't you take Kate? Sydney's her home town.'

'You think she'll want to stay on the program after this? I would have thought a Level 4 laboratory would be the last thing she'd want to go back to.'

'You might be surprised,' Imran replied, and he smiled his thanks to the duty sister as she showed them into Kate's room.

'You had us worried there for a while,' Imran said. 'Feeling any better?'

'Much, although I'm beginning to wonder who I've got to influence to get off this show! Do I really have to stay here another week?' Kate's face was still a little pale but her green eyes had regained their mischievous sparkle.

Curtis and Imran exchanged glances. Dr Kate Braithwaite was clearly back to her old self.

'I'll see what I can do,' Imran promised. 'In the meantime, I've got to get to the airport. The Secretary of the United Nations has asked me to brief him on a few things, so get well soon,' he said, blowing Kate a kiss, then turning to shake Curtis' hand.

'I am well, Imran, that's the problem,' Kate grumbled. 'Safe trip.'

Curtis sat down on the edge of Kate's bed. 'Given what's happened I will understand if you want to pull out,' he offered.

'This has only made me more determined to stay, Curtis. What we're attempting to do is extraordinarily dangerous, but beautiful creatures like Maverick shouldn't be sacrificed in vain.'

Curtis O'Connor nodded, total understanding in his eyes.

'And thank you for the flowers,' she said. 'They're lovely.'

'Thank you for staying with the project and for what it's worth, I agree, this Administration has lost the plot, but if you ever repeat that, I'll be forced to kill you,' he said with a grin. Breaking with protocol Curtis O'Connor leaned over and kissed Kate on the cheek.

CHAPTER 56

HALLIWELL TOWER, ATLANTA

A week after Kate had been discharged, Richard Halliwell buzzed Simone, annoyed that Eduard Dolinsky was late for their pre-luncheon discussion. 'Where's Dolinsky?'

Simone Carstairs took a deep breath and glared at the intercom on her desk. Even with the volume turned down low, she recognised Richard's mood, a mood that matched her own. Ever since he had been invited to run for the Republican nomination for the Presidency, Simone sensed he had placed her outside his inner circle. Esposito had not returned her calls, and she and Richard slept together far less regularly. Not that she missed the sex, if it could be called that, but sex was one of the most important holds she had over Halliwell. Nor was she concerned with secrecy in the labs; Simone accepted it was not necessary for her to know the details of classified medical research, but lately the aura of secrecy around Richard had extended well past the laboratories, and for the first time since she'd been his personal assistant she'd not been invited to lunch. Simone's antennae were finely tuned and she was wary about what Richard might be up to. She got up from her desk determined she was not going to conduct a conversation over an intercom.

'I'm not Dolinsky's keeper, Richard,' Simone said defiantly, taking the seat beside Halliwell's desk without being asked. 'For whatever reason he's in Alan Ferraro's office.' Simone knew that the Russian scientist had been there for over an hour. She had taken a dislike to Alan Ferraro from the first day she'd met him but tolerated the shifty accountant for the same reason Richard did – his expertise at keeping the share price high and the authorities none the wiser as to the contents of the company accounts.

'Perhaps you'd like to ask him what he's doing there?' Simone suggested.

'Some time ago he asked me if he could browse through some of Ferraro's accounting books that are hard to get in Russia, and I don't see anything wrong with that,' Halliwell barked. 'What's eating you? Get out on the wrong side of the bed today?'

'Not that you'd notice,' Simone said, 'but since you've asked, is there some reason why I'm not invited to lunch today?'

'Oh I see! It all becomes clear.' Halliwell was becoming increasingly tired of Simone's all-pervasive presence. Lately she was looking her age, he thought, glaring at her. Once a woman reached forty she was on the downhill run and Simone had reached that milestone two months ago, something she had not been backward in reminding him of when he'd let the occasion pass without the usual bunch of flowers. 'This may come as a surprise to you, Simone, but there are some things around here you don't need to be involved in!'

'I'm fully aware of that, Richard,' Simone replied icily, 'but I wouldn't have thought a lunch would be classified top secret. For what it's worth, although why I'm bothering to protect you in your present frame of mind is beyond me, I wouldn't trust your new Russian scientist any more than I would trust Alan Ferraro. It's not the first time he's been in Ferraro's office, but if you're happy with that be it on your own head.' Simone stormed out of Richard's office, almost bumping into Dr Dolinsky on her way through.

Richard Halliwell's luxurious private dining room was on the same floor as his office suite, next to the lavishly appointed Halliwell boardroom. A Picasso and a Rembrandt, part of the stunning Halliwell art collection, were included on the panelled walls, as well as the odd Caravaggio and a sculpture by Bernini. Exotic pot plants and lampshades in the Halliwell colours of gold and black had been added to the gaudy trappings of power. The far wall was plate glass that stretched from floor to ceiling. The twenty-seat dining table was polished silky oak, and today there was a setting for four at one end of the table. Each dining chair had a Halliwell seal sewn into the backrest – a black circle with two bright gold crossed syringes and a test tube positioned through them, the seal edged in gold with the words 'Philanthropy before Profit'. Beyond the dining room a set of double doors led to a large kitchen equipped with state-of-the-art stainless steel appliances. Three chefs, as well as a small army of young, slim waitresses and kitchen hands, all personally selected by Halliwell, were standing by; the waitresses linked by a common denominator of a D-cup.

Imran and Kate waited in the large entertainment foyer at a bar that would not have been out of place in any five-star boutique hotel. The two scientists had decided that it would be a waste not to sample some of the Halliwell cellar and in the afternoon they would work in their offices on the thirty-sixth floor rather than return to the hot lab.

'Doesn't do things by halves, does he?' Kate observed, sipping her Clos des Goisses Philipponnat champagne as they waited for Halliwell and Dolinsky to appear.

'Ah, there you are, Kate,' Richard Halliwell said smoothly, ushering Dr Dolinsky into the dining room. 'Welcome back. I trust you're fully recovered?'

'Fully thank you, Dr Halliwell,' Kate replied. Once again she had that strange feeling about Halliwell that sent a shiver down her spine.

'Please, it's Richard, and this is Dr Eduard Dolinsky.'

Kate extended her hand towards Dolinsky. He was slim and of just average height. His handshake was unassuming but Kate knew from what Curtis and Imran had told her that the Georgian scientist was often intolerant of those who might not meet his exacting standards, and very ambitious for both himself and Islam.

'Shall we?' Halliwell gestured towards the table as Karen, his young maître d', hovered in the background.

'Here's to a very successful program,' Halliwell said, raising his champagne flute towards Kate. 'I trust everything is satisfactory in the laboratories?' he asked, when the staff had withdrawn having served the first course of crab chowder.

'The laboratories are first class, Dr Halliwell,' Imran replied.

'Please, it's Richard,' Halliwell offered again with a quick, mechanical smile. 'We're going to be family by the time we've finished working on this.' Kate froze as Halliwell placed his hand on her thigh. She was about to remove it when he slowly ran his hand down to her knee and removed it himself before resuming the conversation.

'And the monkeys?'

'They're still restless, Dr Halliwell,' Kate said, deliberately using his title. 'But I would be too if I was part of this program. I think what we're doing is extremely dangerous.' Kate made no attempt to hide the anger flashing in her green eyes.

'Very dangerous,' Halliwell agreed urbanely, 'but in Dr Dolinsky here, and in you and Professor Sayed, I couldn't wish for the experiments to be in more capable hands.'

'What will your role be in this,' Imran asked, sensing that his young protégé was about to give the CEO of Halliwell Pharmaceuticals her legendary 'rough end of the pineapple'.

'As you're aware, Eduard will be leading the research and I'll be watching at a distance, putting on a biosuit occasionally to see how you're getting on, just to keep my hand in,' Halliwell replied. 'I still have a day job,' he added, turning to look at Kate and smiling mechanically again, 'but I'm sure you've been told that our mission is to try to find out what might be possible because if we can do it we have to assume that the terrorists may be able to do it as well.'

'What's your view, Eduard?' Kate asked, keen to determine whether the Georgian scientist had a voice, let alone an opinion.

'We live in very dangerous times,' Eduard replied. 'I think it is possible we will be building a virus from scratch before too long,' he opined, echoing Kate's, Imran's and Curtis' fears.

'In our discussions before lunch, Eduard and I were talking about the coming threat from terrorists. It's not only here that Americans are vulnerable. I'm particularly concerned at what might happen overseas, including the Beijing Olympics,' Richard Halliwell said, steering the group in the direction that he intended to focus on. 'It will also be important for us to develop effective vaccines against genetically engineered viruses.'

'Which may not be all that easy,' Kate said, this time lifting Richard Halliwell's hand off her thigh and placing it firmly back on his own.

BOOK TWO

THE FIRST WARNING ATTACK

CHAPTER 57

THE TARGET CITY

Amon al-Falid waited patiently among the mass of humanity that had charged off the aircraft and were now jostling for position behind the long yellow line that marked the arrivals barrier in the target city's main international airport. al-Falid kept his face impassive as he took in every detail. No fewer than six jumbos had arrived within minutes of each other, just after the curfew had been lifted at 6 a.m., yet for some reason known only to the authorities, barely a third of the Customs and Immigration desks were manned. The queues stretched back up the ramp into the duty free area, where an overweight female Customs Officer was waddling back and forth, officiously directing people into various lanes as if she was herding cattle. From the looks of bewilderment on some of the faces of the weary passengers, she might just as well have been herding cats.

'Non-citizens in that lane over there!' she barked at a group of Muslim women.

People of 'Middle Eastern appearance'. It was the same in this country too, al-Falid reflected, fingering the Egyptian passport he'd used to depart Islamabad.

'What's the purpose of your visit?' the young woman in the booth demanded.

al-Falid refrained from arguing that he'd clearly indicated that in the box marked 'Purpose of Visit'.

'I'm an academic on sabbatical,' he said, smiling politely. 'My specialties are the history of architecture in this region and in South Asia.'

The Customs Officer made a final check of the screen in front of her, stamped his passport and handed it back. 'Enjoy your stay,' she said curtly, her face devoid of any emotion.

al-Falid smiled to himself. Clearly the crosschecks had not connected his American passport with his Egyptian one.

Jamal Rabbani was waiting for him as he cleared the final baggage check and came into the arrivals hall. Rabbani was short and muscly, with a round face and short black hair; his eyes were dark and alert. He was in his early twenties, highly intelligent but impressionable, and he'd been one of al-Falid's most important recruits. The two had met over five years before during one of al-Falid's recruiting visits. Taunted and bullied at a beachside high school that was not known for its acceptance of difference, the young Rabbani had descended into a state of deep depression by the time al-Falid had been introduced to him. Jamal's devotion to the Islamic faith and his insistence on performing the midday *dhuhr* and the mid-afternoon *asr*, two of the five prayers or *Salat*, had been his downfall. The bullies of the school had only been further encouraged when teachers refused to allow Rabbani time out of class for prayer.

al-Falid knew that Muslims were seen by many in this country as a threat to the country's established values, and that schoolboys like Jamal were seen as foreigners, even though they had been born and raised here. al-Falid also knew that in this country, the presence of Muslims was often the subject of heated debate, especially on talk-back radio where many of the presenters reflected the prejudice and intolerance of the majority of the community. It was an intolerance that had made al-Falid's job of recruiting very much easier; the highly intelligent Rabbani was now his right-hand man. al-Falid had not only put Rabbani in charge of the boatshed cell, he had also given him the responsibility of coordinating all of the other cells involved in the first warning attack.

'The warehouse is not far from here, Amon. On the way into the city,' Jamal said with a smile, as he pushed the parking ticket into the machine. As the boom gate rose, Jamal eased the nondescript second-hand Mitsubishi Pajero out of the car park.

Being a Sunday, the traffic was light. The city, with its towering high-rise office blocks, was clearly visible a short distance away from the airport and al-Falid pursed his lips in anticipation. Today, the people might be strolling in the parks and relaxing on the beaches, he thought, but very soon, if Allah the Most Kind, the Most Merciful was willing, this city would be thrown into absolute chaos.

al-Falid nodded with satisfaction as Jamal pulled up outside an inner city warehouse and got out to open a set of rusting wire gates that had a lopsided sign that read 'Acheson's Trucks' wired to one of them. The old warehouse, in a rundown part of the industrial area close to the airport, was perfect. The secondary targets were only minutes away.

'There's no interest from the authorities?' he asked.

Jamal smiled. 'Apart from the mountain of paperwork that is required for running a small business in this country, none at all. I've warned all of our people that they're not to do anything that might draw attention. There are one or two outspoken clerics in this country that have already drawn fire from the authorities, and I've ordered that no one goes to those mosques.'

'They have them under surveillance?'

'Yes, as well as a bookstore that has prompted the government here to review the laws on banning books, so I've put the bookstore out of bounds as well.'

'And the trucks?'

'I did exactly as you requested, Amon, and purchased fourteen trucks second-hand from four different dealers; 5-ton Hinos and Isuzus. They're all in good condition. Seven of them have been modified so that each can take 2.5 tonnes of explosive. The floors have all been replaced with hardened steel and the interiors have been shaped into a cone. The other seven will be used for normal activities. We've already done several runs to the targets,' Jamal said. 'At the time you want us to detonate the trucks the traffic is still heavy, but flowing pretty well.'

'Communications?' al-Falid asked as Jamal unlocked the small metal door that was part of the main roller doors of the warehouse.

'Text messages on mobile phones. In an emergency I've authorised my men to use open speech but by then it will be too late for the authorities to react,' Jamal said with a slow smile. He flicked on the main light switch and the power hummed as the big arc lights above them warmed up. Seven large trucks were lined up in the front part of the warehouse with another seven behind them. A big workshop at the rear had been sealed off from view.

'We finished modifying the last of the seven delivery trucks last week,' Jamal said, opening the back of the one closest to the work-shop. 'This is the last truck to be filled and I'm expecting the final delivery of fertiliser tonight from our fertiliser company in the south. It's not your ordinary agricultural fertiliser,' Jamal explained. 'In order to provide sufficient oxygen for the fuel oil, we need mining grade ammonium nitrate,' he said. '94 per cent ammonium nitrate and 6 per cent no. 2 diesel. I've increased the ratio of diesel a little to make it more effective.'

'You had no problem with the fuel oil?'

Jamal shook his head. 'We use it in the trucks,' Jamal said, unlock-ing the big workshop.

At the back of the workshop there was another area that was sealed off and locked. 'This is the mixing area,' Jamal explained, pointing to three 44-gallon drums that had been positioned under a bench to which three industrial paint stirrers were anchored.

'What's that?' al-Falid asked, pointing to a long, thin aluminium cylinder on the floor of the workshop.

'That's our solution for getting explosives onto the floor of the harbour,' Jamal replied. 'We finished packing it yesterday but I'll explain all of that when you visit the boatshed.'

'And the paint?' al-Falid asked, looking at several big cans of Dulux that had bright yellow spillage on the sides.

'A little of that is stirred into each batch of ANFO – ammonium nitrate fuel oil – explosive,' Jamal explained. 'That way we can tell when the fertiliser and fuel oil are thoroughly mixed.'

'You're confident this will work, Jamal?' al-Falid asked.

'Timothy McVeigh used a variant of it to destroy the Alfred P. Murrah building in Oklahoma City in 1995. I've studied his methods, Amon, and they were very effective. That explosion killed 168 people, injured more than 800 and damaged 324 buildings in a sixteen-block radius. The mining industry uses it all the time,' Jamal added confidently. 'They normally mix it on site. Essentially the ammonium nitrate reacts with a long-chain hydrocarbon. I can explain the chemistry on the whiteboard if you like.'

al-Falid shook his head. 'As long as you're confident, I trust you, Jamal,' he answered with a smile.

'We pray here in the workshop. That way we are hidden from the outside world,' Jamal said, looking at his watch and handing al-Falid a beautifully woven prayer mat. He put his own on the workshop floor, facing towards a mark that had been scratched on the corrugated iron above the benches where the ANFO explosive was being mixed.

'After prayers I'd like to use your computer, and when I return from down south I'm looking forward to seeing the boatshed and your arrangements for the harbour attack,' al-Falid said, laying his prayer mat beside Jamal's.

The cell al-Falid had formed in a city further to the south had been given a task that some thought impossible. Several groups had planned a similar attack in the past but all had failed. al-Falid knew that the target had immense value as a symbol of the Great Satan's power, and he was confident that, given the right circumstances, where others had failed his cell would succeed. If they did, the attack would send shockwaves around the world.

CHAPTER 58

WASHINGTON

Curtis O'Connor glanced at the clock on his office wall. The intervening days to the conference in Sydney seemed to have flown. Imran had already left for Sydney the previous day and it was almost time to pick up Kate and head out to Dulles airport. He reached for the last file in his tray, marked 'Top Secret – Echelon'. Echelon had been set up during the Cold War by the United States, Britain, Canada, Australia and New Zealand to eavesdrop on the Russians, but now, thousands of operators around the world scanned the electronic spectrum for private emails, faxes, mobile phone calls and any other electronic communication ordinary citizens made as part of their daily lives. The big dishes at top secret satellite stations at Fort Meade in Maryland and Yakima in Washington State, as well as overseas stations like those at Menwith Hill in Yorkshire, Bad Aibling in Germany and the remote bases at Shoal Bay in the Northern Territory and Geraldton in Western

Australia pulled the transmissions in like giant electronic vacuum cleaners.

O'Connor's brain kicked into high gear as he read the email intercept that had been flagged by an alert analyst:

Authorities reacted to TCDD and community worries. Half-life a concern. Normal activities suspended and no longer able to use them as cover. Cork in bottle approach may now be limited and will need to concentrate on HEAT for surface attack.

'Half life a concern'. Did that mean al-Qaeda was attempting to launch another series of dirty bombs, or did it mean Dr Kadeer was planning to go nuclear, as his colleagues, bin Laden and al-Zawahiri had threatened twice before him. O'Connor wondered.

As he rushed out of the office on the way to pick up Kate and get to the airport, he knew that it was only a matter of time before a terrorist set off a bomb packed with radioactive material. Given the availability of the stuff in hospitals and industry, both he and Tom McNamara had been surprised that one hadn't been detonated already, but with such a high-volume workload, even experienced operators like O'Connor could miss the clue that was contained in the first line of the email: 'Authorities reacted to TCDD and community worries'. It would have led O'Connor to the target. Of all the dioxins, TCDD or 2,3,7,8-Tetrachloro dibenzene-para-dioxin was one of the most lethal, with a half-life of nearly ten years. At high levels it caused cancer in humans and it had been dominating the target city's media for months.

The ramp outside the departures hall of Washington's Dulles International Airport was crowded with yellow taxis disgorging passengers into the mêlée that had become the usual for post-September 11 travel.

'Pamela!' Curtis waved to a taxi further beind them in the rank, turned back to his own and gave the cheerful taxi driver unloading the bags a generous tip. The taxi driver had regaled Kate and Curtis with proud anecdotes of his nine children for the entire trip. Curtis strode down to the taxi behind them and Kate watched as he embraced an older, elegant woman in a Qantas uniform. He then beckoned Kate over. She smiled, shook her head, and pointed to the bags on the terminal apron.

'Very nice,' Kate said, when Curtis returned. 'Old flame or current model?'

'You make it sound like I'm running a car franchise,' Curtis replied. More like a small boy in a candy shop, Kate thought as they headed for the queue at the counter for Flight QF 3082 to Los Angeles and then on to Sydney.

'Pamela is a very useful person to know,' Curtis said, his attempt at looking hurt only partly successful. 'She just happens to be the Purser on this flight so you should've come across to meet her.'

'I'm sure I'll meet her on board. It would have been very bad form for a man in your position to have his bags unattended on the sidewalk,' Kate chided. 'The way Homeland Security is these days, the bomb squad would have been there in an instant.'

It took nearly an hour to check in and get through customs and by the time they were on the departures side, the 'go to gate' sign had changed to 'boarding'.

'I'm looking forward to Business Class,' Kate said, as she took out her ticket and boarding pass. 'We scientists are not used to this sort of luxury.'

Curtis smiled as they handed over their tickets.

'Dr O'Connor, Dr Braithwaite, welcome aboard.' The flight attendant was young and attractive, and Kate grinned as Curtis flashed a warm smile.

'You won't be needing these,' the flight attendant said, her attention on Curtis. She put the boarding passes in the bin. 'Unfortunately I'm working in Business Class but I'm sure Pamela will look after you,' she added, as the machine churned out two replacement passes with their distinctive gold First Class stripe.

'That is unfortunate,' Curtis replied with another warm smile.

'That is unfortunate.' Kate mimicked Curtis' soft Irish brogue as they headed toward the for'ard door of the 747.

'Very ungrateful,' Curtis responded. 'This way you and I can have a bed all the way to Sydney,' he added mischievously.

'Two single beds,' Kate said quickly, shaking her head. She was finding herself strangely attracted to Curtis. His irreverent attitude and sense of fun made her wonder what it would be like to . . . Steady on, girl, don't get involved, she told herself. A relationship with a work colleague was not professional. For both of them, the research program was more important and the work ahead was going to be complex and dangerous. She needed to keep her wits about her.

CHAPTER 59

SYDNEY CONVENTION CENTRE, DARLING HARBOUR

The flight from the east coast of the United States to Australia had taken nearly 24 hours, but the trip was worth it. The three-day program for the International Conference on Bioterrorism promised to be a full one. Kate was having a coffee with Curtis in a quiet part of the foyer of the Sydney Convention Centre at the southern end of Darling Harbour.

'I wonder how our friend Dolinsky's going?' Curtis mused.

'In the short time I've been with him in the lab I'm amazed at how quickly he's working. It's almost as if we're covering old ground.'

'That's Imran's view as well,' Curtis replied.

'And if this ever got loose . . .' Kate let her voice trail off. She knew the implications were horrific. 'I guess all we can do is keep warning people in the hope that those in power will come to their senses, although I don't see that happening anytime soon. Halliwell's been in the lab a dozen times to see how we're going. It's weird, Curtis, it's almost as if he's got some sort of vested interest.'

Curtis nodded. 'He asked about what intelligence I might have on the Olympics the other day but I've put him off while I do some checking. Something is not quite adding up with our friend Halliwell.'

'Or Dolinsky for that matter. He gives me the creeps. I guess this conference is pretty important, although the time will go so quickly,' Kate observed, conscious of how close she and Curtis were standing and how easily they enjoyed one another's company. Again she warned herself not to get involved.

'Too quickly,' Curtis said enigmatically, 'but we've got an extra day at the end of it for the visit to the State Crisis Centre. I'm looking forward to catching up with my old buddy, Brigadier Davis, who will no doubt bring us up to date on Australia's counter-terrorist arrangements. Then it's the big freedom bird home.'

'You to Washington to do whatever else you do, and me to Atlanta.' Kate immediately regretted the remark, annoyed that her personal feelings kept surfacing. She found herself thinking about what Curtis might be involved in when he wasn't worrying about Operation PLASMID and the security of the Olympics.

'Sorry. Didn't mean to pry,' Kate said, breaking the awkward silence.

'You're not prying,' Curtis said, looking at her and gently touching her arm. 'One day I'll tell you,' he added. Curtis was struggling with his own feelings. For the first time in his life, he found himself drawn to a woman for more than the thrill of the chase.

'How about dinner tonight at one of those little restaurants at the Rocks,' Curtis suggested, a touch of mischief in voice. 'I'd ask Imran to join us if he wasn't flying out.' Curtis knew he was throwing caution to the winds. Any thought of a relationship would make his profession even more dangerous. Emotional feelings could threaten his judgement, and it wouldn't be fair on Kate either.

'That would be nice,' Kate replied, as she accompanied Curtis back into the auditorium.

It was not every day that delegates had the opportunity to listen to a virologist of the international standing of Professor Imran Sayed. The main auditorium in the Sydney Convention Centre was packed, every scientist in the room acutely aware of the dangers that bioterrorism and genetic engineering posed to humanity if deadly viruses ever got into the wrong hands. Kate and Curtis were sitting two rows from the front and both listened attentively as Imran opened the conference with a warning.

'Not to put too fine a point on it, the human race now stands at the edge of a vast precipice. Too often the western world has resorted to war as a first, rather than a last resort. Unless we change course, bioterrorism will provide other cultures with a means of retaliation that may well destroy a significant part of our civilisation. Later on in this conference the Chinese delegation will be giving a presentation on the security they are putting in place for the Beijing Olympics. One of the greatest threats facing the world today comes from Islamic fundamentalists and the Beijing Olympics is a prime target,' Professor Sayed said. 'As a result of the West waging a war in Iraq that has taken the lives of hundreds of thousands of Muslims, support for the fundamentalist cause has risen immeasurably and al-Qaeda have an inexhaustible supply of suicide bombers. People in the United

States, Britain and Australia are much *less* safe than we were before we invaded.'

It was a rare departure from the more polite form of public address for which the Professor was known. His frustration at western politicians' reckless commitment to war was palpable.

'I am a Muslim and I have nothing but contempt for Islamic fundamentalist groups who completely misinterpret *Jihad* to suit their own evil purposes, but by creating chaos in Iraq we've played right into their hands.'

Michelle Gillard, a young, accredited *Sydney Morning Herald* journalist sitting next to Kate was furiously taking notes.

'As tragic as this American, British and Australian invasion of Iraq has been,' Professor Sayed continued, 'it's a sideshow compared to that which awaits us. Many of you will have seen the warnings from Dr Khalid Kadeer. The West brands him as a terrorist and we refuse to discuss his grievances, but to him and his followers those grievances are very real. To cite just two examples, from where he sits, we are seen to be favouring Israel at the expense of the Palestinians. I happen to think he's right.' Imran paused to emphasise his point. 'And the presence of American forces in the lands that contain the two most important cities in all of Islam, Mecca and Medina, is a grave affront to Kadeer. It's akin to us having to put up with an Islamic army camping on the shores of the Potomac around Washington, or around the harbour here in Sydney. I think we should at least sit down and talk with him.'

Michelle Gillard wrote the quote down word for word. Coming from such a distinguished Muslim professor, it would be a front page story.

'The White House isn't going to like that, but I think he's right,' Curtis whispered to Kate.

'Nor is the Australian Prime Minister,' Kate replied.

'Not so long ago,' Professor Sayed said, 'someone published the entire genome of bird flu on the internet, which enabled every bio-terrorist in the world to download what would normally take twenty years of research to decipher. An Islamic fundamentalist, or any other terrorist with a PhD in microbiology, can now alter that virus to suit their own dark ends. Our friends from China who are responsible for protecting everyone at the Beijing Olympics have every right to be both alert and alarmed. If the Islamic fundamentalists and other ter-rorist groups are ever to be defeated it will take the combined efforts of the West, the Han Chinese, *and* the moderates in Islam, but we need to sit down at the negotiating table. Fighting unnecessary wars will lose those few friends we have left in the Islamic world.

'I wish you all well for what will be one of the most important conferences of the modern era, and I make no apology for a simple concluding observation. It is but one example in the devastating sce-nario of untold misery that awaits us if we don't come to our senses as a species. Filoviruses like Marburg and Ebola have no cure and we've never been able to develop a vaccine. The only saving grace is that they're not easily transmitted from human to human, other than through close personal contact. Were these viruses ever to be com-bined with another more easily transmittable pathogen, the death toll could be in the hundreds of millions.'

Imran's closing statement highlighted the frightening truth. Advances in science meant the threat from bioterrorism was a terrifying reality.

CHAPTER 60

THE TARGET CITY

'The boatshed is upriver,' Jamal said, as he and al-Falid left the warehouse near the airport and headed towards the city, 'but I thought you might like to see the target at close range.' Jamal turned onto the road that led to the tunnel under the harbour. He headed north up the gradually rising exit and negotiated a route through the satellite city on the northern shore, turning off to a fashionable harbourside suburb.

Jamal parked near a small ferry wharf and they both got out of the Pajero and walked down to the harbour's edge. al-Falid stared up at the underside of the massive bridge that connected the northern and southern shores.

'The area on this side of the harbour together with that one over there are two of the most populated suburbs in the city,' Jamal said, pointing across the harbour past a naval base to the high-rise apartments on the southern shore. A distant rumble grew louder and louder. A train was going across the bridge and al-Falid looked back at the massive pins securing the steel arch to their stone pylons.

'You were right, Jamal. The infidel's design is good, but if Allah, the Most Kind, the Most Merciful is willing, we will still succeed.'

Thirty minutes later Jamal unlocked a wire gate that opened onto a path covered with oyster shell leading down the side of a big wooden boatshed upriver from the main harbour.

'We've rented the boatshed from a deceased estate,' Jamal explained, unlocking a big padlock that secured a small door beside a wooden ramp. A river cat sped past, its wake rippling against the concrete pylons supporting the ramp and the two rusting rails that led from the boatshed into the water.

Jamal switched on the lights hanging from the roof of the shed to reveal a huge ocean-going fishing trawler supported by old and scarred wooden blocks on top of a rusty but well-greased slipway trolley. Two gleaming silver shafts protruded from the trawler's hull, connecting with twin bronze propellers either side of a recently refurbished rudder. The hull had been freshly painted with salmon-coloured anti-fouling paint, and 'LFB 15011' was painted prominently either side of the bow and on the stern. al-Falid nodded approvingly at the name *Destiny* that was painted beside the wheel-house, but it was the inside of the trawler that interested him most. He followed Jamal up the paint-spattered wooden ladder that was leaning against the transom.

'We've remodelled the deck and the bow to accommodate the change of plans,' Jamal said, leading al-Falid down a narrow steel ladder into the hold. Steel sheets had been fastened to the sides and

the keel and welded together into a cone at the bow. 'We will begin
filling the hold tonight. When it's detonated all of the force of the
explosive will be directed through the cone in the bow.'

'And the anti-tank rockets?' al-Falid asked.

'We've engineered the mountings for the rockets just aft of the
bow,' Jamal explained, leading the way back up to the deck, 'and
we're using the infidel's own rockets,' he said, his eyes gleaming
with satisfaction at the irony of it all. The disappearance of Army
M72 anti-tank rockets had caused a huge storm in the media, but he
had assured al-Falid that the police would never trace them to the
boatshed. His brilliant young pupil was truly deserving of his place
in heaven, al-Falid thought.

'On the day of the attack two of the infidel's anti-tank rockets will
be secured in the mountings and covered with old tarpaulins until
the last minute,' Jamal said. The wheelhouse was crammed with
sophisticated equipment that included radar, depth sounders and a
plethora of electronics.

'What's that?' al-Falid asked, pointing to a black laser screen
mounted on the marine ply.

'A screen for showing the position of the laser beams,' Jamal
explained. 'I will be at the helm in the final attack, but before we
detonate the fishing boat I want to make sure I've breached the hulls
of the tanker. Because it's a double hull the missiles must arrive at
the same point a split second apart; that way, the first missile will
breach the outer skin, and the second will breach the inner hull that
protects the crude oil. The camera mounted on the roof is wired into
the aiming systems of the missiles,' he said, 'and the first missile will
be fired when the laser dots come together on the screen. The second

will be fired a fraction of a second later; and tonight, we will position the last of the canisters on the harbour bed.'

Later that night al-Falid returned and he watched as Jamal's divers suited up and assisted one another with their state-of-the-art rebreathing units. The LAR-V units were used by US Navy Seals and Dräger, the German manufacturer, had steadfastly refused to sell them on the open market. It had been a relatively simple matter to obtain them from a less than scrupulous dealer; money always talked. al-Falid didn't understand all the technical details, but he knew that the fully enclosed system of the Dräger meant there would be no telltale bubbles, which was critical for where the divers would be working.

The cigar-shaped canisters filled with ANFO were designed with neutral buoyancy but the divers needed time to manoeuvre them into position, and the LAR-V units gave up to four hours endurance on each dive. So far, al-Falid thought, that had been more than enough time. Over a period of six weeks, eleven canisters had been locked into position on the harbour bed, and tonight the divers would connect the final canister. al-Falid and his al-Qaeda explosives experts had calculated this might be enough to achieve the 'cork-in-a-bottle' that Khalid Kadeer had wanted.

The canisters were equipped with recoverable mini-propulsion systems and the four divers swam easily beneath the inky waters of the darkened harbour. Without lights, visibility below the surface was almost zero, forcing the lead diver to check his compass. He made a small correction to bring his divers onto a heading for the first of the long-life pinger beacons they'd pre-positioned along the route to the target. The small ULB-364 'Extended Life' was a commercially available underwater location beacon with a pulse rate of one pulse per second and it was powered by simple 9 volt lithium batteries. Using GPS satellite navigation the divers had positioned enough of them to guide them unerringly along the bottom of the harbour.

The volume, sensitivity and frequency controls were already set and the lead diver moved forward with his small DPR-275 handheld receiver. It locked on to the first pinger almost immediately and the lead diver again made a slight adjustment to his heading as he zeroed in on the direction of the strongest signal being picked up in his head-phones. On the surface, the harbour traffic continued uninterrupted, oblivious to Allah's superbly trained frogmen moving stealthily and silently towards the target.

CHAPTER 61

THE ROCKS, SYDNEY

Curtis had reserved an outdoor table at 'Waterfront', a restaurant in the converted wool stores that had been built by convicts on the foreshores of The Rocks. A replica of the *Bounty* rode the gentle swells of Campbell's Cove. Beyond the historic ship, Sydney's green and gold ferries travelled past the sails of the Opera House on their way to and from Circular Quay.

A young waiter seated Kate and Curtis at a table with a view of one of the world's greatest harbours. He was about to pass the wine list to Curtis when Kate intercepted it. 'You're in my country now,' Kate said, looking at the list.

Curtis rolled his eyes and turned to the young waiter. 'Are you married?' he asked.

'No Sir.'

'Fiancée?'

'Yes,' the waiter replied, his face breaking into a broad smile.

'We're getting married next March.'

'Take my advice young man, don't!' Curtis said with a wicked grin. 'We've only been married a week and she's already taking charge. I shudder to think what she's going to be like in ten years time.'

'Oh stop it, Curtis! Don't believe a word he says,' Kate said to the waiter. 'We'll have the Affleck Cabernet Sauvignon, thanks.'

'You're incorrigible!' Kate chided when the young waiter had left, looking more than a little confused. 'I *was* married once, and that was quite enough, I can assure you.'

Curtis was quick to see the momentary shadow reflected in Kate's eyes. He could have kicked himself. He was about to apologise when the waiter returned with the wine.

'Shall I pour or would one of you like to taste it?' the waiter asked, unsure of who should be offered the wine.

Curtis smiled and gallantly waved his hand to indicate that he was deferring to Kate.

'That's outstanding,' Curtis said. 'How do you say it here – good health?'

'Not bad is it!' Kate enthused, pleased that the wine from the cool climate vines near Lake George had met with Curtis' approval. 'Affleck's one of my favourite vineyards so I'm glad you like it.'

'It's superb, and I'm sorry if I raised any uncomfortable memories a moment ago,' Curtis offered. 'Sometimes my sense of humour gets me into trouble.'

Kate grinned. After the intensity of Malcolm, Curtis' sense of humour was one of the things she found so attractive about him.

'Don't be sorry. The memories are ghastly, but I guess we learn these lessons the hard way. Essentially I married my bloody father,' she said, remembering her strict upbringing at the hands of her puritanical father. 'Steak and three veg every night, Christ's the head of his church, I'm the head of the house, and my word is final.'

'You want to expand on that?' Curtis asked gently.

Kate decided that it was time Curtis knew a little more about her.

'Malcolm is a member of the New South Wales Liberal Party, the equivalent of your Republican party, but he's also a born-again Christian and here in New South Wales and in Canberra the Christian Right is doing its best to take over politics.'

'Sounds a bit like 1600 Pennsylvania Avenue,' Curtis quipped. 'Do the Christians have much say in politics in this country?'

'More than people realise. A mega church was opened by the Prime Minister, and the Christian lobby groups are not only gaining a lot of power in the parliament in Canberra but here in Sydney as well.'

'Move over Jerry Buffett!'

'Got it in one,' Kate said. 'It all went to hell and back in a hand-basket on our third wedding anniversary. I'd been out and bought a lovely bottle of Château Latour and two prime fillets of beef. Malcolm arrived home with two of his political cronies in tow and they proceeded to have a bloody prayer meeting in my living room, and then they drank the wine! After the prayer meeting the three of them moved onto pre-selections. Anyone who was divorced, pro a woman's right to choose, wasn't married or – horror of horrors – supported gay rights, didn't get a look in.'

'As you've probably noticed it's pretty much the same with a lot of the Republicans back home. Was politics the only reason?'

'Not really,' Kate confided. 'About two years into the marriage, Malcolm started nagging me to have children. Said it would be good for his image.'

'Not a great reason to start a family,' Curtis sympathised gently.

'Exactly, so after he cut off conjugal rights, I went off to Yale.'

'Has he remarried?'

'About a month after the divorce came through, to another politician,' Kate said with a wry smile. 'They're welcome to each other. I felt like I'd won a "get out of jail card".' Kate reached for her wine. 'What about you, mystery man?'

'Marriage?' Curtis shook his head. 'I've been close a couple of times and sometimes I think it would be nice to come home to someone, but it would take a special kind of woman to team up with someone in my line of work.'

'Afraid you're going to talk in your sleep?' Kate teased.

Curtis grinned. 'We take a vow to be silent, even in our sleep, but from what you've told me being married to a politician couldn't have been easy either.'

Kate looked thoughtful. 'You know, I don't think it was just the politics, although I was never cut out to be a politician's wife. It was more the mixture of politics and religion and the belief that theirs is the only tram to be on that really started to turn me away. They're such hypocrites.'

'It can be quite an extraordinary force, this religion thing,' Curtis observed. 'The problem with religions is that they're all based on faith rather than logic. You can no more argue with a Muslim terrorist who's convinced he or she is going to heaven for blowing up a bus stop on behalf of Allah than you can with a president or prime minister who is convinced he or she is being guided by God.'

'Yet as a species we've always needed something greater than our-
selves to believe in,' Kate replied. 'Look at the bloody Greeks and
Romans, they had a raft of Gods to go to war for – Apollo, Mercury,
Zeus – and heaven help you if you offended them, yet who believes
in them now?'

'I'm not sure we're any more enlightened,' Curtis responded. 'The
Muslims think the Christians are wrong and the Christians think the
Muslims are on the wrong trolley bus, although I've often wondered
what the women suicide bombers are going to do with seventy vestal
virgins,' he added with a grin.

After dinner, as they walked back to the Park Hyatt, Curtis put
his arm around Kate's slender waist and she found herself thinking
seriously about getting to know him a lot better.

At Sydney's Kingsford Smith Airport, al-Falid was boarding the last
flight to Melbourne. In the morning, he would link up with Cathay
Pacific's direct service to Beijing.

CHAPTER 62

THE HARBOUR OF THE TARGET CITY

The sinister signal emitted from the last of the pingers embedded in the rocks covering the cross-city tunnels on the bottom of the harbour echoed quietly and relentlessly in the lead diver's headphones. He swung the receiver through an arc of 20 degrees to confirm the direction of the last pinger's signal. He checked the bearing with his compass, but as he reached for the communication cord to signal to those behind he was moving on, something knocked the receiver from his hand.

The diver froze and waited, forcing himself to keep calm, and mouthing a silent prayer to Allah for protection of the mission. Whatever it was didn't return. Probably a small shark, the diver thought, and he reeled the receiver's safety line in and re-established his bearings. He gave a short tug on the communication cord, signalling again that it was time to move forward.

The long and painstaking journey along the bottom of the

harbour had taken over an hour and a half. The lead diver signalled that he'd reached the final pinger and the team gently descended to the rocks that marked the top of the western cross-city tunnel. Getting the negative buoyancy of the canisters right and working in the dark had not been easy, but the team had practised for weeks, perfecting their deadly art off a deserted beach on the south coast. The team leader felt his way to the last of the cylinders and the team unhurriedly manoeuvred their cargo into position. A Port Jackson shark scurried out from the rocks while above the divers, the deep throb of twin outboard motors could be heard as one of the rich and powerful infidels brought a large boat back to its berth. Leaving his team to connect the last container to the others, the lead diver checked his depth gauge and compass and swam off on a predetermined bearing to the north, slowly paying out a long line of detonation cord from a lightweight reel. Each cylinder was shaped to direct the blast upwards, and each contained 50 kilograms of ammonium nitrate. 2.5 kilograms of plastic explosive were embedded in the centre of the ANFO and the detonators were all connected to the detonation cord. The lead diver knew that explosives behaved differently under water and the deeper the cord was laid down, the faster it would burn. He had learned his trade in Iraq, near the headwaters of the Persian Gulf, and he'd calculated the timing of the blast down to the last second.

The al-Qaeda frogman felt for the pylons underneath the Jeffrey Street wharf, in the shadow of the harbour bridge. He surfaced beneath the wharf and reached for the bag on his belt that contained a mobile phone with special circuitry that would set off the detonation cord as soon as the phone was rung. He located a steel strut beneath the centre of the wharf, connected the detonation cord to the phone and hid it among the barnacles just above the high water mark on the strut. He looked out across the dark surface of the harbour where he could see the *Destiny* passing beneath the massive bridge and heading towards Clarke Island. The harbour island was uninhabited at night and the shallow waters around it provided a perfect rendezvous to collect the team. He gave the phone on the strut a final check and slipped beneath the water.

CHAPTER 63

THE PARK HYATT HOTEL, THE ROCKS, SYDNEY

Curtis guided Kate into the lift. The dinner, the wine and Curtis' ability to make her laugh had weakened Kate's resolve.

'We should have a nightcap,' Curtis whispered.

'And just what might your definition of a nightcap be, Curtis O'Connor?' Kate challenged. Curtis' face was close to hers. She could see that his eyes were a smoky blue.

'Champagne or whiskey,' Curtis replied in the Irish brogue she found so attractive.

Kate Braithwaite, this man is trouble. Remember the rule. Don't get involved with someone you work with, Kate reminded herself.

'I think whiskey,' she said softly, deciding to rebel against 'the rule', parting her lips as he kissed her very slowly and very softly.

Kate wandered out on to Curtis' balcony while he cracked ice into two crystal glasses. The ferries had stopped running for the night and Sydney Harbour was quiet but beautifully powerful and captivating. Kate took a long, relaxing breath, taking in the smell of the sea breeze that was coming through the Heads and ruffling the waters below in swirling 'cats' paws'. To the south, dark clouds were gathering, signalling a storm was on the way.

Kate glanced back into the hotel room. Curtis had finished pouring the drinks. His tanned face was relaxed and his dark hair slightly tousled as he put a CD into the machine. The soft tones of Madeleine Peyroux drifted out to the balcony. If she was honest with herself, Kate thought, she'd been attracted to him from the day he'd met her in the foyer of the CIA Headquarters, and it wasn't just his lean, fit body and mischievous blue eyes that drew her in. The physical attraction had only deepened as she'd discovered his agile mind. Kate smiled inwardly at how well he'd handled her angry lecture on DNA and she decided she was entitled to a fling.

She glanced to her left, up towards the massive bridge that towered over the hotel. A lone fishing vessel, the *Destiny*, was passing slowly underneath the bridge as it headed towards the outer harbour. Opposite Curtis' balcony, the huge white sails of the Sydney Opera House reached majestically toward the night sky. Kate soaked up the city harbour she loved.

'Twelve-year-old Jameson's. The proper Irish stuff,' Curtis said, handing Kate a glass and standing closely beside her on the balcony.

'Prost,' Curtis whispered, softly clinking his tumbler with hers.

'Prost. Mmm. That is *so* good. Like malted honey.' Kate could feel the old whiskey warming her, dissolving any last minute misgivings.

Curtis' hand moved lower and she felt a surge of warmth between her legs as she let him slowly explore her thigh. He put his glass down and when he reached for hers, she relinquished it willingly, and pressed herself against his body. He kissed her gently, his lips soft, warm and tasting of whiskey, then he kissed her more urgently and she responded with her tongue as he held her tight. Kate parted her legs to allow his thigh between hers.

Kate groaned as he slowly undid the zip on her white linen pants and she moved against his finger as he gently explored her. She reached for his zip but it caught; unhurriedly, he helped her pull it down. He was growing in her hand and she groaned again as he kissed her.

'I think we should do this,' Curtis whispered.

'I think we should too.'

Kate leaned her head against his shoulder as they walked towards the bedroom. He stepped back and slowly unbuttoned her shirt.

The small voice was back, annoying and persistent. 'This man has too much finesse. He's bad news. You're just another conquest.' Kate banished the voice by concentrating on undoing Curtis' leather belt. He released the clip on her bra.

Kate closed her eyes and groaned again as she felt Curtis run his hand very slowly down her back and over the outside of her thigh.

Curtis kissed Kate's breasts and slowly licked and sucked her hard, erect nipples. He searched Kate's tongue with his own and as she reached for him, she found that he was hard and wet.

Curtis moved his hand slowly between her thighs and caressed her, gently at first, and then more powerfully.

'Fuck me, Curtis,' Kate whispered, guiding him into her.

As their tongues found each other, Kate could feel herself rising on a huge wave.

'Oh fuck me, Curtis! Fuck me!' she urged softly, her voice catching in her throat as the wave took her still higher.

She wrapped her arms more tightly around his broad shoulders and pushed against him in perfect harmony with the increasing power of Curtis' lean, muscled body, the wave taking her higher and higher.

'Oh fuck,' she whispered urgently. 'Oh fuck! I'm going to come! Oh fuuu . . . ck!' Kate's lightly tanned and freckled face was contorted in exquisite pain as Curtis too, let out a muffled cry and she felt him convulsing inside her.

Kate basked as she slowly surfed the wave into the beach. Curtis held her for a very long time, kissing her softly, and gently stroking her back.

CHAPTER 64

SYDNEY HARBOUR CONTROL TOWER, SYDNEY

Deputy Harbour Master Murray Black drove along Hickson Road in the pre-dawn darkness, past the stone convict buildings and on towards Dock No. 5 and the main entrance to the container docks that lined the west side of the central business district of Sydney. The headlights of Murray's battered Saab probed through the rain that was falling in silvery sheets. It was going to be one of those foul weather days that made control of the busy harbour even more difficult, but not even the rain or the 45-knot westerly that was blowing could diminish Murray's good spirits. Today marked his tenth year as a deputy harbour master. After a stint in the Australian military Murray had finally agreed with his wife that a young family shouldn't be pushed from pillar to post, and he'd joined the Sydney Ports Authority. It had been a wrench to leave the Army but his experience as an operations officer had been a good match for Sydney Ports, who needed men and women trained to be calm in a crisis and make instant, common sense decisions.

The entrances to Sydney Harbour and the nearby Port Botany were strictly controlled to the extent that ships' masters often complained about excessive red tape, but Murray knew that it was one of the safest maritime environments in the world and he intended to do everything he could to keep it that way. Fit, wiry and not overly tall, Murray Black had a rugged face and light blue eyes. His blond hair was kept short in a regulation military haircut; some habits died hard.

Today was his daughter Louise's eighth birthday. As Murray approached the security gates and the guardhouse that marked the entrance to the container dock and the port control tower he smiled to himself, recalling his daughter's pleas the night before as he was watching television after the family had been out late-night shopping.

'Can we go to Luna Park for my birthday, Daddy? Please, please, pleeeeease. Can we?'

'We'll see, little one. Daddy has to work tomorrow so we wouldn't get there until after lunch.'

Louise crawled onto his lap, put her arms around his neck, rested her blonde head on his shoulder and whispered, 'I love you Daddy, can we go please?'

Murray glanced out towards the kitchen where his wife Anthea was preparing dinner. Anthea rolled her eyes and raised her eyebrows, as if to say 'Daddy's girl has you wrapped around her little finger. How are you going to get out of this one?'

' Please, Daddy, please, pleeeeease?'

'Okay. If that's where you want to go, little one, that's where we'll go. Mummy can bring you and the boys in on the train in the morning and I'll meet you there after I finish my shift,' Murray said, giving his daughter a kiss and again looking across to Anthea.

She shook her head and smiled warmly.

Murray pulled up behind a semi-trailer in the waiting bay in the middle of Hickson Road, the traffic sloshing past intermittently on either side. It had been over thirty years since he'd been to the fun park in the shadows of the northern pylons of the bridge. It was a toss-up as to who was more excited – Louise or the six-year-old twins, Jonathon and Matthew – and although Anthea wasn't letting on, Murray knew that she was pleased too. It was about creating family memories. As they'd made love together that night, Anthea had whispered, 'We're so lucky, Murray. I love you.'

'I love you, too,' he'd replied.

CHAPTER 65

THE APPROACH TO SYDNEY HARBOUR

As the dawn broke over the Pacific Ocean, Captain Arne Svenson, the Swedish captain of the *Ocean Venturer*, stepped quietly onto the bridge of the massive tanker. Svenson was a tough professional who had dedicated his life to the sea; no matter what time of the day or night he was always on the bridge hours before any ship under his command entered a port. He glanced in the direction of the helmsman and was mildly irritated to find that Mussaid ibn Khashoggi was on duty. Not that the swarthy Saudi Arabian wasn't competent, quite the reverse. He was arguably one of the most professional and reliable men in the tanker's entire crew, but Arne had been around seamen and the sea for nearly forty years and there was something about Khashoggi that made him uncomfortable. The Saudi never relaxed and Captain Svenson was convinced he had some sort of chip on his shoulder, but his early attempts to find out what that might be had been met with surly denial.

Acknowledging the greeting of his first officer, the Captain checked the tanker's position on the GPS and then checked the chart. They were abeam of Point Perpendicular, less than 100 nautical miles from Port Jackson and the entrance to one of Captain Svenson's favourite harbours. More importantly, the tanker's arrival in the port would coincide with the high tide. The *Ocean Venturer* had a draft of 14.2 metres and the UKC, the under keel clearance, was critical. He knew that Port Jackson's next high tide was 1.7 metres and that it would occur at 10.05 a.m. He also knew that the Western Channel of the harbour was dredged to a minimum of 13.7 metres at mean low tide. The critical points were the tops of the two tunnels the authorities had built on the harbour floor; even at high tide the massive tanker would clear them by barely a metre.

Captain Svenson thanked the duty steward for the mug of hot coffee and sank into the big leather chair that he'd worked a lifetime to win. Driving rain was lashing the reinforced glass on the bridge that towered over the *Ocean Venturer's* wide deck, with its jigsaw puzzle of interconnecting pipes and winches. A great mass of foaming water exploded over the tanker's huge bow but the *Ocean Venturer* barely registered the vibration. Svenson had a deep respect for the awesome power of the sea but the waves would not trouble him or his ship today. As if to underline his judgement the *Ocean Venturer* smashed through another wave, causing dark, foaming water to cascade over the decks only to disappear into the scuppers, spent and defeated. He glanced at the radar screen. There was a small blip on the screen, about 10 nautical miles further inshore.

'She's a bit bloody close in this weather,' Svenson observed.

The First Mate nodded. 'Small cargo vessel. The *Jerusalem Bay.*

She's due to dock just after us. My guess is that she's making heavier going than we are and probably doesn't want to be out in this weather longer than necessary. I've been keeping an eye on her.'

Svenson grinned. A 3-metre swell could make life very uncomfortable aboard a small container vessel. He glanced at the radar again. Well to the north, off the tanker's starboard quarter, one and occasionally two fainter blips were showing on the screen.

'And those?' the Captain asked.

'A couple of ocean-going tugs, the *Montgomery* and the *Wavell*, also due in Sydney at the same time as us.'

'Who'd be a tug driver,' Svenson observed sympathetically. He'd started out in tugs and he knew the sheer hell of a watch spent strapped in and hanging on through a long night, the deck pitching and rolling relentlessly beneath you.

'A warship, the *HMAS Melbourne*, is due out of the harbour this morning as well and she'll be followed by a car ship, the *Shanghai*, but otherwise, there's nothing else to bother us,' the First Mate said.

CHAPTER 66

SYDNEY HARBOUR CONTROL TOWER, MILLER'S POINT

The semi passed through security and Murray Black inched forward in the rain. The hydraulically controlled posts in front of the gate disappeared into the road, the light turned green and Murray drove off Hickson Road and pulled up at the guardhouse.

'Morning, Frank.' Murray flashed his Sydney Ports Authority identification card and gave the security guard a smile. Frank waved and a second set of security posts disappeared, opening the entrance to the vast concrete dock. Murray drove onto the secure area of the docks and turned right towards the Sydney Ports Authority Control Tower at the far northern end. Slowly, he swung his car into the small parking compound at the base of the control tower.

'Bugger!' he muttered as the wind blew his umbrella inside out. The Best and Less $2 special was no match for the westerly that was driving rain across the open docks. Murray bolted up the narrow staircase on the outside of the tower, unlocked the door, wiped his face and stood dripping rainwater onto the carpet in the lift well. The tower might be an engineering marvel but it had one of the slowest lifts in the world, he thought, as he waited for the tiny capsule to come down from the operations centre, 76 metres above him. After what seemed an eternity, Murray stepped into the lift and pressed the button for it to return to the top. He could feel the lift rocking as it ground its way up the middle of the concrete tower. He stepped out and made his way up a few stairs into the operations centre – a large round capsule on top of the tower that provided 360 degree vision around the city and the harbour. The tower had been deliberately sited above the most dangerous part of the harbour where ships were blind to each other's movements around Miller's Point.

'Morning, Bob.'

Bob Muscat, the duty operations officer, waved a greeting from his desk. He was leaning into one of several microphones arrayed in front of him, talking to the Captain of a Royal Australian Navy guided missile destroyer that was just rounding the sea buoy at the Heads.

'Harbour Control, *HMAS Melbourne* is rounding junction buoy, over.'

'Romeo, *Melbourne*, this is Sydney Harbour Control, report departing Line Zulu and have a safe voyage.'

'A pleasant overnight leave?' Bob asked, leaning back from the microphone. The two had served together in the 5/7th Battalion, a mechanised cavalry regiment and there was an easy camaraderie between Murray and the short, dark-haired ex-Major.

'Late-night shopping,' Murray said, rolling his eyes. 'Why is it that most women at shopping centres are fourteen pick handles across the arse?'

'With husbands and barge-arsed kids to match,' Bob replied. 'You can't have your ice-cream until you finish your bloody hamburger!' he said with a grin.

Murray steadied himself against the roll of the tower, which was designed to flex in high winds, and then made a move towards the coffee that was quietly percolating near a whiteboard that held the current information on arrivals and departures. The whiteboard was there as a backup in case any of the four big computer screens on each duty officer's desk ever crashed. Each officer had a split screen with a detailed display map of both Sydney Harbour and Port Botany. Another screen held arrivals and departures, and at the flick of a cursor either Murray or Bob could haul up the information on any ship. A third screen was controlled by a joystick linked to dozens of cameras that covered every part of both ports from the tops of buildings and other critical points. The image on the screen on Murray's desk was beamed in from a camera near Sydney Airport; it was shaking even though the camera was anchored in an armoured box to protect it on days like today. Despite the weather, Murray had no difficulty in seeing the details of a tanker that was preparing to depart from Port Botany.

He scanned the digital meters above the whiteboard. No wonder the camera was shaking. The wind was touching 53 knots from the west. The tide had turned and at 0.8 metres, it was on the flood. Two more digital displays showed local time and Greenwich Mean Time. It looked like it was going to be a pretty light day. Only one large car ship was departing in the morning. He looked towards the west where the car ship was berthed a kilometre or so from the control tower. The *Shanghai*, a huge grey box towering over the loading dock at White Bay, was straining at her moorings and the wind was whipping grey smoke from the stubby smokestack at her stern. She had been emptied of the last of nearly 3000 cars from her eighteen decks and the engineers were firing up the huge diesels in preparation for departure. A break in the driving rain allowed Murray to scan the horizon. As the night sky gave way to the grey of the dawn he could just pick out the long jagged peaks of the Blue Mountains, and he noticed that another bank of thick black clouds was rolling in from across the Western Plains. To the east he could see Shark Island and beyond that South and North Head; between them, a Manly ferry was smashing its way past Bradley's Head, one of the tree covered promontories that marked the turn towards the inner harbour.

He looked back to the whiteboard. The arrivals board was a little busier with the 80,000-ton tanker, the *Ocean Venturer* scheduled to berth just across from the tower at the big oil terminal at Gore Cove. She would be closely followed by the *Jerusalem Bay,* a regular visitor to the port.

'Who are the *Montgomery* and the *Wavell?*' Murray asked.

'A couple of ocean-going tugs on their way to Vanuatu. They're coming in to refuel,' Bob replied.

'They must be having quite a time of it out there,' Murray observed. The waves were rolling powerfully and relentlessly across hundreds of miles of the Pacific, venting their fury against the jagged but unbowed face of North Head in thunderous explosions of boiling green water and foam.

'Who'd be a tug boat driver,' Bob said, echoing the words of Captain Svenson. It seemed to be a universal view.

'Or a pilot,' Murray replied, as he focused his binoculars on the small but powerful boat that was heading out to sea from its base at Watson's Bay. The bright yellow pilot boat rose momentarily on the crest of a big wave before ploughing defiantly into the base of the next one. The passage to the rendezvous point with the *Ocean Venturer*, 4 nautical miles off the Heads, would be rough and arduous. 'It's bad enough up here,' Murray added, lowering his binoculars and glancing at the photograph of Anthea, with Louise and the twins, that he kept on his desk.

In a few short hours it was going to get unimaginably worse.

CHAPTER 67

AN INNER-CITY WAREHOUSE, SYDNEY

Jamal had been at the warehouse since before dawn calculating the extra time he would need to allow for the stormy weather and reflecting on the first part of the attack that was to be launched with the trucks. One by one, his drivers arrived, all of them suicide bombers, all of them sombre and determined. The videos with their last messages to family and friends had all been completed. They had woken to their last day on earth. Soon they would all be reunited with Muhammad, peace be upon him, and they would receive the rewards of heaven that were promised to all those who martyred themselves for the Faith.

Jamal disappeared into the warehouse's small bathroom to conduct the ablutions that were mandatory before a Muslim could get in touch with his creator. First he washed his face, then his arms to the elbows, then he wiped his head with his wet hands and finally, he washed his feet. When the other cell members had completed washing, they laid out their prayer mats on the floor of the workshop where they'd loaded the trucks with ammonium nitrate. Jamal began the dawn prayer.

Allahu Akbar! Allahu Akbar!
God is Great! God is Great!

Bismillah ir-rahman ir-rahim
In the name of God, the Most Gracious, the Most Merciful . . .

Ash-Hadu Allaa Elaaha Ellaa Allah, Wahdahu Laa Shareeka Lah –
I bear witness that there is no other god beside God. He alone is God; He has no partner.

Assalaamu Alaikum
Peace be upon you.

Jamal stored his prayer mat beside a battered filing cabinet in the office at the back of the workshop. He spread the big map of the city streets over his grimy wooden desk and switched on the scanner that was tuned in to the channel the tow-truck operators used to monitor police responses to traffic accidents. As a back up, he switched on a local radio station that encouraged people to call in with information on the traffic. Unbelievers, he thought bitterly. Soon the information on the traffic would jam the airwaves but so far the roads seemed remarkably clear. One truck had been allocated to the first target and the other six would attack in pairs with the routes to each of the four targets being worked out to the last second. Nothing had been left to chance.

Just before 8 a.m., Jamal kissed each one of his seven drivers three times on the cheek.

'Your place in heaven with the Prophet, peace be upon him, is assured,' Jamal said, and he pointed toward the seven trucks lined up at the front of the warehouse. 'It's time for you to start your engines. May Allah, the Most Kind, the Most Merciful go with you.'

Less than an hour later, Jamal parked his car at the boatshed to which the *Destiny* had returned after picking up the divers from Clarke Island. After final prayers, he and two other crewmen opened the old boatshed doors and one of them started the winch motor. Jamal took his position at the wheel as the *Destiny* slid down the greased rails into the water. He pressed the starter button and the big re-conditioned diesel throbbed into life, and he waited until his two crew members had rolled the doors on the boatshed shut. As he pushed the heavy chrome throttle levers forward, Jamal switched on the radios that operated on the Police and Harbour Control channel. Almost immediately, there was a transmission on Channel 13.

'Harbour Control, this is the pilot aboard the *Ocean Venturer*; we are now rounding the sea buoy and inbound on the Western Channel with four tugs in attendance.'

'Romeo *Ocean Venturer,* you are cleared to proceed to Gore Cove.'

Jamal nodded to himself in satisfaction. The trap was closing. The first truck was due to be detonated at 10.05 a.m., followed by the others in quick succession.

CHAPTER 68

THE PARK HYATT HOTEL, THE ROCKS, SYDNEY

K ate stirred, her head still on Curtis' chest. Curtis brushed her
blond locks away from her forehead and kissed her gently.
There was a faint aroma of whiskey on her breath.

'We smell of sex,' Curtis whispered, as he ran his hand slowly over
her back, moving down to Kate's small, firm bottom.

'Mmm,' Kate responded dreamily.

The rain was lashing the balcony where they'd stood the night
before, and Kate moulded herself against Curtis' body. It was one of
those mornings where they both would have preferred to stay in bed.

'Come inside me,' she said softly, caressing his hair.

Back in her own bathroom, Kate set the shower nozzle to 'pulse' and
let the warm water massage her back. Her thoughts were in turmoil.

The sex the night before had been urgent and passionate but this morning they had taken their time. The roguish Irish-American she'd decided to have a fling with had also turned out to be a wonderfully caring lover. As she stood in the shower she reflected on the early morning. She had felt very comfortable and safe with this man but she tried repeating her mantra with more conviction. 'This is a one night stand and I can't get involved with him.' But Kate knew Curtis was different and realised her mantra had come a little too late.

The rain lifted momentarily as Kate and Curtis arrived at the State Crisis Centre on the southern side of the city. Kate spotted a postbox as she waited for Curtis to pay the taxi fare.

'Won't be a second. I'll just post this off to Richard,' she said, waving a postcard. In an instant Curtis recognised the photograph. He remembered he'd seen it years ago at the time of the Sydney Olympics. Taken when the smoke of the fireworks heralding the start of the 2000 Olympic Games had cleared, the word 'Eternity' was illuminated in the middle of the arch of the Sydney Harbour Bridge.

'Wait. Can I see that?'

'Want to read my mail now that we've slept together?' Kate saw that Curtis was serious. 'What's wrong?'

'Do you remember Kadeer's first warning attack – "beneath Eternity"?'

'You think this is what he was referring to?' Kate frowned as she suddenly recalled something else Kadeer had mentioned in his broadcast.

'It's possible,' Curtis replied. 'Is there a significance to the relationship between Sydney and the sign of Eternity?'

'It has its origin in the 1930s,' Kate explained, remembering a
long-forgotten history lesson. 'Arthur Stace was a homeless alcoholic
who lived on the streets of the city. One night he went in to the Baptist Tabernacle in Darlinghurst where he listened to a sermon from
a minister called Ridley. Ridley was urging his congregation to think
about their mortality and the promise of eternity with God and he
concluded his sermon with something like "Eternity! Eternity! Oh
that this word could be emblazoned across the streets of Sydney!"
For the next forty years, while the city slept, Arthur Stace wrote
'Eternity' using yellow chalk in an immaculate copperplate hand in
every doorway, and on every footpath, train station and ferry wharf
where he thought people would see it.'

Curtis shook his head.

'You don't think this has anything to do with the warning?'

'On the contrary, I think it might have everything to do with it.
It's just that you seem to have swallowed the Britannica.'

'I'll take that as a compliment but if you're right, Kadeer is going
to attack the Sydney Harbour Bridge, and now that you mention it,
there was something else in Kadeer's video. Didn't he say that his first
warning would take place where we least expect it, beneath Eternity
where the windmill has been stolen?'

'The stolen windmill has always confused me,' Curtis admitted.

Kate looked thoughtful. 'Can we get access to a computer at the
State Crisis Centre? I vaguely remember that the area known as
Dawes Point was once called Windmill Hill.'

'Let's go,' Curtis said.

By the time they reached the foyer, Brigadier Anthony Davis, the Australian Defence Force's senior liaison officer in the State Crisis Centre was waiting for them.

'Curtis! Welcome back. Great to see you again.' The Brigadier shook his old friend's hand warmly. 'Still travelling in the company of beautiful women?' he said, turning to Kate.

'Brigadier General Anthony Davis,' Curtis said, introducing him to Kate.

'I prefer Anthony,' Davis said, shaking Kate's hand firmly and smiling. 'Welcome to Fort Fumble. We're preparing for a major anti-terrorist exercise so you've come at the right time. The Prime Minister's hosting APEC next week and the politicians are in a flap,' Davis said as he pressed the lift button for the sixth floor. 'The State Police Minister's here at the moment,' the Brigadier said, 'and right now he's arguing with Cecil Jensen, the Defence Minister's minder over who has responsibility for announcing the exercise. Since responsibility is something that the politicians here only take when the news is good it's really an argument about who gets their mug in front of the cameras.'

Curtis grinned. 'Who's winning?'

'Last time I looked, the Police Minister. Right royal little turd he is too. Pardon my French,' Davis added, holding his arm against the lift door for Kate.

'I've heard it all before,' Kate replied easily.

'But I wouldn't think he'll be winning for too long,' Davis continued as he swiped his card at the door to the State Crisis Centre. 'I'm putting my money on the Defence Minister. He's an even bigger turd with an ego the size of the Great Wall of China and when he finds out, he'll be in front of a camera in a flash.' The Brigadier closed the door and led them into a large room. Two big plasma screens were operating on the far wall.

'Paul! Great to see you again, buddy!' Curtis and the senior policeman shook hands.

'Assistant Commissioner Paul Mackey,' Brigadier Davis said, introducing Kate to the Commander of the NSW Police Counter Terrorism Group. Mackey's handshake was firm. He had a strong jaw and a craggy face, etched with the lines of nearly forty years' experience as a tough, no-nonsense policeman. He was one of the most respected men in the force.

'Paul kept me sane when we worked on the Olympics together and if he wasn't so fond of politicians, I could learn to quite like him,' Davis explained to Kate.

'I have a file on the brigadier and one day I'm going to make it public,' Mackey replied. 'This is the nerve centre for the city. There are several hundred cameras in Sydney, and sometimes we pick up things going on at bus stops that the participants would rather we didn't.' He glanced at the left-hand screen and gave Curtis a wink. The images on the screens were constantly changing, and the one on the left had rotated to a bus stop in North Sydney. Oblivious to the hidden camera, a well-dressed man in his early fifties and a much younger woman in an elegant black suit were in a steamy embrace in a bus shelter. As the man's hand disappeared down the front of the woman's pants the cameras rotated and an image of traffic gridlock in Market Street appeared. The other screen showed an image from a camera focused on the waters around Bradley's Head.

'These people in front of us,' Mackey continued, pointing to the occupants of two long rows of desks with computers that were linked to various other headquarters around the city, 'are from the police, ambulance, fire brigade, the military, health department and any other experts we need to call in; and behind us is the conference table for the main participants. When it's up and running, as it will be for APEC in the next few days, the State Crisis Centre is chaired by the Premier and it includes the Ministers for Police, Transport, Roads, Emergency Services – all the usual suspects.' Commissioner Mackey glanced at the group near the main conference table where a heated discussion was still going on between the Police Minister and the senior advisor to the Defence Minister.

'Have you got an office where we can get online?' Curtis asked.

'Sure. Follow me. Anything I can help you with?'

'More the other way around, although I hope we're wrong.'

Kate googled 'Sydney Observatory' and 'Dawes Point'. 'Bingo,' she said as she pulled up a web page that referred to Windmill Hill. Next to a photograph of the Sydney Observatory taken in 1874 was an explanation of the early history.

'Here it is,' Kate said. 'In 1796 a windmill was built on the hill overlooking the first settlement in Sydney Cove and it became known as Windmill Hill, and later Observatory Hill when a fort built by Governor Hunter was turned into the Sydney Observatory.'

'But more importantly,' Curtis said, looking over her shoulder, 'the canvas sails of the windmill were stolen. Did you ever have a problem with TCDD in this town?' Curtis asked, remembering the email Echelon had intercepted.

'Tetrachloro dibenzene-para-dioxin?' Davis replied, a quizzical look on his face. 'As a matter of fact we have. They found some pretty alarming levels among the fishing community so they've banned prawning and trawling in the harbour. Why?'

Curtis reached into his leather briefcase and took out a copy of the intercepted email.

'This is too much of a coincidence,' Davis said. 'Stolen windmills might sound a bit far-fetched but when you couple it with Eternity and this email, Sydney might be the curtain-raiser to whatever Kadeer's planning for his final solution. No offence, mate, but our government's decision to get involved in this clusterfuck in Iraq has made Australia a much more likely target and, as targets go, they don't come any bigger than Sydney Harbour. I'm not sure how much time we have but if you're right, we need to sharpen our readiness. TAG East is on its normal notice to move but we can bring that down as a precaution,' Brigadier Davis said. He picked up the secure phone and pushed the speed dial button for the Vice Chief of the Defence Force in Canberra.

'TAG East?' Kate whispered to Curtis.

'Tactical Assault Group. These guys have got two of them. One in their Special Air Services Regiment on the west coast and one here on the east coast in their commando battalion.'

'His minders are here now in the middle of a shit fight with the Police Minister,' the brigadier explained, winking at Curtis. 'Always polite . . . Sir.' Davis grinned as he put down the receiver. 'The Vice Chief is Navy and oversees operations. Member of the Commonwealth Club, wears leather patches on the elbows of his tweed jacket and reminded me I wasn't flavour of the month in Canberra.'

'Off the PM's Christmas card list again?' Curtis asked.

'I doubt I'll ever get over it but life must go on,' Davis said with a wicked grin. 'The Vice Chief will brief the Chief of the Defence Force and he'll speak with Little Lord Fauntleroy.'

'Little Lord Fauntleroy?' Kate asked, bemused.

'Defence Minister. Likes to be kept informed if we so much as change our underpants, let alone readiness states. These days you need his permission to fart,' Davis said. 'At least we can brief his minder on our plans to get the TAG ready to move, which might save us some time down the track.'

'Out of the question,' Cecil Jensen, the Defence Minister's chinless, pasty-faced advisor insisted pompously. 'If it ever gets out that we've brought forward readiness states because the earlier low life in this country stole the canvas sails from a windmill,' he said, glaring at Curtis and Kate, 'we're going to look as if we've panicked over a "maybe" based on history.'

'It's not about how you or the Minister "look" Cecil,' Brigadier Davis responded coldly. The longstanding animosity between the military man and the jumped-up advisor was obvious. 'It's about taking a sensible precaution until we can investigate this more thoroughly. Right now we're in a very fortunate position. Normally a lot of our Blackhawk helicopters are based in the north,' he explained to Curtis and Kate, 'but they arrived down here yesterday for APEC.'

'We've already taken a decision to base some of them in Sydney,' the Minister's advisor sniffed.

The Brigadier looked to the right and then to the left. 'Nope. No media around to catch that one, Cecil. And it's irrelevant. The point is they're here and so are the Tigers.'

'Tigers?' Kate said to Curtis.

'Armed reconnaissance helicopters,' Curtis replied. 'They pack a powerful punch.'

'Even on the present notice to move,' Brigadier Davis argued, 'there's no guarantee we can get either the Tigers or the TAG in the air quickly enough if something happens. See that, Cecil,' Davis said, pointing to the screen on the right. 'That's the *Ocean Venturer*.' The massive bow of the tanker had come into view with no fewer than four tugs shepherding the great ship around Bradley's Head and lining her up for the passage where she would pass under the bridge and move on to her berth at Gore Cove.

'That's the largest crude oil tanker ever to berth in Sydney and you'll notice it's almost high tide. At low tide she would hit the bottom of the harbour. That's a huge target, and if these guys are right,' he said, glancing at Curtis and Kate, 'I'd be a damn sight more comfortable if the TAG was sitting in those choppers with their rotors spinning.'

'Fortunately those decisions are not up to you, Brigadier,' Jensen said haughtily, picking up one of the secure phones that would connect him with the Defence Minister in Canberra.

'For once I agree with Cecil,' the NSW State Minister for Police said, reinforcing his claim while Jensen was distracted. 'It's way too early to involve the Commonwealth. This is a State responsibility and I'll be holding a media conference to make that point very shortly.'

Tony Davis, Paul Mackey and Curtis O'Connor exchanged glances. The *Ocean Venturer* was in full view making a slow but inexorable run down to the bridge.

The small, dark-skinned man picked up his mobile phone. The foremast of the cruiser *HMAS Sydney* had been positioned as a memorial to the men who had taken part in Australia's first naval engagement of World War I. As the colossal bow of the *Ocean Venturer* went past, the man pushed the send button on a text message: 'Passing the war memorial now'. Modern technology meant that Jamal would be able to read the exact moment the message was transmitted and calculate the precise time the tanker would pass over the tunnels. The man's mobile phone beeped and he read Jamal's reply: 'May Allah, the Most Kind, the Most Merciful, be with us'.

Further down the harbour, another of al-Falid's men standing near the Jeffrey Street Wharf at Kirribilli read the message as well. The text on the location of the tanker and Jamal's response had also been copied to seven other mobile phones.

Every driver had calculated his start based on the exact time that the tanker's bow passed the memorial, all designed to get each of them to their targets at the right moment, all linked to the tanker passing over the tunnels on the harbour bed.

The operation had begun.

Further to the south, the weather had thrown the flight schedules at Sydney Airport into chaos and the controllers were battling to clear the backlog.

CHAPTER 69

THE CONTROL TOWER, SIR CHARLES KINGSFORD SMITH AIRPORT, MASCOT

Mick Hammond was on the third-last shift of his career. He was a big man with a moustache to match and he had a relaxed view of the world; a temperament that made him ideally suited to the extraordinary stresses associated with being an air traffic controller. With forty-two years up next month, he was the longest serving controller among Sydney's team of highly trained professionals.

The tower had been built at the edge of the main runways, alongside General Holmes Drive, less than 300 metres from where the freeway passed into a tunnel under the taxiways and the main north–south runway. In three days, the little holiday shack at Sussex Inlet on the south coast would become home for him and his wife of thirty-seven years, but at the moment, Mick had no time to reflect on fishing or pottering about in his tool shed.

All of the control tower's nine operator consoles were at full capacity. Although the weather of the morning was lifting a little and controllers could now see the ends of the runways jutting into Botany Bay, the backlog was fierce. Across the road in the Terminal Control Building, another team of controllers was battling to get aircraft out of their holding patterns and onto final approaches where they could be handed over to the tower. The director for 'Runway 34 Left' focused on one of a dozen radar blips on the screen in front of her. The blip that was slowly moving to the point where she'd vectored it for final approach into Sydney was Qantas Flight 12 from Los Angeles with 458 passengers and crew onboard.

'Qantas 12 you have 6 miles to touchdown. Wind is 15 knots from the west, gusting to 20 knots. Contact the tower on 120 decimal fife when established.'

'Qantas 12.' The Captain reached up to change frequencies as his co-pilot prepared to land. On the ground the queue for take-off was getting longer.

'Qantas 438, heavy, ready.'

'Sydney Tower, G'day. Expect a delay, there are twelve aircraft in front of you.' Even when the pressure was intense Mick Hammond was unfailingly polite and good humoured. Qantas 438 lined up behind a Singapore Airlines 747 bound for London. There were now thirteen aircraft waiting to take off and Mick glanced at the 'Maestro Ladder', a computerised schedule which showed the landing sequence on the radar screen in front of him. Every rung was occupied.

As the controllers battled to get aircraft on the ground, seven non-descript trucks rolled along with the morning traffic. The first truck turned into Missenden Road near Sydney University, heading for Dunblane Street. Two more trucks headed west towards the M5, destined to pair up with two others heading east on the same expressway. The last two trucks had reached their positions; one at Woolloomooloo and one on the north side of the harbour at Neutral Bay.

'Sydney tower, Qantas 12 established.' Mick allowed himself a smile. Inbound aircraft were stacked up like poker chips in the dark clouds above the tower and the pilot sounded a little terse. Being forced into a long holding pattern after a 16-hour flight from Los Angeles would not have improved the mood on the flight deck.

'Sydney tower, G'day.' Mick's voice was calm as he looked to the south. Through the gloom he could see the powerful landing lights of the big 747. Several sets of lights were lined up behind it. Mick Hammond was about to clear the big inbound 747 when his headphones crackled again.

'Sydney Tower, this is Lifesaver One. Request immediate departure. We have a Medical One at the Light Horse Interchange on the M7.'

Mick glanced over his right shoulder towards the heliport on the eastern side of the airfield. With a priority clearance from the ground controller, the brightly coloured red and yellow rescue helicopter was already moving towards the threshold of the east–west runway. The weather and impatient driving was being blamed for a horrific accident involving a semi-trailer, a bus and three cars at the intersection of a dozen twisting overpasses that connected the M4 and

M7 near the foothills of the Blue Mountains. Seven people had been critically injured, and three of these were fighting for their lives. To clear Lifesaver One would mean it would have to cross the path of the incoming 747.

Mick weighed up his options in an instant. The 747 was just inside the separation required for the chopper to cross in front of him, but was probably getting low on fuel and to send him around again would do nothing to ease the controlled chaos in the clouds above him. Mick calmly reached towards the big console in front of him and pressed the button that connected him with one of the departure directors in the terminal control unit across the highway.

'I'm going to clear him direct but he'll need to stay below 3000 feet, Shelley, if you can do that?'

'No problem, I'll whack in a quick flight plan.' All of the controllers were under enormous stress but they took the load off one another in whatever way they could. It was one of the most professional operations in the world.

'Lifesaver One, you're cleared direct to the Light Horse Interchange below 3000 feet. Rapid departure on Runway 25, Qantas 12 inbound from the south on 34 left. Winds gusting to 20 knots from the north-east, contact departures when airborne.'

'Lifesaver One, much obliged.' As the medevac chopper tilted forward and powered down the cross runway, Mick shot the hastily made-up flight stick around the slide that connected adjacent controllers.

'Qantas 12, you're cleared to land runway 34 left. Lifesaver One crossing in front of you. Rapid exit Bravo.' Mick Hammond glanced at the needles on the weather computer on his console. 'Crosswinds are now gusting to 25 knots,' he added.

'Qantas 12.'

'Damn it.' The captain of the Qantas 747 peered through the fast-moving windscreen wipers and the driving rain. In the distance the white lighting that marked the edges of the main runway stretched into the gloom but on the left, the lights of the visual approach system flashed in and out of sync as the onboard computers adjusted the glide path and the weather played havoc with the instrument approach being flown by his co-pilot.

'25 knots, I'll take her, Jim.'

'Handing over,' his co-pilot said good-naturedly. The two worked well together. One day, Jim thought, he would be sitting in that left-hand seat and he'd be qualified to land this baby in a strong crosswind, but not today.

CHAPTER 70

SYDNEY

On board the *Destiny* Jamal was monitoring the police channel and commercial radio. The traffic on the M5 was heavy, although moving freely, but the lead item on the 10 a.m. news bulletin was a sign of things to come. 'In breaking news there have been reports of an explosion outside the Chinese Consulate in Dunblane Street near Sydney University. As yet there is no information on casualties but police and ambulances are on the way and police are advising motorists to avoid the area around Church Street and Parramatta Road.' Allah be praised, Jamal thought. Hopefully the casualties would be heavy.

The driver of the second eastbound Hino checked his odometer as he entered the short tunnel that dipped down and then flattened out underneath the Cooks River. He was confident that the truck in front had already passed through on the way to the airport. It was precisely 300 metres to the point where the tunnel crossed under the middle of the river and as the number '3' tumbled into position on the odometer, the driver heard the muffled roar of an explosion in the westbound tunnel next to him. Slamming on the brakes and oblivious to the small car that rammed into the rear of his truck, he raised his fist in defiance, and shouted '*Allahu Akbar*! God is Great!'. In his last act on Earth he pressed the button on the firing mechanism. Two tonnes of ANFO exploded in a deafening roar of flame and smoke. Most of the ferocious blast was directed upward towards the roof of the tunnel, breaching it and sending a plume of debris through the river above. In both of the tunnels the desperate screams of the injured and dying, many with limbs torn from their bodies, could be heard above the roar of water pouring in. Near the exits of the tunnels, drivers and their passengers were abandoning their cars and struggling to escape the rising waters. Many of the victims didn't make it, pushing against the concrete of the tunnel roof in a desperate search for air.

In the State Crisis Centre, Brigadier Davis, Curtis and Kate watched in dismay as the cameras switched from the shattered Chinese Consulate to the devastation in the flooded tunnels under the Cooks River, then just as quickly, the left-hand screen switched to the short tunnel under the main runway. It was engulfed in flames, flying debris and billowing clouds of black smoke.

The explosion under the runway tunnel rocked the control tower but Mick Hammond's years of training only took a fraction of a second to kick in.

'Qantas 12, Sydney Tower, Abort! Abort!' but his commands came too late. The 747 had settled its nose wheel onto the runway and the Captain had already applied reverse thrust.

'What the—' The Captain of Qantas 12 stared in disbelief as the main runway erupted in front of him. He increased the big engines to full emergency reverse thrust and the passengers were thrown forward as the 400-ton aircraft hurtled towards the clouds of smoke. Concrete and shards of steel-reinforcing rods were raining down on the runway.

'Jesus Christ!' The Captain swore as a lump of concrete bounced off the hardened windscreen, cracking it from top to bottom.

'120.' '110.' The co-pilot kept calling the speed but it was not dropping fast enough and in a moment they disappeared into the boiling black inferno that had engulfed the airstrip from below. The hole in the runway sheared off the bogies under the port wing in an instant and as the Captain felt the big aircraft slew to the left, he instinctively applied opposite rudder and eased the reverse thrust on the port engines, but to no avail. The port wing hit the ground, tearing off the port outer engine and puncturing the wing tanks. The 747, with 458 passengers and crew, careered across the grass verge of the main runway slamming into the Singapore Airlines 747 bound for Heathrow. It was fully laden with fuel.

Kate held her hand to her mouth as she watched the two 747s explode in a ball of fire, the distinctive white kangaroo on the red tailfin protruding from the inferno. A short while later, passengers with their clothes on fire could be seen jumping from one of the rear doors that was over 6 metres above the ground.

Assistant Commissioner Paul Mackey was on the phone to the Police Operations Centre. 'Close all tunnels in the Sydney metropolitan area,' he ordered quietly.

Brigadier Davis was on another phone talking to General Howard, the Commander of Special Forces whose command post did not have the images from the RTA cameras. The Minister's advisor tapped the Brigadier on the shoulder.

'The Minister wants those helicopters in the air – now!'

'One more word, Jensen, and I'll fucking deck you,' Davis replied, a cold anger in his blue eyes. 'Not you, Sir,' he said calmly, resuming his conversation with the Special Forces Commander. 'From what I've got on the monitors here, they've attacked the east- and west-bound M5 tunnels under the Cooks River and under the main airport runway. A 747 was landing at the time and it's collided with another one on the ground. The police are closing all tunnels in the metropolitan area but their greatest concerns are the tunnels under the harbour. You should also be aware that an 80,000-tonne oil tanker is in the harbour en route to Gore Cove. You'll get a message down the command chain from the Minister to scramble whatever you've got.'

'Thanks to the fucking Minister's office, not much, and I doubt we can get our hands on more than three or four Blackhawks,' General Howard replied bluntly. 'The Tigers are doing some minor maintenance but I'll put a cracker up their arse and see what we can get airborne. I'm also scrambling two RHIBs out of *Waterhen*,' the General said, 'so between us and the NSW Police, the harbour will be as safe as we can make it, although I'd like a lot more firepower and those Tigers might have been handy.'

Both General Howard and Brigadier Davis knew that the Black-hawk helicopters were only lightly armed with 7.62mm machine guns, and the RHIBs – the sinister, black Rigid Hull Inflatable Boats – each carrying ten Special Forces troops were also lightly armed. Hopefully it would be enough, but the attack seemed to be thoroughly planned. Without the Tigers they might be in trouble, Davis thought, as he watched the images of the two burning 747s on one screen and the ambulances and fire engines struggling to get through the traffic chaos around the eastern and western entrances to the tunnels, on the other.

'I think we should close the harbour,' Assistant Commissioner Mackey said to the Police Minister after the Brigadier had briefed them both.

The Minister looked uncertain.

'And cancel the ferry services?' the Minister's advisor asked.

'We don't know the extent of this attack yet,' Mackey replied, and 'if the bridge is also a target the ferries might be an unnecessary complication,' he said, giving the ministerial advisor the benefit of a steely glare.

On board the *Destiny*, Jamal's monitoring of the police and Harbour Control channels was interrupted. He nodded in satisfaction as another series of beeps on his mobile phone announced that the two remaining trucks were on their way to their detonation points.

Earlier in the day, Anthea Black had stood in front of the mirror on the back of her wardrobe door. She was tall and slim, her jeans fitted snugly and she'd put on the white cotton shirt Murray liked. 'Not bad for an old girl,' she said to herself. She had turned thirty-four a month ago. Anthea had looked up the City Rail timetable on the internet and the 9.47 out of Strathfield would get them to Milsons Point just after 10 a.m. From the train station, it was a short walk down to Luna Park and hopefully the kids would've had nearly enough by the time Murray joined them for lunch. Anthea shook her head and smiled. Who am I kidding? she thought. She'd already suggested to Louise that they postpone Luna Park to another day because of the rain. 'The weatherman said the showers will ease later in the day,' Louise had said. Eight going on forty-eight, Anthea had thought.

'Come on, birthday girl, are you nearly ready?'

'Coming, Mummy, I'm just doing my hair the way Daddy likes it.'

'The boys, dressed in their yellow raincoats and hats, pulled faces in the direction of their sister's room.

Bob Muscat and Murray Black stared at the scenes shot from outside the Chinese Consulate that were being relayed to the Harbour Control Tower. Firemen were desperately trying to bring the blazing building under control but a burst gas main was fuelling the fire, while ambulances were rushing the wounded and dying to the Royal Prince Alfred Hospital a short distance away. There, as at other hospitals around the city, the medical staff were on full alert. A second camera was relaying images of the carnage at the airport. The intense heat from the burning aviation fuel was preventing the fire trucks from getting as close as they wanted to, and despite massive amounts of foam being sprayed over the burning wreckage, the fire was still out of control. Murray Black's thoughts for those still inside the aircraft were interrupted by the ring of the red phone that connected the Harbour Control Tower with the State Crisis Centre.

'Paul Mackey here, Murray; the harbour is to be closed to all shipping until we get a better handle on the extent of this attack. What have we got moving at the moment?'

'The *Ocean Venturer* is abeam Fort Denison en route to Gore Cove,' Murray said. 'A big tanker can't be stopped so we'll have to let her berth. The remaining traffic is the *Jerusalem Bay*, a small container vessel already in the Eastern Channel and two tugs, the *Montgomery* and the *Wavell*, just astern of her. I can turn the tugs around easily enough but at best I can only hold the *Jerusalem Bay* where she is.'

'Thanks, get her to stop and let me know if there's a problem.'

'Understood, Paul. I'll get her to drop anchor in the channel.' Murray Black put down the phone and brought Bob Muscat up to date.

As he reached for the Channel 13 mike, Murray Black could see first one, then another RHIB tear out of *HMAS Waterhen* just to the west of the Harbour Bridge. Commandos armed with light calibre weapons, including a MAG-58 machine gun mounted in the bows, clung grimly to the safety ropes. The boats were powered by twin

Mercury 250 outboard motors, reaching well over 50 knots; their blunt bows rose off the choppy harbour before crashing back on to the surface, foaming spray exploding either side.

'All Ships. All Ships. All Ships. This is Sydney Harbour Control. Port Jackson from the Parramatta River in the west to Line Zulu in the east is closed until further notice. There is to be no, repeat no maritime movement of any description without the express authority of Harbour Control. *Ocean Venturer* you're exempt. Proceed to Gore Cove, acknowledge.'

Captain Svenson and the pilot on the bridge of the *Ocean Venturer* exchanged glances.

'Very odd,' the captain said, looking back towards the *Jerusalem Bay* and the two big tugs following her. 'I wonder why they're closing the harbour?'

'Not sure,' the pilot replied, 'but we should be thankful they don't want us to try and stop.' The distance required to stop a fully laden tanker of this size at full speed was measured in nautical miles, and even at slow speeds, she couldn't be stopped quickly.

Captain Svenson nodded to the First Mate, who reached for the radio mike and transmitted the response.

'This is the *Ocean Venturer,* received and will comply.'

The only other person on the bridge was the helmsman, Mussaid ibn Khashoggi, who maintained his inscrutable expression as he looked towards Kirribilli Point. When they were abeam of the Prime Minister's residence coming up on the starboard side, he would act. Keeping one hand on the helm, he felt for the .380 Beretta pistol in the pocket of his dark blue overalls.

'Romeo, *Ocean Venturer*, out to you,' Murray replied. *'Jerusalem*

Bay, you're to go astern immediately and drop anchor in your present position, acknowledge.'

Murray Black lifted his binoculars and focused them on the bridge of the *Jerusalem Bay* as he waited impatiently for an answer. The cargo deck was packed to capacity with 10-tonne containers.

'Might be fairer to hold the tugs off Balmoral?' Bob ventured. 'It's still bloody rough outside the Heads.'

Murray Black nodded, his attention still on the *Jerusalem Bay.* The container vessel was now abeam of Clarke Island.

'*Jerusalem Bay,* this is Harbour Control, acknowledge my last transmission.'

Murray Black's eyes narrowed; something was not right. The *Jerusalem Bay* was silent and she kept coming.

Bob Muscat raised his binoculars to the west. A fishing boat, the *Destiny,* was powering past Darling Harbour towards the bridge.

'*Jerusalem Bay. Jerusalem Bay!* This is Sydney Ports. You're to go astern and drop anchor where you are and await further instructions. Acknowledge!' Murray Black's voice held a note of urgency as he let go of the transmit button.

'Don't stand on the seat, sweetheart. People have to sit there,' Anthea Black said to her daughter as the 9.47 from Strathfield arrived at Town Hall station in the city.

'Harbour Control, this is the *Jerusalem Bay,* can you read me, over?'

'About bloody time,' Murray Black muttered as he pressed the transmit button on his radio mike.

'She's speeding up,' Muscat observed, as he watched the container ship through his binoculars, the *Destiny* momentarily forgotten.

'My apologies, Harbour Control, we've been having trouble with our radios. Could you say again?'

The captain of the *Jerusalem Bay* had a thick, Middle Eastern accent, something that would not normally have bothered Murray except that his gut feeling that something was amiss on the *Jerusalem Bay* was getting stronger. As he focused his binoculars past the ship's stern he realised that Bob Muscat was right. The wake turbulence behind the container ship was increasing alarmingly and she was now headed for Fort Denison. If she passed the fort Murray knew that it would be impossible to anchor her before she reached the bridge.

'The port is now closed to all traffic. You are to go astern immediately, drop anchor and await further instructions. Acknowledge and comply.'

'The two tugs have speeded up as well,' Bob said, still sweeping the harbour with his binoculars, 'and there's a fishing vessel approaching the bridge from the west,' he added. The *Destiny* was moving out from the entrance to Darling Harbour. 'She's got to be doing about 12 knots as well. What the bloody hell's going on, Murray?' Harbour speed limits were strictly enforced and when they were exceeded the culprits were almost always pleasure craft operators. Commercial operators were well aware of the heavy penalties and breaches by them were very rare.

'I've got a nasty feeling about this, Bob,' Murray said, glancing at the images of the blazing 747s before refocusing on the bridge of the *Jerusalem Bay*.

'Harbour Control, this is the *Jerusalem Bay*, we have a very sick crewman on board with acute appendicitis. Request permission to continue on course.'

Murray Black shook his head. 'I'm not buying that, Bob. Their radio was working perfectly in the approach to the Heads. If he's that sick they would have radioed ahead hours ago.'

Muscat nodded grimly. 'I agree, the police will need to board her.'

'It'll have to be the military, she's too high for the police to board while she's underway.' Murray Black reached for the direct line to the State Crisis Centre.

At the Army's big military base at Holsworthy, 40 kilometres to the west of the city, the commandos were working furiously to try and reverse a readiness state that had allowed them leeway to train on the ranges adjacent to the base. Without any warning, 'four hours notice to move' had suddenly dropped to 'move now!'. Normal activities had been cancelled and with the professionalism for which they were renowned they had managed to assemble their personnel, issue live ammunition and get three of their big Blackhawk helicopters airborne, each carrying ten commandos. Over at Luscombe Field the aviation mechanics were working as fast as safety would allow to get the two Tiger armed reconnaissance helicopters they'd been maintaining back on line, and the soldiers were racing against time to configure the gun turrets with 30mm rounds and 68mm rockets.

The pilot of the lead Blackhawk scanned the harbour ahead as the three aircraft powered towards the city. They were staying low, just above the water, and at 190 knots the airspeed indicator was nudging into the red. The co-pilot turned back towards Major Gould, the commander of Team Delta, who was still finalising his plans and speaking on another frequency to the section commanders in the other two aircraft.

'Eagle is trying to contact you on Channel 3,' the co-pilot said.

Gould acknowledged the message with a double squelch on the internal mike and he switched channels.

'Sunray Delta over.'

'Good morning, this is Eagle.' Major Gould didn't need the General's call sign. He would have recognised the deep modulated tones of his commander anywhere, not to mention the eccentricity of General Howard's radio procedures. No matter what the crisis, General Howard always managed to sound as if he was contemplating a Sunday afternoon stroll in the park.

'In addition to escorting the *Ocean Venturer* to her berth at Gore Cove we have another small problem.'

Major Gould grinned. General Howard's definition of small problems invariably meant you were about to be issued with a very large shit sandwich.

'There's been a slight change of plans. The *Jerusalem Bay* is being difficult. She's refusing to comply with the Port Authority's orders to drop anchor and is still heading up the harbour, just reported passing Clarke Island. Board her and, short of garroting the captain and his miserable crew, persuade the little pricks to comply. They're claiming they've got a sick crewman onboard but Harbour Control's not buying that and neither am I. And be careful, the way this morning's shaping up, they may not be all they seem.'

'Roger Eagle, out to you. Blackhawk 02, Blackhawk 03, proceed with the escort of the *Ocean Venturer* and take up your positions on the port and starboard side of the bridge. I'll deal with the cargo ship.'

The two Blackhawks acknowledged the altered plan as all three choppers climbed to get over the Harbour Bridge. The lead Blackhawk and Major Gould's men veered to the south, using the Opera House for cover as they lined up for a risky fast roping drop onto the decks of the *Jerusalem Bay*. The other two Blackhawks vectored on towards the big tanker that was now halfway between Bradley's Head and Kirribilli Point, 2 kilometres from the bridge.

In the State Crisis Centre, Curtis and Kate were looking at the left-hand plasma screen which had been switched to track the big tanker and the *Jerusalem Bay*. The *Destiny* was lurking behind the northern lee of Fort Denison.

'As well as the tunnels, I think we should also shut down the bridge and the trains,' Assistant Commissioner Mackey said to the Minister for Transport, who had arrived with his advisor in tow.

'All of them?' the Minister asked.

'Certainly those trains that are running in the city.'

'That will effectively shut down the entire network across every electorate,' the Transport Minister's advisor warned.

'Trains are not my long suit, Minister,' Brigadier Davis interjected, ignoring the political advisor, 'but let me give you a feel for what's going on here. We've been attacked in three separate locations. As yet we don't know for sure that it's Khalid Kadeer, but like the attacks on September 11, these have got Kadeer's stamp of careful planning all over them. There's no guarantee this operation is over or that it won't include a subway attack along the lines of the one in London. We're talking about the protection of people's lives and if closing the network under the city means the rest of it comes to a halt, I think people in the other electorates will understand.'

As the 9.47 from Strathfield pulled into Wynyard, the train driver looked at his watch, still angry over the bawling out he'd received from his supervisor earlier in the day. He'd tried to explain that on the day in question there'd been a succession of red lights all the way from Parramatta to Hornsby. To make up lost time he would have had to exceed the speed limits. 'I don't give a shit,' his supervisor had said, his own job on the line. 'Get it through your thick head that we run on time.'

The officer on duty at Wynard leaned into the microphone.

'The train on Platform One goes to Hornsby. The next stop is Milsons Point. Alight at Milsons Point for Luna Park.'

The driver of the northbound Hino could hear the sirens as he left Woolloomooloo and headed towards the western harbour tunnel. Jamal had ensured that the detonation point for both 5-ton trucks was towards the southern ends of both tunnels, so that they did not interfere with the explosives on top of the tunnels at the northern end.

Across on the north shore, the other driver, Abdul Azzam, could hear the sirens too. He calmly drove down the main approaches that led to the Bridge and the eastern harbour tunnel, smiling as he contemplated the carnage he was about to inflict on those who had taunted him. Even though it was past peak hour the traffic was still heavy. Abdul's one regret was that the infidel's buses didn't use the tunnel.

'*Allahu Akbar*. God is Great,' he whispered, touching the detonator in his pocket. The entrance to the tunnel under the harbour symbolised his entry into heaven and it had just come into view. Down on the harbour, he could see the huge bow of the *Ocean Venturer* but the sirens behind him were getting closer and, as he glanced in his rear-view mirror, he began to worry that he might not make it to the tunnel.

As the police car sped past with its siren wailing and blue lights flashing, the officer in the passenger seat signalled angrily for Azzam to pull over. Two hundred metres further on, the police car slewed to a halt across the entrance to the tunnel. An officer leapt out and held up his hand. The traffic in front of Azzam began to slow down.

Murray Black dialled Anthea's mobile. He'd left two messages asking her to ring him but for some reason she hadn't answered.

'Hi. You've reached Anthea Black. If you leave a nice message, I'll get back to you as soon as I can.'

'Sweetheart, please call me when you get this,' Murray said. There'd been no answer at home and he wondered if she'd been listening to the news. 'I need to know you're all okay.' Murray put his mobile back on his desk beside the photograph, reassuring himself that she'd just forgotten to turn her mobile on. He turned back to the *Jerusalem Bay.* The two tugs were still ploughing along behind her and he reached for the radio again.

On the *Montgomery,* Malik al-Falid directed his helmsman to hold course behind the *Jerusalem Bay* as three Blackhawk helicopters appeared over the top of the Bridge. One helicopter disappeared towards the city and Malik watched as the other two took up positions protecting the *Ocean Venturer.* Through his binoculars he could see the infidel's soldiers sitting in the back and in the side seats. 'SAS or perhaps commandos,' Malik mused. With four missiles they could only afford one miss. He reached for the microphone dangling above him.

'*Wavell,* this is *Montgomery,* take out the helicopter on the starboard side of the tanker, we'll take out the one on the port side,' he said, nodding to the missile teams who were out of sight in the aft area of the *Montgomery's* bridge. The time for subterfuge had passed.

'It will be a pleasure, *Montgomery. Allahu Akbar!*'

Murray Black swung his binoculars onto the *Montgomery* and then the *Wavell*. He stared in disbelief as men dressed in black suddenly tumbled from the tugboats' bridges. On each of the powerful tugs crew members raced forward and tossed tarpaulins to one side to reveal .50 calibre heavy machine guns mounted in the bows. On either side of each bridge crew members were hoisting missile launchers onto their shoulders and bracing themselves against the heavy steel gunwales as the tugs ploughed on towards the city. The missiles were instantly recognisable.

'Jesus Christ,' Murray muttered, reaching for the red phone to the State Crisis Centre.

'Davis.'

'Murray Black, Tony, Harbour Control. Get your cameras on the tugs. They're both armed with .50 calibre machine guns in the bows and I've counted four stinger missile teams, two on each tug. *Montgomery* is maintaining a westerly course behind the *Jerusalem Bay* but the *Wavell* is altering course towards the northern side of the harbour and is heading towards the *Ocean Venturer.*'

'Thanks, keep me posted,' Davis replied evenly, as he reached for the direct line to the Special Forces Headquarters.

The orange sensor light flashed urgently on the instrument panel in front of the pilots in Blackhawk 02 and an alarm shrieked in their headphones.

'Missile inbound! Bearing 1800!' the co-pilot yelled and instinctively the young captain at the controls of the Blackhawk hauled on the collective and banked the aircraft in a sharp turn, turning the heat of the engine cowlings away from the missile. The warning and the manoeuvre had been carried out quickly and calmly by one of the world's best trained pilots but it was too late. Travelling at over 1500 kilometres an hour, the deadly missile slammed into the side of the helicopter's engine cowling.

Murray Black watched in horror as the Blackhawk disintegrated in an explosion of flame and smoke. As if in slow motion, the giant blades separated from the aircraft, lifting into the air before falling into the sea, narrowly missing one of the RHIBs escorting the *Ocean Venturer.* The tail rotor flew across the harbour, disappearing into a luxury penthouse not far from the Prime Minister's residence. The fuselage broke into three jagged pieces. The bodies of the commandos and the pilots fell into the harbour as first one RHIB and then the other broke from their escort positions. From the decks of the *Montgomery* and the *Wavell,* cheers of celebration and defiance could be heard across the harbour, accompanied by shouts of '*Allahu Akbar*! God is great!'

The nose on Blackhawk 03 tilted forward sharply as the pilot powered forward in search of cover. As the aircraft banked and disappeared from view behind one of the northern pylons of the bridge, the missile warning alarm on the instrument panel lit up. Suddenly deprived of the heat signature of the helicopter the guidance system on the stinger automatically searched for another target. Having given priority to the harbour tunnels, more police were now racing to close the bridge and although they'd successfully shut down the myriad of lanes from the city side, traffic was still coming on to the bridge from the north. Murray Black watched helplessly from the control tower high above the harbour. The deadly smoke trail left by the missile's rocket motors was surreally graceful. The missile curved to the south as its guidance systems locked on to the exhaust of a 30-ton semi-trailer. The guidance computer onboard the missile wasn't about to make any subtle distinctions over heat signatures and the huge truck exploded in a flash of flame and smoke. A bus and several cars travelling either side of the semi collided and veered across four lanes of the Bridge.

'Harbour Control, this is the pilot on board *Ocean Venturer*, a Blackhawk has just exploded on the port side!' Not sure what was happening, both the pilot and the captain of the *Ocean Venturer* were acutely aware that they were standing on over 60,000 tonnes of light crude.

'Romeo, *Ocean Venturer*,' Murray replied calmly. 'The harbour is under terrorist attack. As yet we're not sure what the main target is but maintain your present course.'

Ibn Khashoggi again felt for the cold steel of his Beretta.

Abdul Azzam judged that there might just be enough room to get past the front of the police car and he floored the accelerator. Veering around the slowing traffic, he raced for the gap between the police car and the tunnel wall, aiming at the policeman waving frantically for him to stop. Abdul said a silent prayer to Allah as the policeman standing in the middle of the gap stopped waving and drew his pistol. Sixty metres, 40 metres – his jaw was set as the truck gathered speed down the ramp. Two bullets whistled past the truck and then the left side of the windscreen shattered as one of the policeman's bullets found its mark. Two more shots ricocheted off the top of the cabin roof as Azzam held his nerve, the detonator in his right hand. The policeman was desperately loading another magazine and the side window of Abdul's truck shattered as his partner opened fire, but in an instant the speeding truck was on them both. The heavy bumper struck the front fender of the police car, spinning it in a grinding crunch and a shower of sparks, killing one of the policemen instantly. The truck was now up on two wheels and Azzam fought desperately to bring it under control. He braked, bounced off the wall and fishtailed down the long ramp towards the bottom of the harbour tunnel and the heavy traffic ahead. Coming the other way in the western tunnel, the driver of the other truck was closing on his detonation point.

The earlier attacks were being covered live on the Hino's radio, but suddenly the broadcast was interrupted. 'This is a message from the Sydney Harbour Tunnel Authority. We are closing both tunnels. All vehicles are to clear the tunnels as soon as possible.'

Azzam once again put his hand on the detonator as he approached the southern end. 'You are too late, far too late,' he said, and as his brothers had done before him, he raised his fist in defiance.

'*Allahu Akbar*! God is great!' he screamed. Ten kilograms of plastic explosive detonated nearly 2 tonnes of ammonium nitrate and the heavy steel casing directed the massive blast towards the roof of the tunnel.

In the control tower Murray Black and Bob Muscat were watching the tugs and the *Jerusalem Bay* and neither noticed the stubby plume of dirty seawater, carrying rocks, concrete and steel , rise only a metre or so above the harbour; nor did they notice a second plume moments later. The twin plumes of boiling water subsided, leaving two widening circles of oily foam on the surface of the rain-lashed harbour, belying the death and devastation below. Thousands of tons of water were pouring through the holes torn in the tunnel casings. As black smoke was forced out of the ends of both tunnels, the fires in the burning vehicles, along with the screams of the dying were slowly extinguished, replaced with the sound of the sea splashing eerily against the tunnel walls.

As the *Ocean Venturer* reached abeam the Prime Minister's residence on the end of Kirribilli Point, Mussaid ibn Khashoggi kept one hand on the helm and took out his Beretta with the other.

The blast was deafening. The pilot collapsed onto the steel deck, blood spurting from his neck. Khashoggi fired again and the First Mate collapsed beside the pilot. The Saudi helmsman calmly turned his pistol on the Captain and fired twice more. Captain Arne Svenson was dead before he hit the deck, a look of chilling understanding in his eyes.

Khashoggi moved the big throttles forward to full ahead. The engine on the *Ocean Venturer* was the size of a small building and weighed over 2000 tonnes. She only had ten cylinders but each of them was the size of a household water tank and the chief engineer looked up in alarm as the electronic telegraph suddenly registered maximum revolutions. He reached for the microphone dangling above him in the control room.

'Bridge, this is the engine room.'

Locking the rear access bulkhead, Khashoggi ignored the call from the engine room and the increasingly urgent calls from the tug captain of the *Wilberforce*. With override activated and control of the engines transferred to the bridge, 90,000 horsepower turned the massive 304 tonne crankshaft ever more quickly. Deep below the surface the *Ocean Venturer's* huge propeller thumped in ever-increasing revolutions. Khashoggi swung the small, stainless steel helm hard to port, transmitting 10 tonnes of hydraulic pressure to the big rudder. For a while, nothing happened, then degree by degree, the bow began to turn towards the city and the pylons on the southern shoreline. Mussaid ibn Khashoggi raised his fist. '*Allahu Akbar*! God is great! God is great!'

'Where are we, Mummy?' Louise asked.

'Wynyard, sweetheart. We get out at the next stop which is Milsons Point and guess what?' Anthea said, adjusting the yellow hat that had slipped over Matthew's eyes. 'We get to go over the big bridge!'

The twins' eyes widened as they looked at each other in delight, big smiles on their little faces.

General Howard weighed up his options. To use the lightly armed Blackhawk behind the pylon against the tugboats armed with stingers would be the modern equivalent of the Charge of the Light Brigade, but it was looking more and more as if the *Jerusalem Bay* was part of the plan. If Major Gould and his men were to have any chance of getting onboard, the tugs would have to be distracted. Whoever was behind this was a brilliant military planner, Howard thought grudgingly. If only he'd had the Tigers on line they could have engaged the tugs with missiles and heavy cannon. 'Fucking Minister. Fucking minders,' the General muttered as he prepared to issue fresh orders to the commandos in the powerful boats searching for life among the debris of the downed Blackhawk. General Howard reached for the radio handset.

'Team Charlie, this is Eagle, over.'

'Sunray Charlie, over.'

'This isn't going to be a picnic but I want you to distract those tugs and cover Team Delta for their assault on to the container ship, over.'

'Sunray Charlie, Roger, over.'

'Sunray Delta, copied, H-Hour in two, over.' Major Gould and his men on Blackhawk 01 were making final preparations for a fast rope assault, hovering behind the sails of the Opera House just above the water in Sydney Cove.

'Eagle, good luck, out.'

The General let out a deep breath. There was only one thing he hated more than not being in the middle of the action and that was sending his troops in to do a task that they weren't properly equipped for.

Captain Jeffery was in command of the two RHIBs and he didn't hesitate. He was angered by the loss of his mates in the Blackhawk and he'd hoped to find some of them alive, but the mission came first and he knew the dead and dying in the water would have it no other way. The *Jerusalem Bay* had just passed Fort Denison and in another few minutes she would reach the Opera House. Jeffery scanned the harbour with his binoculars. The rain was still coming down but beyond the Naval Base he could make out the dark shapes of the big tugs charging towards them. Jefferey called his second-in-command in the other RHIB.

'Charlie 2, this is Charlie 1, I'll take the tug on the right, you take the one on the left,'

'Charlie 2, Roger, over.'

'Charlie 1, Go Go Go!'

The RHIBs were capable of a staggering 60 knots and with the outboards screaming, the bow gunners hung on and opened fire on the tugs with their 7.62mm MAG-58 machine guns. They might as well have been firing at two charging elephants with a pop-gun.

Dozens of terrified residents in apartments in Kirribilli took cover on their floors as the bow gunners onboard the *Montgomery* and the *Wavell* returned fire. The sound of the heavier and far more stable .50 calibre machine guns was unmistakable, but Malik and his terrorists had an even bigger shock in store for the commandos. White-faced security guards at the Prime Minister's and the Governor-General's residences on Kirribilli Point crouched behind the biggest trees they could find. Dealing with unarmed protestors climbing onto roofs with banners was one thing; their training had not equipped them for this.

With the tugs distracted Major Gould didn't wait any longer.
'Go, go, go!'

The pilot powered Blackhawk 01 out from behind the Opera House, skimming the water and keeping the *Jerusalem Bay* between him and the tugs. At the last moment the commandos were crunched into their seats as the pilot shot the aircraft skywards over the container ship's bow, flaring and coming to a hover above the containers behind the foremast.

Major Gould grabbed the m-biter on his fast rope and leapt out of the helicopter, leading the rest of the commandos onto the containers nearly 6 metres below. The terrorists on the *Jerusalem Bay* opened fire from the bridge and two commandos fell from their ropes, their bodies bouncing off the containers into the harbour. The commandos who made it to the top of the containers raced forward, returning fire with Heckler and Koch 9mm sub-machine guns.

'What the fuck . . .' The captain of the *Wilberforce* swore as the massive tanker veered to port, away from the westerly course that would take them clear of the gunfire on the harbour and to Gore Cove.

'Pilot aboard the *Ocean Venturer*, this is *Wilberforce*, over.

'Pilot, this is *Wilberforce*, do your read me, over?' the captain of the *Wilberforce* asked urgently. There'd been no response to his query about gunfire on the bridge and if the tanker continued to turn it would eventually ground on the southern shore. For a tug captain to take over the pilot's control of a vessel in the harbour was unprecedented and it could cost him his ticket, but Captain 'Blue' Gilchrist had spent over twenty years on tugs and he'd never been involved in anything like this. He didn't hesitate.

'*Woolwich, Waverton, Werombi,* this is *Wilberforce,* am assuming command from the pilot,' Blue said calmly. He eased the throttles forward slowly to avoid ramming the big tyres on the tug's bow into the side of the turning tanker. The rain was heavier now, sheeting against the tug's windscreen and hissing onto the wind-whipped water. Blue Gilchrist applied maximum power and the twin 2500 hp Daihatsu diesels responded immediately.

'Give me full reverse on the starboard quarter, *Waverton,*' Gilchrist said.

'*Waverton,* romeo.' The young captain on the *Waverton* had only been certified the week before, and he was rattled by the downing of the Blackhawk and the carnage on the Bridge. As he pulled the steering joystick to the rear, the young captain pushed the *Waverton's* twin throttle levers too far forward. The engines responded instantly and beneath the big tug, the propellers that were surrounded by thick bronze casings spun through 180 degrees in an instant. The *Waverton* surged away from the tanker and the young captain realised his mistake. With a breaking strain of over 170 tonnes, the state-of-the-art nylon hawser was twice as thick as a man's arm but as the momentum of the powerful tug met the immoveable momentum of the massive tanker turning in the opposite direction, the hawser snapped like a piece of cotton and whipped back with the force of an artillery shell leaving the barrel of a gun. The crewman on the fore-deck had no chance. He was decapitated, his head making a ghastly bloodstained arc over the *Waverton's* bridge. The 80,000-ton tanker, its engines approaching full revolutions, kept turning towards the southern shore.

As the 9.47 from Strathfield climbed out of the subway under Sydney, the train driver could see a red light just past the tunnel exit. The track ahead looked clear. Still angry over his supervisor's stinging rebuke, the driver slowed the train but he continued across the Bridge towards Milsons Point on the far side.

'Shall we call Daddy and wave to him?' Anthea asked. Louise's and the boys' eyes lit up. Surprised to find four messages waiting for her Anthea pressed the speed dial for Murray.

'Where are you?' Murray demanded.

'On the train, darling, what's wrong?'

'Where's the train!'

'Just coming out of the tunnel on to the Bridge, why?' Anthea asked, bewildered by the tone of her normally calm husband.

'Can we speak to Daddy? Can we speak to Daddy!' the twins demanded.

Murray looked across to the Bridge, horrified by the sight of train carriages coming slowly out of the tunnel.

al-Falid's man standing above the Jeffrey Street Wharf had checked and double-checked the compass bearing until he could picture the imaginary line in his sleep. The Western Tunnel had been laid on a bearing of 178 degrees magnetic, and the 'line' ran through the right-hand corner of a bus shelter near the harbour's edge and across to a point on the Cahill Expressway, near where the expressway turned towards the Conservatorium of Music. The man waited until the centre of the turning tanker crossed his imaginary line and he pressed the green call button on his mobile. The mobile phone strapped to the pier beneath the Jeffrey Street Wharf at the bottom of the hill rang just once. The detonators ignited the detonation cord that ran across the bottom of the harbour towards the lethal cylinders on top of the tunnels.

Seconds later, all ten cylinders exploded in a muffled roar and a plume of foaming water shot up the starboard side of the tanker, like an anti-submarine depth charge. Only five of the cylinders were directly underneath the turning tanker's keel but the clearance was less than a metre, and it was enough. The blast ripped a jagged hole in the *Ocean Venturer's* outer hull.

Had it not been for a warning light flashing on the console in front of him, Khashoggi would not have even noticed the blast. 'Allah be praised,' he muttered. Several of the compartments that were designed to protect the environment from an oil spill were being flooded with seawater. With a full cargo of crude on board, this flooding would be enough to ground the tanker under the bridge, sealing the harbour like a cork in a bottle.

Curtis O'Connor and Brigadier Davis exchanged glances as the camera on the roof of one of the city's tallest buildings showed a wide shot of the harbour. At the top left of the screen, the tanker was still turning, the bow passing under the bridge at an oblique angle. At the bottom right of the screen, the *Jerusalem Bay* was almost abeam the Opera House, and there were several small black figures running across the top of the containers on the foredeck. In the middle of the screen, a fishing boat had just left Fort Denison where she appeared to have been sheltering from the firing. The *Destiny* was now heading west towards the tanker at full speed.

Davis reached again for the direct line to General Howard's Special Forces Headquarters a short distance away.

'I know you've got your hands full at present, General,' he said, 'but a large fishing boat's just broken out from behind Fort Denison and she's headed straight for the tanker.'

'Not exactly a good news day,' Howard grunted as he hung up the phone and reached for the radio.

'Tiger 01, this is Eagle, are you airborne yet, over?'

'Tiger 01, negative, loading ammunition, over.'

'As soon as you are, contact me on this frequency, out.'

'Fuck,' Howard muttered. Well, if they couldn't do anything about the tanker, at least they might be able to stop the *Jerusalem Bay*.

With the *Destiny*'s big diesel engine thundering beneath him, Jamal centred the laser beams on a point about 2 metres above the water line. As the two red dots came together on his computer screen he fired the port anti-armour rocket and then the starboard one. The first rocket breached the outer hull of the *Ocean Venturer* and exploded against the inner hull, a metre further in. The second rocket exploded as it breached the inner hull. The weight of millions of litres of oil in the amidships tank was immense and a powerful geyser of Kuwaiti crude shot out of the side of the tanker, spewing on to the surface of the harbour, blackening the white caps.

Further down the harbour, Captain Jeffery and his commandos onboard the flying RHIBs had their hands full as they pressed on towards the tugs. Both of the RHIBs still had more than 300 metres to cover and Malik al-Falid had one more weapon.

Malik ducked behind the control console as a burst of machine-gun fire ricocheted off the side of the steel bridge of the *Montgomery*. He nodded to the crew member crouching in the starboard wing with the rocket-propelled grenade launcher.

'The closer the better; wait till they get within 100 metres then hit them,' he commanded quietly.

The young Palestinian cell member raised the RPG-7 grenade launcher to his shoulder. The return fire from the commandos was continuous but they were struggling to get accuracy as the big RHIBs bounced off the water at high speed.

Steadying himself against the bridge, the Palestinian calmly aimed just in front of the bow and fired. Seconds later, the anti-tank grenade exploded with a deafening roar against the hull, killing three of the infidels instantly. As the shattered RHIB fell back to the choppy water, the big outboards were still screaming at full power and the commandos' boat was driven under the surface in a ball of exploding foam.

'*Allahu Akbar*! God is Great!' Malik clenched his fist as he drove the big tug at the men struggling in the water.

Fifty metres. Forty metres. Jamal raised his fist in defiance as he adjusted his course to avoid the geyser of oil spewing from the side of the tanker. Willing the *Destiny* to go even faster, he aimed the heavy boat towards the breach in the tanker's hull.

With a cry of '*Allahu Akbar*!' and confident of his place in heaven, Jamal calmly pressed the detonator moments before the bow of the *Destiny* slammed into the side of the stricken tanker. The shaped charge penetrated deep into the bowels of the *Ocean Venturer* and exploded in a deafening roar. Thick, black smoke and fuel-fired flames shot 70 metres into the air, engulfing the roadway above and the emergency crews who were working desperately to save those who'd been hit in the earlier missile strike. As the intense heat from the oil fire softened the asphalt on the roadway, people ran from the Bridge, fleeing from what had turned into a blazing car park. The fire generated temperatures in excess of 1000 degrees and the steel walls separating the amidships tank compartment from the others on the *Ocean Venturer* began to twist and buckle.

'Anthea, you're to pull the emergency brake now. Don't ask questions sweetheart, just do it,' Murray said quietly.

'But . . .'

'DO IT!'

Anthea found the yellow emergency handle near the doors. Above it was a warning of severe fines and imprisonment for improper use but Anthea trusted Murray with her life. With the distant gunfire on the harbour faintly audible, she pulled the handle and the train slid to a halt on the greasy tracks.

'What the—' The driver reacted angrily as he lost control of his train.

The captain of the *Jerusalem Bay* fingered the detonator in his right hand as he crouched below the shattered windows of his bridge.

'Cover me!!' Major Gould broke cover and fired several bursts from his MP-5 as he stormed forward towards the foot of the companionway that led to the bridge above him.

As he peered above the shattered port side glass, the Sydney Opera House was so close the captain could see the bars and entertainment areas inside. Reluctantly he realised that he would not be able to get his ship as far as the ferry terminals in Sydney Cove, but it was better to detonate now than not at all.

'*Allahu Akbar*! *Allahu Akbar*! God is Great! God is—

The detonator tumbled from the captain's hand as Major Gould burst in through the bridge's rear bulkhead, his MP-5 blazing.

Kate Braithwaite stared numbly at the plasma screen in the State Crisis Centre showing the fiercely blazing tanker.

'Jesus Christ!' Curtis said softly, as he put his arm around Kate's shoulder.

On the bridge of the *Montgomery,* Malik al-Falid tightened his seat belt as the *Montgomery* and the *Wavell* charged towards the Heads and the safety of the Pacific Ocean beyond.

'Keep a sharp lookout,' he ordered. 'The infidel will try to mobilise his forces.'

Onboard the *Melbourne* Keke Newbold steadied himself in his captain's chair on the starboard side of the bridge. As soon as he'd received word of the attack on Sydney, he'd turned the powerful frigate around and headed north back towards the Heads, demanding from his Marine Engineering Officer every last horsepower out of the *Melbourne's* big gas turbines. Her huge prop was throwing a 3-metre high rooster's tail of white water behind the stern. The phone beside him rang as the *Melbourne's* Principal Warfare Officer called from the operations room two decks below.

'Captain, this is the PWO, we've got an update on the situation here, Sir. You'd better come down and have a look.'

'On my way,' he replied brusquely, leaving the ship in the hands of the officer of the watch.

The operations room was lit with a green glow from the radar and fire control screens and as soon as he entered through the bulkhead Captain Newbold put his headphones on and took a call from General Howard.

'*Melbourne,* over.'

There was more than a touch of restrained anger in General Howard's voice. 'The two tugs are running for the Heads and they're presently west of Line Zulu. All commercial shipping's been suspended and you are cleared to destroy them, over.'

Keke glanced at the two blips on the radar operator's screen.

'PWO, sound action stations,' Keke said calmly.

'Hands to action stations, hands to action stations.'

'PWO,' Captain Newbold commanded, 'these are harpoon targets, let me know when we're in range.'

'Captain, Sir, harpoon targets 2412 and 2413 confirmed, ready to engage.'

'Engage,' Keke said without emotion.

'Birds away.'

Captain Newbold and his PWO watched while first one missile and then another left a track of phosphorescent blips across the ship's radar screens.

On the bridge above, Lieutenant Campbell focused his binoculars on the tugs that were now clear of Sydney Heads.

'Bastards,' he exclaimed, as he watched the *Montgomery* and then the *Wavell* explode into separate balls of flame.

Even among the chaos it had taken Murray Black barely 15 minutes to get across to Observatory Hill, a short distance from the train tracks. As he ran towards Anthea and the children the tears streamed down his face.

CHAPTER 71

CANBERRA

CNN's television images of the tanker fire and the burned out fuselages of the two 747s faded in front of a packed media conference in Canberra. The Prime Minister of Australia was visibly shocked as he addressed the nation. Flanked by a confused-looking Defence Minister and a grim-faced Chief of the Defence Force, the Prime Minister brought his speech to a close.

'These terrorists are murderous barbarians who have no respect for human life and human dignity, and my government will leave no stone unturned to bring the perpetrators to justice.'

The Prime Minister faced a flurry of questions about the ability of hospitals to cope, what might happen to Sydney and how people who were still employed might get to work. Michelle Gillard, the journalist who had covered Professor Imran Sayed's opening address at the bioterrorism conference, ignored the tabloid newspaper approach as to how the attack might affect the average worker in the street. She was asking the deeper questions about why this had happened.

'Prime Minister, we've all seen the declassified reports in which no fewer than sixteen intelligence agencies in the United States have concluded that the war in Iraq was a very big mistake. Those reports claim that the war is providing a training ground for terrorists and is attracting more and more young Muslim suicide bombers to the fundamentalists' cause. Will you finally concede that we're now a bigger target because of our unqualified support for the United States war machine and that as a result of our policies in the Middle East, the Muslim fundamentalists are gaining strength around the world?'

The Prime Minister looked rattled. He responded angrily. 'Now is not the time to be cutting and running from the war on terror. Now is the time to be redoubling our efforts to bring these terrorists to justice.'

'We've heard reports, Defence Minister,' another journalist asked, 'that you and your advisors blocked the military's decision to reduce their notice to move. I've heard claims that, had the military been authorised to move earlier, this attack might have been prevented. Can you comment on that?'

The Defence Minister blinked several times and looked even more confused. 'Those sorts of questions are best answered by the military,' he responded, looking at the Defence Chief.

The Chief of the Defence Force's left eyebrow rose quizically. It was one of those classic media moments and another flash lit the room as one of the *Herald's* most experienced photographers caught it for posterity. The relationship between the Defence Chief and his egotistical minister had just reached a new low and every journalist in the room knew it.

'I think it would be unwise to speculate on rumour before we have a full and thorough report on what has been a dreadful and dark day in Australia's history,' the Defence Chief replied diplomatically. 'I extend my personal condolences to those military families who've lost loved ones serving their country today and on behalf of the military, I extend our condolences to the wider community who've also suffered so tragically as a result of these attacks.'

BOOK THREE

THE SECOND AND THIRD WARNING ATTACKS

CHAPTER 72

THE SITUATION ROOM, THE WHITE HOUSE, WASHINGTON DC

As the enormity of the attack on Sydney dawned, the mood in the Situation Room beneath the Oval Office was again tense as President Denver Harrison and his war cabinet watched the video released on al-Jazeera.

'The loss of life in Sydney is to be regretted,' Dr Kadeer said, 'but of all the governments in the West, the Australian government is the most enthusiastic supporter of the United States war machine. This was just the first of three warning attacks. If the West does not change course and start to negotiate, more lives will be lost, on both sides.' Kadeer's face was expressionless.

'Even by the West's own figures,' he continued, 'over 3000 people, more than the total number killed in the Twin Towers on September 11, die every month as a result of your free-wheeling invasion of Iraq. The attack on Sydney is a small taste of what is to come if you don't take the opportunity to redress this. Sit down and negotiate with

Syria, with Iran, and with all of the Arab nations in the Middle East. Hold a summit and agree to a way forward. It looks complex but the fundamental principles are not difficult. The establishment of a viable Palestinian State should be the first principle the West must support. There will be a need for compromise on both sides with an exchange of Israeli land for the illegal settlements that continue to be built on Palestinian land with the support of you in the West, and there will need to be funding for the return of Palestinian refugees to the new State of Palestine. If you in the West genuinely get behind this, you will find that the ordinary Israelis and Palestinians crave peace and they will support it.'

'Arrogant bastard,' Vice President Bolton muttered.

'The only way you will solve the horror you have created in Iraq is by political negotiation. Extra troops will not solve your problems and many more of them will be killed. Persian Shiite Iran doesn't want a hotbed of terrorism on her borders, any more than Arab Sunni Syria does, but you won't solve your problems without inviting both of these countries to the negotiating table. Finally, you must stop ignoring the murder and imprisonment of ordinary people in China and the thuggery and human rights abuses of the Chinese Communist Party. If you do not we will deliver two more warnings. When the opportunity presents itself we will attack you when the alpha rotates for the first time, then we will attack you when the alpha rotates for the second time. One of the most powerful prime numbers, through which we are all intimately connected, is the prime of 137. Verse 137 of the noble Qu'ran makes it very clear that we are all believers in what was given to Abraham, Moses, Jesus and all the prophets. When the alpha rotates for the second time the prime of

137 will be turned against you. For you, Western infidels, time is running out. If Allah the Most Kind, the Most Merciful directs it, then as Noah was commanded 6000 years ago, the final solution will be implemented where the single strand meets its double.'

As the video faded to black, President Harrison's face was set more stubbornly than ever. It was Vice President Bolton who broke the silence.

'We can't be seen to be negotiating at the whim of some two-bit terrorist, Mr President.' With Curtis O'Connor in Sydney there was no one in the room to challenge the Vice President's view.

'I agree, Mr President,' the Defense Secretary said, adding his weight to stay the course. 'The President of Iran's price for helping out in Iraq will be endorsement of their nuclear capability.'

'That's not going to happen on my watch,' President Harrison agreed, turning to his press secretary. 'No negotiation.'

In the NSW State Crisis Centre, images of the death and devastation in Sydney were suddenly replaced by CNN's anchor announcing a live broadcast from the White House Rose Garden. The image of President Harrison of the United States standing behind the White House podium took over the screen.

'These latest attacks show that these terrorists, these fundamentalist Muslims, will stop at nothing. They hate decent, freedom-loving people like my good friends in Australia and other like-minded people, and they're trying to break our will. They're trying to destroy us and our civilisation and everything we stand for. Let me assure the

Australians and my fellow Americans that we're not going to stand by and let that happen. God is not going to stand by and let that happen. We're winning in Iraq. We're winning in Afghanistan and now is not the time to surrender. We're winning this war on terror. The terrorists are being defeated on every front and we're going to keep fighting until every one of them is brought to justice.'

The President's refusal to even consider changing a policy that was clearly not working left the most sycophantic of the journalists in the White House press corps shaking their heads.

Curtis turned to Kate. 'Doesn't look as if Denver Harrison's going to negotiate anytime soon,' he said.

'Neither will our Prime Minister,' Kate replied. 'One's as stubborn as the other.'

'Yet they must realise that Kadeer is deadly serious.'

'He's an unusual man, this Khalid Kadeer,' Kate said quietly.

'Highly intelligent and more moderate than people think. I suspect we could do worse than sit down and talk to him to see if we have any common ground,' Curtis said.

'I wonder if it will have any effect on the Chinese torturing their citizens?' Kate mused. The preliminary attack on the Chinese Consulate in Camperdown had been all but forgotten by the media, but the significance of the target had not been lost on either Kate or Curtis.

'Hard to tell but the Chinese can be just as stubborn as the West and I can't see any movement on the human rights front. They execute you over there at the drop of a hat, although,' Curtis reflected, 'if this starts to affect the success of the Games, the Chinese may shift ground. Nothing's going to get in the way of them getting "the best Games ever" tag; it will be a matter of saving face. What do you make of the alpha and 137?'

'Not sure about the next warning and the alpha rotating for the first time,' Kate responded, 'but the prime number 137 is an interesting one. The fine-structure constant of the universe is very close to 1 over 137.'

Alpha, the universe's fine-structure constant had been puzzling some of the finest minds in the world of physics for nearly a hundred years. It had been introduced in 1916 by the German physicist Arnold Sommerfield as a constant that characterised the strength of electromagnetic reaction. Several formulae had been developed, the simplest of which was:

$$\alpha = \frac{e^2}{4\pi\epsilon_0 \hbar c} = 1/137.035$$

where 'e' was the charge on the electron, 'c' was the speed of light, h-bar was Planck's constant and the epsilon represented the permittivity or effect of an electric field on free space.

'Arguably the most important number in physics,' Curtis agreed. 'If it varied in the minutest amount life on this planet wouldn't exist. I wonder if that's what Kadeer is saying to us.'

'That life will no longer be possible,' Kate wondered, 'or is it related to the number itself? If you rotate the alpha you get 137, and if we're talking about an attack that is even more deadly and more explosive than what Kadeer's just carried out in Sydney, he might be threatening a dirty bomb.'

'The radioactive isotopes,' Curtis offered, following Kate's logic with intense interest.

'Exactly. The isotopes having two elements with mass numbers of 137 are barium and caesium, and if either of those elements were rotated into their radioactive form Kadeer would have the ingredients for a dirty bomb,' said Kate.

'I hope you're wrong but we'll need to follow this up. The consequences of a radioactive dirty bomb in a crowded city would be horrific,' Curtis said thoughtfully.

'Now that you and I are flying back to the States out of Melbourne, I'd better see if I can organise something to get us down there,' said Kate.

Nearly an hour later, Kate leaned back from one of the computer screens and stretched her neck wearily as she received confirmation of the online booking. 'We're on the XPT to Melbourne,' she said to Curtis, 'but I feel really bad about leaving these guys.'

'We'd only be in the way,' Curtis assured her. 'You're far more valuable back at Halliwell. What time does the train leave?'

'8.40 p.m.'

'Single or double beds?' Curtis asked, eyes dancing. Even in the middle of a crisis he hadn't lost his sense of humour.

'First Class, but they're seats. We don't run to an Orient Express here,' Kate said with a smile.

'Pity, I was looking forward to a nightcap,' Curtis replied, winking at her.

The Vice President, Secretary of Defense and Dan Esposito accompanied the President up to the Oval Office. The Secretary of State had not been invited.

'It might be a good idea if you were to pay a flying visit to Australia, Mr President, to show the Australian people that we're grateful for their support,' Dan Esposito offered, moving the focus away from Kadeer's video threats.

'For fuck's sake, Dan, the Australians have only got three men and a dog in Iraq and Australia's at the bottom of the bloody world. Even if the President only stays there for 24 hours, it's a three day round trip at least,' the Defense Secretary added pointedly.

'It's not how many they've got there, Mr President,' Esposito responded, giving the Defense Secretary a steely glare, 'it's the fact that there's another flag on the coalition flagpole. Right now this coalition of ours is shaky and the Australian Prime Minister is looking pretty rattled. He's stubborn and he'll ignore any protests but on his past form, if he thinks something's going to cost him an election, he'll do a U-turn. We can't afford for the Australians to cut and run like the bloody Spanish or Italians. That would look pretty bad in the run up to the next election,' Dan Esposito concluded, pushing the meaning of 'hypocrisy' to new heights.

'I think Dan's right, Mr President,' Vice President Bolton said in a rare display of support for the President's advisor. 'They need to stay with us and if that means a little arm-twisting, now's the time.'

CHAPTER 73

BEIJING

Beijing might have been designed in accordance with an ancient feng shui grid, but to al-Falid's disgust the city pulsed like any other decadent city in the West. Twenty floors below his room in the five-star hotel on Wangfujing Avenue, not far from QianHai Lake, Tiananmen Square and the Forbidden City, Beijing's equivalent of Fifth Avenue and the Champs Élysées throbbed with the heartbeat of a capital that was keen to match the avarice of the West. As the city's nightlife gathered pace, the bars and restaurants with their 陪小姐 or *sanpei xiaojie,* the 'ladies of the three accompaniments' began to fill up.

Tomorrow al-Falid would travel east to Shandong Province and the Qingdao bear farm where he would brief his team leaders on what was required for the final solution, but later tonight he would go online to receive reports on the arrangements that were in hand for the second and third warnings. al-Falid couldn't understand why

Kadeer didn't move straight to the final solution, release the deadly virus and eliminate the Chinese and Western infidels, but he went along with Kadeer's warning approach out of a grudging respect for the Islamic philosopher. Kadeer might be going soft, he thought as he went over the arrangements he'd put in place. The success of the second warning attack would depend on al-Falid having cells in sites close to where the alpha rotated if the opportunity arose. It was an opportunity that didn't arise very often. al-Falid had chosen locations in five countries to maximise the chances of being able to take advantage of it if it did.

The British al-Qaeda cell had rented an apartment close to where the infidel had been on 18 November 2003, but that had been the first time the infidel had been there since 1982, so the chances of it happening again any time soon were probably remote.

The Frankfurt am Main cell, al-Falid knew, had overcome their earlier problems with the Rhein-Main military base. That was now closed, which left Schönefeld as a possibility and the cell members had rented an apartment with good coverage of the area.

For the Moscow cell Sheremetyevo was unlikely; when they were there in November 2006 both infidels had preferred Vnukovo.

The Chaoyang District cell was also ready, but again the sightings had been a long way apart. The first had been on 21 February 1972, and at the time it had caused headlines around the world. The last one had occurred exactly thirty years later on 21 February 2002, which left the fifth cell.

The small cell in Australia, al-Falid knew, was reconnoitering the final attack locations but again, the chances of a successful attack there were slim. The infidel had visited just three times in the

02 ADRIAN D'HAGÉ

country's entire history: on 23 October 1966, on 19 November 1996, and again very briefly on 23 October 2003, exactly thirty-seven years after the first visit. On the last occasion the local residents had been left holding a $30 million bill for damages. al-Falid and the leader of the Australian cell, Ahmad Rahman, a solidly built young man with a neatly trimmed beard, were of like mind. The chances might be slim but if Allah wished it, they would surely get another opportunity. Al-Falid smiled. 'When the alpha rotates for the first time.' Kadeer's coding had been exquisite.

Ahmad Rahman stood at the lookout and immediate ruled it out. Although this spot commanded sweeping views of the target, if the chance to strike arose, the infidel's puppets would almost certainly put patrols in this area. Ahmad scanned the target area and then swung his binoculars towards another smaller hill further to the south. It offered even less opportunity as it was located just above a military barracks.

Ahmad drove back down the narrow winding road that provided access to the mountain and turned left onto a highway that connected the main city with a satellite city to the east. He followed the road until he came to the sign he'd been looking for. The Air Disaster Memorial was near the top of a hill in the middle of a pine forest, but when Ahmad tried to drive up the dirt track he found the way blocked. A sign reading 'Wilson Security' and a telephone number had been erected beside the heavily padlocked barrier that was blocking the way. Ahmad parked his older model black Jeep Cherokee and set out on foot, taking his map and binoculars. If anyone challenged him he would claim he was bushwalking.

Forty minutes later, he reached a site among the pine trees that was also less than perfect. The range was fine but the visibility wasn't good and, worse still, the pine forest was a little more open than he'd expected. If the infidel were patrolling this area, he might be discovered. Ahmad scanned the mountain range on the far side of the target area and then stopped and focused his binoculars on a vineyard on the side of hill about 5 kilometres away.

As he walked back to the jeep, Ahmad reflected that of all the targets around the world, this one was surely the most open and the hardest for the infidel to defend. To the south, the foothills of another mountain range came into view where he'd already selected a position if the weather necessitated an attack being made from there. He was in good spirits as he headed back to the highway. If the weather dictated a strike from the north, the hills above the vineyard looked promising.

al-Falid poured himself a mineral water and turned his attention to the third warning, for which caesium chloride would be critical. It was not easy to obtain in its highly radioactive form, but Khalid Kadeer had overcome that problem.

Teletherapy used radioactive sources to irradiate and treat tumours and it was very common in developed countries, with over 10,000 machines worldwide. The later machines used cobalt 60 as the radioactive source. Cobalt 60, being a metal, could not be used in an aerosol attack but Kadeer had pointed out to al-Falid that the early machines had been manufactured using caesium chloride and it was these discarded machines he had ordered al-Falid to get hold of. Many of the early machines had been donated as part of well-meaning aid programs for third world countries with ineffective record systems, and even less effective records of disposals. In the late 1990s in Goiânia in Brazil, over a hundred thousand people had been tested for radiation exposure after scavengers had broken into an abandoned building that housed an old teletherapy machine. After smashing it apart they distributed a powder that was glowing a deadly blue. The powder was caesium 137.

The *Churchill* had been successful in picking up a consignment of eight teletherapy heads from the port of Arica in Chile and another six teletherapy heads from Wewak in Papua New Guinea, as well as a much larger load from al-Falid's contacts in Georgia. There was enough for six large backpack bombs – two for each of the three cities Kadeer had ordered to be attacked if the West ignored the second warning.

As he closed the curtains to shut out the bright lights and the noise on the streets below, al-Falid fervently hoped the West would ignore the next two warnings. Beijing would not have been his choice for the final attack, but the Olympic Games was a huge drawcard and al-Falid was confident that the Beijing authorities' predictions would be close to the mark. For a critical two weeks, more than 3 million spectators, athletes and team officials would be concentrated in the city. With the exception of the devoted warriors of Allah, the Most Kind, the Most Merciful, who would be vaccinated, the western world and other unbelievers would be wiped off the face of the Earth.

CHAPTER 74

PARLIAMENT HOUSE, CANBERRA

Forty-eight hours after the attack on Sydney, the news of the US President's flying visit to Canberra was being greeted with mixed views.

'For security reasons, the Americans don't want the visit announced until the last minute,' the Prime Minister said, looking around the cabinet table, 'so for now it doesn't go outside this room.'

'Bugger me,' the Liberal Party's campaign director muttered from his seat against the cabinet room wall. He had an election to worry about and with Sydney in ruins, a visit by the American President was the last thing he needed. 'A couple of things, Prime Minister,' he said, resolving to do what he could to put the visit on hold, but wary of his boss's stubborn allegiance to Australia's great and powerful ally. 'My research is showing that President Harrison is not going down too well in the electorate, which will play right into the hands of the Opposition. Given the preparation for one of these visits we're not going to be able to keep it a secret for long.'

'The White House wants the President's visit kept quiet, and that's what I've agreed to,' the Prime Minister replied angrily. The strain of the past two days was clearly evident.

Sydney had been brought to a standstill. With the CBD effectively isolated from the north shore, the transport system was in chaos and traffic was in gridlock. The huge Royal North Shore hospital was isolated, as was the North Sydney business district. Thousands of people had been laid off work and divers were still recovering bodies from the flooded tunnels. The Australian stockmarket had plunged based on fears of further attacks and Wall Street and London had also fallen sharply. The State's economy was in tatters, threatening to have an impact on the national economy. Anger over Australia's close ties to the United States was growing, but the Prime Minister stubbornly refused to distance the country from President Harrison's policies.

'There's to be no announcement on President Harrison's visit until I say so,' the Prime Minister added, closing the meeting.

The next day, alongside the pictures of the fallout from the carnage in Sydney, *The Sydney Morning Herald* carried a companion story on the front page:

PRESIDENT HARRISON TO VISIT CANBERRA

Michelle Gillard was one of the best-connected journalists in the country. She had had an exclusive scoop, much to the annoyance of the rest of her colleagues in the Parliamentary press gallery. News of the impending visit only served to further alienate Australians, already in a state of shock over an attack launched against them because of Australia's unswerving support for an American Administration that was increasingly despised in many parts of the world.

Ahmad Rahman picked up the papers from his local newsagent at the Ainslie shops. For the past eighteen months, al-Falid's young recruit and the other two members of his cell had been renting a house in the quiet leafy suburb near the Australian War Memorial. They had kept to themselves, working shift work at a call centre, never missing a rent payment and making sure that their lives appeared perfectly normal. To the neighbours they were just ordinary, fit young men with an interest in bushwalking.

As Ahmad read Michelle Gillard's report on President Harrison's impending visit, he sent a silent prayer of thanks to Allah. The chance that the five cells around the world had all been preparing and praying for had come to him. Ten days from now the President of the United States would be in Canberra for just 24 hours, but Ahmad was sure it would be long enough.

The President will be accompanied by a 650-strong entourage and is expected to attend an official dinner hosted by the Prime Minister at The Lodge, a short distance from the American Embassy where he will be staying. The following day, before flying out from Canberra in the afternoon, the President will address a joint sitting of Parliament. The Australian Federal Police are refusing to comment and Defence didn't return *The Herald's* calls but sources close to those involved in the planning have indicated

there will be more than 500 police officers on duty, supported by members of the military's Special Forces Tactical Assault Group, as well as other military and police personnel trained to deal with any chemical and biological threats. Protesters are expected to number in the thousands but they will be kept well away from the official residences and from the Parliament which will be closed to the public for the duration of the President's stay. The Prime Minister's office is refusing to confirm or deny the visit.

Ahmad smiled. Whenever a government refused to confirm or deny it was a sure sign that a story had credibility.

CHAPTER 75

QUINGDAO

The drive to Qingdao in the Province of Shandong, nearly 800 kilometres to the south-east of Beijing took a full day, but al-Falid wasn't concerned. He'd insisted on a very early start and his driver handled the chaotic traffic around Beijing with ease. Clearing the thick smog of the capital they travelled south-east across the vast flat areas of the North China plain where for centuries the peasants had grown wheat, cotton and maize. They reached Huang He, the great Yellow River, at midday and shortly afterwards, the city of Ji'nan, the province capital. To the south-east, the sacred Taishan Mountain rose majestically, and further south lay Qufu, the birthplace of Confucius. After a short break and fried dumplings at a roadside stall near the main railway station, they turned due east towards the bustling port of Qingdao.

It was after dark by the time they wound their way down into the foothills of Lao Shan, an ancient Taoist mountain 40 kilometres to the east of the port. Kadeer had been right, al-Falid mused, as the driver veered off onto a track that eventually led through a thick pine forest. A bear farm would be the last place authorities would be checking for terrorist activity.

The next morning, al-Falid rose early and went for a walk to explore his surroundings. The 2-hectare compound was situated on the side of Lao Shan and hidden from view. The sleeping quarters were in a low, dirty building at the top of the slope. Pines ran all the way to the bottom far corner of the property where the bear compound was surrounded by an earthen wall. The site had once been an ammunition bunker when the Germans had occupied Qingdao at the time of the Boxer Rebellion. Now it was the site of even more unimaginable suffering for the gentle moon bears, imprisoned in cages in which they could neither stand nor sit, their bile ducts kept permanently and painfully open.

In the far left-hand corner of the compound another dirty building housed the administration block. Most of the staff were Han Chinese workers, including the farm manager, Peng Yu, a short, cruel and thoroughly corrupt Han peasant who'd been around bear farms since he'd left school at the age of ten. Today the staff had been given the day off and the accommodation had been taken over by ten of Kadeer's best men who had been entrusted with organising the teams that would be trained to distribute the lethal Ebolapox into airconditioning systems in dozens of key buildings in Beijing. They were yet to be vaccinated. This would be done as soon as the vaccines arrived along with the deadly vials of Ebolapox.

'I trust you sleep well, Mr 'Flid,' Peng Yu said in broken Eng-lish as he met al-Falid in the compound outside the accommodation block.

'Thank you. When was the last time we sent General Ho some bear bile?' al-Falid asked.

'Not for while. You want more?'

al-Falid nodded. 'Make sure the driver has a package on ice before we leave tomorrow morning. He can deliver it personally. And make sure it's from a young bear.'

Peng Yu headed off towards the stinking compound where the bears had been imprisoned for years. He unlocked the store at the back of the compound, retrieved a blunt knife and a catheter and headed back into the main area where nearly fifty bears were in cages. Oblivious to the deep groaning of the older bears, Peng Yu hooked a thin rope around the youngest bear's front and rear legs, pulling them through the cage, and tied the rope off.

'This is a typical airconditioning system,' al-Falid explained to the young Uighur men he'd gathered around a large table at the back of the accommodation block. 'The substance will come in vials like this,' he said, holding up a vial of pink-coloured water. 'Our people need to be trained to gain access to the airconditioning ducts in their particular building. You will be given a number of dates on which you can strike and apart from the airport, which day you choose is not important,' he said, looking at the cell leader for Beijing's Capitol

International. 'The airport is to be struck over three successive days at the start of the Games, for maximum effect.' Suddenly the training session was interrupted by the high-pitched squealing of the young moon bear, his agonised cries carrying up the hill as Peng Yu attacked the bear's stomach with the blunt knife.

CHAPTER 76

CANBERRA

The President of the United States' visit had received maximum coverage in the national media. Although the protests against Australia's involvement in the disaster that had overtaken Iraq had been some of the biggest in the country's history, the protesters had been kept away from a stubborn President Harrison and an equally immoveable Australian Prime Minister, both of whom were in final discussions as the visit drew to a close.

Ahmad Rahman froze as he caught sight of the patrol entering the pine forest 500 metres below his hide above the vineyard. He watched the soldiers through his binoculars until they disappeared from view. Turning back towards the other two cell members, he gave the thumbs down – the signal for 'enemy'. The commandos were heading up the hill towards the cell members' location.

The al-Qaeda cell had been in position for three days and as the first rays of the sun broke over the gum trees on the hills to the east, Ahmad Rahman had checked the camouflage around the hide and carefully replaced any of the eucalyptus that was wilted. The fissure in the rocks above the vineyard wasn't deep but it was just big enough to hold the three of them, together with the stinger missiles they'd brought in before Ahmad judged the area would be swept to ensure the safety of President Harrison.

In his earlier reconnaissance, Ahmad had realised that the problem facing any soldiers assigned to protect the President was one of geography. Apart from some new construction around the airport and a lengthening and strengthening of Runway 35, the area around the Canberra airfield hadn't changed much since April 1940 when DC-3s had flown in and out of what had been a small military air station. Horses and cattle still grazed in the open fields, and the whole airport was surrounded by densely wooded hills and mountains. To search such a vast area properly would have taken many more soldiers than could be spared for a 24-hour visit, something Ahmad Rahman had taken into account. The day before, one patrol had passed within 100 metres of the hide, but that had been as close as they had come until a few minutes ago when he'd spotted the latest patrol.

Rahman scanned the area beyond the airfield. A kilometre to the north, a police car had stopped the traffic from using Majurah Lane, a major access road that ran along the side of the airfield connecting Canberra's satellite city with the freeway to Sydney. To the south, another major highway had been sealed off and the traffic banked up for several kilometres. Further towards the city, dozens of police cars had been deployed along the route the President would use to get to the airport. The President must be on his way, Rahman thought, and he motioned to the two young men behind him to make a final check on the missiles.

Ahmad Rahman trained his binoculars back on the pine forest below. Through the trees he could see the occasional movement of the forward scout. The patrol was closer and still heading up the side of the mountain towards his position. Rahman focused back on the airfield to the area just in front of the control tower at the RAAF base. The area on the opposite side of the runway to the commercial terminals was under heavy guard. In addition to the police presence, sniper teams had been positioned at key points around the airfield and special response force teams had been assembled in nearby hangers, while dogs and their handlers patrolled the special perimeter that had been established around the president's distinctive aircraft and the refuelling trucks. Rahman could see the pilots going through their procedures in the cockpit and the warning beacon on the aircraft's underside was rotating.

Ahmad swung his binoculars past the commercial airport on the far side of the airfield towards the long drive that led to the Air Force Base. Police motorcycles, their blue lights flashing, were escorting a big white car with the Australian flag fluttering on the bonnet. The Prime Minister and his wife, Ahmad thought, as he focused his binoculars further south. A phalanx of police motorcycles headed the motorcade that had just reached the turnoff from the main highway; black Suburbans were followed by two armoured Cadillacs. Ahmad knew that these were part of the 'secure package' that was designed to break away from the ten vehicles following behind and the rest of the motorcade in case of attack. One was a decoy but both had run-flat tyre systems, an environmental sealing system for protection against chemical and biological attack, as well as more than 12 centimetres of ballistic armour to protect the President from anti-tank grenades. Ahmad again focused on the pine forest. The soldiers were getting closer.

'We've had a departure,' President Harrison's Chief Steward announced. 'The President and the First Lady will arrive in the next few minutes.'

'Thank Christ for that,' one of the journalists from the press corps muttered. The President's discussions with the Australian Prime Minister on the devastation in Sydney and Australia's support for America in Iraq had gone well over time. The journalists and other staff that had been assigned seats in the rear of Air Force One had been waiting for nearly an hour.

'Canberra Ground, this is Air Force One, request start.'

'Air Force One, you are cleared to start.'

The President's chief pilot, Air Force Colonel Mike Munro reached towards the bank of switches on the control panel above him.

'Start number four.'

'Valve open,' the First Officer replied.

'Pack valves closed, N2 rotation. Oil pressure.' The engineer watched as the oil pressure light for the number four engine extinguished. It was a procedure the crew could carry out in their sleep.

'Valve closed on four.'

'Number four stabilised, start number one,' Colonel Munro ordered, satisfied that the bank of gauges for the starboard outer engine indicated it was operating normally.

'Guard! Present Arms!' The 100-strong honour guard came to a crashing salute. On the hill above the Royal Military College the guns of the ceremonial artillery battery boomed out over the capital. The Governor-General, the Prime Minister and their wives stood on the tarmac as the President's plane started to roll.

'Canberra control, Air Force One, ready.'

'Air Force One, you are cleared for an immediate departure on Runway 35, contact departures when airborne. We've enjoyed having you here. Have a safe and pleasant flight.'

'Air Force One, thank you and good day.'

Mike Munro lined up the President's aircraft on the centre line, applied the brakes and advanced the throttles halfway, allowing the engines to spool up. Satisfied, he released the brakes and slowly pushed all four throttles forward.

'EPR set, 80 knots,' the First Officer called. 'Vee-one.' Air Force One, the 'alpha' of the world's aircraft and the icon of the power and prestige of the United States of America had passed the point where the flight could be aborted.

'Rotate. Vee-two . . . ' The alpha had rotated for the first time.

Ahmad Rahman glanced nervously to his right. The soldiers were now barely 100 metres from his position. One or two of them, in contravention of their orders, turned to watch the President's aircraft take off.

'Hold your fire until I tell you,' Ahman said as loudly as he dared. They'd practised many times for this moment but Ahmad felt his heart pounding as he watched Air Force One approach. It was the most vulnerable time for any aircraft; it seemed that it was moving so slowly it would fall out of the sky. Ahmad had to resist the urge to fire immediately. He waited until the big aircraft lumbered past.

'*Allahu Akbar*! One, two, three fire!' he counted.

The three sophisticated heat-seeking missiles shot out of their launchers and a short distance later their rocket motors fired.

The loud tone in the crew of Air Force One's headphones sent a chill through the cockpit as the missile warning light flashed on the instrument panel. Unlike ordinary 747s, Air Force One was equipped with the most advanced missile defences of any aircraft and the crew had trained for just such an attack. Air Force Colonel Mike Munro reacted in an instant and he flicked the switch to activate a modulated beam of infra-red energy designed to lock on to the incoming missile and defuse it.

'Flares,' he ordered calmly.

'Flares gone.'

'Chaff.'

'Chaff gone.'

The sophisticated defences of Air Force One might have been sufficient if the aircraft had not been so low and if there had only been one or perhaps even two missiles. One missile had been confused by the aircraft's infra-red defences and a second one by the sudden explosion of flares. Both missiles missed the target, exploding a kilometre or so away on a military training ground just to the north of the airfield, but the first missile was already too close to the port inner engine and it exploded in a blinding flash.

Mike Munro struggled at the controls of the stricken aircraft but, with half the port wing gone, the big 747 flipped on its back and went into a steep, spiralling dive.

Air Force One, laden with fuel, hit the ground at an angle of nearly 45 degrees, exploding in a huge fireball.

Back on the ground the faces of those in the official party who'd watched the take-off were ashen. A pillar of thick smoke rose from the hills just to the north of the airfield as fire engines roared towards the access gates. The fire-fighters were grim-faced in the knowledge of what they would find. More than a billion people around the world would watch the television footage of the black plume of smoke among the gum trees being broadcast over and over.

CHAPTER 77

THE OVAL OFFICE, THE WHITE HOUSE, WASHINGTON DC

The day after the images that shocked America had been shown around the world, they were followed by another image of a different kind, one that sent a shiver through Arab and Muslim communities. As Vice President Lyndon Johnson had done when President Kennedy had been assassinated, Vice President Charles Bolton repeated the words of the Chief Justice of the United States as he was sworn in as President. 'I, Charles William Bolton, do solemnly swear . . . that I will faithfully execute the office of the President of the United States . . . And will, to the best of my ability . . . preserve, protect, and defend the Constitution of the United States . . . So help me, God.'

'Good luck,' the Chief Justice concluded. Unlike a normal inauguration on the steps of the Capitol, there was no band music and the applause from the small group of solemn onlookers in the Oval Office was muted. As soon as the group had dispersed, President

Bolton tested the chair behind the desk. 'Now we'll show the Muslims and the Chinese who's boss,' he muttered, gaining no satisfaction that it had taken the death of a President for him to gain office. It wasn't that he mourned the passing of his former boss. He'd always thought President Harrison was weak and indecisive; it was more that he would have liked to win an election in his own right.

'Let's see these lily-livered bastards on the Hill criticise the war in Iraq now,' he said to himself.

'I want some advice on where we stand on appointing a Vice President,' President Bolton said, after he'd summoned the White House Legal Counsel and Dan Esposito to the Oval Office. President Bolton's first order of business was to get the right person into the Vice President's position; someone who would not show him up in terms of style and charisma but someone who would support him in taking advantage of the renewed outrage in the American community at the downing of Air Force One. His second priority was to kick start a campaign to gain the Republican nomination for the Presidency; not necessarily in that order. Halliwell, he knew, was ambitious and would likely run and that challenge had to be negated, and quickly. Incumbency of office was an advantage he fully intended to capitalise on, although he knew only too well that it didn't always mean election, as Ford had found out when Carter beat him in 1976.

'The 25th Amendment allows you to appoint whoever you wish, Mr President.'

Bolton nodded. He had already thought about appointing Halliwell, not because he wanted him in the job but because it would likely stymie any presidential ambitions. It would be near impossible for a Vice President to challenge a sitting President.

'Of course whoever you nominate will have to be approved by both the House and the Senate,' the legal counsel said. 'If I may, Mr President, at this unsettling time in the country's history, it might be wise to select someone who is not going to run into a lot of flack on the Hill,' the legal counsel concluded, reading the new President's thoughts.

Bolton grunted. Halliwell might not be such a wise choice. The Democrats would have a field day over his own relationship with Halliwell and his share portfolio would re-surface. In any case, the Chinese weren't going away any time soon and that was something that as President he had the power to do considerably more about than his predecessor. Halliwell was probably more useful where he was and, for the moment, he would leave the position vacant. After all, it had taken over five months before Rockefeller was confirmed after the downfall of Nixon. 'That'll be all,' he said, dismissing his legal counsel.

'I intend to run for the Republican nomination, Esposito,' President Bolton stated flatly after the White House Counsel had left, 'and I intend to win. If you value your job around here, you'll see that it happens.'

'I have a plan, Mr President, which I'll be happy to brief you on once you've attended to the funeral of President Harrison and other more immediate issues.'

Ever since President Harrison's untimely death, Esposito had been in no doubt as to the precariousness of his position. On the surface he would appear to support the incumbent but very soon he would get Halliwell to declare his hand.

CHAPTER 78

THE SITUATION ROOM, THE WHITE HOUSE, WASHINGTON DC

Tom McNamara, the CIA's Director of Operations, and Curtis O'Connor looked thoughtful as they sat down to watch al-Jazeera's video of Dr Khalid Kadeer's third and final warning. They were not the only ones watching. Undetected by the system, al-Falid had flown back into the United States on his American passport.

President Bolton had assembled his war cabinet, although this time the numbers in the Situation Room beneath the Oval Office were smaller. Bolton was not going to tolerate the sort of discussion that had taken place under President Harrison's stewardship. For a start, the new President had declared that only one intelligence representative would be present – the newly appointed Director of National Intelligence. Bolton had a very clear idea of where he was going without the waters being muddied by analysis of intelligence by the CIA, especially officers like Curtis O'Connor. Dan Esposito was furious as he had also been excluded and told to concentrate on the President's re-election.

'The alpha has rotated for the first time and soon it will rotate again and the prime of 137 will unleash its fury,' Kadeer began. As usual, his manner was calm and reasonable.

'As the great Prophet, peace be upon him, will attest, the loss of any life is unfortunate but doubly unfortunate when the solution is in your hands. We do not wish to change your society yet you seem to think you have a right to change ours. Your leaders talk about imposing democracy on us. In your democracies you allow notorious prisons like Abu Ghraib and Guantanamo Bay without any hope of a fair trial for those who are incarcerated. Some have been held there for over five years. For Muslims in China, the position is the same and torture is commonplace. We are beginning to wonder whether freedom and human rights are privileges that are available for all or only to those of you who agree with your governments and their imperialistic views of the world.' Kadeer paused to allow his message to take effect.

'Our demands are simple and fair. Firstly, we want to see an end to the suffering of the Palestinian people and the establishment of a viable and prosperous Palestinian State at peace with her neighbours.'

'Secondly, we want you to withdraw your forces from our holy lands. You do not have a right to use military force to secure oil for your gas guzzling SUVs and four-wheel drives. Thirdly, we want you to withdraw your support for corrupt regimes like those in Saudi Arabia and Egypt where our people are persecuted. Fourthly, the West is to stop turning a blind eye to the Beijing government's relentless murder of innocent Muslims and other ordinary citizens. The Han Chinese see the Beijing Olympics as their entrée card into global society. If you in the West continue to support this event without demanding the freedom of speech and religion you are so keen to impose on the Middle East, you will all pay a terrible price. Finally, just as we do not wish to interfere in the affairs of Christianity, we seek an agreement that you will cease interfering in the affairs of Islam. You have a choice. You can sit down and negotiate the peace we all desire, or you will meet us again when the alpha rotates for the second and final time. This is your last warning.'

No one spoke. The cabinet members were keen to hear the new President's views although few were prepared for the vehemence of what followed.

'These little bastards are going to regret this,' President Bolton began. He turned to the Chairman of the Joint Chiefs. 'I want a report on how soon we can double the Armed Forces,' he said.

The Chairman of the Joint Chiefs struggled to hide his alarm. 'That would involve the draft, Mr President.'

'I know that General, goddamn it!' President Bolton spat back, slamming his fist on to the table. 'Let's get one thing straight,' the President demanded, his cold eyes staring down each member of his cabinet in turn. 'This is war and this cabinet's going to be very different from the last one. No more debates. No more roadblocks and speed humps, and no more negative analysis. This year's only got a few more weeks to run but by the time I give my State of the Union address early next year, I want to map out a war footing for the whole nation,' the President snarled, convinced that where the previous President had failed, he would succeed.

'This country faces two threats, and if they're not dealt with and crushed they will overwhelm our civilisation as we know it. The first one is Islam. They're already running for Congress and parliament in other countries like Australia. If these little bastards get their way we'll all be in a fucking mosque attending prayers every other hour of the day and our women will be stumbling around in burqas. I'm not going to stand by and let that happen. Instead of leaving the problem to a few thousand in the military, the whole nation is going to be geared to defeat them, and that includes taking on Syria and Iran,' the President added, turning back to the Chairman of the Joint Chiefs.

'I want your options for attacks on both those countries. If the President of Iran thinks he can develop nuclear weapons to wipe Israel off the map he's got another think coming. Those plans are to include options for ground invasion. In the meantime, I want another nuclear carrier group deployed into the Gulf.'

Bolton was making sure his defiant military message could not possibly be misread.

CHAPTER 79

LONDON

In the face of the West's intransigence and China's silence on human rights, Kadeer had reluctantly ordered al-Falid to execute the plans for the second rotation of the alpha within seven days.

Like the London bombers of 7/7 who had met at Luton station before taking a train to Kings Cross and then separating to detonate their rucksack bombs, Kadeer's cell in London were all 'home grown'. All of the members of this cell were second generation Britons; graduates of some of the best universities in the country, including one from Oxford who had a blue for cricket. The only common denominator was their faith. All of them were Muslims angry at the treatment they were getting in their own country, and angry at the lies the British government had told them about the invasion of Iraq.

The first words of the plans that Thames Water had thoughtfully provided on the internet for all their consumers read: 'The Thames

Water Ring Main is one of London's best kept secrets'. The irony had not been lost on Kadeer's men, each of them prepared to die for their spiritual leader as part of the new *Jihad* sweeping Europe. The Thames Water map showed the precise detail of the 83-kilometre tunnel that had been built under London. It gave the locations of the advanced water treatment works like those at Ashford Common, Walton and Hampton, and it detailed exactly where all the pump-out shafts were in places like Holland Park, Battersea and Brixton. Thames Water had provided a free CD that the members of the Leeds cell had watched many times. They had one of their own working in the advanced water treatment plant at Hampton. They were ready to strike.

The cell leader, Mahmood al-Masri, and his cell were ecstatic. They had watched Dr Kadeer's video and were in admiration of the man who could devastate a city like Sydney and bring down the most famous 747 in the world. The might of Islam was on the rise and the timing was perfect. In a week's time, London would play host to a rock music festival that had been organised as a peace rally dubbed 'Peace Rocks'. Some of the world's most famous international bands had given their support and Trafalgar Square would be packed. Before the barriers and magnetometers went up, a thousand pellets of the glowing blue caesium chloride would be dissolved into each of the famous fountains. The flashing lights playing on the stage would be joined by an iridescence of a far more deadly variety.

Mahmood also planned to introduce 2000 pellets into two of the water treatment works and the final 4000 pellets would be exploded in three backpacks. The smallest would be detonated as close to the Chinese Embassy in Portland Place as possible. Mahmood had reconnoitred the area thoroughly and the Embassy was in the centre of London near Regents Park, not far from the BBC Headquarters in Broadcasting House and one of the infidels' most famous churches, Nash's All Souls. The location was perfect. Mahmood planned for a second backpack to be detonated in one of London's other famous parks. The final decision as to which one would depend on the prevailing wind but, because of its size and central location, Mahmood was leaning towards Hyde Park. The final backpack would be exploded on the roof of a building in the financial district. The eight rusted teletherapy heads were still under the bed in the spare room of the cell leader's nondescript tenement house in Leeds. Each member of the cell knew they would die once the heads were dismantled, but they were looking forward to their next life when they could join their great Prophet. A life free from persecution in their own country where Muslims were reviled and a life free from having to watch the news every night and witness the slaughter of their brothers and sisters at the hands of the West in places like Iraq and Lebanon. Together the cell members placed their prayer mats on the floor of the cell leader's lounge room, and faced towards Mecca.

'*Allahu Akbar*. God is Great,' the cell leader intoned, as he began to lead them in prayer. Halfway across the world, two more of Kadeer's cells were completing their preparations for similar attacks, one cell in one of the largest cities of the United States, another in a city belonging to one of the United States' staunchest allies.

CHAPTER 80

THE OVAL OFFICE, THE WHITE HOUSE, WASHINGTON DC

'The second problem is China,' President Bolton continued, glaring at his Secretary of State. Like everyone else in the room, the Secretary of State could sense he was on borrowed time and he held his tongue.

'I want a threat analysis prepared immediately and that's to include their likely influence in space as well. Space is absolutely vital to the defence of the United States and let there be no doubt, as long as I'm in the White House, we will control it. Any threat to our satellites will be dealt with first and we'll ask questions later.' Bolton looked around the room, daring anyone to disagree with him. China had already sent a shot across the bows of the United States' space program, firing a 40-tonne KT-2 ballistic missile and destroying one of their own satellites 860 kilometres above Xichang, a major Chinese launching pad in the far south of the country. The ageing Feng Yun weather satellite was well past its use-by date, but that was not the

point. China was looking very closely at the vulnerability of the satellites of the United States. Used for a myriad of top-secret tasking,
the big US satellites were vital for GPS navigation in the military,
guidance of smart bombs and for any surveillance the President and
his military might order.

'One of my predecessors had the wisdom to sign an order denying
our adversaries the use of space,' President Bolton declared. 'We will
continue to reserve our right to deny access to space to any country
which even looks like being hostile, and that includes the Chinese.'

Not wishing to risk any publicity over his discussions with Richard Halliwell, the President met with him in the now-vacant Vice
President's residence at Number One Observatory Circle later that
evening. The heavily guarded, turreted nineteenth century mansion
in the grounds of the Naval Observatory in Washington DC overlooked Massachusetts Avenue.

'Congratulations, Mr President,' Richard Halliwell offered
without sincerity as the two men settled on the couches in the cosy
first-floor library. 'I wish it were under happier circumstances.'

President Bolton took a sip of bourbon before he replied. 'Are you
planning to run, Richard,' he asked bluntly.

Richard Halliwell smiled deprecatingly. 'I haven't decided, Mr
President,' he lied, 'but if I do, rest assured, you'll be the first to
know.'

'You'll be wasting your time,' Bolton warned, 'so be it on your
own head. More importantly, how are we doing with the Ebolapox
research?'

'I'm due to have another meeting with Dolinsky shortly but

getting him onboard has been a masterstroke,' Halliwell enthused, his coming battle with Bolton and the Republican nomination for the White House temporarily forgotten. 'He's confident he's overcome the last of the technical difficulties with the cutting enzymes, and he's produced several different combinations of DNA and RNA. Even more pertinent is his work on a vaccine. Several of the monkeys have now been immunised and I'll let you know the results. If it's successful we have the means to mass produce the vaccine very rapidly and make it available to our embassies around the globe, but I think we should ensure that our Olympic team and officials are vaccinated well before they leave. I'm still going to need to get the Ebolapox vials into Beijing and the only foolproof way will be through the black bag.'

'That won't be a problem,' Bolton replied. 'When do you think you'll be ready?'

'No later than three months before the Games. I met with my planner in Beijing the last time I was there and he's assured me that any substance can be distributed throughout the city, for a price,' Halliwell added meaningfully. The well-connected leader of the Sānhéhuì, the Triad Society, had not come cheaply but getting the vials to the right targets would be crucial.

CHAPTER 81

THE TARGET CITIES

The suburb was one of the wealthiest and oldest in the city, it's big colonial homes overlooking a meandering river from the sides of a substantial hill. As night fell, another of Kadeer's cells was at work in a quiet backstreet, gaining access to the ageing hydrant outlet that was connected to the fresh water mains. Their uniforms had been tailored to look like those of the local fire brigade. The specially adapted stand-pipe had been bought through one of the many companies that sold fire-fighting equipment on the internet and the 64-milimetre screw fitting would have fitted perfectly were it not for the appalling condition of the hydrant base and the complete lack of maintenance by the City Council. At least there had been a blue marker in the middle of the road to indicate where the hydrant was, otherwise Kadeer's men might never have found it. The team leader, Muhammad, used a shovel to clear away the matted grass from the top of the rusted iron plate that was marked FH. As he

prised it open, a frog leapt to safety; he reached in to clean the mass
of debris from the clogged well.

'I wonder what they do when there is a real fire, Abdullah,'
Muhammad said, as Abdullah, one of his cell members, wrestled
the stand-pipe into the well and locked it onto the two lugs at the
bottom.

'I don't know but it's just as you predicted, up here the pressure is poor,' Abdullah said as the stand-pipe spindle depressed
the concave pressure disc in the base of the hydrant and the water
flooded up and into the specially fitted pressure gauge. 'Only 200
Kpa. The compressor will overcome that easily,' he said, connecting the other side of the T to the pressure vessel containing the
caesium chloride. '*Allahu Akbar*! God is Great!' Abdullah muttered
fiercely as he started the purpose-built compressor and opened the
valve. A hundred litres of dissolved caesium chloride was forced
into the city's fresh water mains. Abdullah bent over and vomited
in the gutter. The deadly gamma radiation he'd absorbed when
he'd dissolved the blue pellets was beginning to have a devastating
effect on his body, but both he and Muhammad knew the radiation would not end their lives before they were able to carry out
their final mission. Tomorrow, Allah be praised, they would still
be able to explode their backpacks of blue powder in the centre of
the city. Muhammad would take the lift to Level 9, 79 Adelaide
Street and explode his pack in the reception area of the Chinese
Consulate. Abdullah and a third cell member would head for the
top of a building that overlooked the flame of remembrance in the
CBD, an area that was dedicated to those who had fought for their
country. Both men knew that the winds would take the fine, deadly

powder and distribute it for thousands of metres. The city would become a gravesite.

Nearly 12,000 kilometres away, one of al-Falid's most important recruits had clocked on shift at the San Francisco Public Utilities Commission water treatment plant in Millbrae. Two years before, the cell member from the Muslim community in the Bay Area of San Francisco had secured a job at the plant. In April 2006, he had reported back to the cell leader that the Commission had installed a tank containing nine bluegill fish. Sophisticated banks of computers had also been installed to monitor the fishes' breathing. Just as humans coughed to get rid of food or liquid that might have 'gone down the wrong way', fish flexed their gills to clear particles of sand and other matter from their breathing passages. This system was designed to monitor the way fish coughed; if any of the bluegills were upset by foreign or toxic matter in the water, the computers could sense which fish was breathing abnormally and trigger a pager and email alarm to those on duty and to senior management. The team leader of Kadeer's San Francisco cell was not in the least perturbed. By the time the fish sounded the alarm it would be too late.

The 'Peace Rocks' concert was a sell-out. 15,000 people had packed around the stage beneath Nelson's column and for nearly four hours, as rock stars strutted their stuff on the temporary stage, dissolved caesium chloride cascaded from the famous fountains. A strong breeze whipped a fine spray into the air but the frenzied crowd were oblivious to the lethal mist drifting over them. Red, green and yellow strobe lights played over the stage as the bands sent the crowd wild. The water and mists from the cascading fountains glowed a deep and beautiful blue.

The President of the San Francisco Public Utilities Commission, Hank Arkell, was enjoying a round of golf when his beeper warned him that all was not well with one of the bluegills. Passive electrodes in the tank, amplified 10,000 times had picked up the distressed breathing of one of the 'fish police'. The Vice President and three other Commissioners were also paged but none of them had been unduly alarmed. If one of the fish was breathing erratically, the system was designed to automatically sample and analyse the water for chemical impurities. By the time the analysis had revealed the presence of caesium chloride and gamma radiation, all of the fish were dead.

Mahmood al-Masri's backpack was faded, matching his jeans and white T-shirt. No one took the slightest notice as he exited the Tube at Hyde Park Corner at the start of another working week. The morning after the Sunday concert the underground was crowded with early-morning commuters. The sky over London was unusually clear and blue as Mahmood walked through the Queen Elizabeth Gate. He headed past the bandstand and on to The Lookout, the former police observation point. As the last seconds of his life ticked away, he said a silent prayer, thanking Allah for the success of the operation and the moderate breeze that was coming from the west. Raising his fist in the air, he turned away from the Serpentine towards Mecca and shouted '*Allahu Akbar*! God is great! *Allahu Akbar*! God is Great!!' The blast sent shockwaves around the park as the wind picked up the cloud of deadly caesium chloride and whisked it towards the crowded city.

Ten minutes earlier, Mahmood's companion, Abu Zayyat had walked out of Blackfriars Station and headed for an access to the roof of the building where he worked as a sales consultant, not far from St Paul's Cathedral and overlooking the great city's financial district. For one last time Zayyat stared out across the city he had lived in all his life, turned towards Mecca and as he raised his fist and shouted '*Allahu Akbar*! God is Great!' a second blast rocked the city. A cloud of superfine radioactive dust drifted out across Threadneedle Street, the Bank of England and the Stock Exchange. A short distance away, a third explosion destroyed the front of the Chinese Embassy in Port-land Place. Apart from the death of the suicide bomber and some minor injuries to the staff in reception, there appeared to be little damage.

A little earlier, and over 16,000 kilometres away, the evening peak hour was beginning. Just before close of business, Muhammad, buoyed by early reports of an outbreak of sickness in the wealthy Brisbane suburb of Hamilton, took the lift to Level 9 at 79 Adelaide Street and detonated his deadly bomb. Seconds later, Abdullah and the other cell member gained access to the roof of the hotel overlooking Brisbane's Central Railway Station. As the sound of sirens filled the streets of Brisbane, Abdullah paused to vomit again, and both men moved to the edge of the roof. They stared down on the clocktower of the station and the sandstone dome surrounding the Flame of Remembrance. Turning north-west to face Mecca and a fiery sun that was setting over the city's rush hour, they raised their fists in unison and shouted '*Allahu Akbar! Allahu Akbar!* God is Great! God is Great!'. As they'd practised many times before, they pressed their detonators together.

Monika Spalding, the attractive CNN anchor, swivelled towards the camera with the red blinking light. Not yet aware of the explosions in Brisbane, she interrupted the coverage of the London bombings to cover a growing disaster closer to home. 'In news just to hand,' she said, 'several more explosions have been reported in San Francisco and we cross live to our reporter Wayne Diaz at Fisherman's Wharf. What can you tell us, Wayne?'

The CNN reporter was standing on Fisherman's Wharf in front of the big wooden boatwheel where tens of thousands of tourists had their photo taken each year. Behind him people were running from their stores and restaurants, some crying hysterically.

'Three explosions have been reported just minutes ago, Monika, and as you can see behind me, given what's happened in London, panic has taken over.' The camera panned towards the centre of the CBD where the streets were gridlocked as people tried to flee the stricken city.

'Two of the explosions occurred on the tops of buildings quite close to where I'm standing and a third when a security guard stopped a young man of Middle Eastern appearance outside the Chinese Embassy, also very close to here in Laguna Street. There are fears that this might be part of a well-coordinated worldwide warning that was foreshadowed by the terrorist, Dr Khalid Kadeer. Back to you, Monika.' The images of the chaos in San Francisco faded as the CNN newsroom crossed to their London bureau.

At first the London authorities had reported that the only casualty from the blasts in Hyde Park and the city's financial district had been the suicide bombers themselves, and there had been speculation that both bombs had gone off prematurely before the bombers had had a chance to enter one of the teahouses in the Park or the office block crowded with workers. The great city hardly missed a beat. The tourists had been inconvenienced when the park had been sealed off but the authorities were quick to re-open it, restoring as much normality to city life as possible so the terrorists were not seen to be winning. The bombers had detonated their bombs just ten seconds apart, the first at 7.50 a.m., but at the same time Hyde Park was being re-opened, Dr Paul Templeton, the Head of Porton Down telephoned the Prime Minister with the unwelcome news. These were no ordinary bombs. Clouds of radiation were being detected in busy Oxford Street and Park Lane in Mayfair, Shaftesbury Avenue in Soho and as far east as Fenchurch Street Station and the Tower of London.

The CNN anchors, Monika Spalding and Efram Brooks, were used to covering world catastrophes, and this looked like a routine terrorist attack that had failed. They crossed to CNN's London correspondent Michael Duffy.

'What can you tell us, Michael?' Monika asked. The image of CNN's news desk faded to that of a tall man in a woollen overcoat and black scarf standing in Hyde Park with a double line of London plane trees devoid of leaves in the background.

'This attack still has authorities puzzled, Monika. Apart from the suicide bombers themselves and some minor injuries in the Chinese Embassy, no other casualties have been reported. Although, as you can hear, there are a large number of sirens sounding and the police presence in the city is increasing.'

'A fear of more attacks?'

'Perhaps, but we've had no word on that yet, Monika.'

'And these bombs went off prematurely?'

'That was the authorities' first impression but that theory is coming under increasing pressure from several experts, particularly as the bombs went off within seconds of one another. We're also getting some unconfirmed reports of large numbers of people turning up at doctors' surgeries and hospitals with extreme vomiting, nausea and diarrhoea. It would seem that most, if not all of these people either attended the 'Peace Rocks' concert in Trafalgar Square on Sunday night or they're from the Hampton area.'

'Michael,' Monika said, breaking in. 'We're going to have to leave it there, we're getting a feed from the Prime Minister's Office in Downing Street.' The pictures of Hyde Park faded to figures in biowarfare suits outside Number 10 – suits that were entirely useless against gamma radiation. Those images were replaced with a stony-faced Prime Minister, flanked by the Home Secretary and the Mayor of London.

'Until we know the extent of this situation the authorities have advised that it would be prudent to evacuate the city. The Home Office will coordinate the evacuation and we're appealing for calm. I can confirm that a radioactive substance, caesium chloride, has been detected in the bomb blasts and we're now monitoring the extent of the plume. I'm also advised that caesium chloride has been found in both of the fountains in Trafalgar Square, and in the water supply around Hampton. We're confident that the radioactive water is confined to the Hampton area and is unlikely to affect any areas beyond that. The Home Secretary will confirm this as soon as possible.'

The Prime Minister's words fell on deaf ears. With every television and radio station in the country broadcasting the disaster live, the news of the dirty bombs had spread through the city at the speed of light. There was a silent and unseen killer in the air and the stoic citizens of London were unnerved. The terror was palpable. People rushed onto the city's streets, jamming the tube stations and fighting to get on the buses. Supermarket shelves were emptied of bottled water as panic overtook the entire country. Stocks on the London Stock Exchange plummeted.

Monika Spalding was obviously shaken as she turned to her co-host. 'And we have some early reports of what looks like a similar situation in Australia, Efram?'

'This is increasingly looking like a coordinated worldwide attack, Monika,' Efram said, turning towards the camera. 'We cross now to Brisbane, Australia, where more explosions have been reported in that city. What can you tell us, Kimberly?'

Efram's swarthy face was replaced by a young CNN reporter standing beside the Brisbane River.

'That's right, Efram. We've had a total of three explosions here. Two on the top of a building in the centre of the city and the third in the Chinese Consulate on the ninth floor of a building in Adelaide Street.' The reporter's face faded to images of people running towards Roma Street Station, a sea of blue and red flashing lights of ambulances, police cars and fire engines in the background. In another image, a crowd of people, some of them crying, some vomiting, some nearly hysterical, were queued at the entrance to the city's largest hospital. These images faded to Parliament House in Canberra and a Prime Minister who was clearly flustered .

'The evacuation of Brisbane is purely a precaution,' the Prime Minister insisted in answer to one journalist's question from the packed media conference.

'Do we know how they got into the city's water supply?' asked another.

'Look, I don't want to speculate on that right now, Michelle. The important thing is that we take immediate steps to ensure the people of Brisbane are safe and then investigate this thoroughly before we draw any conclusions.'

'Can you accept that as a result of Iraq we're a bigger target now, Prime Minister? Khalid Kadeer wants to negotiate. Shouldn't we at least meet with him?' shouted another journalist.

'We don't negotiate with terrorists and now is not the time to cut and run from places like Iraq,' the Prime Minister replied angrily, closing his folder and finishing the conference. The vision moved back to the CNN reporter beside the Brisbane River.

'With what looks like radioactive bomb attacks on the cities of London, San Francisco and Brisbane in the countries that first invaded Iraq, as well as poisoning their water supplies, this has all the hallmarks of Khalid Kadeer's final warning, Efram, and the attacks on all three Chinese Embassies and Consulates contain a terrifying warning for a country staging its first ever Olympic Games.'

'Thanks, Kimberley,' Efram responded and the camera switched to Monika Spalding.

'We have with us in the studio, Professor Edward Barton, Professor of Nuclear Medicine at Johns Hopkins University. Professor Barton, thank you for joining us.'

'Pleasure, Monika.'

'Professor, we've seen the earlier reports from San Francisco and the death of the bluegill fish at the Millbrae water treatment plant. What's the risk of nuclear radiation from the water supply in the Bay City?'

'It depends on the strength of that radiation, Monika. While there appears to be no doubt that caesium chloride has been introduced into the San Francisco water supply as well as London and Brisbane, and we know that caesium chloride is one of the most water soluble radioactive substances on earth, it would take a substantial amount of this powder to affect other than the area immediately around the treatment plant itself.'

'Some of the staff at that treatment plant have been hospitalised, Professor, and given that London and Brisbane have also been blanketed in a radioactive cloud, it will be a huge issue in those countries. What are the actual dangers of exposure?'

'Again it depends on the dose that people receive but gamma

radiation from 137-caesium chloride causes the cells of the body, or at least the atoms that make up those cells, to become electrically charged. Our white cells that fight infection and the crypt cells of the intestine are especially vulnerable. People will experience the nausea, vomiting, headaches and dehydration symptoms that have been reported in all of the affected cities. We can expect the more serious cases – and unfortunately there may be thousands or perhaps tens of thousands in this category – to develop further symptoms, including rapid heartbeat, internal haemorrhaging, a darkening of the skin, hair loss and shortness of breath. If the radiation is severe, and by that I mean greater than ten sieverts or joules per kilogram, death can follow in a matter of days.'

'For those who have perhaps suffered a lesser dose, are there any long-term effects, Professor?'

'Unfortunately, yes. I'm sure most of us are familiar with the melt-down of the Russian nuclear reactor in Chernobyl in the Ukraine in 1986. Already there's been a significant increase in cancer cases in the Ukraine, and in the surrounding countries of Belarus and Russia. The long-term effects are still being felt as cancers from exposure to radiation tend to show up about ten years after the event.'

'Professor, thank you for joining us at such a difficult hour.'

al-Falid flicked off the coverage he'd been watching on the computer in his office. 'Allah, the Most Kind, the Most Merciful be praised,' he whispered. Compared with what he had organised for Beijing the dirty bombs were insignificant, and with the reckless President

Bolton in the White House al-Falid was convinced there would be no negotiations. At last Islam would rise to its rightful place in the world. He turned his mind to the final solution and the vaccines al-Qaeda would need to protect the organisation. It was time to meet with Eduard Dolinksy to check on his progress.

BOOK FOUR

THE FINAL SOLUTION

CHAPTER 82

HALLIWELL LABORATORIES, ATLANTA

As the full impact of the worst attacks on the West since September 11 became clear, for those in the United States, Britain and Australia the 'Year of the Chinese Olympics and the Greatest Games Ever' had opened in an atmosphere of fear and apprehension, and that apprehension was not confined to the West. The messages of Khalid Kadeer and the attacks on the Chinese embassies and consulates around the world had not gone unnoticed in Beijing.

The central business districts of London, San Francisco and Brisbane were still largely deserted as the authorities struggled to decontaminate tens of thousands of square metres of office space, rail and bus stations, parks, hotels, swimming pools and public buildings. Thousands of people still didn't trust the water supplies, tourism was non-existent and thousands more people had lost their jobs. Losses on the stock market threatened a recession and economic confidence was at its lowest since 1929.

In Sydney, the burned-out hulk of the *Ocean Venturer* grounded under the Harbour Bridge was a grisly reminder of Kadeer's first warning. The state government had wisely abandoned the initial spin of 'it could have been much worse, had it not been for the bravery of the Commandos' in favour of concentrating on getting the stricken city back on its feet. In the months since the attack, progress had been painfully slow. The intense heat from the burning tanker in the harbour had caused severe structural damage to the bridge and the engineers were unwilling to give an exact date for the re-opening. The news on the tunnels was a little better, with engineers confident they could replace the damaged sections, but that was going to take time and both the harbour tunnels remained closed, as did the M5 at the Cooks River. The trains were running, but only on either side of the harbour and the government had hired as many additional ferries as the harbour could accommodate. Hundreds of businesses had gone under and thousands of people were out of work as well. Worse was to come with the American President's State of the Union Address that would send shockwaves through Arab, Muslim and western communities alike. Evangelicals like the Reverend Jerry Buffett and other Christian leaders were warning millions of their followers of the approaching Armageddon, an Armageddon that was being quietly orchestrated right under their noses.

Dr Eduard Dolinsky inserted first one key and then the other into the specially designed locks on the Halliwell vault. It was a breach of procedure that would never have been tolerated at CDC. The reasoning was to guard against a rogue scientist having access to pathogens for which there was no cure, so access to the CDC smallpox vault always required two scientists.

Imran and Kate helped Dolinsky with the stainless steel trolleys. Kate put an insulated mitten over her spacesuit glove, opened the freezer and stepped back as a cloud of liquid nitrogen vapour poured over the sides of the portable freezer, swirling around her boots and the trolley wheels. At Halliwell, the filo virus Ebola was stored in the same trolley as smallpox. At CDC there had been a strict protocol to keep the two viruses separate for safety.

Kate could see the look of concern on Imran's face as they watched the Georgian virologist. There was no doubt that Eduard Dolinsky had already done a considerable amount of work towards combining the harder to catch but more deadly single-stranded RNA Ebola virus with the much more easily transmittable but not quite so deadly smallpox. With India-1 smallpox, only 90 per cent of those who contracted it were likely to die.

On Dolinsky's left, Imran had placed the seed vials of smallpox into a specially designed water bath that was kept at a constant temperature of 37°C, the same temperature as the human body. Dolinsky carefully took out one of the vials and held it against a bench light, checking to see that the frozen liquid had completely melted. Kate shivered involuntarily. No matter how often she looked at prepared slides of the crinkly bullet-shaped pox viruses under an electron microscope, or handled the live viruses in their shimmering pale pink soup, Kate couldn't help thinking that one vial was enough to wipe out the whole of New York City. On Dolinsky's left, another 37°C water bath had melted the even more lethal contents of vials containing millions of the spaghetti-like strands of Ebola. In the centre of the bench Kate had set up rows of plastic well plates and beside them were the small dark bottles that had come from one of several ordinary domestic refrigerators. Inside the bottles were the microscopic enzymes that were used to splice sequences of the double-stranded DNA of smallpox and reverse-transcriptase enzymes that could synthesise DNA from the single-stranded Ebola. Kate shivered again. It was a complex process that could not be seen by the human eye but over the past months, Dolinsky had produced vial upon vial of Ebolapox, a man-made virus far more deadly than any of the pathogens found in nature. Here, in the Halliwell laboratories, paid for by the taxes of the American people, the single strand had met its double.

al-Falid and Eduard Dolinsky both knew that the FBI had assigned close surveillance to the Georgian scientist from the day he'd arrived in the country. Surveillance was manpower intensive and as Dolinsky never went out, that surveillance had been dispensed with in favour of bugging his apartment, although al-Falid was not taking any chances. The one place Dolinsky was free to move around was the Halliwell Laboratories, and once he had gained a clearance to be in the building al-Falid met with Dolinsky in a quiet, unoccupied office.

'The program is on track, Amon,' Dolinsky assured al-Falid. 'The laboratory resources have been first class and I've overcome the final technical hurdles to combining smallpox with Ebola.

Several chimpanzees have been tested and the results have been, how do you say it, impressive,' Dolinsky said with a slow smile. 'More importantly I have made progress on the vaccine and several more chimpanzees are showing immunity, but this virus is far more deadly than smallpox or Ebola on their own. Once it gets loose, unless it's in a small area that can be contained, it will kill hundreds of millions.'

Dolinsky had no way of knowing that the Olympics were the target, and once he realised the sinister purposes his research could be put to, it would be too late.

CHAPTER 83

THE WHITE HOUSE, WASHINGTON DC

The US House Sergeant at Arms cleared his throat.

'Mr Speaker, the President of the United States!' Senators and Representatives stood and applauded President Bolton as he marched down the centre aisle of the House towards the Speaker's podium.

'My fellow Americans,' the President began, 'we are now facing the most serious threat to our freedom since the Japanese attacked us in Pearl Harbor. Back then, the Japanese made a grave mistake, just as the Muslim fundamentalists have made a grave mistake attacking us in San Francisco, as well as in London and Australia. It was a fatal mistake to murder our President. This country is now on a war footing and tomorrow I will be mobilising the National Guard and re-introducing the draft for all eligible men and women between the ages of eighteen and twenty-six.' There were audible gasps from the gallery but the Republicans rose to their feet and applauded. President Bolton glowered at those who remained seated and when the applause slowed, he resumed his speech. 'I can assure those who seek to destroy all that we stand for – our democracy and our freedom – that this nation and its people will not be intimidated. I am also announcing today that I will be seeking the Republican nomination for the Presidential election so that I can lead you to a greater victory against our enemies.'

The combined Senate and House applauded again but several Senators and Representatives were doing so without enthusiasm, aware that the prestige and international reputation of the United States had sunk to historic lows in Europe and in other parts of the world. More than one member of Congress harboured private doubts that President Bolton's 'bring it on, go it alone' approach would work. The view of ordinary Americans would be reflected at the New Hampshire Primaries in the not too distant future. After nearly an hour, President Bolton concluded his speech with a blunt message for the Arabs, the Iranians and the Chinese.

'In the Middle East I have deployed no fewer than five carrier groups, one of the greatest naval task forces ever assembled. For those who think they can take on the might of the United States in space I would urge them to think again. Just as we will prevent any nation from gaining nuclear capabilities that can be used against us or our interests, so we reserve the right to deny access to space to any of our adversaries.

'I am confident we will win this war on terror and I intend to muster every resource at our disposal to ensure victory.'

The combined House and Senate rose to their feet and applauded as the President left the building.

Richard Halliwell was in his office, wondering how Bolton's announcement might affect his own campaign which he was about to formally announce. He would need to discuss things with Esposito. The situation on the ground in Iraq was worse than at any time since the invasion, and Esposito's polling was showing that the anti-war sentiment was growing. The announcement of the draft might be the final straw that would put many of the President's supporters in Halliwell's camp, although the view that it should not only be the soldiers bearing the brunt of war but the whole of the nation was still strong and the polling over the next few days would bear careful watching. At least the Democrats were in their usual disarray, Halliwell thought to himself. The New Hampshire Primary would be like the charge of the Light Brigade. Hillary Clinton had long ago declared she was 'in it to win', and with Bill Clinton campaigning for her, Halliwell did not underestimate her chances. Senator Barack Obama had also captured the public's imagination. He was black, Halliwell mused, and with a name like 'Obama' surely unthinkable, even to the donkey vote. No fewer than six others including Governor Bill Richardson of New Mexico and John Kerry's old running mate, the former Senator John Edwards, had entered what was rapidly becoming a very crowded field. That had its advantages as it would split the votes and increase the chance that those who had the biggest war chest would win, especially on the Democratic side. Halliwell's war chest was vast. It was almost time for the announcement.

Halliwell turned his mind back to Beijing. The vaccines would be made available through the embassy network and, for the distribution of the Ebolapox, Halliwell had set up a secure communications line between the Triad leader and Halliwell's office in Shanghai.

He'd been assured that everything was ready.

Halliwell's target list included Beijing's Capitol Airport as well as the underground and key airconditioning systems. Unbeknown to Halliwell, Kadeer's list was remarkably similar. It would come down to which of the final attackers could get their hands on the deadly vials first.

Halliwell locked the plans for Beijing in his safe and headed towards the lift. Dolinsky had succeeded in combining the RNA and DNA viruses and the chimpanzees subjected to the Ebolapox supervirus had all died violent deaths. It was time to find out if the virus had a similar effect on humans.

Halliwell paid the pound man in cash and watched him leave. After the delivery door slid back into place, he turned his attention to the first of the drug-addicted vagrants strapped to the steel trolleys – a black woman in her late twenties, needle marks visible on her arms and legs. Being black, she would have a smaller brain than her white counterparts, Halliwell mused, moving to another trolley where a second woman lay. This one had dirty matted hair and mud-stained legs and when he saw the fear in her wide blue eyes, Halliwell felt a surge of power. He paused and then decided against it. She had small breasts, and in any case, she was in her early forties. That said, the human flotsam in front of him on the trolley was white, so there would be no decision needed as to which one he would inject with the vaccine.

Halliwell began to suit up. He was particularly interested to see if, in addition to the bloody pustules of smallpox, the symptoms of Ebola might also appear – blinding headache and muscle aches, excruciating abdominal pain, nausea, searing sore throat, dizziness, tachycardia, vomiting of blood and continuous bloody diarrhoea. With the prognosis for Ebolapox and the viability of the vaccine looking promising, Halliwell felt an intense satisfaction as he wandered over to the CD player, selected Beethoven's Fifth Symphony and turned up the volume. Beethoven always enhanced his feeling of power and destiny.

In China, General Ho Feng, who was chairing the monthly Olympic Security meeting, had also watched the American President's address with interest and derision. For this meeting, Ho Feng had chosen the Qingdao Olympic Sailing Centre. The huge banner on the wall read: 同一个世界，同一个梦想 – 'One World, One Dream'.

A wooden board hung beside the banner. Under the heading 'Days to Go' was the number 212.

'I see the Americans are not too pleased with our space programs,' General Ho said as he opened the meeting. In addition to the representatives from the Beijing Organising Committee, the Police, the Peoples' Liberation Army and Intelligence, Ho was focusing on the Qingdao Sailing Test Event and the Chinese Navy was also represented. 'They had better get used to it,' Ho said with a sinister smile. 'They think they own it but not for long. Now, what progress on security of the harbour?'

The Naval Captain bowed and switched on a PowerPoint presentation with a satellite photograph of the harbour defences. 'The principle we are following is one of "above and below",' the Captain said, 'and while the police will look after things above the water, we will have 125 divers to look after the wharves and pontoons, and before any races or presentations we will do a thorough check for bombs and mines. Outside the harbour we will patrol with destroyers and other vessels.' Even at this meeting not all of the officials were cleared to know the locations of China's submarines but as the briefing progressed anyone present could not help but be impressed with the thoroughness of the Chinese preparations.

'Good,' General Ho said after the Naval Captain had finished his brief and the Chief of Police had outlined the plans for security on the surface. Even the lifejackets on the ferries would be inspected to ensure one had not been substituted with a look-alike bomb. 'You will also be pleased to know we are training 10,000 mice to taste the athletes' food before every course.' No one laughed because General Ho was deadly serious. 'And we have vaccinated 550,323 dogs in Beijing against rabies. This will not only be the greatest Games ever, it will also be the safest.'

'You've seen the reports on the planned protests?' Ho asked the Qingdao Police Chief after the meeting had finished.

'The Human Rights groups?' the Police Chief sneered.

Ho nodded. 'Including the Uighurs and the Animal Rights activists, although it is hard to tell the difference between those two,' Ho added sarcastically. 'Crush them, but out of sight of the cameras. Make sure they are not allowed to even gather here and I want special protection paid to the big bear farm near Lao Shan. I'm sure you will be able to do that without difficulty.'

'It will not be a problem, General Ho,' the Police Chief said with a knowing smile. Chinese *guanxi* worked both ways.

CHAPTER 84

HALLIWELL TOWER, ATLANTA

Simone pressed the intercom reply button. She was in a foul mood. 'I'll be with you in a moment, Richard.' She knew that would irritate him immensely; it was meant to, although this morning she would make one last attempt.

'Yes, Richard,' Simone said, as she stepped into his office.

'Is everything in order for New Hampshire,' he asked, without looking up from the papers he was working on.

'I've checked the accommodation. You and Constance are booked in at the Metropole. Esposito still refuses to take my calls so I'm not sure what his arrangements are,' she added pointedly.

Halliwell looked up from his desk, a cold anger in his eyes. 'Enough! Esposito is booked in at the same hotel I gave you to organise.'

Simone turned and walked out of the office, the fire in her eyes the same colour as her hair.

Dan Esposito, while ostensibly on President Bolton's team, had been a very busy man. No one knew better than Esposito that the New Hampshire primary would be crucial. Even though other states had now moved their primary dates forward, there had always been a debate as to whether New Hampshire was more important than Iowa, the next primary on the election calendar, but as a previous New Hampshire Governor had once put it, 'the people of Iowa pick corn, the people of New Hampshire pick Presidents'.

'My values in life are those my parents taught me, values that have made America the great nation we are today,' Halliwell began. The crowd, many of them handpicked broke into wild, flag-waving applause. Esposito's contacts had organised the layout of the podium, covered in red 'Halliwell' posters, down to the last camera angle. Constance Halliwell was on the Presidential candidate's right. Halliwell's son and daughter, together with their young families stood further to the right. On Halliwell's left, but still well in shot, stood America's most famous evangelist, the Reverend Jerry Buffett. Sally McLeod, Richard Halliwell's new but yet to be announced executive assistant, was well out of shot to the side. McLeod, a leggy, tanned, blue-eyed blonde had just graduated in political science from Georgia University and Dan Esposito had been none too impressed with Halliwell's insistence that she accompany them on the campaign trail. Esposito had acquiesced with a warning. 'Keep her out of camera shot and stay out of her pants, Halliwell, or you're fucking dead in the water.' Halliwell vowed that once he made the White House, it would be Esposito who would be dead in the water.

'We need a new face in Washington,' Halliwell continued, pausing to smile broadly the way Esposito's PR team had coaxed him.

'A face that is not tainted by the corruption we've seen in Congress. Someone who understands what it's like to live and work outside the beltway, someone who started at the bottom.' It was a carefully crafted strategy, designed to turn charges of Halliwell's lack of experience in Washington to an advantage, and if the early polls were anything to go by, it was working. Halliwell was leading President Bolton by fifteen percentage points.

'I stand before you today as a champion of family values, fidelity and freedom, and as the next President of the United States of America, I look forward to taking those values into the White House and the wider world,' he concluded, and the crowd went wild. New Hampshire was in the bag but, as Esposito had warned him, the race for the White House was a marathon, not a sprint.

'I'm very glad you could join us at such short notice, Sally. It's a real bonus to have someone with your qualifications on the team and if there's anything I can do, just ask,' Halliwell said smoothly, raising his champagne flute and clinking it with his new assistant. It was past midnight and Constance had long since retired to the suite Simone had booked in the fashionable old New England hotel. Halliwell and Sally were standing close together at the window of Sally's suite.

'It's a wonderful opportunity, Richard. I'm enjoying every moment,' Sally replied, smiling seductively and making no move to put any distance between her and her new boss. 'The crowd seemed very enthusiastic today, don't you think?'

'Couldn't be better. We're leading Bolton by a clear fifteen points,'

Halliwell replied, re-filling Sally's glass with Krug.

'That champagne is just wonderful,' she enthused. 'Do you think the other challengers are any threat?'

'Not if what Esposito tells me is right, and he ought to know,' he replied, confidently. Esposito did indeed know, and in six months time, with the Beijing Olympics a bare 30 days away, the only two to be left on the Republican side would be Halliwell and Bolton. Halliwell put his arm around Sally's waist and pointed towards the lights of Concord, New Hampshire's small but elegant capital. 'What we got from the people here today is just a taste of what's to come over the next six months, Sally. We're on our way to the White House,' Richard whispered, his hand beginning to wander.

CHAPTER 85

TIAN SHAN, THE HEAVENLY MOUNTAINS, XINJIANG

There was less than a month to go until the Games; white clouds streamed off the lower granite peaks of the Tian Shan, Xinjiang's heavenly mountains in the northern part of the autonomous region near the Chinese north-western border with Kazakhstan and Kyrgyzstan. The higher peaks, the Jengish Chokusu and the Khan Tengri or 'Lord of the Spirits' rose above the clouds and, at over 7000 metres, they were the most northerly peaks over that height anywhere in the world. The setting sun had touched the magnificent, craggy peaks and the snow was tinged with soft hues of orange and red.

In a safe house in the heavily wooded Alatau foothills, guarded by the same fiercely loyal tribal warriors who had escorted him into Peshawar, Khalid Kadeer weighed up his options, but his mood was bleak. The infidel had taken no notice of the warnings and the final solution would now be necessary. al-Falid, his firebrand lieutenant, had given him a message in one of their chat rooms that Dolinsky had perfected the Ebolapox and developed a vaccine. The news that Richard Halliwell had ordered a trial run of several thousand vials of the vaccine was puzzling but Kadeer had determined that could be put to al-Qaeda's use. Once al-Falid, Dolinsky and the vials of Ebolapox had reached the bear farm, there would be enough vaccine for his people in Xinjiang, Qingdao, Beijing and other selected cells around the world.

As the snow started to fall, coating the tall Alatau conifers with white crystals, Kadeer's thoughts turned to the United States and her allies. President Bolton had turned out to be far worse than Harrison, if that was possible, and there had been no response to Kadeer's demands for negotiation since the caesium chloride attacks. Instead, the Olympic fever that had been gripping Beijing for months had now engulfed the rest of the world. Beijing was a sea of flags and colourful bunting and with the Olympic torch just twenty-three days out from Beijing, the expectation of a nation was rising. Hundreds of millions of yuan had been spent on sporting stadiums, fireworks for test events, and opening and closing ceremonies, while the majority of people in the world didn't have water that was safe to drink, Kadeer thought sadly. The war in Iraq was costing over a billion dollars a week and the world continued to ignore the Chinese Communist Party's murderous persecution of the Uighur Muslims and other minority groups.

In Urumqi, the capital of Xinjiang, and in the other cities like Kashgar, the passage of the Olympic torch saturated the news, even when the Han Chinese had made another major oil discovery. Reporting on the US Presidential election was also scant, although

Kadeer had been following it very closely online. It remained to be seen what would happen if either a woman or a black Senator got up, but Bolton and Halliwell were only separated by a few percentage points and Kadeer knew he had no choice. It would be another four years before the unique circumstances of the Games came around again. With the opening ceremony timed for 8 p.m. on 8 August 2008, Kadeer knew he couldn't afford to wait until the Presidential elections. The first Tuesday in November would be way too late.

CHAPTER 86

HALLIWELL TOWER, ATLANTA

In the large office she shared with Imran, one floor below Halliwell's office, Kate listened with a sense of foreboding as Imran briefed Curtis on the secure STU phone the CIA had installed.

'The single strand has not only met its double, Curtis,' Imran said, his voice grave, 'but it's working every time. You and I both know that one of the major problems in genetically engineering a super virus is that once the RNA is incorporated into a bacterial plasmid, the reverse transcriptase enzyme often makes errors. That doesn't occur in nature because living cells contain proofreading mechanisms. Dolinsky is using reverse transcriptases that have much higher fidelity. Every chimpanzee that has been injected with Ebolapox has died within four days.'

At the memory of the experiments Kate fought to control her anger. When she'd assisted Imran with the necropsies, both of them had been sickened by the viciousness with which the Ebolapox had attacked every organ in the bodies of the chimps, turning their hearts, livers, spleens, kidneys and lungs into a dark, bloody mush. None of them knew that Halliwell had produced identical results on the vagrants.

'And Dolinsky's progress on vaccines?' Curtis asked, his voice reflecting the worry he shared with Imran and Kate.

'That's the chilling part, Curtis. Normally it would take over a year, perhaps more to develop an effective vaccine, but since he's arrived he's produced several, although only one of those is effective.'

'One is enough to give this administration the confidence to use this as a weapon,' Curtis replied.

'Halliwell has directed that several thousand doses be prepared, which I find very odd, but Dolinsky's rapid progress is even more disturbing. The Russians might have removed him from this sort of program but looking at the way he's worked, you get the feeling we've not so much been involved in research here as helped to put the finishing touches to a program Dolinsky might have already been close to finishing. If the White House wanted proof that this could be done, I could have explained that on a whiteboard,' Imran said, frustrated.

'I agree,' Curtis said. 'I think perhaps it's time you and Kate came to Washington to bring Tom McNamara, the Deputy Director of Operations up to date. When do you and Kate get back from Singapore?' he asked, disappointed that pressures of work would prevent him from going to the International Bioterrorism Conference this time around.

'We'll be away for a little over two weeks,' Imran replied. 'The World Health Organization has a conference in Kuala Lumpur two days after Singapore.'

'Swing by Washington on your way home. Enjoy,' he added wistfully.

The day after Imran and Kate left for Singapore, al-Falid arranged to meet Eduard Dolinsky inside the Halliwell Laboratories. With Halliwell away campaigning there was even less chance of being disturbed.

'The ocean-going tug, the *George Washington* is berthed at the ocean terminal in Savannah,' al-Falid said quietly, pulling up the overhead photographs of the port that had been published on the internet. 'It is just here, east of the oil terminal and not far from the maintenance dock. After the surveillance team clocks off, a vehicle will pick you up from your apartment tomorrow night. It's going to take two weeks to get there, and even though it is summer in China, it can still get very cold where you're going so pack some warm clothes.'

'The vials of Ebolapox, Amon?' Dolinsky asked, worried. 'They are extremely dangerous.'

'You are to crate the liquid nitrogen trolleys and mark them 'medical supplies'. They're to be in the loading bay at precisely 4 p.m. tomorrow afternoon. I've arranged for one of Halliwell's vehicles to pick up the crate. The drivers will be instructed to make sure it's securely fastened to the floor of the truck but on no account are they to be told what's in it. The paperwork being prepared will release the vaccines and the trucks will be met outside the port, as you will be, and I've arranged for your paperwork as well. Familiarise yourself

with what is in this and destroy it,' al-Falid commanded, handing
Dolinsky a brown envelope. 'This contains your new identity papers,'
he said, handing Dolinsky another smaller envelope. 'Keep them on
you at all times.'

The moonlight was reflected on a placid Savannah River as the
George Washington, her cargoes safely loaded, eased away from the
Ocean Terminal. Eduard Dolinsky felt some satisfaction at having
achieved what many scientists a few years before thought was impossible; he also felt a strange sense of foreboding. He was confident in
the vaccines in the hold but very worried about what might happen to the deadly vials stored in the big freezers alongside them. As
they passed the Tybee Lighthouse and the tug's massive bows rose
to meet the swell of the Atlantic beyond, Eduard Dolinsky's foreboding increased.

Sixteen days later, as Kate and Imran flew back into Washington
and with just one week before the Opening Ceremony of the Beijing Olympics, the captain of the *George Washington* eased the twin
throttles back and the tug steamed slowly into the Chinese port city
of Qingdao. Situated on the Yellow Sea roughly 800 kilometres east
of Beijing, Qingdao was the sixteenth largest port in the world with
vast warehouse storage and loading facilities capable of handling
more than 100 million tons of cargo and containers each year.

Dr Eduard Dolinsky scanned the shoreline, contempt in his dark eyes. In the city of seven million people the western influence was unmistakable. Terracotta tiles dating back to the days when the city was run by the Qing dynasty in the seventeenth century were over-shadowed by crowded apartment buildings and soaring high-rise office blocks. Further to the north-east, clouds obscured the top of the 915-metre Mount Lao, the highest mountain on the Chinese coast. The Qingdao Bear Farm nestled in the foothills below the mountain's ancient Tao palaces and temples.

The captain of the *George Washington* felt relaxed and confident. al-Qaeda tentacles reached into hundreds of large cities around the world, and given the Chinese government suppression of the Muslim Uighurs in Xinjiang, an al-Qaeda presence in Chinese cities had been inevitable and Qingdao was no exception. The sealed silver trunk with the vials of lethal Ebolapox was stored at the bottom of the tug's big freezer near the galley. With over 100 million tons of cargo coming in every year, the authorities focused on containers, and even then they were only able to physically check a fraction of them. Like their western counterparts, Chinese customs officials relied on intelligence and tip-offs for interceptions of drugs, pornography and any western publications that might be considered harmful to the State.

al-Qaeda's finances ensured that both Dr Dolinsky and the trunks marked 'medical supplies' were driven out off the wharves in a Qingdao Port Authority four-wheel drive without inspection. After a simple vehicle change in nearby Mengzhang Road, Dolinsky and the Ebolapox were taken north through the big Renmin Road roundabout and then east towards the Qingdao Bear Farm 30 kilometres away at the base of Lao Shan in rural Shandong Province.

CHAPTER 87

CIA HEADQUARTERS, LANGLEY, VIRGINIA

'Welcome back guys,' Curtis said, refraining from giving Kate a kiss on the cheek. He shook hands with her and Imran as they arrived at his office. 'Coffee? It's my own machine you know,' he said, giving Kate a wink.

'So what's been happening while we've been away?' Imran asked.

'Usual suspects on the TV,' Curtis replied. 'President Bolton's closing the gap on Halliwell but if either of those get up it'll be bad news in my book. I suspect the average American is beginning to get very nervous about Kadeer's final solution threat and Bolton's taking a hard line. We're not getting anything definitive on Beijing but the hooplah is in full swing and the American athletes leave for the Games shortly. How was Singapore and the world of microbiology?'

'Singapore was a good break but the world of microbiology is more dangerous than ever I'm afraid,' Imran said somberly. 'I think we should be suggesting that this program be shut down. Dolinsky's proved it can be done and we can store his vaccine; that's been a truly remarkable achievement, but I think the Ebolapox stocks should be destroyed.'

'I suspect we won't have much more luck with that than we've had with smallpox but we can give it a shot. The DDO's still tied up, he'll give me a yell when he's ready.

'I grabbed this before I left Halliwell just in case your in-tray gets low,' Kate said with a grin, retrieving 'The Halliwell Report' from her bag and handing it to Curtis. She relaxed back into a chair that would not have been out of place among the relics in Tom McNamara's office. 'The latest piece of extravagance to come out of the thirty-seventh floor.'

'Must have cost a fortune,' Curtis said, as he idly thumbed through over a hundred glossy pages covered in marketing hype and coloured photographs. A sizeable proportion of them were of Richard Halliwell presenting cheques to charity organisations or hosting luncheons and dinners for visiting dignitaries. He was about to put the report back on his desk when he came to the start of the financial pages. The section began with a letter confirming the outstanding financial position of the company and predicted even greater growth for Halliwell in the years ahead. At the end of the letter was a signature – Dr Alan Ferraro, Chief Financial Officer, but it was the photograph of Ferraro that caught Curtis' attention.

'Have you met Halliwell's Chief Financial Officer, this Dr Ferraro?' Curtis asked.

Kate shook her head.

'I've been introduced to him very briefly; he works on the floor below us so we don't have any contact. Why?' Imran asked.

'I have the distinct feeling I've seen a photograph of this guy or someone very like him somewhere before,' Curtis said, racking his brain, then he remembered. It was the nose.

'I wonder.' With a mixture of anticipation and rising anger at the memory of it all, Curtis turned to his computer and called up the gruesome images of the young agent's burning car outside the Taliban *madrassa* in Peshawar. Although Dr Alan Ferraro was no longer sporting a beard, the resemblance was uncanny.

'Have a look at this,' Curtis said to Kate and Imran, turning his screen so they could see the images. 'Some time ago we lost a young agent near Peshawar. We've been looking for that guy there,' Curtis said, pointing to the image of al-Falid's bearded face and hooked nose, 'and I'm wondering if Dr Alan Ferraro might also be Dr Amon al-Falid.'

'There's a strong resemblance,' Kate agreed. Curtis knew only too well that al-Falid had left the country on an academic sabbatical but despite extensive efforts to track his return, he hadn't shown up on any of the Customs or Homeland Security's crosschecks and Michigan University had never heard of him.

Curtis typed in a request to Homeland Security for a report on Alan Ferraro's movements in the past two years. Even with the most sophisticated checks, if the two passports had never been matched, it was still possible for someone to leave as Dr Amon al-Falid and return as Dr Alan Ferraro.

CHAPTER 88

HALLIWELL TOWER, ATLANTA

On the front page of Atlanta's major daily newspaper, *The Atlanta Journal-Constitution,* two headlines shared the front page:

SEVEN DAYS UNTIL BEIJING OLYMPIC OPENING CEREMONY: TIGHT SECURITY SURROUNDS OLYMPIC FLAME

SOME HARD CAMPAIGNING AHEAD: BOLTON GAINS ON HALLIWELL AS REPUBLICAN CONVENTION LOOMS

The advantage of incumbency and the fear of another attack was beginning to tell. President Bolton's position and rhetoric against Muslim terrorists had moved even further to the right than the tough stance he'd been renowned for when he was Vice President. In many parts of Europe, his refusal to negotiate with anyone who was not with America in the war on terror, including Iran and Syria, was seen as arrogant. He was known as the 'ugly American' in Europe but his speeches had started to resonate with the American people who increasingly saw themselves under siege from the rest of the world.

'Richard Halliwell might have a big smile,' Chuck Bolton was fond of saying, 'but this is war and this country needs more than dental floss to defeat an enemy who's hell bent on destroying our way of life.'

With just five primaries to go, the Republican Convention was going to be won and lost in the next few weeks. The photograph on the front page of *The Atlanta Journal-Constitution* showed Richard with his arm around Constance, campaigning in Louisiana. He'd dismissed the latest polls but Simone thought he looked to be in trouble and she decided she would give it one last try to get on the team. She picked up the phone and pressed the speed dial for Richard's mobile.

'Halliwell.'

'Richard, it's Simone,' she said. Knowing that her name would have come up on Richard's phone she kept her anger at his curt response in check. 'I saw the vote tallies and I thought I'd let you know that the offer of help on your campaign is still open.' Simone couldn't remember feeling this powerless.

'How many times do I have to say this, Simone. If it were up to me that would be fine,' Halliwell said irritably. He wasn't quite ready to fire her as he needed her to run things back in Atlanta, but the time was fast approaching. 'I've discussed this with Esposito before. He's given a flat no and you've as good as said it yourself, image is everything. I'm running a campaign on family values, and

Constance is going to be in every photo opportunity we get. Unless there's a problem down there, don't interrupt the campaign.' The line went dead.

Simone glared at the photograph. Despite Esposito's instructions, the well-endowed blonde she had seen in some of the earlier campaign photographs was there again, almost out of shot. When Simone had asked what the woman's role was Halliwell had been defensive. 'For Christ's sake, Simone,' Halliwell had exploded. 'She's a political science graduate from Georgia University.'

The reminders of the man she had hoped she would one day accompany into the White House were everywhere. The previous month's copy of *Pharmaceutical*, the industry's major glossy magazine had a picture of Richard on the front cover. Simone had already read the article, but she picked up the magazine again and had begun to flick through it when a small advertisement in the classifieds caught her eye. 'Executive Assistant For High Profile CEO'. The company wasn't named but the job description seemed uncannily like the one she'd applied for eight years before; then she saw Richard's private box number. Jealous and angry, Simone searched for the spare set of keys she had for Richard's desk drawers. Up until now she'd never felt the need to search them but if there were any job applications in the drawers or in his safe, Simone was determined to find them.

Other than some of his personal papers, the first drawers drew a blank. In the larger bottom drawer, there was a file containing the folders from applicants for her job. The first five had been rejected. Probably wouldn't come across, Simone thought angrily. The sixth file contained a letter of appointment as Executive Personal Assistant to Dr Richard Halliwell, Chief Executive Officer of Halliwell

Pharmaceuticals. The letter was a copy of one that had been sent to Ms Sally McLeod. On the inside of the file was a photograph of a leggy blonde matching the one on the front page of *The Atlanta Journal-Constitution*. Simone pushed the button on the side of Halliwell's desk. As the liquor cabinet swung out from the wall, she walked over and reached for the bottle of Chivas Regal.

CHAPTER 89

CIA HEADQUARTERS, LANGLEY, VIRGINIA

'From the boys in imagery – Dr Amon al-Falid alias Dr Alan Ferraro,' Curtis said darkly after they'd returned from the DDO briefing. The computer-enhanced photographs of the senior Halliwell executive matched the satellite images of the man beside agent Bill Crawford's car in Peshawar. 'Amon is a variation on the Egyptian *Amun*, meaning hidden, which is pretty bloody apt.'

'Doesn't seem much doubt there's a link between al-Falid and the Taliban *madrassas*, but I wonder if that link extends to al-Qaeda?' Imran mused.

'We're about to find out. I've asked young Corey Barrino to come up.'

'An expert on al-Qaeda?' Kate asked, puzzled as to how the CIA would have a young expert on the complex and sinister workings of the Islamic fundamentalists.

Curtis shook his head. 'In a previous life he was a computer geek.

Used to get his rocks off hacking into the Pentagon and NASA's classified networks and leaving messages for them. He hacked into here once and left a message for the Director and I think you can still see the spot where the paperweight hit the wall. He got caught when he went into a big merchant bank. They wouldn't accept their systems had been breached until he left a message for their CEO with a list of all his top clients' bank account numbers and then the shit really hit the fan. Fortunately for us, after he served out his good behaviour bond, we found a better use for those talents and I'm hoping he might be able to get into Ferraro's computer at Halliwell. The al-Falids of this world keep dual identities for a reason but sometimes they think they're infallible and they keep encrypted files as well.' Curtis was interrupted by a knock on the door.

'That'll be him. Corey, come on in. Professor Imran Sayed, Dr Kate Braithwaite – Corey Barrino.'

'Hi, good to meet you,' Kate said, holding out her hand.

'Hi,' Corey said shyly. Kate thought he looked about sixteen, but to be working for the CIA he was probably quite a bit older.

'Any particular area you want in Halliwell,' Corey asked after he'd taken over Curtis' computer and dialed up the website.

'Several but we'll start with a Dr Alan Ferraro,' Curtis said.

'The Chief Financial Officer?' Corey asked, his fingers tapping the keys.

'He's the one.'

'Access Denied' flashed up on the computer screen and Kate watched, fascinated, as Corey's hands flew across the keyboard, a look of concentration on his face.

'They've added a salt to the DES,' Corey muttered, totally

absorbed by the lines of numbers, letters and symbols that to Kate, as mathematically savvy as she was, looked like a jumble. 'Salt to the DES?' she whispered to Curtis, her inquiring mind frustrated that she didn't have the vaguest idea of what Corey was talking about.

Curtis grinned. He'd had the same problem until Corey had put him through 'Hacking 101'. 'A "salt" is just another layer of data that makes it harder to crack the Data Encryption Standard or DES algorithm. It is two characters that are added to either end of a password. They can be chosen from upper- and lower-case letters of the alphabet or the numbers 0 to 9 or a full stop or a forward slash. With a choice of sixty-four characters either end, you get a possible 4096 different salts to use on your password, making it a lot harder for your average hacker.'

As Curtis already knew, and Kate and Imran were about to find out, Corey Barrino was anything but an 'average hacker'. In real life, hackers were often shy but still sought recognition from their fellow hackers. If they managed to hack into a particularly sensitive target like the Pentagon or the CIA, as Corey had done back in the days when his handle was 'Byte Blaster', those feats would be posted on cybernet bulletin boards. Proof was provided by posting a piece of information that could only have been obtained from within that organisation's system. The more protected the system, the greater the recognition. In the murky world of cyberspace 'Byte Blaster' had been a hero.

Corey ran a program that would have crashed most medium-sized networks but it only required a fraction of the big Cray computers in the CIA's basement. In a matter of minutes, Corey had cracked Halliwell's password file. Ferraro's name was in clear but his password was encrypted. After several more minutes and millions of computations the blur on the screen suddenly stopped.

'Welcome Dr Ferraro' was displayed on the screen. They were in.

'Where do you want me to start?' Corey asked as dozens of folders appeared on the file library.

'I'm looking for a file that probably looks fairly innocuous but won't be able to be opened, even if someone happened to obtain Ferraro's password.

'Two possibilities,' he said finally. 'Either "Silk Road Architecture" or "Duple".'

'"Duple" is Latin for double,' Kate offered.

'Where the single strand meets its double,' Curtis said. 'Something tells me that Ferraro would be more subtle than that, although it could also be a second set of accounts for Halliwell. Let's go for the Silk Road Architecture.'

'Whatever he's got behind here, he doesn't want anyone else to see it, or certainly not anyone in Halliwell,' Corey said twenty minutes later, as the big Cray computer continued to make millions of high speed calculations in parallel with one another. Suddenly the screen calculations stopped.

'Cold-blooded murderous bastard,' was all Curtis said as he scanned down the subfolders headed with names like 'Air Force One' and 'Caesium Chloride'.

'Shall I check if he's encrypted these as well?'

Curtis nodded and Corey clicked on 'London'. The file contained a series of documents, including diagrams of the Thames Water reticulation systems and locations of water treatment plants and maps of Trafalgar Square.

'All open source stuff but when you put it all together it will be enough to put him away for the rest of his life,' Kate observed.

'In this country we send them to the electric chair.'

'Barbaric and too good for him,' Kate responded. 'He should rot in jail.'

Curtis leaned over and clicked open the folder marked 'Travel'. It looks as if our friend is in Beijing,' Curtis observed, opening a sub-folder that showed confirmation of a departure the previous day.

'Do you want me to bust in to "Duple"?' Corey asked, a smile on his face.

A short while later the complete accounts for Halliwell Pharmaceuticals were on the screen, but this time they were the real accounts.

'Corey, you're a genius, you can leave the rest with us,' Curtis said, noticing a folder headed 'Bolton' towards the end of the library and not wanting the young man to be exposed to what a folder on the President might contain.

'I get paid for this now,' Corey said, giving Kate a grin and writing down a series of code words that would get Curtis back into the systems. 'As long as you're careful not to change anything they probably won't notice you've been in there, although if Ferraro is the only one that opens some of these files, the date/time group for the last usage could alert him.' With that Corey headed back towards the basement.

'Jesus Christ!' Curtis muttered. The bribes to the then Vice President Bolton ran into the tens of millions, all directed to a bank in the Bahamas. Curtis clicked on a subfolder headed 'Meetings' and opened the most recent file. The audio took a few seconds to spool up but the voices of Bolton and Richard Halliwell were unmistakable.

CHAPTER 90

CIA HEADQUARTERS, LANGLEY, VIRGINIA

Tom McNamara shook his head in disbelief after Curtis had shown him the bank accounts and played the tape of the conversation. In a career spanning nearly forty years, McNamara had seen President Nixon resign before he was impeached for criminal conduct and he'd seen Vice President Spiro Agnew resign over corruption. For McNamara, corruption in high office was nothing new, it had been going on since the dawn of time, but the sheer magnitude of the payments to Bolton made Nixon and Agnew look like amateurs.

'Well, I suppose if you're going to rob a bank, you might as well rob a big one,' McNamara said cynically.

'It's not the bribes I'm worried about, Tom, it's the conspiracy to attack the Chinese in Beijing and murder half the human race in the process. In a few days time, Beijing's Capitol Airport will be handling more than eighty aircraft an hour. And at the end of the Games we might be faced with Ebolapox being transported to hundreds of thousands of cities and towns as people return home.'

'Every time I think I've seen everything in politics, some power hungry asshole proves me wrong and from what Professor Sayed and Dr Braithwaite have told us, Dolinsky was a lot further down the track than we thought. Where's Halliwell at the moment?'

'Campaigning in Louisiana. Kate says he's due back the day after tomorrow.'

'And the Ebolapox?'

'Ferraro alias al-Falid left for Beijing yesterday and although he wouldn't be stupid enough to try and get vials of a deadly virus through an airport, or I hope he wouldn't, I've scrambled one of our jets. Imran's got some debriefing to do at the UN, so I've sent Braithwaite down to Atlanta to check it's all still there in the Halliwell vaults. This is every bit as dangerous as you and I thought it would be.'

'I think Imran's right. We should shut this fucking Ebolapox program down immediately,' Tom said, angry at the short-sightedness of those who'd refused to destroy the smallpox stocks when they'd had the chance. 'Although that's only half the problem. After we've arrested Halliwell, all hell's going to break loose because it will just about sink the Republicans. Given wunderkind's relationship with the President,' Tom said, looking up towards the seventh floor, 'I wouldn't be surprised if they try and find a way of keeping this quiet until after the election. As for arresting the President . . .'

'Impeachment?'

'That's what it will come down to, but can you imagine the impact of a trial in the Senate? Thanks to our "bomb now, ask questions later" foreign policy, not to mention the conviction in some quarters that God is on our side, somewhere in the world, someone burns one of our flags every day of the fucking week. I'm not one for covering up the stinking cesspits some of our politicians swim in, but if it ever comes out that the American President was part of a plot to poison half the world's population, Islam versus the West will go into meltdown.'

'I think you're right,' Curtis agreed. 'The fact that he wasn't President at the time is not going to save us, although I have a suggestion. Before you go up to the seventh floor and give them a chance to put the lid on this, there is one man on the Hill we can trust.'

'Name him,' Tom responded grumpily, 'or is it a her?'

Curtis grinned, ignoring the bait. 'Professor Sayed is very good friends with the Speaker of the House.'

'Didn't you say Speaker Burton is Halliwell's father-in-law?'

'Even if his daughter is up to her neck in this, and I suspect she hasn't the faintest idea what her psychopathic husband's been up to, he wouldn't flinch. More importantly, he might have an insight into how best to handle this. Davis Burton is a man of great principle and a Vietnam veteran.'

Tom nodded. 'I remember, Congressional Medal of Honour when his platoon bumped into 200 VC on a track in the jungle. Very cool under fire and effectively saved their lives.' Tom McNamara looked thoughtful. It was a risk, but he'd been in that business all his life. Wunderkind could wait a little while longer. 'Twenty-four hours long enough?' was all he said.

CHAPTER 91

THE HOUSE SPEAKER'S OFFICE, CONGRESS, WASHINGTON DC

Randy Baker's ears pricked up as the young congressional page in the House Speaker's Office watched the flurry of activity around the Speaker's personal secretary. Appointments for meetings with some of the most powerful people in Washington were being re-scheduled at very short notice and that could only mean something of importance. Baker was surprised when they introduced themselves. He'd never heard of a Professor Sayed or a Curtis O'Connor but in a moment they were hurried into the Speaker's Office.

'I must admit,' Davis Burton said solemnly after Curtis had played the tape and briefed him on the possibility of a cover-up, 'this is argu-ably the gravest constitutional crisis the United States has ever faced. And I mean no disrespect, gentlemen, but if you hadn't brought that recording with you I would have found it hard to believe,' he added. 'Although it wouldn't be the first time men in high office have been seduced by power and money.'

'I think Tom McNamara and Curtis are right though, Davis,' Imran responded. 'I'm not one for covering things up either, but exposure of the President's involvement in something the magnitude of the Beijing conspiracy would do immense harm, not only to the United States, but to other nations around the world. The economic implications would make the Wall Street crash of 1929 look like a small bump in the road and anti-western sentiment would explode. This is one of those rare occasions when disclosure is not in the public interest. The trouble is, Davis, if Bolton is impeached – and he clearly should be – I don't see how you and your colleagues can prevent it from becoming public.'

The great southern statesman was silent, wondering how he might deal with the crisis in a way that would best serve his nation and the wider world.

'Not only that,' Curtis added, 'if I understand the impeachment process correctly, President Bolton would continue to act as President until the Senate decides he's guilty or they acquit him. We can't just bowl in to the Oval Office and arrest the President.'

'If this was not so real it would be the stuff of movies,' Davis Burton said. 'You've actually given me an idea. It will depend on whether I can get my colleagues on side. It will be important for them all to remain silent until we're prepared to act. There is a little-known section of the Constitution that allows just one person in this country to arrest the President. But you're right,' he added, 'it would be unwise to attempt that in the Oval Office.'

It was a very risky strategy and one that could only be justified by the extraordinary circumstances that prevailed when a President or Vice President became involved in criminal activities.

As soon as Burton's visitors had left, Randy Baker became even more intrigued. All of the Speaker's appointments were suddenly cancelled. Randy wandered down the corridor to find a quiet place to use the mobile phone his generous mentor had provided. He felt a surge of excitement. Politics was where it was at and he knew that this was going to be a very exciting career.

As he was leaving, Curtis switched on his phone to find an alarming text from Kate. The vials of the deadly Ebolapox, together with those of the vaccines, had vanished and Dolinsky was nowhere to be found.

CHAPTER 92

HALLIWELL LABORATORIES, ATLANTA

Kate Braithwaite turned on the decontamination shower and let the water run over her face plate and the rest of her biosuit. She felt sick but she forced herself to remain calm and resisted the urge to cut the shower short, kicking herself that she hadn't raised the alarm earlier when she'd questioned Dr Dolinsky about why he was preparing so many vials of the virus, and why there had been a semi-commercial production run of the vaccine.

Kate took the lift to the thirty-seventh floor and pressed the button beside the combination lock and swipe-card track. Neither she nor Imran had been given an access card that was programmed for Halliwell's inner sanctum.

'Can I help you?' Simone Carstair's voice sounded slurred.

'It's Kate Braithwaite.' After an audible click, Kate pushed the heavy red door. Simone was not at her desk, but the door to Halliwell's office was ajar. Simone was standing beside Halliwell's desk with a large glass of whiskey in her hand, staring out at Stone Mountain.

'Do you know where Dr Dolinsky is, Simone?'

'No and I don't care. Dolinsky hasn't been around for the past two weeks,' Simone said, swaying on her feet as she turned around. Kate realised she had been crying.

'Are you alright?' Kate asked. Simone Carstairs had not struck her as the type to give in to tears.

'I will be, although I may not be around for much longer. I suspect I'm about to be replaced,' Simone said thickly. The job application she had found in Richard's drawer lay on the desk.

'I'm sorry to hear that, Simone. Do you mind me asking why?' asked Kate, surprised to find that Simone had been drinking heavily.

'No, it will be public knowledge soon enough. Dr Halliwell has decided to replace me with a younger woman,' Simone said, the alcohol loosening the grip she normally kept on her private life, 'which is a bit rich after all the years I've given him here but that's life on a rubber raft, honey. I told you he was a ruthless, ambitious bastard, I just didn't think it would happen to me.' She walked unsteadily towards Halliwell's liquor cabinet and returned with the half empty bottle of Chivas.

'Aren't you going to fight?' Kate asked, puzzled at the sudden change in demeanor of the fiery Simone.

'I thought about it. I've got enough on that miserable, hypocritical prick to send him up the river four times over, but you know what? I'm over him.' Her words were running into one another. 'He's a lousy fucking lover and if someone else wants to crawl over that prissy little wife of his when she becomes First Lady to get to him, then they're welcome. I have myself quite a nice place in the Bahamas and I'm out of here.'

Kate didn't hear Simone's diatribe. She was staring at the roof of the Halliwell Level 4 laboratories. Something wasn't quite right, then she realised what it was. When viewed from the thirty-seventh floor the area of roof was considerably bigger than the area she and Imran had shared with Dolinsky; not only that, Kate could count twice the number of venting systems.

'Is there more than one entrance to the Level 4 laboratories?' Kate asked.

'Why do you want to know?' Simone asked, sobering up a little.

Simone hadn't denied it and Kate decided to probe further. 'Can we sit down,' she said, moving towards the leather lounge chairs. 'Look, I know you're upset at the moment,' Kate began, 'and I'm genuinely sorry to hear you might go but some of the programs that are running here are not all they seem. My colleagues and I think Richard Halliwell might be involved in some dangerous and illegal activities. If he is and you protect him, then your chances of getting to the Bahamas will be about zero. On the other hand, if you help us then you'll be home free,' Kate said, flashing her CIA badge.

Simone stared out at the gathering dusk. 'Why not,' she said, retrieving the key to the lift from Halliwell's still-open desk drawer. 'I've always wondered what was down there but first I gotta go to the bathroom, honey.'

It was amazing how alcohol could remove a veneer, Kate thought, as she punched in Curtis' speed dial.

'I can't talk for long,' she said. 'I'm in Halliwell's office. Simone's legless but she's about to show me a lift which I think leads to another lab at the back of the Level 4 complex.'

'Where's Halliwell?'

'Not due back until the day after tomorrow, got to go,' Kate said, not willing to risk Simone coming out of Halliwell's private bathroom and finding her on the phone.

Halliwell negotiated the steps to his private jet almost before they hit the tarmac of Atlanta's Hartsfield-Jackson Airport and he strode over to his McLaren that the valet parking service had brought around to the front of the VIP terminal. As he sped back to his headquarters Halliwell's mind was racing. In two days time he had planned to return to supervise the dispatch of the vials of Ebolapox and vaccines to Beijing, and a visit by Professor Sayed to the office of the Speaker in Washington would normally not have concerned him. Halliwell knew the two men shared the same flawed views against the war in Iraq, but for him to be accompanied by the CIA agent in charge of PLASMID, and for the Speaker to cancel his entire program as soon as they'd left had rung alarm bells. Halliwell had already decided that Dolinsky and that stuck-up bitch Braithwaite would be meeting with a nasty laboratory accident as soon as the vials of Ebolapox were aboard his jet and on their way to Beijing, but Halliwell needed to be sure they were still safe.

It took Simone three attempts before she got the key in the lock but eventually the lift took them down to a small basement area where they were stopped by another heavy stainless steel door protected by a combination lock.

'He changes his combinations on the first day of every month but he always uses the same series of numbers on all of the locks, so unless this is any different . . .' Simone said, feeling for each button before she pushed it. '*Voila* . . .' The door swung aside, revealing the long tunnel to Halliwell's private laboratories. At the far end of the tunnel, when they opened the second heavy door, Kate gasped as she was confronted with surroundings she was all too familiar with.

'This is a Level 3 preparation area,' she said, looking at Halliwell's blue biosuit with its regulator and boots ready for use.

'A what, honey?'

'Never mind,' Kate said, preparing to leave.

'Don't you want to see what's on the other side of that door?' Simone asked, pointing unsteadily to the airlock door marked with the international biohazard warning.

'I've seen enough,' Kate said, locking the door and guiding Simone back up the long tunnel they'd just come from.

Richard Halliwell's steely grey eyes narrowed as he saw the half-empty whiskey bottle and the open desk drawer. The key to the lift was gone. Halliwell unlocked the other drawer to his desk and took out the Luger pistol he kept there. He slipped it into his pocket and pressed the button for the lift, putting his ear to the doors. The lift mechanism was humming. Whoever was down there had left the key in the lock. Two minutes later he stepped out of the lift and into the tunnel to find Kate and Simone about 200 metres away, walking towards him.

'Well, well, well, what do we have here?' Halliwell sneered.

Simone staggered to the side of the tunnel. Kate's heart sank as she turned and looked back behind her. It was nearly 800 metres to the far door and on the other side was a hot lab. Halliwell's slow and deliberate steps rang hollow on the concrete floor of the tunnel as his voice echoed off the walls.

'You'll be back there soon enough, I can promise you, Dr Braithwaite.' Ignoring the sight of Simone slumped against the wall of the tunnel, Halliwell felt a surge of power as he got closer to Kate and another idea took shape.

'Before I inject you with Ebolapox, you bitch, we'll see what you look like naked and strapped to a trolley,' he whispered under his breath. He could feel his erection hardening as he took the Luger from his pocket.

CHAPTER 93

HALLIWELL LABORATORIES, ATLANTA

Curtis felt the pit of his stomach tighten as the white, unmarked CIA Learjet taxied to a halt beside the black Learjet 60 with the unmistakable gold 'H' on the tail fin. Could Halliwell have returned early? he wondered.

Special Agent Rob Bauer, a rugged-looking veteran FBI operative Curtis had known and worked with for over twenty years, was waiting for him with a search warrant for Halliwell Tower and a warrant for Halliwell's arrest.

'Halliwell arrived a quarter of an hour ago,' Rob said, as they climbed into his unmarked car. 'I've got back up from the Atlanta Police Department but I kept them at a distance until I knew how you wanted to play this one.' Two dark blue patrol cars with the familiar red stripe of the Atlanta Police Department had taken up positions some distance from the entrance to Halliwell Pharmaceuticals. Rob Bauer was well aware the entrance was under continual surveillance. 'You know better than I do that if we arrest this guy the shit's going to hit the fan big time,' Rob said, as he swung out of the VIP arrivals area at the airport.

Curtis nodded. The trust between the two was rock solid. 'That's putting it mildly, buddy, but you're going to have to trust me on this one. Halliwell is not the only high flyer mixed up in criminal activities here, but we need to get there in a hurry, Rob. I've a feeling that the life of one of my officers is on the line.'

Rob Bauer put a portable flashing blue light on the roof of the car and switched to the frequency of the two patrol cars. The time for subtlety had long disappeared, both men gambling that the sounds of sirens might make Halliwell think twice.

Deep in the tunnel underneath the Halliwell Tower, neither Dr Halliwell nor the two women he was shepherding towards the hot zone at the far end heard anything other than footsteps echoing eerily off the reinforced cement walls.

Halliwell pointed his Luger menacingly at Kate. 'You first! Get on the trolley!' he demanded. Keeping the pistol pointed at Kate's head, he clipped and tightened the straps around her ankles with one hand, then anchored her wrists.

'You're next,' Halliwell snarled, turning his attention to Simone. Simone fell off the trolley at her first attempt, the stainless steel gurney running into the far wall of the preparation room with a loud clang. Halliwell put the pistol back in his pocket, retrieved the trolley and manhandled Simone onto it. 'A pity you let your curiosity get the better of you,' he sneered as he wheeled the trolley into a waiting bay. 'From the research I've done, Ebolapox works even better on humans than it does on the chimps, but we can always do with a healthy specimen like you to confirm it. It's one of the cornerstones of scientific research.' Simone's red hair was in disarray and her green eyes reflected her fear of Halliwell. She had always known Halliwell to be ruthless, but even she had not detected the mind of the monster standing over her. 'Any hypothesis requires very rigorous testing before it is proven and the tests must be able to be replicated many times,' he snarled.

Simone fought against the nylon straps holding her down as the effects of the alcohol started to wane. There had been many times when she'd witnessed Halliwell exercise charm to control people, but now he was showing he was equally at home with violence. Simone shuddered. A psychopath, running for the highest office in the United States.

Halliwell left the curtain open. 'You should watch this,' he said, as he moved back to the other trolley.

He ran his hand slowly up the inside of Kate's thigh.

Kate spat at him as he caressed her crotch. 'You filthy deranged bastard. Get your hands off me.'

'You're going to regret that,' Halliwell said coldly, as he wiped his face and went in search of some tape.

Rob Bauer screeched to a halt at the Halliwell guardhouse. The sirens of the two Atlanta Police Department patrol cars died as they stopped behind.

'FBI. Open the gate,' Bauer said, flashing his badge.

The guard hesitated and turned towards his supervisor, who was trying to reach Halliwell on the phone. The supervisor shook his head as Halliwell's phone rang out. The man's orders were explicit, no one got in without authority and he would need to hold the police until he could get in touch with the boss. Curtis could see Halliwell's red McLaren sports car parked in front of the Tower entrance.

'He's here and he was in a hurry,' Curtis said calmly as the senior security guard came over to the window.

'You can't—'

For as long as Curtis cared to remember, Special Agent Rob Bauer had shared his own preference for the Ruger .44 Magnum as his weapon of choice. 'Open the gate or you'll spend the next fifteen years of your life in a penitentiary protecting your butt from some very nasty inmates.'

Curtis forced himself to focus on what he had to do and detached himself from his feelings for Kate as the lift shot up to the reception area on the thirty-seventh floor. Finding the combination locked, Curtis drew his revolver and blasted it off the door. Seconds later they were in Halliwell's office. A mobile was ringing on the desk where Halliwell had left it. The guardhouse was still frantically trying to reach him.

'A couple of your guys might like to check the floor below,' Curtis said to Bauer. 'Dr Braithwaite's office is at the far end, but I've got a feeling she won't be there,' he added and he strode over to the walnut-panelled lift doors on the far side of Halliwell's big office. Simone had not been the only one to leave the key in place and deep below the lift doors closed silently.

Kate spat at Halliwell again and he slapped her face.

'Mustn't do that,' Halliwell said, slowly and deliberately. 'Naughty girls get injected with Ebolapox and you're being very, very naughty.'

Despite her bravado, fear filled Kate's gut with ice. Halliwell's grey eyes were devoid of emotion and she came to the same conclusion as Simone. Not for the first time in history had a dangerous psychopath, driven by a lust for power, got close to obtaining leadership of his country. Richard Halliwell was just a few primaries away from winning the Republican nomination for the White House. Kate winced as he stretched the thick industrial tape over her mouth.

'Perhaps this is best done to Beethoven's Fifth?' Halliwell said, switching on the stereo. 'Such majestic music. Da da da dah . . . Da da da dah . . .' he sang along with the opening stanzas.

'Very nice,' Halliwell leered, his erection growing. His hands wandered inside Kate's bra then slid down inside her pants. Kate willed herself to remain calm so that she didn't choke on the bile rising in her throat.

CHAPTER 94

CAPITOL INTERNATIONAL AIRPORT, BEIJING

'Business or pleasure, Mr Ferraro?' the young Chinese immigration officer asked, her English greatly improved. The Chinese government had introduced an English program for everyone likely to be involved with international visitors almost as soon as they'd won the Games. Nothing was going to stand in the way of the Beijing Olympics being 'the best games ever'. The Games were China's passport into the twenty-first century.

'Business,' Ferraro replied politely.

She smiled again as she checked his face against the photo in his American passport. 'Enjoy your stay.'

The Beijing arrivals hall was packed with thousands of people coming in for the Opening Ceremony of the Games, due in just six days time. al-Falid headed straight for the car park at Terminal 2 where one of Khalid Kadeer's men was waiting for him.

'Everything is in place?' al-Falid asked, taking the bag containing the Walther P38.

His driver nodded. 'All of our people have been briefed and all of them have access to the airconditioning systems. We picked up the vaccines from the docks at Qingdao and they are being distributed to those who need them here and in Xinjiang,' he said as they drove out of the airport.

It was nearly midnight by the time they arrived but Peng Yu, al-Qaeda's sadistic bear farm manager was up and waiting for them.

'Has Dolinsky arrived?' al-Falid asked.

'He a'seep, Mr 'Flid,' Peng Yu replied.

'And the staff?'

'Bear farm crosed for two weeks, just as you request, Mr 'Flid and staff given day off for Games.'

'What about Dolinsky's luggage?'

'Many trunks, Mr 'Flid. In storehouse behind bears.'

'You have done well, Yu. You can have the holiday as well but I will need your keys,' he said as he turned to the driver. 'Pick me up tomorrow.' For what al-Falid had in mind, he wanted to make sure there were no witnesses.

After the manager and his driver had left, al-Falid returned to his room and took the Walther P38 from the small khaki bag. He checked to see that the magazine was loaded and smiled as he fitted the silencer. Khalid Kadeer was wrong, al-Falid thought. Like Osama bin Laden before him, the Uighur microbiologist had become a rallying point for many in the downtrodden Muslim world, but Kadeer was mistaken in thinking that you could negotiate with the

West, just as he was wrong in thinking someone like Dolinsky should be spared. al-Falid feared that once the Georgian scientist realised the utter devastation of the virus he'd created there was a danger that, like those who'd worked on the Manhattan project and the nuclear bomb, he would talk. Anything that might lead back to Amon al-Falid's identity in the United States had to be eliminated.

He crept up to Dolinsky's room and inserted the manager's master key. The door squeaked as he opened it but he need not have worried. The Georgian scientist's snores were rattling off the thin walls. al-Falid placed the end of the gun barrel centimetres away from the back of Dolinsky's head. The Walther kicked savagely – twice.

CHAPTER 95

HALLIWELL LABORATORIES, ATLANTA

Halliwell stood near the stainless steel bench seat. He picked up his biosuit and waved it at Kate in time with the symphony, a sinister smile playing around his thin lips as he mimicked squeezing a needle with his free hand. Kate felt sick as Halliwell moved towards her, unzipping his fly.

As soon as Curtis and Special Agent Bauer, together with two of the patrolmen, got out of the lift they could hear the sounds of the first movement of Beethoven's Fifth Symphony. Gun drawn, Curtis sprang into the opening of the tunnel. It was empty. The music was coming from beyond the half-open door some 800 metres away, echoing loudly through the tunnel.

Fitter than the other three men, Curtis was nearly 20 metres in front when he slowed, using the cover of the music to approach the door. What looked like a receiving bay was empty but beyond it another vault door was wide open. Halliwell had his back to Curtis and his hand was on someone strapped to a stainless steel trolley. Curtis realised that someone was Kate. As the first movement of the famous symphony came to a close, Halliwell applied the wheel brake and started to climb onto the trolley. Curtis approached silently, wishing he had a short length of wire to garrote him. In one movement Curtis wrenched the precariously balanced Halliwell from the trolley, throwing him to the concrete floor.

'You're a dead man, O'Connor,' Halliwell snarled as the surprise on his face was quickly replaced with unbridled hatred. Halliwell sprang from the floor with surprising agility but Curtis' boot smashed into his jaw. Seconds later Halliwell was face down, roaring like a wounded lion as the patrolmen snapped his wrists into cuffs, subduing Halliwell's wildly flailing legs with the roll of industrial tape Curtis found on the trolley next to Kate.

'I'll join you in Halliwell's office shortly,' Curtis said to Kate and Rob Bauer, after Kate and Simone had both refused Curtis' suggestion they be examined for shock. Curtis donned Halliwell's biosuit, which was baggy on him, but it would protect him from whatever was on the far side of the vault-like door.

As he plugged his regulator in to the air hose and went through the airlock the hardened CIA man was sickened by what he found. For no reason other than unfortunate circumstances, these three human beings had been taken from the streets of a civilised western city. All three were still alive and strapped to their trolleys, but with no morphine or other medication they were suffering excruciating pain. Curtis stared at what appeared to be an eleven-year-old girl with a feeling of helplessness. With a body temperature of 37°C, the human species was the perfect host for a filo virus and the man-made virus she'd been injected with was multiplying at an astounding rate. He could see the dark blotches underneath her skin as the Ebolapox turned her organs to mush and her lungs slowly filled with blood and foul fluids. Curtis knew that unless they could find the missing vials, hundreds of millions of people were going to die the same horrible death as the filo virus was released into the wider world.

He checked a freezer beside the trolleys. Inside he found frozen packets of bear bile from the Qingdao Bear Farm. A more thorough search of Halliwell's dark world would later reveal a supply of anthrax spores with a sophisticated coating of silicone particles engineered down to microns. The spores would prove to be identical to those found in the Daschle anthrax.

The door to Halliwell's office opened and one of the patrol officers came in to report that Halliwell had been taken away under heavy police guard. The security guards were being taken in for questioning and the Chief of the Atlanta Police was on his way up the drive.

'Split personality schizophrenic?' the young patrol officer asked, genuinely shocked that such a dark side could exist in a man running for the Presidency of his country.

'It's too early to make that judgement,' Curtis said. Young patrol officers like this had to learn on the job, and even in the middle of a crisis Curtis found a few seconds for his education. 'No doubt

Halliwell's highly paid lawyers will come up with a defence along those lines but don't be too shocked when people in powerful positions turn out to have fatal personality flaws,' Curtis added, accurately reading the look of disillusionment on the young officer's face. 'Power and corruption often go hand in hand.'

While Kate sat on one of Halliwell's couches with Simone, her hands no longer shaking as the Chivas calmed her, Curtis sat at Halliwell's desk, waiting for his connection to the CIA's internal computers to spool in. He turned to Rob Bauer.

'For the moment it will be best if the administrative areas and pharmaceutical laboratories of Halliwell are allowed to operate normally,' he said, 'but I want the entrances to both of the Level 4 laboratories sealed off.' When the pound man returned with two more vagrants the following day he would get a nasty shock, but the vagrants would be given another chance at life. 'You're going to have to trust me on this one again, Rob, but there's another activity in Washington that we've yet to close in on and if any of this becomes public, that might be at risk.'

'You got it, buddy,' Rob replied, and as Simone was led away for questioning by one of the patrol officers, Special Agent Bauer disappeared to meet the Chief of the Atlanta Police Department.

'You sure you don't want a medical examination?' Curtis asked Kate as the results for the checks on Alan Ferraro's movements appeared on Halliwell's computer, together with movements of the *George Washington*.

'I'm fine,' Kate said as Curtis scanned the movement schedule from the Port Authority of Savannah. The west coast port of Georgia was the nation's sixth largest container port, and Curtis knew the departure of the ocean-going tug two weeks earlier would not have raised a ripple. Despite the demands for imagery over Baghdad and the border regions of Afghanistan, Pakistan and the Hindu Kush, the Administration kept a very careful watch on the growing threat from China, and the latest US satellite surveillance of Chinese ports had found the *George Washington* not far from the headquarters of the Chinese Northern Fleet in the harbour of Qingdao.

'I've got to get going,' Curtis said. 'The packets of frozen bear bile in Halliwell's freezer came from the Qingdao Bear Farm but I've got a hunch there's more to that bear farm than meets the eye.'

'Why don't you get the Chinese to raid it?' Kate suggested.

'Because they'd keep the Ebolapox for their own research. This virus needs to be destroyed, and that goes for the world's stocks of smallpox as well. I'm almost certain that I'm going to find al-Falid at this bear farm and probably Dolinsky as well. There's no guarantee that Kadeer hasn't infiltrated the Chinese police force and that they'll be tipped off. I won't be happy until I've got these vials back in our Embassy in Beijing and in the black bag.'

'I'm coming with you,' Kate said firmly.

Curtis shook his head. 'It's too dangerous.'

'Haven't I earned my spurs yet,' Kate snapped, but then her anger subsided quickly. She could see that Curtis was only trying to protect her, and for that she was grateful.

'Look,' she said, 'we haven't seen enough of each other for me to have had time to tell you this, but much to my father's annoyance I used to be a member of a pistol club. I can handle that .44 Magnum of yours probably better than you can.'

Curtis grinned and raised his eyebrows as if to say 'really?'

'You and I both know there's a very strong chance that if those vials are at the Qingdao Bear Farm, they're headed for a Beijing crammed with three million extra people from God knows how many hundreds of thousands of towns and cities around the world. You might know a bit about polymerase chain reactions,' Kate said, her green eyes recovering their sparkle, 'but I'm the expert on viruses and I'm coming with you.'

'What about Imran?' Curtis suggested in a last but futile attempt.

'Because he's a man?' Kate responded.

'I'll need to use the secure phone in your office,' Curtis said, not entirely disappointed Kate would be accompanying him. 'Tom McNamara will need to hold off the Wunderkind and getting a CIA jet to Beijing is a bit above my pay grade, although it might have a double bed!'

Kate punched him in the shoulder as they made their way to the floor below.

CHAPTER 96

CAPITOL HILL, WASHINGTON DC

President Bolton was surprised to find the Speaker of the House, Davis Burton, waiting for him as he arrived on Capitol Hill to address a history-making joint sitting of the Senate and the House of Representatives. He'd been briefed that procedures would be identical to those employed when a President delivered a State of the Union address and that he would be escorted by the Sergeant at Arms. No President could enter the House Chamber without first being issued a formal invitation and being escorted to his place at the podium.

'I apologise for the break in procedure, Mr President, but a matter of the utmost importance has arisen that you need to be briefed on.'

'Can't this wait, Burton, I have a speech to make,' President Bolton replied irritably.

'No it can't, Mr President. I need to brief you in my office before you enter the chamber.'

'This better be good, Burton,' President Bolton snapped.

The Sergeant at Arms followed at a discrete distance, determined to do his duty, but still struggling to come to terms with the enormity of the conspiracy to attack the world in Beijing and his President's involvement. A short distance away, an unusual silence had descended on the packed and normally vocal chamber.

'Are these yours, Mr President,' Davis Burton asked, pushing a document across his desk towards President Bolton seated on the other side. The document contained details of the nearly $50 million in bribes that had been deposited in Bolton's account under the name of Charles Boardman.

'How dare you!' President Bolton exploded. 'I'll have you flung out on the street for this.' The President had turned a peculiar shade of pale.

'I don't think so, Mr President.' Right to the last, Davis Burton adhered to the protocol of calling the disgraced and criminally negligent President by his title. Speaker Davis Burton pressed a button on the high fidelity recording the CIA had provided of the conversation between Bolton and Richard Halliwell in his office. As the tape finished, President Bolton had become paler still.

'A super virus is no respecter of international borders, Richard. I don't give a shit how many millions of these slanty-eyed Chinese we wipe out, the more the better, but we'd want to make damn sure we had a vaccine to protect Americans, especially our athletes before we released it.'

'You've hit the nail on the head, Chuck. Dolinsky is one of the few people, and perhaps the only one who could develop both the virus and

*its vaccine quickly. I can look after the distribution in Beijing, but I'd
need your help to get the virus in through the black bag.'*

At the last moment, Tom McNamara and the Speaker of the House
had briefed both the Director of the United States Secret Service and
the Director of the CIA. Two Secret Service agents normally charged
with protection stood outside the Speaker of the House's office, ready
to assist the Senate's Sergeant at Arms, the only man empowered
under the Constitution to arrest the President. The Director of the
CIA had been apoplectic at not being told but McNamara had looked
him squarely in the eye. 'I've seen a lot of Directors in my time, but
you're arguably the worst and if you want proof, just look up the file
on Bill Crawford. He was decapitated because you refused to give
young agents enough training to equip them to operate in some of
the godforsaken places we send them. By the time we get to the bottom of this cesspool, you're the one who's going to need re-training
because your mates in the White House aren't going to save you.'

The Sergeant at Arms need not have worried about having backup. The last of the evidence on the tape was not as damning as the
plans for Beijing, but it would be enough to put the President behind
bars for a very long time.

*'The fewer people that know about this, the better, Chuck. Genetic
engineering's come a long way and provided they're at the top of
their field, two scientists will be enough. You think you can sell it in
Washington?'*

*'I sold the idea of a new $500 million bio-level four complex for
you, and I'll be working on the contract for the production of smallpox*

vaccines as well, which comes in at half a billion; and the last time I
looked, your contracts in Iraq this year topped $300 million.'

'You will find there will be $10 million of that in your Bahamas
account by the end of the week.'

The President of the United States of America slumped in his chair.

'I intend to see to it that you face the full force of the law, Mr President,' demanded Davis Burton. 'For the moment that will be restricted to the bribes you've taken over the years. The members of the Senate and the House have only been given enough detail to ensure their cooperation and silence on this extraordinary conspiracy in Beijing. You've been a party to one of the most sinister plots in the history of mankind. My colleagues and I agree that it is in neither America's nor the world's interest to make this public, but that will depend on whether or not we can recover the vials.'

President Bolton's eyes widened in horror.

'No, Mr President, they have not, as you previously authorised, been delivered through the American Embassy's diplomatic bag to Halliwell's paid thugs. Two weeks ago they were stolen from Halliwell's laboratories by Dolinsky, the man you insisted we give assistance to defect. Dr Eduard Dolinsky works for al-Qaeda. Curtis O'Connor is going to attempt to recover these vials. If he doesn't, I can't think what the outcome might be, except for one certainty. You will die in the electric chair. Either way, may the Lord have mercy on you for your betrayal of the high office to which you were entrusted.'

The President nodded in a daze.

The Sergeant at Arms, accompanied by the two Secret Service agents escorted the President to a side door where a car was waiting.

Davis Burton had insisted that the images of a President under arrest not be beamed around the world by the mass of media waiting for the President to re-emerge after his speech on the Hill. With a grim determination, Burton walked towards the chamber to deliver a history-making speech of his own.

'It is with a deep sense of sadness that I announce to my fellow Americans, and to the world that the President of the United States has been arrested.'

Gasps of disbelief could be heard in the visitors' gallery.

'As Vice President, and as our chief executive, President Bolton has been involved in serious criminal activities, including the acceptance of millions of dollars in bribes.' The carefully worded statement allowed for further elaboration on those activities should the Beijing conspiracy ever become public.

'I expect many in the wider community will want to know why impeachment proceedings have not been brought. In this case, the crimes are so serious and the evidence so compelling that when confronted with that evidence a short while ago in the Office of the Speaker, the President had no defence.' Davis Burton waited while the murmurs of shock and amazement died down in the gallery.

'In the absence of a Vice President, the office of President falls to me as Speaker of the House and the next most senior person in line. Although I have sought this office in the past, I would never have wanted to assume the position under these circumstances; but just as the democratic process that is the backbone of this great country determined the results of the elections I fought and lost, under a little known section of our Constitution, it allows for the arrest of a wayward President by the Senate Sergeant at Arms. Now is not

the time for electioneering, now is the time for healing, but, if my
colleagues so wish it, I will once again put my name forward for this
great office. In the meantime, I do not intend to introduce any substantial items of domestic policy in the months remaining until the
next election. In the area of foreign policy, I will do everything I can
to restore the good name we once had among those with whom we
share this planet. I am reminded of what the great President Harry S.
Truman once said from this very spot. In his 1951 State of the Union
address, when he was referring to the threat from Communism, he
said, and I quote: "The United Nations, the world's greatest hope for
peace, has come through a year of trial stronger and more useful than
ever. The free nations have stood together in blocking Communist
attempts to tear up the charter."

I am sad to say that, in recent months, it has been the United States
of America that has been trying to rip up the charter. I read a report
the other day from the Peres Centre for Peace where 70 per cent of
Palestinians *and* Israelis favour reaching a peace agreement and a
surprising number of those are in favour of a Palestinian state. That
report suggests to me that one of the greatest obstacles to peace in the
Middle East has been self-serving politicians and minority groups
on both sides. The Peres Centre is one organisation that is bringing
Palestinians and Israelis to work together, sharing ideas in fields like
agriculture and business, but more importantly, enabling Israelis and
Palestinians alike to get to know, understand and respect each other's
different cultures. You will not find it reported in the mainstream
media but young people are bonding amidst the camaraderie on the
sports field. Mixed teams of Palestinians and Israelis are being pitted
against other teams of Palestinians and Israelis. Like an effective

United Nations, if that sort of good will can be harnessed on a greater scale, and if I can move towards spending a billion dollars a week on health and education instead of bombing the populations of Iraq and Lebanon, then whether my fellow Americans decide I should stay put or leave the White House, I will be a very happy man.' Burton paused again as the Democrats and many on his own side of politics applauded. The shock of the arrest of the President had certainly not subsided, but Davis Burton was widely respected as a man of vision by both sides and already he seemed to be providing hope for a far more peaceful future, not only for the United States, but for the world at large.

'I don't agree with Dr Kadeer's methods but he is right in insisting that Palestinian families have the same aspirations as anyone else. We take for granted in this country that we are able to enrol in a school or a university. Many Palestinian children would give their right arm to have the same opportunity. There's been far too much bloodshed, and we need to find common ground with other cultures. Just as we would not tolerate an Islamic army camped on the shores of the Potomac, perhaps withdrawal of our armies from around the Islamic holy sites might be feasible. I intend to try and find a way to do that through intermediaries in the United Nations.'

Thousands of kilometres away, Dr Kahlid Kadeer watched the address and wondered if this was an infidel who could be trusted, although Kadeer knew that it was now too late. He had received word from al-Falid that all the teams were in position and the final rehearsals for putting the virus into the airconditioning systems had begun.

'Finally, to the fundamentalists of all religions who believe that theirs is the only path to salvation, I would ask them to ponder what sort of a God would oversee the creation of a billion Christians, a billion Muslims and over four billion people of other paths and faiths, then in some obscene cosmological joke, declare that only one group had been given the map. What sort of a God would rapture up a small proportion of his creation and leave the rest to burn in a sulphurous chasm? What sort of a God demonstrates his Greatness by destroying thousands of innocent women and children? That is not the sort of God I want to worship, and those who think their God sanctions horrific violence have not read the script, and it comes in more than one language,' he concluded, mirroring the views of Kadeer.

'In the time available to me I will do everything I can to negotiate a meaningful peace in the Middle East that is fair to all sides, but I cannot do it on my own, and I would appeal to the moderates of all cultures and faiths to meet me halfway. Compromise is not a weakness but a wisdom.'

As the distinguished Davis Burton left the podium, the members of Congress got to their feet and applauded. Not all Americans would agree with his decision to try and find common ground with someone like Khalid Kadeer, but given the alternative, they were prepared to let him try. America had not seen a politician of such vision in a long time.

CHAPTER 97

QUINGDAO BEAR FARM, SHANDONG PROINCE, CHINA

Curtis parked the car the US Embassy had lent him and he and Kate covered the last 500 metres to the entrance on foot. The bear farm was in darkness and Kate followed Curtis as he kept close to the pine trees surrounding the compound. Neither needed the satellite maps and imagery they'd been poring over to know when they'd reached the bear compound; the stench was enough. Curtis propped just past the gap in the mound and signalled Kate to stop.

'Wait here,' he whispered.

The continuous satellite surveillance of the bear farm had provided imagery of people coming and going between the administration building on the left and the accommodation building at the top of the small rise above them. The big KeyHole satellites had provided night vision of one or two guards patrolling but tonight the whole place seemed deserted, except for the vehicle outside the accommodation block. Curtis moved forward cautiously across the open ground and was nearly two-thirds of the way to the vehicle when a big set of sensor lights flooded the compound. Curtis ran towards the trees and dived into cover as three bullets whistled past his ears.

From behind the mound Kate could see whoever had come out of the building moving towards the edge of the trees and, holding her pistol against the mound to steady it, she fired off three quick shots.

Earlier in the evening, in the city of Shanghai, the residents had gone wild as the Olympic torch was paraded along the Bund beside the Huangpu River, past elegant and imposing buildings that reflected Shanghai's colonial past. Across the river in the Pudong New Area, the viewing platforms in the Pearl TV tower and one of the world's tallest buildings, the Jin Mao, had been packed.

Further north in a warehouse on the outskirts of Beijing, the team leaders al-Falid had trained at the bear farm were being issued with syringes.

'Under no circumstance are the vials to be opened until you're ready to use them,' al-Falid's commander in Beijing directed, picking up a cheap plastic syringe which could be bought in any drugstore. 'The nozzles on these syringes have been modified slightly to produce a fine mist in the shape of a fan.' He opened a vial of coloured water, filled the syringe and, holding it about 10 centimeters from the intake duct of an air conditioner, sprayed it with an even coat of the liquid. 'Once you and your teams have completed putting the virus into the systems you've been allocated, wipe the syringes and vials clean of any fingerprints and dispose of them in a rubbish bin as far away from the building you work in as possible.'

Confused as to how the intruder might have got back to the bear enclosure so quickly, al-Falid fired three more shots towards the gap on the mound.

Kate winced as a bullet grazed her left shoulder. Ignoring the pain she lay on the ground and returned fire.

Curtis counted the shots as he worked his way up through the pine forest, circling back towards his quarry. He was 10 metres above the man when Kate fired again. Go girl! Curtis thought. He could see his quarry through the trees and as the man returned fire, his face was silhouetted by the sensor lights. Curtis would have recognised that nose anywhere. al-Falid fired at Kate twice more, then there was a resounding click. Less than 5 metres from the man who had set out to destroy civilisation, Curtis calmly took aim and fired. al-Falid grabbed his stomach, his pistol and the new magazine tumbling onto the pine needles.

'Kate! It's me, don't shoot!' Curtis yelled, conscious that Kate would be firing at any movement.

al-Falid made a move towards his pistol but Curtis kicked it out of the way.

'This one's for Bill Crawford, Mr Ferraro-al-Falid.'

al-Falid's eyes widened in fear. Curtis felt no emotion as he fired once between them.

'Kate! Up here and stay low!' Curtis ordered as he turned towards the accommodation block, wondering where Dolinsky was hiding.

'Cover me,' he said to Kate when they reached the edge of the pine forest close to the building. With his back to the wall, Curtis eased his way along the covered walkway, kicking open each door in turn. As he entered the last room, he found Dolinsky's body on the blood-soaked bed.

'Shot twice through the back of the head. More of al-Falid's handi-work, I suspect. No sign of the vials. I only hope they're still here.'

It took just one shot to blast the flimsy lock off the administra-tion building, but a search only revealed a rudimentary sales area for powdered bear bile products and a café with bear bile soup featuring prominently on the menu. A soup made from bear bile powder cost a mere US$2.50, but if the bile was fresh from the bear, the soup would set you back ten times that amount or 200 yuan. Kate and Curtis both knew price would be no obstacle to those who valued it for its supposed medicinal qualities.

'And they want a leading place in the twenty-first century,' Curtis muttered. 'Fucking barbarians.' As he turned back towards Kate, Curtis noticed blood seeping through her shirt.

'You've been hit,' he said, concern in his voice.

'It's just a graze,' Kate replied, almost defensively.

'I'll be the judge of that,' Curtis said, sitting Kate on a wooden bench and unbuttoning her shirt. Kate looked up at him and smiled. 'Not now, darling,' she whispered.

'You're right,' Curtis said with a grin. 'Although when we get out of this shitbox, there's a first aid satchel in the car. The only place we haven't searched is the bear compound.'

Kate felt sick, not so much from the stench of bear bile and excrement, but from the low howls of agony from the caged bears. She and Curtis had paused briefly at one cage where the beautiful creature was trapped in a mediaeval truss, bleeding from where metal had gouged the skin away. Like Maverick and the other Great Apes, there was a look of 'Why?' in the tortured bear's eyes that neither she nor Curtis would ever forget.

'They're all here,' Curtis said, after he'd counted the lethal vials, each with a plastic syringe attached, but neither he nor Kate felt like relaxing. Beijing was still 800 kilometres to the west.

They reached the first police Games checkpoint on the outskirts of Ji'nan, the provincial capital.

The young Chinese policeman waved Curtis to a stop, and was about to ask for his papers when an older policemen approached. A short exchange in Mandarin followed and the older man pointed to the diplomatic plates.

'Very sorry,' the younger policeman said with a smile, handing Curtis back his passport and waving him and Kate through. The next checkpoint was at the great Yellow River; again they were waved through.

The CIA jet was waiting for them when they arrived at Beijing's Capitol Airport. Kate and Curtis boarded with a sense of relief, but only after they had both watched the embassy staff complete the paperwork for the diplomatic bag and they had supervised the loading into the hold.

CHAPTER 98

THREE MONTHS LATER, THE OVAL OFFICE, THE WHITE HOUSE, WASHINGTON DC

'I know you people in the CIA have some crazy rule about not being decorated in public,' President Davis Burton said with a warm smile towards Kate, Imran and Curtis, after they'd been shown into the Oval Office, 'so I've reluctantly decided to do this here.'

'To be awarded the Presidential Medal of Freedom for outstanding devotion to duty and exceptional courage in the face of enemy fire. Dr Katherine Diane Braithwaite.' It was the civilian equivalent of the military's Congressional Medal of Honour.

Kate gasped as the Marine Corps aide stepped forward to the President with a velvet cushion holding one of America's highest awards of honour.

'Kate, if you'd like to step forward,' President Burton said. He smiled broadly as he place the ribbon around Kate's neck, a smile not entirely due to his ability to reward those who so richly deserved it. The Grand Old Party had overwhelmingly endorsed him as their candidate and if the most recent polls were anything to go by, the American public had as well. When it had become known that their President had entered into a dialogue with the Presidents of Syria and Iran and the other Arab nations, seeking the creation of a Palestinian State, as well as their assistance to stabilise Iraq, most Americans had supported the change in course.

'Congratulations.' The President shook Kate's hand. 'And I've had a word with the Chinese Ambassador,' he said. 'He's promised me that the Chinese government will finally shut down these barbaric bear farms and I intend to insist on an international delegation being allowed in to see that they do.'

Kate felt like hugging him. She stepped back and watched the President present the Medal of Freedom to the two most important men in her life. To Professor Imran Sayed for exceptional and outstanding service to the world of medicine, often at great personal risk to his own safety, and to Curtis Brendan O'Connor for exceptional courage in the face of enemy fire and outstanding devotion to duty.

'The country owes all three of you a great debt and my only regret is that it won't be recognised more publicly, although these things have a way of getting out, and our policy is to neither confirm nor deny,' the President said with a conspiratorial grin as he nodded to the Marine Corps aide to lead the way. 'If you'd like to come with me, the First Lady and I would be honoured if you'd join us for dinner.'

'I didn't know your middle name was Brendan,' Kate whispered, as she and Curtis followed the President and Imran out of the Oval Office towards the main house.

'There's a lot of things you don't know about me,' Curtis replied mischievously. 'Fancy a nightcap after dinner?'

Kate glanced at him, her green eyes just as mischievous. 'That depends entirely on your definition of a nightcap, Curtis O'Connor.'

AUTHOR'S NOTE

I have approached this novel as if I was a terrorist, without access to the top-secret files which used to land on my desk. All the information that a terrorist might require to launch such attacks is available on the public record. For example, when I went searching for information on harbours and the water supplies of major cities, the internet and other sources provided a wealth of detail. In some cases, authorities even included engineering designs. This is perhaps as it should be, but it underlines the difficulty of preventing this information falling into the hands of terrorists.

During the early stages of researching this book, I wondered whether I should write it, conscious that it might give terrorists ideas. But during my discussions with some of the world's leading virologists, it became clear that the possibility of genetically engineering a super virus is now a chilling reality, well known to both sides. The genie is out of the bottle. I have therefore written the novel as a warning of what we might face if we don't change course. While most of the characters in this book are fictional, the scenarios are very real.

The weak points in any great city are also well known, and they include the underground railways, aircraft on takeoff and landing, tunnels, water and power supplies, and air conditioning systems. During the Sydney Olympics for example, in addition to the police, there were over 5,000 troops hidden around the city, yet despite this and other measures, which included sampling the air and the use of sophisticated mobile laboratories, we could not *guarantee* we could prevent an attack. Cities can never be completely protected, which underlines the need for intelligence. That intelligence will not be forthcoming if foreign and domestic policies alienate and isolate different ethnic and cultural groups.

Those Muslims who misinterpret the Qu'ran and *Jihad* and use violence in their efforts to create a pan-Islamic world are to be condemned; but so, too, are the Christian fundamentalists who would have us believe that the

Messiah cannot return until all of Palestinian land is returned to Israel, that Islam is an evil religion, and that God is somehow directing Christian nations and foreign policy against the rest. It would be a very strange God who would create a world as diverse as ours, only to turn around and say, 'You Christians are okay, but the rest of you – sorry, unless you convert, I'm finished with you.' The same can be said for Allah, and Yahweh; yet we are increasingly ready to wage war on behalf of various versions of a god who share the same lineage of revelation traced back to Abraham. As my CIA agent, Curtis O'Connor, puts it: 'The world is going barking bloody mad.'

As a former soldier, and now a research scholar at the Centre for Arab and Islamic Studies at the Australian National University, I am of the view, and many far more distinguished soldiers than I share this view, that the invasion of Iraq by the United States, Britain and Australia has been an unmitigated disaster. Iraq spans an area of 432,000 sq km, four-fifths the size of France yet, arrogantly confident of post-war success, we invaded with just 140,000 troops. When the much-respected Chief of the US Army, General Eric Shinseki had the temerity to disagree over the numbers of troops it would require to stabilise Iraq, he was sacked. To go in with so few troops was not, as the American Secretary of State would have us believe, a minor 'tactical mistake' but a strategic mistake of the first magnitude. In terms of winning the hearts and minds of the population subjected to our invasion, we have learned little from the war I and my brothers-in-arms fought in Vietnam. As I write, every month more civilians die in Iraq than were killed in the attacks on September 11. Iraq is now a haven for terrorists and an inspiration for suicide bombers all over the world; and having destroyed the country and its infrastructure, the West is telling Iraqis that if they don't do more to sort it out, we're out of there. As a result of one of the most poorly planned operations in modern military history, and our refusal to even talk with countries like Iran and Syria, the peoples of the West are now at much greater risk of attack, especially in our big cities.

Unless we develop not only greater tolerance but *acceptance* of different cultures, race and religion, the attacks portrayed in *The Beijing Conspiracy* are not only possible, but probable.

ACKNOWLEDGEMENTS

A great many people have helped me unstintingly with the research for this book, but a number of them did not wish to be acknowledged. You know who you are, and I am indebted to you all. I consulted with distinguished and internationally recognised professors of microbiology and virology, as well as nuclear scientists, who are very worried, but many of them are unable to speak out. As I write this in early 2007, the incumbent governments of the United States, Britain and Australia, the original trio of the coalition of the willing in Iraq, do not take kindly to anyone who is critical of their policy, especially foreign policy in the Middle East.

In no particular order, I am indebted to: my editor, Jody Lee. A good editor generates spirited discussions, and our discussions have been very spirited. My thanks to the highly professional team at Penguin, who have all given me tremendous support, amongst them: Bob Sessions, Ben Ball, Belinda Byrne, Sally Bateman and designer Dave Altheim who, as usual, has produced a fantastic cover. Thanks also to proofreader Sharon Nevile for her wonderful eye for detail, and to my agent, Jane Adams.

A big thank you to Kate, Nic and the team at The Stockmarket Café at Leura, where advice is freely given on characters and plot, and the problems of the world are constantly solved, if only the politicians would listen. To Lisa, for long discussions, and to Lou for her wonderful insight and her work in the world of the Great Apes. To the highly trained tugboat crews, it was a pleasure to meet you. To the air traffic controllers, Australia is very fortunate to have men and women of such high calibre; Air Services Australia can be justly proud of their calm professionalism. To the staff at Qantas, I was privileged to spend time in the 747 simulator, and I am not surprised that the airline's safety record is second to none. To Jack Pommeato, for things that go bang in the night. To Ian Deeds, for advice on aviation matters; Rob Ennever, for reviving my love of languages; Leon Andrews, for computer hacking 101; Ivan McTavish, for his intimate knowledge of matters maritime and Sydney harbour; for all those at 'Fighter World', near Richmond Air Base; Caroline Ladewig, for her insightful views on characterisation; Chris Cameron, who read one of the early drafts; Antoinette and friends; Mark and his partner Amanda, whose insight into the female mind is always illuminating; and to Dobie and Carolyn, for discussions over excellent red. Clare Forster worked with me on the earliest ideas, and her advice was, as always, much valued. To Jill Robinson, Animals Asia and the many others who are working so hard to free the Chinese moon bears, caged for life in shocking conditions on bear farms in China – thank you.

And finally, to my two boys, David and Mark, who though they may have scratched their heads at times over what their father was up to, have always encouraged my desire to make a difference, and in their own ways make a greater contribution – the former as a senior fireman, the latter as a detective.

Also by Adrian d'Hagé

The Omega Scroll

A Dead Sea Scroll has lain undisturbed in a cave near Qumran for nearly two thousand years. The Omega Scroll contains both a terrible warning for civilisation and the coded number the Vatican fears the most.

The Pope's health is failing and the Cardinal Secretary of State, the ruthless Lorenzo Petroni, has the keys to St Peter within his grasp. Three things threaten to destroy him: Cardinal Giovanni Donnelli has started an investigation into the Vatican bank; journalist Tom Schweiker is looking into Petroni's past; and the brilliant Dr Angela Bassetti is piecing together fragments of the Omega Scroll. While they fight for their lives in a deadly race for the scroll, the Vatican will stop at nothing to keep the prophecy hidden.

At the CIA's headquarters in Virginia, Mike McKinnon suspects a number of missing nuclear suitcase bombs are connected to the warning in the Omega Scroll.

In the Judaen Desert a few more grains of sand trickle from the wall of a cave. The countdown for civilisation has begun.

'A provocative book in which every sort of dogma is questioned and every preconceived idea turned on its head' *Sunday Mail*

'A classy action thriller' *Sunday Times*

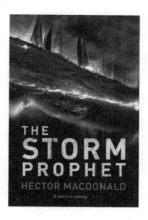

The Storm Prophet
Hector Macdonald

'In the time I knew the boy called Moses, he made three terrible predictions. The first was his own death; the last was something personal to me. But the prediction everyone still talks about is the Sydney Hobart storm.'

The Sydney Hobart yacht race is world famous: the crowds at the Boxing Day start; the Harbour full of colour; giant super-maxis competing for line honours and glory. But in the wrong weather, it can be deadly. No one will ever forget the carnage of 1998.

This year, Kirsten McKenzie must win. The bank she's inherited is in trouble, and desperately needs the PR boost of a race victory. Everyone thinks she'll do it - she's got the fastest boat and the best record. Everyone, that is, except a boy called Moses who claims to be able to see the future. He doesn't foresee victory. He sees a storm, mountains of water. He sees disaster.

Petra Woods is Director of the Sydney New Coastguard. She doesn't want to believe Moses' warning, but as the race draws closer and his other predictions start coming true, she might not have a choice. The only option may be to plunge in between the perfect race and the perfect storm.

The Storm Prophet is a truly gripping thriller about a vision, a race and the merciless power of the sea. It reveals Hector Macdonald as a master of suspense.

Subscribe to receive *read more*, your monthly newsletter from Penguin Australia. As a *read more* subscriber you'll receive sneak peeks of new books, be kept up to date with what's hot, have the opportunity to meet your favourite authors, download reading guides for your book club, receive special offers, be in the running to win exclusive subscriber-only prizes, plus much more.

Visit penguin.com.au to subscribe.